LOUIS L'AMOUR'S
Lost Treasures:
Volume 1

Bantam Books by Louis L'Amour

LOUIS L'AMOUR'S
Lost Treasures:
Volume 1

Unfinished Manuscripts, Mysterious Stories, and Lost Notes
from One of the World's Most Popular Novelists

Louis L'Amour
with
Beau L'Amour

BANTAM BOOKS · NEW YORK

Louis L'Amour's Lost Treasures: Volume 1 is a work of fiction.
Names, characters, places, and incidents are the products of the author's
imagination or are used fictitiously. Any resemblance to actual events,
locales, or persons, living or dead, is entirely coincidental.

2018 Bantam Books Mass Market Edition

Copyright © 2017 by The Louis D. & Katherine E. L'Amour 1983
Trust and Beau L'Amour

Published in the United States by Bantam Books, an imprint of
Random House, a division of Penguin Random House LLC, New York.

BANTAM BOOKS and the HOUSE colophon are registered trademarks of
Penguin Random House LLC.

Originally published in hardcover in the United States by
Bantam Books, an imprint of Random House,
a division of Penguin Random House LLC in 2017.

ISBN 978-0-425-28443-8
Ebook ISBN 978-0-399-17755-2

Cover design: Scott Biel

Photograph of Louis L'Amour by John Hamilton-Globe Photos, Inc.

Printed in the United States of America

randomhousebooks.com

2 4 6 8 9 7 5 3 1

Bantam Books mass market edition: September 2018

To my father, Louis L'Amour,
whose world was so much wider than the West he loved.

What Is Louis L'Amour's Lost Treasures?

L ouis L'Amour's Lost Treasures is a project created to release some of the author's more unconventional manuscripts from the family archives.

Currently included in the project are *Louis L'Amour's Lost Treasures: Volume 1* and *Volume 2*, which will be published in the fall of 2017 and 2019 respectively. These books contain both finished and unfinished short stories, unfinished novels, literary and motion-picture treatments, notes, and outlines. They are a wide selection of the many works Louis was not able to publish during his lifetime.

In 2018 we will release *No Traveller Returns*, L'Amour's never-before-seen first novel, which was written between 1938 and 1942. In the future, there may be a selection of even more L'Amour titles.

Additionally, many notes and alternate drafts to Louis's well-known and previously published novels and short stories will now be included as "bonus feature" postscripts within the books that they relate to. For example, the Lost Treasures postscript to *Last of the Breed* will contain early notes on the story, the short story that was discovered to be a missing piece of the novel, the history of the novel's inspiration and creation, and information about unproduced motion-picture and comic book versions.

An even more complete description of the Lost Treasures project, along with a number of examples of what is in the books, can be found at louislamourslosttreasures.com. The website also contains a good deal of exclusive material, such as even more pieces of unknown stories, personal photos, scans of original documents, and notes.

All of the works that contain Lost Treasures project materials will display the Louis L'Amour's Lost Treasures banner and logo.

LOUIS L'AMOUR'S LOST TREASURES

CONTENTS

INTRODUCTION

By Beau L'Amour

This book may drive you crazy.

What it contains is mysterious and fascinating, frustrating and, more often than not, tragically incomplete. It is a look behind the curtain into a world of what might have been. It is a look under the hood at how the machinery of a writing career that lasted over half a century functioned. It is also a look at the struggle to express an idea, and how difficult it can be to bend the unruly process of creativity to one's will. This is the story of the debris, the chaff, the waste heat that a writer produces. The stuff that never makes it to the editor's desk. The stack of pages never graced by a final "The End."

It is humbling to think that, with a career that produced ninety-one novels and nearly four hundred short stories, articles, screenplays, and poems, Louis L'Amour also left behind hundreds of unfinished works. It is comforting to know that, regardless of how prolific he was, he was human, that he had failures, weird ideas, and dreams he couldn't quite fulfill. It is amazing to realize that his imagination stretched well beyond the tremendous variety of work that he eventually published, from Westerns and crime stories, high adventure and historical romance, to stories he planned in science fiction, horror, and what can only be called the genre of mystical or spiritual adventure.

You may not find a hidden literary masterpiece between these covers, but you will get a sense of the entirety of a prolific writer's journey, an idea of the scope of all a truly creative person can struggle to wrap his or her mind around.

Within these pages I have included some of the most interesting material from what is a considerable archive. Many examples are stories that Dad discussed with us around the dinner table; others were completely unknown to me and inspired a good deal of research. I am reluctant, however, to do too much explaining, reluctant to organize this book too carefully. Exploring these manuscripts for the first time gave me a wonderful feeling of surprise and discovery. It is an experience that I do not wish to deny to others.

But I will try to create some context. . . .

It is still dark. Early morning. A late 1960s winter and the previous night's rain is still dripping from the eaves.

The neighborhood is just off the Sunset Strip in a neglected sliver of Los Angeles County sloping down from the Hollywood Hills. It is a community of nightclubs, gas stations, and small offices where, up narrow flights of stairs, the agents of rarely employed actors ply their trade.

West Hollywood is the dark sibling of Beverly Hills, which lies right next door. Beatnik poets and hungover movie stars frequent the coffee shop on the corner. The Doors, Led Zeppelin, and Buffalo Springfield play at clubs like the Whisky a Go Go, the Roxy, and Gazzarri's, and crowds clash with police when the neighbors complain about the noise and traffic. The edges of parking lots and the overgrown hillsides, even the sidewalks themselves, are dotted with hippies, camping (for lack of a better word) any place they can find a spot where no one will hassle them. They have come to this part of LA following a dream, or the music, or just one another. The place is a motley riot of counterculture, creativity, and confusion.

The sound of typewriter keys clacking greets me as I wake. I come downstairs dressed for school. The hallway that leads to the kitchen ends in three doors. Ahead, a bathroom; to the left, my father's office, a small room choked with books and papers in a small house choked with books and papers. The light is on above his desk, but his chair is empty. To the right is the kitchen, the coffee percolating and my mother delivering eggs and broiled bacon, condensed strips with the fat cooked off (my favorite), to the breakfast table.

In a few minutes my sister will join us. My mother doesn't have to dress her anymore; she's old enough to manage by herself. Then, Dad will put down the newspaper, take up a book, and read to us while we eat. It's a morning routine that will not end until I start driving myself to school nearly ten years later. The books he read were things he was interested in, Thor Heyerdahl's The Kon-Tiki Expedition, Adventures in the Apache Country, *or something from his youth, like* Tarzan and the Jewels of Opar. *We were surrounded by stories in every manner imaginable.*

By the time Mom was backing our aging and road-weary Cadillac out of the garage, Dad was back at his desk, typewriter rumbling, keys whacking out an irregular pattern. He'd still be there when I came home from school, after dinner, and sometimes, long past my bedtime.

This is how I remember my dad at work.

I would wake up to that sound the next morning and the next and the next. . . .

Louis's schedule, to be specific, was to always be the first one in the house out of bed. He took great pride in this, no matter what the circumstances. He wrote before breakfast and then immediately afterward. He worked until lunch, which, unless he had a business meeting, didn't last long. In the afternoon he would break to exercise, lifting weights in the backyard, whirling a jump rope, or shadowboxing. Before we got home from school he was back at it, and after dinner would often work until the late news came on the TV. He wrote seven days a week. He never took a vacation that wasn't a research trip . . . and sometimes, when we did travel, he would pack a tiny portable typewriter that had been "liberated" in Germany, and would write then, too.

I'm not sure when he took on this type of schedule, but I think it started in Oklahoma in the late 1930s. There was a certain point when he got serious; you can see it in his work. At first he wrote poetry and stories that were both personal and dark. Louis Lamoore (the way he was spelling his name when the Lamoore family arrived in Choctaw) was a bit of a pretender, an "artiste." He was a young man who, though he had talent, traded a great deal on his personality and good looks. In many ways he seemed to be writing more to augment his social life than to found a career.

Then something happened. Perhaps it was a sudden sense of vulnerability, of the years passing, of the realization that, though he had roamed the world, he was over thirty, living with his parents, and there were few things he could actually *do* that would earn him any money. Maybe it was the advice of a mentor or a warning from his father or elder brother. Maybe it was some small success that made him recognize that his future could be realized, rather than simply dreamt about. Whatever it was, it left him a changed and highly motivated man.

The point of view of his writing shifted. In the early period, the characters were stand-ins for himself, the stories drawn from his life or those he had known. In *some* ways these stories were actually better written, and certainly more polished, than some that came later ... but to succeed professionally, he was going to have to learn to communicate in a manner that was more universal than personal. He would need to entertain the masses rather than members of writers' groups and readers of minor literary magazines.

It was just before this moment, through accident or the hand of destiny, that Louis also met an angel. In *Education of a Wandering Man* he said:

> At one time, trying desperately to write something that would sell, I rented a typewriter. For several months I paid the rent. Then came a time when I could not, so I wrote him a note and explained. I never heard from him again. No bill, nothing. That typewriter meant more to me than anything. . . .

Being able to write every day opened the creative pathways and kept them open. Becoming good at it wasn't quick or easy, but eventually Dad had practiced so much that creativity became somewhat automatic. He set himself detailed goals and worked hard to achieve them, crossing projects off of typewritten lists with a proud, red grease pencil. By the late 1940s his goal was to sell a short story a week.

Not to *finish* a story a week. Sell.

Even though he'd had a fair amount of success by then, publishers would not take everything he wrote, so he had to complete quite a few more than fifty-two stories a year in attempts to make his quota. The work didn't pay much. Even that volume of writing did little more than pay the rent. Speed was essential.

I have no memory of how we were trained, my sister and I, but we knew how to approach my father if he was working and we wanted his attention. We would enter his office, picking our way through the piles of books and papers. We would stand to one side of him, just within his peripheral vision, and silently wait while he worked. Sometimes he would lift his fingers from the keys and say, "Just a minute." Then he would go on and complete a thought or get himself to a place in the story that would remind him what he had been intending to say next. Then he was yours . . .

. . . for about ten minutes. Before long, you could see the story or some innate discipline calling him back. We never had to worry about interrupting him because, while he was happy to be briefly distracted, he guarded his work time very carefully, and it never occurred to us that he might behave in a different way. "You run along now, I have to get back to work." He would lean forward then, hunting and pecking at the keyboard, back in the story and perfectly in tune with where he had left off. It seemed as if he always knew exactly where he was going and no interruption could confuse him or even make him pause for very long.

* * *

The descriptions of Louis L'Amour's writing process were legendary. According to publicists and popular myth, he did not outline and did not rewrite. He embodied every young writer's fantasy of what the process would be like. He cranked a page into the typewriter, started typing, and with absolute confidence, didn't look back until he reached the end of the story. All action, no agonizing.

Everything he wrote was good enough to immediately sell, or so the story went. The words simply flowed out of him. He did not get writer's block. He was not temperamental.

These may have been exaggerations, but they were not utter falsehoods or public-relations hype. He bragged he could sit with his typewriter on his knees and write a novel in the middle of Sunset Boulevard ... and when a German magazine asked to shoot some pictures of him doing so, he did it, producing half of his day's output during the photo shoot. He was already so well-known for that particular boast that a motorist leaned out the window of his car and yelled, "You've *got* to be Louis L'Amour!"

* * *

Mom and Dad in their apartment in West Hollywood.

Before I was born, Louis made the transition from writing short stories to writing novels. The length of the stories changed, the publishers changed, the way the material was distributed changed, but Dad's work habits did not. His income grew, but he also had a family to support. We had a very comfortable middle-class lifestyle as long as he could write three or four books a year. If he sold a movie, then maybe my mother could redecorate a room, or we'd buy a new car. Financial considerations aside, Dad still took great pride in having a lot of story ideas and in the speed with which he could produce a page or a chapter or a novel.

Progress was his byword. Louis claimed he could "simply" put himself and his characters in a situation and the story would take off, virtually telling itself. He loved beginnings . . . loved them to the point that he occasionally short-changed the ending of a story because he was so excited about starting the next one. He was powerfully optimistic, focused on productivity, the future, whatever was next. His frame of mind was such a potent force that, occasionally, Dad would announce stories that he had only just thought of as if they were finished. . . . In the reality he made for himself, there was little difference between thinking of something and completing it.

His presence was big and happy and generous. He made what he did look easy and, for the most part, it was. A great deal of the magic behind his sales was that he wrote so effortlessly that the material read the same way. . . . The energy that *any* writer puts into their work is the energy a reader will take out of it. And rare among writers, Louis loved the writing process.

Smoggy summertime. The early 1970s. A major transition in our lives. The L'Amour family—my father, mother, sister, dog, bird, and myself—are leaving West Hollywood for a new home in another part of town.

After many years of hard and constant work, Dad's fortunes have changed. The new street is quiet and elegant, not far from the campus of UCLA, the opposite of the bohemian funkiness of our old neighborhood. Louis is ensconced in the new house, typewriter set up on a carpenter's bench in a room just off the entrance hall. The boxes containing the books and papers he needs most are stacked around him. It will be a couple of years before the new house is fully furnished, before my dad's new office is built. Right now the move and the stress of buying a bigger home is enough for all of us.

My mother and I trek back and forth across town. Packing Dad's papers and books is not something she is willing to trust to the movers. She's got a borrowed station wagon and a twelve-year-old kid, me, to help her haul a considerable amount of stuff. Dad stays home and works.

It's not three or four trips we have to make, it's dozens. There are nearly eight thousand books, most of them hardback. I have always wondered what the new owners of the West Hollywood house thought; every wall was covered in shelves. We had nearly been forced out of the house by the sheer volume of Dad's books and papers.

The job takes weeks, moving from the echoing, dusty rooms of our old home to the new one, which, though larger, is rapidly filling with piles and boxes. To be sure, most of the boxes are full of books, but many contain papers, notebooks, and random stacks of manuscripts. It's hard to believe Dad actually fit all this stuff in our old place.

For a few years after the move that "stuff" remained stacked in the living room of our new house, and I occasionally saw my dad sorting through it, searching for one thing or another. Later, after his new office was built, most of those materials migrated down there, and the new room was big enough for him to add exponentially to their number. I can't say that the rest of us thought much about what this mass of papers contained. "Dad's work," or "Dad's mess"—that was as far as we went with it. It was only after his death, over fifteen years later, that we discovered many unexpected things. . . .

In the 1970s and '80s, after paying his dues for forty years, Louis L'Amour was the rock star of the paperback-book business. No title he put his name on had ever gone out of print, and his books were translated into more than twenty languages. When he appeared to do a signing, lines stretched around the block. The movie business has given a name to that kind of success: blockbuster.

Critics and commentators were either swept away by his infectious writing style or they struggled desperately to explain away his popularity. If audiences had found his work to be no more than disposable, momentary entertainment, dismissing it would have been easy—but those readers kept coming back, not only buying every new book, but rereading the old ones until they fell apart and were purchased again. By 1980, Bantam Books estimated he had sold one hundred million copies. By the time he passed away in 1988, that number was topping two hundred million.

His success, though long in coming, was also limiting. Since the end of World War II, Louis had made his name writing Westerns. He loved the West, and he loved being successful and making so many people happy with the entertainment he provided . . . but he also felt trapped. Trapped in the Western genre. Trapped by his own success.

The Walking Drum, Louis's epic twelfth-century adventure novel, was published late in his career. However, it was written in 1960, a time when no publisher wanted anything but a Western from Louis L'Amour. It was not his only attempt to break away into new territory during that era. All of them failed, at least in the short term, though the blow of not being able to expand his horizons was softened considerably by the increasing success of what he eventually began to call his "frontier" stories.

By the time the mid-1970s rolled around, Louis was a lot smarter about his approach to working in other genres . . . and he had become a good deal more successful, which made publishers feel less need for caution. Incrementally approaching the issue of change, he published *The Californios* in 1974, a Western to be sure, but one that included some strange and otherworldly elements. He followed that with *Sackett's Land,* utilizing the characters of his popular Sackett family to open the door to novels set in the sixteenth and seventeenth centuries, long before the classic "Western" period. By the 1980s, his publisher was happy to experiment with tales like *Last of the Breed,* a contemporary thriller about an American military pilot escaping from the Soviet Union, and *Haunted Mesa,* a science fiction novel that adapted elements of Native American lore. Like *The Walking Drum,* both of these stories were conceived twenty or even thirty years earlier. By the time of his death, Dad was finally able to sell stories in a wider array of genres than just the Western.

Certainly, what held Louis back, when it came to the more adventurous and interesting material that he dreamed of writing, wasn't just the conservative nature of publishers or his core audience—his own limitations played a part, too. To complete many of the ambitious projects he envisioned, a great deal of planning and revision would no doubt have been necessary.

As you will see in this book, and contrary to popular myth, Louis *did* outline to a certain extent, and he *did* rewrite, or at least *restart*, stories that hadn't taken off in that magic way that would carry him all the way through to the end. But writing was not as intellectual an experience for him as it may be for many writers; over the years it had become instinctual and reactive. To complete some of these projects, which in their personal nature and distance from the Western genre were more like his earliest work, Louis might have needed to relearn the planning and revision skills he had developed at the start of his career.

For Louis, the key to almost every story was the beginning. He was both renowned for and proud of how he started stories. Using action or mystery or a particular turn of phrase, he would propel the audience into a situation in a way that made them lean forward, eyes leaping ahead to the next sentence. Getting *himself* to react to that moment was a trick he used to unlock the story. If the narrative "took," then he went with it, forging ahead until he had followed his characters through to the end. After a certain point he rarely looked back, and the story wrote itself in an unstoppable stream of the *un*conscious.

> One day I was speeding along at the typewriter, and my daughter--who was a child at the time--asked me, "Daddy, why are you writing so fast?" And I replied, "Because I want to see how the story turns out!"

Working all day, every day, for decades on end had pretty much programmed him to write this way; having a story in the back of his mind for months or years before he put it down on paper allowed him to work out many of the details unconsciously. Once he started work, he really had little idea what was going to come out, and that kept his approach and the reader's experience consistently fresh.

Although he was occasionally accused of writing in a formulaic manner, by the 1950s Louis found it difficult if not impossible to accept *any* influence imposed from the outside. Whatever his formula was, it was based on some internal and little-understood aesthetic. This made working under the direction of publishers and movie executives nearly impossible. A number of the stories that you will read within these covers were victims of those limitations. At times of financial stress, or in moments when he dreamed of doing something different, Louis would hammer out a treatment (a "treatment" is much like the description of a story, rather than the story itself) and then try to get a publisher or movie studio to pay him up front for executing the final, finished story.

However, if he was lucky enough to receive that advance, he would soon become frustrated by corporate executives' attempts to get him to conform to their "creative" expectations or their schedules. It is true that very few writers of any sort like writing treatments, and even fewer do them well. In Louis's case it was so antithetical to the way he liked to work that on a number of occasions I remember him returning the money, regardless of how much we needed it, and going back to the methods he came by naturally. Writing a treatment was nearly always a recipe for disaster; if Louis was lucky enough to work out the story all the way through to the end, he was not very interested in doing so again when the time came to write the finished version. He knew what was going to happen. He was ready to move on to something else.

The day after my father died, I walked down into his office. It was shuttered and dark; for the previous four months, Dad had rarely left the second floor of the house. The room was more than four times the size of the space he had worked in in our old house in West Hollywood. The walls were lined with double bookshelves, twelve feet tall, the outer set mounted on huge hinges to allow it to swing out of the way, like a giant pair of doors, in order to access more books behind them. Few of these could be opened, however. The floor, his desk, and a sofa at the far end of the room were all stacked two to three feet high with papers and books and odds and ends of various sorts, left over from the different aspects of Dad's life.

In the preceding decades, the mess, like an occasionally rising tide, had moved up the hallway and into my mother's dining room. It happened a couple of times a year. We have never been able to prove that the expansion of that great mass of Dad's papers was connected to the phases of the moon or to solar weather, but sooner or later Mom would put her foot down and tell him to clean it up. His work space always looked like a disaster area, but she kept the rest of the house squared away in a manner that would have made the navy envious. If she had taken on the job of cleaning up his office after his death, it would have been both horribly emotional and completely exhausting on top of the crushing weight of settling his estate and renegotiating our publishing contracts. I knew this particular job was going to be up to me.

It was literally tons and tons of material, thousands and thousands of pages, and the sorting and copying had to be done with extreme care. Eventually, after two or three years, all that was left was our dining room table, piled high with random unidentified manuscript pages, some with numbers, some without. None were titled. The challenge was to match them to existing stories by recognizing the name of a character, or finding the continuation of a

*sentence at the top of a page or the beginning of a sentence at the
bottom of another, in this way we pieced together unfinished and
unknown manuscripts, all going into their own individual folders,
the pile of which grew larger and larger. By this time a number of
friends and family had joined in the effort, and it was like a giant
game of literary Concentration.*

It had never been easy to keep track of what Louis was working on. He kept lists of everything: what he had sold, what
he planned on accomplishing in the next six months, what
physical exercises he did and how many repetitions, his
weight, what books he had read and the ones he planned
on reading. He made several journal entries a week. And he
made hundreds of pages of notes on unlined paper with a
felt-tipped pen. He outlined speeches and articles and even
jotted down jokes and poetry. The number of pages he gen-
erated was substantial even before adding the things he considered to be his actual work. A great many of the projects in

The new office. Louis L'Amour surrounded by his work.
(Nancy Ellison ©1985)

this book had been hidden from us by the avalanche of paper he was constantly producing.

Somehow, even with all that *and* the novels that actually got published every year, he managed to write quite a few treatments and start scores of stories we had never heard of. In addition, we found partial manuscripts where Dad had made several different attempts to start many of his now well-known works, and piles of notes relating to that same successfully published material.

In some cases, he tried to start over and over. Often he would produce nearly identical drafts, each attempt allowing him to forge a few pages—or sometimes just a few words—further. Other times he would explore whether a completely different beginning, or different characters, would get a story to take off. On occasion he even considered changing a story concept from a novel to a TV series or even a play in order to see if he could make an idea work. Dad never *seemed* to agonize over anything, yet as I explored the materials he left behind, I realized that his writing was a much more laborious process than I had ever imagined. Possibly it was a more laborious process than he would even admit to himself! Working through these mysterious fragments of stories made us all realize how much we had taken for granted.

However, as this book will show, some of his most interesting material came to a halt after a few pages or a few chapters. In some ways, this is the archive of his most ambitious work . . . and, of course, that is *why* it was difficult to write. In my opinion, what Louis was unable to complete is often more revealing than what he *did* complete.

Because of the unfinished nature of some of these manuscripts, I am sure that reading this book will be a frustrating experience. For many readers, I suspect two particular questions will come up over and over. I will answer them as best I can right now. . . .

The first: "Yes. That is *really* where that story ended." Sometimes materials in this book will end in the middle of a sentence or thought. Louis either knew what he was going to write next and so didn't need to hint at what it would be, or he *didn't* know what he was going to write next and he ripped the page out of the typewriter and moved on to something else.

The second: "No. With a possible few exceptions, we are *not* going to have anyone finish these manuscripts or otherwise change them from what you see here." We are *intentionally* leaving this as the final form for many of Louis L'Amour's unfinished materials.

I believe deeply that, at its best, fiction is a partnership or collaboration between the author and the audience. Even with a finished work, a good writer hints, suggests, and directs, but then allows the reader to complete the scene, or the character, or the plot, or the meaning of the story. Imagination is the gift that you bring to the work and there is plenty here for you to imagine. In the end, however, *Louis L'Amour's Lost Treasures* is not so much about what these treatments and fragments of stories might have been, but what they tell us about their creator.

I find myself to be content with the unknown, and recognize that what you see (or don't see) here were the mysteries that Louis confronted too, the uncharted waters of unrealized imagination, the ideas that lurked, misty and half-formed, in the terra incognita of his mind.

Ladies and Gentlemen, Here There Be Dragons. . . .

LOUIS L'AMOUR'S
Lost Treasures:
Volume 1

JEREMY LOCCARD

The First Four Chapters of a Western Horror Novel

CHAPTER I

At the top of the rise Duro Weaver pulled
in his team to let them catch their
wind . . . He pointed with his whip. "She
lies right yonder, young feller, and I envy
you none at all."

The valley was several miles wide at that
point, and the tiny huddle of buildings
seemed lost in the vast expanse. On their
left the valley narrowed into the pass, and
beyond the pass lay the Mojave Desert,
stretching into infinite distance.

"Twenty Mile Station they call it," Weaver
said, "and it's a good twenty mile from the
last stage stop. In any direction but along
the trail it's more'n a hundred mile to
anywhere else at all."

The mountains loomed dark and ominous in
the late evening shadows. "Them mountains,"
commented Weaver, "are better left alone.
There's deer in them, and bear, too.
Almighty big ones . . . grizzlies. But that

there ain't the reason. The Injuns tell
queer stories . . . mighty queer. You just
fight shy of them."

Jeremy Loccard shrugged his heavy
shoulders. "I've spent most of my life at
sea, and we're used to strange stories."

"Mebbe," Weaver spat. He was skeptical of
tales from other worlds. He preferred his
own. "Mebbe so. But don't you get to
thinkin' the West is all Injuns and fellers
huntin' gold. This here's a strange, wild
country, with queer tales aplenty.

"You ever hear tell of the Frog People?
Injuns got their tales about them, and
they're said to live yonder in the
mountains. Or the Little People? If you
figure all the ha'nts is in old castles you
got another think a-comin'.

"You just walk them mountains alone. Or
down in the desert yonder, an' you'll _feel_
them. You'll feel _watched_. Yes, sir. You
surely will. You won't see nothin' but
you'll know they're there.

"Somewhere around here there's a canyon
full of writin' on the rocks . . . only this
here is dif'rent writin'. I mean real
dif'rent. No Injun will even _look_ at it.

"A few years back some fellers I knew went
off into that desert. Everybody was findin'
gold an' these fellers decide to have a try
at it theirselves. They'd heard tell of that
canyon and decided there must be gold there,
so they set out huntin'.

"Those who claimed to know said it was
deep an' narrow and couldn't be seen until

you stood right on the rim. Mebbe some folks couldn't see it at all.

"One night they figured they was close, so they went into camp. Come daylight they'd scout around. Johnny Haskins . . . an' I knowed him well . . . he was huntin' firewood when he come on a trail. The others said it could wait until daylight, but it still lacked a mite of bein' dark an' Johnny was impatient. He taken off into the desert.

"Mornin' come an' no Johnny. They come on his tracks, but the trail petered out in the desert yonder. Johnny was gone.

"They told the story their ownselves. I never did see Johnny after, but I heard tell of him.

"He come back, all right. On the mornin' of the fourth day they woke up to see Johnny settin' by the fire. They seen him plain, although his back was to them. They knowed it was Johnny, all right, because he had a funny white scar right back of his ear.

"They spoke to him and he turned around. Now this here is their story, not mine, but they do say Johnny turned into an old, old man. Three days had passed for them, a lifetime for Johnny.

"He wouldn't tell them nothing, but he was almighty anxious to get shut of the desert, and believe me, once he got back he never went into the desert again. Wouldn't go for love or money.

"Of a night they say he wandered in his dreams, and they'd hear him cry out . . .

scared-like. Sometimes he'd whimper like he
was in mortal fear.

"Sometimes in his sleep he raved about
great buildin's . . . castles, like. On'y
thing we could get clear was that he'd been
a prisoner somewhere, held a long time until
he broke loose and got away into the desert.
He found that ol' trail again. He took off
down that trail runnin' until he ran smack
into somethin'. He fell, an' when he got up
he seen the fire and come on in. Three days
for them, sixty years for him. You figure it
out."

Weaver spoke to his team and the horses
leaned into the harness, starting the stage
once more. "There's canyons about here where
no man ever walked, and there's valleys you
can find sometimes that are greener than any
desert should be, but no Injun lives there,
where you'd expect them to be . . . won't go
near 'em."

He paused, spat, and then said, more
quietly, "Was I you I'd not git off the
stage. That there Twenty Mile Station . . .
there's been two men vanish from there. Just
disappeared complete.

"An' don't you get to thinkin' all the
spooky things happen of a night. There's
things happen by day. . . .

"Why, there's a deep canyon back yonder,
cuts off into the mountains. Up that canyon
maybe ten, twelve mile there's a place. You
cross the creek to go into it . . . narrow,
winding canyon between low hills but with
mountains all around . . . digger pine an'

blue oak . . . and some of them ghost
trees . . . you know, they're kind of white
an' misty-lookin' after their leaves shed.
Buckeyes, some call them.

"There's a little basin back up that
canyon. There's a couple of springs there,
too. I heard some mighty strange stories
about that place. Ties in with the canyon I
spoke of."

Loccard listened with only half his
attention. Twenty-six years old and for two
years chief mate on the four-mast bark
Annandale, he had heard such tales many
times before.

He had once sailed on a vessel unlisted in
any port he'd ever come across, and found
her a good ship. Good enough, at least.
Piracy had more than one method, and with
the passing of Blackbeard and Kidd other
ways had been attempted. A quick change of
name and a coat of paint with some altera-
tion in the rig . . . who was to say what
happened after she left port?

Nor was he in any position to choose his
berth now, any more than when he sailed on
the mystery ship.

He had come up from the seaport town of
Wilmington, recently established on the
California coast, to look for an old friend
in Los Angeles. He was hunting no trouble, a
fact that helped him none at all when
trouble came. He emerged from the hospital
to find his ship had left without him. What
money he had carried with him was gone for

the doctor and what care he needed while
recovering.

No ships were hiring off the West
Coast . . . a seaman, perhaps, but no mates.
After a few weeks of trying he accepted the
job no one wanted, to handle the stage
station at Twenty Mile.

Shadows were deep in the canyons when the
stage rolled up to the station. Loccard
looked at the buildings with interest,
crouching dark and forlorn beside the stage
trail.

Duro Weaver tied the lines to the
whipstock and climbed back over the tarp-
covered luggage. From the back he handed
down the sea-chest, a battered carpetbag,
and two heavy canvas bags belonging to the
company.

"There's grub in the bags. I hope you can
cook." Duro straightened up, putting a hand
to the small of his back. Jolting over
rough, rock-strewn roads was hard on a man's
kidneys. "There's a well yonder. Water's
good when used reg'lar. Boss will get you
some horses up here soon's he can find a man
to drive 'em."

"Thanks. I'll do all right."

Weaver looked doubtful. From the boot he
took Loccard's rifle. It was brand, spanking
new. "You're likely to need this. Keep it by
you."

A worn holster and gun-belt followed. The
butt of the gun carried five notches.

Weaver glanced sharply at Loccard. "Five?

I never cottoned to carvin' notches, but five's quite a few."

"They aren't mine. They belong to the man I took it off of."

Weaver looked at Loccard again. Loccard was at least three inches shorter than his own six feet, and Weaver guessed his weight at one-sixty. "You took that gun off a man who'd killed five men?"

"It seemed like a good idea at the time. He was shootin' it at me."

Weaver exchanged a glance with Cottonmouth Porter, who had been riding inside the stage. Porter shrugged. The only other man riding passenger besides Cottonmouth was a slender man in a black broadcloth suit. Loccard picked up his sea-chest, shouldered it, then took up his carpetbag and took them to the stage station.

"I saw it," the stranger commented, biting the end from his thin cigar. "It was in Los Angeles."

"How could anybody miss at that range? It's unbelievable."

"It was Steve Darnell. Loccard was hit, all right, but he just kept coming. He took Darnell's gun away from him and slapped him silly with it. You never saw such a beating in your life. Then Loccard took his gun, stripped off his gun-belt, and walked to the nearest doctor. He spent the next three weeks in bed."

Weaver climbed back to his seat as Loccard walked back to pick up the rest of his gear. "Mr. Loccard, if I were you I'd be sure I had water enough and fuel enough before dark."

He held the lines as if reluctant to leave Loccard alone. "No travelers come this way except by stage, and the stages only come by daylight. So, don't open up for anyone . . . or <u>anything</u>."

His whip cracked like a pistol shot, the horses dug in, and the stage vanished in the pursuing dust. Loccard watched it until it was only a dot in the distance. He glanced then at the mountains, at the looming blackness of them. They revealed nothing, offered nothing, and might conceal much.

The corral, across the road from the stage station, was empty. Until the horses arrived there was no way out of here but to walk, and he had no intention of walking. Or of leaving, for that matter. He had come to do a job and do a job he would . . . at least until he had money enough to take him to San Francisco and keep him there until he could get a ship.

There were three buildings and the corrals. The station itself was of good size, with a peaked roof a story and a half tall and no porch. The side facing the trail had a door and three small windows.

The barn for the housing of the horses was as sturdily built as the station itself. There was a lean-to back of the corrals for the temporary housing of additional stock. Behind the corral was a low hill.

Loccard went to the door. It was fastened shut from the outside with a hasp held in

place by a whittled stick. Removing the
stick, he let the door swing open. It
creaked on rusty hinges and inside the air
felt heavy, the dead air of a room long
closed. For a moment he hesitated on the
threshold, for there was something clammy
and unclean about the smell.

With a shrug, he entered. Glass from a
shattered bottle littered the floor and the
pieces of a broken chair had been brushed to
one side. At the end of the room was a bar,
a long table with two benches, and one
intact chair. On the back-bar were several
bottles and a few unwashed glasses. The
cash-drawer was empty. Nearby was a scale
for weighing gold-dust.

The fireplace was large, occupied by two
half-burned logs.

In back was a kitchen, which housed a
range, a boiler, and a good stack of cut
wood. The pots and pans were clean and
polished. Wonder of wonders, there were a
couple of flatirons.

On the left of the door where he had
entered was a room with an unmade bed, a
bed with a wooden frame and leather straps
for springs. An old coat and a slicker hung
on pegs, and alongside them a gun-belt
and holster. There was a pistol still in the
holster.

All else was dust and cobwebs.

He glanced again at the gun-belt,
frowning. Odd that a man should leave
without his gun.

Returning to the kitchen, he put on water

for coffee, brought in his gear, and closed
the door. Hesitating a moment, he turned
back smiling at himself, and dropped the bar
in place.

Yet he had one more thing to do. He lifted
the bar again and taking the former station
keeper's clothing outside, he set fire to
it. No telling how many lives were lost.

With the water on, he puttered about,
cleaning up, putting things to rights. He
discovered an ax, razor-sharp, and a cross-
cut saw. There were several wedges for
splitting logs as well as a pick, shovel,
and gold-pan.

Suddenly curious, he checked the pistol.
It had been fired not long since . . . three
times. Never liking the presence of unloaded
guns, accidents always seeming to happen
with guns suspected of being empty, he
slipped cartridges into the empty chambers
and returned the gun to its holster.

Outside it was now quite dark. The stars
seemed very close because the mountain air
was clear. Stepping outside, he walked to
the middle of the road, looking both ways.
All was dark and still. Suddenly there was a
swoosh in the air above him; involuntarily,
he ducked. An owl . . . and a big one.

Not since childhood had he lived in the
mountains, and the mountains he had known
were far different from these, for even the
trees and flowers of the eastern mountains
were different. Since that time he had been
at sea, the shallow seas of the Malay

archipelago as well as along the China coast and Japan.

Returning to the station, he rebarred the door, poured a cup of coffee, and sat down at the table. The gun-belt and pistol he had taken from Steve Darnell lay on the table. It was a fine weapon, nicely balanced and easy to the hand. That had been trouble he had not wanted, but Darnell was evidently a known man and considered a dangerous one. Seeing in Jeremy Loccard a stranger and obviously not a western man, he had thought to have some amusement. Darnell had a few drinks under his belt, and in such circumstances, apparently he often became quarrelsome.

Loccard had not been wearing a gun, as he had much of his life, for the islands and the waters where he'd sailed were infested with pirates, and had been from as far back as records existed.

Two men had vanished from this place . . . how?

Of course, there were men who could not accept solitude. A few days of silence and loneliness were all they could stand and they must get away, no matter how. That could have been it.

Uneasily, he glanced at the black squares of the windows. Anybody or anything could be out there . . . or at least that's what Duro Weaver had suggested.

What did he mean by anything?

He went from window to window, checking. Cobwebbed and dirty as they were it was

unlikely anything within could be seen from
without, beyond the light itself. For the
first time he was struck by the smallness of
the panes and the strength of the windows
themselves.

A skilled workman, he realized these were
not the original doors or windows. The doors
were of double thickness and strongly
hinged, mounted obviously by someone who
wanted stronger, thicker doors.

Why?

He tried to recall what Duro Weaver had
said about the Indians of the vicinity.
Pah-utes, and further east the Mojaves.
There were other tribes who lived close
about whose names he had forgotten, and a
tribe called the Tehachapis who lived in the
mountains of the same name. They were rarely
seen, but seemed friendly.

He added fuel to the fire and poured a
fresh cup of coffee. Then he opened his sea-
chest and got out a pair of black dungarees,
a black and white checked shirt, and fresh
socks and underwear. He was taking out the
shirt when something fell to the floor.

It was an amulet, a good-luck charm given
him by an old priest of some obscure
religion of which he knew nothing. Actually,
he heard later, it was a coin of Krananda,
believed by many to be the oldest coinage of
India. On it were several symbols: a Tree of
Life, a swastika, and others. He had worn it
from the day it was given him but had taken
it from his neck while undergoing treatment
for his wounds.

Not one to place faith in luck, either good or bad, he treasured the charm as a memento, not only of the priest and his daughter whom Loccard had helped out of a bad corner, but as a memento of the girl herself.

She had been a dainty, lovely thing with whom he had no means of communication beyond a few clumsy signs. All he had been able to discover was that they had come from some far land, both as a pilgrimage and in flight from some unnamed danger.

Yet, superstitious or not, he had emerged reasonably unscathed from a half-dozen brawls and two dozen hand-to-hand fights with pirates as well as the fight with Darnell, all while wearing the charm.

"What the hell," he muttered, and slipped the charm over his head. "It never did me any harm."

Hours later he was awakened by a faint sound. His fingers closed around the butt of the pistol. Then he lay still . . . listening.

He heard it again. Something outside the station, something silent, stealthy, creeping. Gently he eased himself from under the blankets and swung his feet to the floor.

Very carefully someone was lifting the latch, then pushing against the door. The door itself was heavy, the bar a formidable piece of timber. Nothing happened beyond that first creak. After one push the man or creature desisted.

Pistol in hand, Loccard edged to the window and peered out. He could, of course, see nothing. Vaguely through the unclean window he could see distant stars and the outline of the barn roof against the sky, and nothing more.

Yet something or somebody was out there, something that moved very quietly, something that did not wish to be seen, something with intelligence enough not to waste strength on a barred door.

CHAPTER II

Loccard waited, straining his ears for the slightest sound; moving silently, he went to each of the other doors and windows, but he could see nothing.

He was a tough, hardened young man, and as mate on a windjammer he was accustomed to responsibility, and to facing whatever trouble came. On such a ship it was always the chief mate who checked things out first, then reported to the captain, who usually made the decisions.

Now he was mate and master both, and he considered the situation. He was tempted to go outside and face whatever was there, but if he was wrong about someone trying the latch, and it happened to be a grizzly, he would be in serious trouble. Moreover, at this time he had nothing to protect outside, so there was insufficient reason for taking the risk.

Moving in the dark, he went to the kitchen. The glow from the coals was faint, so he added fuel, then put on the coffeepot.

Taking up his watch, he brought it to the grate, where he could check the numerals. It was two-fifteen.

Restless and curious, he went from window to window, listening. When the coffee was hot he filled a cup and sat down.

Something had pushed hard against the door, but finding it firm, pushed no more. That argued for an intelligence beyond that of an animal. Yet the push against the door had given him an impression of great weight, and what could have such weight but a grizzly?

With the coming of daylight he finished the last of the coffee over a few strips of bacon and sourdough bread. As he ate his eyes studied the doors and the windows.

Whoever had strengthened them had been a cunning workman. He had built strong against whatever might come. . . . Had he known something? Felt some premonition, perhaps? Had he built the windows higher in the walls and the doors to their new strength before or after he began to fear what might be outside?

Before, quite possibly, or he might not have remained to build them.

Obviously they had strength enough, for

they were unbroken. Despite that, the man was gone.

It was unlikely Indians had taken him, for they would have looted or burned the station.

Nevertheless, the man was gone, and another, also.

Which one had done the building? He who had first disappeared? Or the man who followed him?

That they had been taken while outside seemed apparent, which meant that when outside he must be wary at all times.

When he had finished eating he took up the new rifle, loaded it, and went outside, drawing the door to behind him.

There were no tracks on the hard-packed clay around the station. He walked to the barn and found twelve stalls, six on either side. There was a small tack room containing some worn harness, a fairly good saddle, and a rawhide lariat of the type used by the vaqueros of California. There was also a pitchfork and a scythe.

He refilled the water-barrel near the well, carried several buckets of water to the trough in the corral, and while doing so saw the tracks of a deer. There was another track, also, but it was oddly smudged and could not be identified. Yet it was a fresh track.

Mindful of what he had been told, he carried fresh water into the house, filling two buckets and the boiler. As he moved about he kept the rifle in his left hand,

and his eyes strayed from time to time to
the surrounding hills. The hills close by
were bald, covered only by some close-
setting growth that he did not recognize. On
the more distant slopes were trees and
occasional outcroppings of boulders, worn by
wind and blown sand.

Far overhead a bird soared. Twice he
looked at it, brow puckered. It was a
large . . . a very large bird. Perhaps it
was a condor, for it was said condors
inhabited some of the mountain valleys they
had passed coming hence from Los Angeles.

Finally, he returned to the station, got a
broom, and swept out; then, rigging a crude
mop, he took water and swabbed the floor as
he would a ship's deck.

He was a man to whom cleanliness was a
habit, developed over long confinement to
close quarters at sea and the necessity of
setting an example for those who served on
the ships with him. He decided what he must
do was rig a holystone so he could clean the
floors properly.

Loccard walked to the door to wring out
his mop, and was standing there when his
nostrils caught a strange, fetid odor, an
odd scent that made the hair prickle on the
back of his neck.

For a moment he looked about. A skunk? It
could be, of course. The smell was not
unlike that of a skunk, yet different
somehow. He was turning to go back inside
when his eyes caught several long hairs
trapped under slivers on the outer surface

of the door. They were coarse hairs, a kind of a dirty whitish yellow in shade, and unlike anything he had ever seen.

There were three of them, and carefully, he took them from the door and went inside. Why he did so he did not know, but he placed them in a folded paper for future examination.

Certainly, he had never seen such hairs. A silvertip grizzly? No . . . these were different.

When Weaver came next with the stage he would ask him, as being long in this country, he might recognize them. The hairs had been more than two thirds the way up the door, and standing on the flagstone doorstep they would have been at eye level for him, or even a mite higher. He shook his head, irritated by the puzzle.

A grizzly standing on his hind legs could have left them. Probably hairs from the white part of his chest, he thought.

Cleaning up the place took most of the day. He stored his food, gathered extra wood, and made ready for the night. The horses would be coming any day, and he found himself looking forward to their arrival. They meant more work for him, but they would also be company.

He glanced toward the flanks of the mountains, thick with a stand of timber. Suddenly, he thought of his telescope and went within.

When he had been unable to return to his

ship they had put his gear ashore, and the
telescope had been stored in his sea-chest.

Getting the glass from his gear, he
returned to the door, where he spent some
time examining the mountains. They were
rougher than they at first seemed; he saw
among the trees more of the outcroppings of
boulders, and what could be cliffs.

As darkness came on, he found himself
growing uneasy. He retreated within the
station, rebuilt his fire, and settled down
for an evening of reading. As a boy he had
no access to books, and had worked most of
the time from daylight until dark, finally
going to bed so tired he was at once asleep.
Not until he went to sea had he any
experience of reading for pleasure.

He had but one book, a copy of a novel by
Bulwer-Lytton given to him when he lay
recovering from his wound. It was <u>Rienzi,
the Last of the Roman Tribunes</u>. He settled
down to reading, taking time out only to
replenish the fire. Several times he went to
the door or windows but heard nothing, saw
nothing. At last, his eyes growing tired, he
turned in.

At daylight he took his rifle and scouted
the area. He found no tracks, no sign that
anything had come near the station.
Relieved, he went back inside, taking care,
however, to bar the door.

He had fried bacon and put out some bread
and dried apples which he had soaked well
during the night, and was preparing to sit

down when he heard a sound of hoofbeats,
then a shout.

He went to the door, took down the bar,
and glanced out. Seeing a herd of horses and
two men driving them, he put his rifle down
beside the door and stepped outside.

The older man rounded up a bay with three
white stockings that seemed inclined to
stray while Loccard walked across the road
and took down the gate-bars.

When he saw the last of the sixteen horses
through the gate, he looked around at the
riders. "Coffee's on. Come on in. You had
breakfast?"

"We done et," the younger man said. He was
scarcely more than a boy, but tall and
strong. "We camped up the road a piece."

"You could have come on in last night,"
Loccard suggested.

"Never git me to come up here of a night,"
the older man said grimly. "This here's no
place to be once dark comes."

"He stopped away back yonder," the younger
one said. "I'd have come on in."

"Ain't got no sense. Not a durned bit. Not
after what happened to them others."

"What did happen?" Loccard asked,
following them through the door.

"Disappeared, that's what. Vanished. One
day they was here, next day gone. I come up
here bringin' grub an' such. They was gone."

"Well, not both t' onct. Each in his own
time. Jed Slocum . . . he was a good man.
Sharp man, too. He wasn't feared of no
ha'nts, but little good it did him."

"What do you think happened?" Loccard asked.

"Who knows? Somethin' got 'em. Jed, he lived it out for nigh three months. Got thinner an' more peaked by the day. Looked like a dead man last I seen of him, but he wouldn't say nothin' about it."

"He said something to me," the boy said.

The older man stared at him. "You?"

"He ast me if I ever seen a yaller bear." The younger man sat down on a bench and stretched his long legs. "I said I never. There was no such thing. Brown bears, black bears, an' them polar bears. They're white. But no yaller bears."

Jeremy Loccard shrugged. "Who knows what's in those mountains? There could be bears of a kind no man has ever seen."

"Or other things," the older man spat, and Loccard winced. He had just swept and mopped that floor.

He helped himself to bacon from the frying-pan. "You ever really _look_ at this here country? She's good country. Grass, timber, water if you know where to look, but there's no Injuns . . . or mighty few. Now I say that's odd . . . mighty odd. I come west along the Humboldt River. Godforsaken country, but there's Injuns there, so why not here? I say they either was run off or somethin' took 'em."

Loccard got the pot from the stove and filled cups for them. "Those horses out there," he asked, "any of them riding stock?"

The younger man shrugged. "That grulla mustang has been ridden a good bit. Fact is, that's why we brought him along. If any stock gits away you can round 'em up ridin' him.

"There's two or three others been rid some, too, but mostly they're drivin' stock." The older man glanced at Loccard. "Heard your name. Jimmy, ain't it?"

"Jeremy . . . Jeremy Loccard."

"Jed Slocum, he was a nice ol' feller. Good man. I never did cotton to that Zimmerman, though. He looked mean . . . kind of sullen, like."

"He was the man here before Slocum?"

"Uh-huh. He was here three, maybe four months. Always had his nose in a book, big ol' books, like of which I never did see . . . kind of worried pictures in them."

"Worried?"

"Uh-huh. There was devils and such."

"Weird?"

"That's it. Worried. He seen me lookin' at a book left open on the table and he got mad as hell. He come over here and slammed it shut, said something about me bein' nosy. Anybody else an' I'd have took it up, but not him. He was a mean . . . mighty mean."

"He'd of killed you, Tom."

"Mebbe. An' mebbe I don't kill so easy." Tom glanced at Loccard, indicating the gun he wore. "You any good with that?"

"Good enough."

The older man chuckled. "All y'have to be!" he said. "That's all you have to be!"

A thought occurred to Loccard. "That
Zimmerman, now? Somebody come an' get his
gear?"

Tom looked over at his companion. "You get
it, Beak?"

"Must still be around. I know Duro never
brought it down . . . all them books, too.
It would have taken some liftin' to get them
aboard. Heaviest boxes I ever did see, an' I
helped him off-load them."

"Them?"

"There was three . . . not so big but
almighty heavy."

"Hid 'em, prob'ly. He was that kind.
Wanted nobody nosin' around. He said as
much, more'n onct. He had some notion . . .
I dunno what . . . but some kinda notion
about this place . . . these mountains.
Maybe the desert.

"Asked all kinda questions. What was the
Injuns like? Was they on' Paiutes? I ever
see any other kind? Ever hear tell of any
stories the Injuns tell?

"Hell, like I tol' him, these Injuns don't
tell no stories. They don't even talk much.
Anyway, what would they have to talk about?
Nothin' but ignorant savages, runnin' around
with no drawers on."

Loccard nodded. "Maybe so, but I've sailed
on some far waters, and I've seen
things. . . . It doesn't pay to take too
much for granted with any people, no matter
how primitive they seem."

"Bah! The sooner they're all gone, the

better. I seen aplenty of them, here and
there. Good for nothin'."

Loccard did not reply. To protest would do
no good. The man had his mind made up and
what he had decided pleased him, and left
room for no further consideration of the
subject. A neat pigeonhole was often a
substitute for thought and a means of
isolating ideas that might otherwise become
disturbing.

"That Zimmerman, now. He was a canny one.
Mean, but canny. I think he had something,
some burr under his saddle. He didn't come
here just for no job. He was _looking_ for
something, something he figured was worth
plenty."

"How could that be?" Loccard suggested
mildly. "In a country where there was
nothing but savages?"

The contradiction irritated the older man.
"Mayn't always have been Injuns here. Who
knows who was here before? I tell you, I
seen things . . . well, they was things no
Injun ever done."

"What sort of things?" Jeremy asked.

"Mummies, an' such. Seen 'em in caves."

"Probably just the dry air," Loccard
suggested.

"Mebbe. Mebbe so. I was just tellin' you
what I _seen_. I seen aplenty, I have. That
Zimmerman, though. He was no tin horn. He
was a mighty big, mean man but he was
knowledgeable. I never figured nothin' would
happen to _him_."

The older man squinted at Loccard. "We got

us a bet, down to Los Angeles. We got us a
bet on you. I'm sayin' you don't last out
the month. Somethin' will git you, or you'll
run."

Loccard had disliked the man before; he
liked him even less now. "Who'd you bet
with?" he asked.

"Weaver. He says you'll stick it. I say
you won't. I say something's goin' t' git
you."

"I hope it was a good-sized bet," Loccard
suggested. "Something worthwhile?"

"Bet him a month's wages, mine against
his'n." He grinned, showing broken teeth.
"He makes three times what I do, so I got me
a good bet."

"No bet is good if you lose," Loccard
said. "And I am going to make sure you do."

The older man shot him an angry look, then
went outside. The boy lingered. "Mister," he
said. "What he said about that Zimmerman was
true. Those books now . . . There was some
kinda strange signs inside. One book had
some o' these funny signs where one end
points one way, and the other end the other
way."

"A swastika?" Loccard sketched the design
in the air.

"That's it."

Loccard stood in the door and watched them
ride away. He glanced toward the horses, who
seemed at home in the corral, but he went
out and added several buckets of water to
the trough, his eyes restless over the

mountainside and down the trail toward the
desert.

Zimmerman had brought three heavy boxes
and none had been taken away, so either they
were here or they'd been taken by someone.
He hesitated but did not add, some<u>thing</u>.

Slocum had lost weight, had been under
strain, had asked the boy about yellow
bears. Had he seen such a bear? Or was it
something else? Some other kind of creature?

The articles found in the living quarters
of the station had obviously been those of
the last occupant, who was Jed Slocum, so
where were those of Zimmerman, who had
preceded him?

Walking to the corral, he glanced over the
horses. Before going off to sea he had known
a little about horses, and these were good
stock. He located the grulla and offered him
a handful of rich green grass, pulled from
near the well. The grulla took it gratefully
and held still while Loccard rubbed his neck
and talked to him, but shied away when no
more grass was forthcoming.

Yet it was the beginning of a rapport
between them, and Jeremy hoped the grulla
understood who he was: the man in charge,
the man who fed him, the man who would be
riding him.

Nothing had been said as to when the next
stage would come through, but he assumed it
would be today. He had turned back toward
the house when from the corner of his eye he
caught a flicker of movement near the corner
of the barn.

He turned sharply, glancing that way,
cursing himself for not having the rifle.
His pistol, however, was in his holster,
easy to his hand.

For a moment there was nothing, and then
he saw them.

An Indian man appeared suddenly,
ghostlike, at the corner of the barn.
Loccard blinked, and a woman was standing
beside the Indian. Then one by one, a slim,
wiry boy, a girl of perhaps eight or nine,
and one still younger, of perhaps but four.

They stood, silent, staring, their eyes
upon him as though he himself were a ghost.

CHAPTER III

"Hello there," he spoke quietly, not
wanting to alarm them, for they seemed
poised to run. "Come on in!" He swung his
arm at them in a gathering gesture. He knew
nothing of sign language but hoped they
would understand.

They did not move, just watching him. He
smiled at them, and then went about the
corral, checking it for strength. On the far
side he came to an abrupt halt. There in the
earth was a smudged track, a huge track, not
unlike that of a bear, yet different,
somehow.

He glanced at the Indians. The man had
come a little closer, so he motioned them on
again, then pointed to the track in the

earth. This time the Indian came on, whether from curiosity or because he was getting over his fear, Loccard did not know.

When the Indian was only a few feet off, Loccard indicated the track, then stepped back a little, spreading his hands and shrugging, as if to say he did not know what it was.

The Indian took one glance, then stepped back so quickly he almost fell. He backed away quickly. "Bad! Bad!" he spoke hoarsely, obviously frightened.

"Bear?"

"No bear! Bad! Ver' bad!"

"No bear? Then what is it?"

"Bad!" The Indian backed away. His fear was obvious. "More big! Ver' bad!"

Loccard gave it up, for the time being at least. "Eat?" he suggested.

The Indians had been about to walk away; now they hesitated. The man wanted to go, the woman was protesting. Her gestures indicated she was speaking of the children.

"Come!" Loccard said. "There is meat."

Reluctantly, they followed him, avoiding the area near the track. Loccard was puzzled, for their fear was obvious and he had never known Indians to fear any animal. To respect them, to be wary of them, but not to fear. He had known no Indians so far west, yet he had known other primitive peoples, and fear of wild animals was rare among them.

There might be fear, however, if the

animal was possessed of an evil spirit, or
believed to be so.

He thought of that. There was something
here, and he must know more. He must know
more to satisfy his growing curiosity, and
he must know more simply to survive.

He led the Indians back to the station and
sat them down on the bench at the door. Then
he went inside, put together some bread and
meat, and brought it out to them. He did not
know these Indians, and they might only be
scouts for an attacking party lying somewhere nearby, awaiting a signal. Others had
vanished from this place, and no man knew
how. He doubted that Indians were involved,
but who could be sure? He would take nothing
for granted.

He brought out meat and bread for himself,
then squatted on his heels where he could
see the road, and ate with them, asking no
questions, saying nothing at first.

Finally when he did it was in his halting
Spanish. He spoke of a good day, asked if
they'd traveled far.

"Not far," the Indian replied in English.

"You are alone?"

The Indian indicated the woman and
children. "They are with me. We look."

"For a place to live?"

The Indian shook his head. He seemed to be
searching for a word, then gave up and said
it in Spanish. "Amigos."

"Friends? Here?" Then he said quietly, "I
will be your friend."

The woman glanced at him slyly, almost

hopefully, but she said nothing. The
children watched him with large dark eyes.

"I have just come," Loccard said. "I like
it here."

"You go," the Indian said quietly. "It is
not good place for man."

"I serve the stage. The stage goes
through. I help."

"You go."

Loccard was silent. He went inside and got
cups from the shelf and filled them with
coffee.

"You know this place?" He gestured around,
taking it all in. "You have been here
before?"

"I am Kawaiisu. This my land. One time I
live"--he pointed toward a place to the
northeast--"there."

He sipped his coffee. Obviously he had
once known more English, but now was feeling
his way with a language long unused. At
least, that was what Loccard thought. Having
partially learned many tongues himself, he
knew how quickly a language only slightly
known can disappear. That was the trouble of
being a seafaring man. One rarely stayed
long enough in one place to learn a language
well. He knew a smattering of marketplace,
waterfront language from fifty ports.

Suddenly the Indian said, "One time many
mans here. All gone, maybe." He looked at
Loccard. "You see?"

"No . . . not yet. I have not been here
long," he said. "You are the first Indian I
have seen. But," he added, "I was not

expecting to see any yet. Maybe they have
not made up their minds about me yet. Maybe
they look at me to decide what to do next."

"They look, too. Soon they take you."

"'They'? Who are 'they'? And where would
they take me? And why?"

The Indian shrugged. He wiped his hands on
his legs. "Is no good here. Many mans
here . . . where now? Gone . . ."

He finished his coffee and Loccard
refilled the cup, adding sugar. The Indian
sipped his coffee. "All around . . . bad
places here. Ghost places. You no stay. You
go . . . now."

"I must stay."

They sat silent. The children finished
their eating and their mother likewise. They
sat silently beside Loccard while the
minutes passed into a half hour, then an
hour. Finally, Loccard got up. "You
stay . . . rest. We talk."

The Indian stirred a little, but made no
reply. The man seemed lonely, hungry for
more than food. Or was that something
Loccard was simply reading into him? It was
hard to tell with an Indian, for all peoples
do not manifest interest or joy or dismay in
the same manner.

Shortly before noon he harnessed six
horses and led them out of the corral and
tied them to the corral bars to await the
stage.

"That animal?" he said, after a while.
"The one that made the track, he is bigger
than a bear?"

The Indian held up two fingers. "Big like
two bears. Maybe three. Long hair . . .
yellow. No bullet kill him. No arrow."

"He lives in the mountains?"

"No live here . . . other place."

Loccard went back inside and began making
fresh coffee. The stage would be coming
along soon and the passengers would want
some refreshment. He built up the fire and
when he looked outside, the Indians were
gone.

Loccard walked onto the road and looked up
and down. The family, if that's what they
were, had vanished. Well . . . He shrugged
and went back inside. In such a short time
they could not have gone far, and they might
return.

He heard the stage before he saw it, heard
Duro Weaver's halloo and then saw it coming
in the distance. He went out to the roadside
and was standing there when the stage came
wheeling up and stopped. He caught the
horses by their bridles, steadied them a
bit, and then he began unhooking the traces
as the passengers got stiffly down. There
were three men and two women.

One of the women was scarcely more than a
girl, and she looked frightened. The older
woman was tall, slender, and very beautiful
in a cold, somewhat haughty way. The men
moved toward the stage station, and the
younger woman made as if to follow, but was
stopped by a sharp word. The other woman
stood in the road and looked carefully
about.

When the team was taken to the corral and the fresh team harnessed, Loccard walked back to the station with Duro.

"You all right?" The stage driver spoke softly.

"Sure. Everything's fine."

"Didn't know whether to expect you or not," Weaver said, "the way thing's been happenin' up here."

"I'll make it," Loccard spoke with more assurance than he felt.

They went inside and he took up the coffeepot and filled cups. He glanced at the girl, smiling when their eyes met. She seemed startled and shot a quick glance at her companion, who seemed not to have noticed.

She was pretty, Loccard decided, almighty pretty. She was frightened, too, but why he could not guess. All three men were well dressed, and seemed to have no connection with each other or the women.

The older man, who might have been one of those who invested in mining ventures, or began them, waved a hand at the country around. "It must be lonely here. Do you have many visitors?"

"I like wild country," Loccard said, "but visitors? Only some Indians."

"Indians?" It was the older woman who spoke. "I thought . . . I mean, I believed there were no Indians here. It is not true, then?"

"There was a family," Loccard said. "They came by just before you did. It is said there are Indians in the higher mountains. Some call them the Kawaiisu, some the Tehachapis."

"This is excellent coffee," a man whom Loccard took to be a gambler commented. "Better than I expected from the tender of a stage station."

The third man, who wore a black suit, spoke up. "You have not looked at him, my friend. I detect a certain air, a certain style. It is the style of command."

"An Army officer?" The gambler studied Loccard with interest. "I believe not."

"Will you have some more coffee?" Loccard suggested.

Duro Weaver, who sat at the end of the table, knew how Loccard felt. "Better drink up," he said. "We've little time and I want to be out of the pass before dark."

The older woman glanced at him, but her expression did not change. She was, Loccard thought, a remarkably beautiful woman who for some reason was trying not to appear so. . . . Was it simply that she did not wish to draw attention to herself? Her eyes were large, her bone structure delicate yet strong.

The mining man, if such he was, glanced at Weaver. "Any special reason to be out of the mountains before dark? Like the lady here, I didn't think there were Indians in this part of the country."

"Could be outlaws," the gambler suggested. "There's one named Vasquez--"

"I didn't think that was what he meant,"

the man in the black suit commented. "I think our good driver had something else in mind."

Nobody spoke for a minute, and Jeremy Loccard went to the door. The sun was sinking behind the mountains. It would soon be dark here, although light upon the desert, only a few miles away. He glanced toward the corral. The grulla had its head up, nostrils flared, looking north toward the darkest mountains.

He glanced down the pass toward the desert. A weird yellow light showed there. "Weaver?" he spoke in a casual tone. "Got a minute?"

The stage driver got up and walked to the door, wiping the back of his hand across his handlebar mustache. Loccard indicated the yellow look over the desert. "Is that what I think it is?"

"Sandstorm," Weaver said, "a bad one. You're sheltered here, don't get much of it."

"The wind is picking up, though."

Weaver went outside and walked along the road a little, looking down the pass. He walked back. "You got comp'ny, son. No way to get a team to face that. Sometimes the sand'll take the hide right off a man."

Loccard shrugged. "Means you'll have to spend the night at Twenty Mile," he commented dryly.

Duro Weaver swore softly, bitterly. "I'll tell 'em," he said, "then we better put up the team." He paused again. "Put 'em in the barn."

They walked back to the station together, and as they stepped in, the older woman started to rise. "Is it not time?" she asked. "It seems to me we have stopped overlong."

"We'll be here longer," Weaver said. He took out his pipe and began to fill it. "There's a sandstorm blowin' out on the flat, blowin' like the mill-tails of Hell!"

Loccard was looking at the older woman. Her features had suddenly seemed to harden and for a moment he saw something in her face that seemed wholly evil, something so--

She turned toward him, and her expression changed swiftly. She smiled, beautifully. Her teeth were very even, very white. "We will be all right here, won't we? I mean, we don't have to be afraid of those Indians, do we?"

"Of course not." He gestured about. "This place is very strong. . . . Nothing could get in, unless we let it in. And we are well armed."

She looked at him, and he thought her eyes were faintly amused, even taunting. "Are your rifles the answer to everything?"

"Sometimes they have to suffice," Loccard replied quietly, "although I've had no trouble here."

He followed Weaver outside and they led the horses to the stable and stripped off the harness, hanging it on pegs inside the stable. They forked hay into the mangers,

and then went outside. Loccard caught the
grulla then and took him into the stable,
too.

Weaver hesitated in the road. "Loccard,
tell me honest. You seen anything out here?"

"No," he said. "I've seen nothing." He
paused. The wind caught dried leaves and
scattered them down the road, moving a
little ripple of sand along with them. The
wind would get into the pass soon, and
they'd be feeling it. And that was the
trouble . . . they would not be able to
hear.

"I've seen nothing, Duro, but there was
something."

Weaver took his pipe from his mouth,
looking at him.

"Something almighty big, something bigger
than the biggest grizzly you ever heard
of, something that pushed against the door,
something that might have weighed a ton or
more."

Weaver swore, slowly, emphatically,
solemnly.

"I found a smudged track . . . long claws,
and I found some yellow hairs. Long hairs,
maybe seven or eight inches, mighty coarse.
Smelled awful."

He listened to the wind, saw the trees
bend with it. A tumbleweed went rolling by
on the road.

"The Indians saw the track. They were
scared. I fed 'em, tried to get them to
stick around. They disappeared."

"Don't do no good to feed Injuns," Weaver said. "Underfoot all the time."

"I wanted to know what they know. They said I'd better go . . . something would <u>get</u> me, like it got the others, and the Indians."

"Indians, too?"

"That was my impression. There used to be Indians here. Now there are none. Maybe they just went away, but that Indian didn't think so, he didn't think so at all. He was scared."

"What d' you think it was?"

Loccard shrugged. "Look, I've been in fifty countries, talked to a hundred kinds of people. The white man thinks he knows it all because right now he's running ahead of the pack. I came to one conclusion, knocking around in foreign parts, and that was that there was just a whole lot I didn't know.

"Maybe there's animals we've never seen, maybe there are <u>things</u> we've never seen. I had a dog whistle once that I couldn't hear, but my dog could hear it.

"I picked up cargo along the coast of Sumba a couple of times. It's an island in the East Indies east of Java, but off the mainline of those islands. We picked up sandalwood there, bird's nests--the Chinese make soup from them--skins, shells, and sometimes horses. There's a lot of wild horses on the island.

"I went back inland to see the high plains where the horses ran. They were there, all right, but here and there I saw stone walls surrounded by thickets of brush through which no path seemed to go.

"These were said to be villages long deserted, although they were not unlike some of the villages in other parts of the island. The people avoided them. Or perhaps they only wanted me to avoid them. In a thicket near one of those villages I saw a piece of what looked like rocks fitted together into some sort of a floor or platform. There were low trees around, a few boulders. I started to go near but they advised against it.

"Few minutes later I looked back and there was a man standing there beside that flat rock. He was looking at me. Or I thought he was. He hadn't been there a few minutes before."

The wind was blowing harder. Duro Weaver started across the road, then stopped again. "Those tracks you seen? Those claw marks? You ever see anything like them before?"

Loccard looked at him, leaning closer so Weaver could hear over the rush of wind down the pass. "One time. We were loading tar down at those brea pits out there west of Los Angeles. There were a lot of bones in that tar; made trouble for us, as they were always in the way. I came on a forearm or foreleg of some creature with claws like that. Whatever it was, it was mighty big, and it must have had tremendous crushing power in those forelegs."

"I never seen no such animal," Weaver protested.

Loccard gestured. "You ever been back in those mountains?"

"No."

"Well, neither have I."

CHAPTER IV

They went inside, closing the door on the wind, which was now blowing a gale. The fire on the hearth was warm, there was a smell of coffee in the air, and the men were gathered about the table, talking.

At the fireplace the two women sat . . . not talking.

The master of a ship, as Jeremy Loccard had occasionally been, or the chief mate, which he had been since he was nineteen, learned to be reticent, sharing his thoughts but rarely. Such a man learned to judge the shades of feeling among a crew, the way the ship creaked in different seas and winds, the way the lines handled and the look of the sails. There was so much in the handling of ships and men that could be found in no book.

Loccard knew that Duro Weaver was a brave, confident man. In any situation he would be where he needed to be and he would be doing what was necessary.

He closed the door and put the bar in place. They had fuel enough, for the nights were cold at this time of year, and they had food enough. The sandstorm might blow itself

out overnight, but if it followed the way of
storms at sea they might be in for two or
three days of it.

The man in the black suit looked around at
Loccard. "Any bears in these mountains?"

"Lots of them," Weaver spoke up. "When we
built the barn, yonder, we killed a grizzly
had to weigh eight or nine hundred pounds."

"Are they really dangerous?"

"Mister"--Duro Weaver got out his pipe--
"any wild animal is potentially dangerous. I
seen a man badly mauled by a buck deer. Up
Frisco way I saw a woman half-killed by a
cub bear she thought was mighty cute. She
just had to ruffle his fur, she said.

"Wild animals are _wild_, you got to
remember that; also, they're like folks, and
they have their moods. Bears more than most.
Bears are notional. A body has to be wary
where a bear's concerned."

"You've hunted this country?"

"No." Weaver stuffed his pipe with
tobacco. "I never hunted about here and I
don't know of anybody who has . . . 'less it
was Zimmerman."

Suddenly Loccard realized Weaver had
sharpened their attention. Even the women at
the fire were listening.

"Zimmerman?" The man in the black suit was
too casual. "Who was he?"

"Station man here . . . a while back."

"What became of him?"

Weaver had not wanted to answer that
question but had seen it coming. "Disappeared," he replied coolly. "He was here one

day, and the next day he was gone. Maybe,"
he added, "he come onto one o' them cute
bears."

"Disappeared? Did anybody look for him?"

Weaver stooped to the fireplace and took
up a burning twig to light his pipe. "Look?
Where? Mister, there's a sight of country
out yonder. Take a mighty big army with lots
of time to comb it.

"Nobody," he added, "knows what's out
there. Maybe nothing. Maybe things no man
has ever seen. Maybe things no man wants to
see.

"I've heard tell of a canyon back yonder
to the northwest . . . maybe twelve, fifteen
mile from here. Maybe not so far. Injuns
used to go there. Left holes in the rock
where they used to grind acorns. There's two
good springs in that canyon, grass, wood for
the burning, shelter from the wind . . . but
no Injuns. Not no more."

"Why?"

"Your guess is as good as mine. They
follow the creek up the main canyon, but
you'll never catch an Injun going up the
south side of the creek. Least, that's what
I been told."

"Superstition," the mining man suggested.

"That there," Weaver said, "is an easy
word. It's a word used to sidestep many an
explanation, or a belief or idea a man don't
understand."

"Or don't want to take time to study,"
Loccard added.

Weaver nodded toward the outside. "You

ever been out in those mountains <u>alone</u>?
Who's to say what's there? Maybe what the
Injuns believe in is only there because they
believe in it. Maybe in places like this
there's things left over, things that ceased
to be a long time back . . . except in
places like this."

"You're talking nonsense," the mining
engineer commented. "I only believe in
things a man can measure and weigh. Whatever
else there is doesn't matter."

Loccard added fuel to the fire. He
crouched beside it, staring into the coals.
On such a night, in such a wind, they would
hear nothing outside. Maybe it was just as
well. He thought of the horses. If there was
trouble there he must go out.

The older woman came to him. "I am Andrea
Ritter. I must speak with someone who is
familiar with all this." Her gesture took in
the country around.

"I just arrived," Loccard said. "Duro
there, he knows as much as anybody and
that's little enough."

Loccard paused a moment, and then in a
lower voice he said, "What's your interest,
ma'am? If I knew, maybe I could help."

She hesitated, seemed about to speak, then
shook her head. "I cannot. It is too much,
too, too much!"

Duro walked over, a cup of coffee in his
hand. "Heard what you asked, ma'am," he
said, "but there's nobody knows much. Some
figure there just isn't nothing to know.
It's empty country. The first white man

along here so far's anybody knows was a Captain Pedro Fages, exploring for the Spanish folks. Jed Smith come through, but we don't know exactly where. Been a few white men back in yonder huntin' gold, an' that's about it.

"So far's anybody knows the Spanish never paid it much mind. Even the Injuns mostly pulled out an' left."

"Why? Why would they do a thing like that?"

Duro sipped his coffee. He had no answer to that and attempted none. He glanced at Loccard and raised an eyebrow. Neither could understand why a woman such as this was so interested in what was to all obvious view a barren and empty land.

Loccard's eyes went to the girl. She was very pretty, but the scared look was there, too, and she seemed scared of Andrea Ritter as much as anything. Or was he imagining things?

He went back to the kitchen and began putting together a meal. There were supplies enough, and he saw no sense in stinting.

The girl followed him into the kitchen. "May I help?" she asked. "I can cook."

"Sure." He held out a hand. "I'm Jeremy Loccard."

"I am Jennifer Kernaby. . . . Call me Jen."

"I'll do that." He waved a hand about. "We don't have much. For now we'll just make up some cazuela . . . one name for stewed jerked beef. You can chop up some onions for me, if you're of a mind to."

They worked in silence for a few minutes, and he asked, "Goin' far?"

She did not look at him. "Not far. At least, I don't think so. Maybe we'll go back to Los Angeles soon. Andrea wanted to come here."

"Here? This place?"

"I . . . I don't know. She wanted to come here, and she wanted me along. Maybe she's going on up to San Francisco. We talked about it. I think . . . maybe she's looking for land."

Loccard glanced at her. "Ma'am . . . Jen . . . this is no place to look for land. There's land aplenty nigh to the sea, better land than this, I'd say, and it's closer to market. This here is wild country, and it will be for a good time to come."

Suddenly she was close to him. "Mr. Loccard . . . Jeremy? I'm afraid of her."

Instantly she stepped away from him. There was a sound of boot heels clicking, and Andrea Ritter was in the door. "Oh? There you are! I wondered what had become of you."

"I am helping Mr. Loccard," she said primly. "There seemed such a lot to do."

"I am sure he can manage." Andrea's tone was grim. "Come! You'll be all smelling of onions."

She rinsed her hands in the basin, and dried them carefully while Andrea waited, then turned and left the room without a backward glance.

"Make's no sense," he commented, to himself. "Why would she be with someone who scared her? And why would a woman like that be hunting land up <u>here</u>?"

He finished fixing their supper and served it. The mining engineer, whose name proved to be Delphin Rickard, came to the kitchen to help Loccard carry the food to the table. He suspected Rickard came more from a desire to look around than from any desire to help. "That man in the black suit? Do you know him?"

"I never saw any of you before," Loccard said, "and it is unlikely I will see any of you again. I'll make some money here, then be gone."

"Probably a wise choice," he agreed. "This Zimmerman now? Did you know him?"

"No. I don't believe even the man who followed him knew him. Mr. Weaver, your driver . . . he knew him to talk to."

"You've never been out in the mountains?" He took up a platter of sliced beef. "Hunting, or the like of that?"

"I haven't been here long enough."

"Odd that Zimmerman would come here," he mused, looking about. "It's unreasonable."

"You should know enough by now that there's no way of judging people. Just when you think you've got them figured, they'll cross you up. But why Zimmerman? What made him so different?"

"Zimmerman? Ah? There was a strange one! I did not know him, you understand, only <u>of</u>

him. He was a scholar. An authority on the occult, a delver into mysteries."

"You must have him mixed up. This Zimmerman was a mean man by all I hear, a big, strong, and mighty difficult man."

"Of course. He was all of that. I had friends who knew him, or knew of him. He went his own way, shared what he knew with nobody. But why should he come _here_? To such a place as this? What was he looking for? What did he expect to find?"

"Maybe," Loccard said dryly, "he just needed the job, as I did."

"Zimmerman? I doubt it. The man always had access to money. I mean he would seem to be on his uppers, then he would show up with money. And money was a prime requisite with Zimmerman. He liked to live. Champagne and fine wines, the best food, the best women. I think the man loved nothing but his appetites."

Rickard took his platter and went into the next room and Loccard followed with biscuits, cheese, and a pot of stewed fruit.

The puzzle of Zimmerman allied itself to the puzzle of Rickard himself. Why was he here? Where had he come from? What was his connection with Zimmerman?

Yet, he might have given Loccard a clue. Zimmerman could always come up with money, and that implied a source. Was he a wealthy man? Had he wealthy friends or relatives? Or was there some other source for his wealth?

A delver into mysteries, Rickard said. Well, he found his mystery here, surely, and disappeared. Or had he? Suppose he was somewhere about?

Well, suppose he was, thought Loccard. That meant nothing to him. Zimmerman had left his job, gone off on his own. Or been killed.

Killed? By what?

The word brought Loccard up short. Why not by "whom"? Was he already imagining something else? Was he filling his world with creatures of the imagination? Was he not creating a mystery where there might be none?

Once the food was served Loccard sat down with the passengers. The talk about the table seemed so much idle chatter, and only Jen and Duro were silent. That was unusual for Duro, for he was a man who liked people and who talked well, and his long years on the frontier had given him a wealth of stories. Now he merely listened, and if anything, he seemed puzzled.

The fire blazed cheerfully on the hearth and the coal-oil lamps, backed with reflectors, gave added light to the room. Outside the wind howled and sand rattled against the windows.

The coffee smelled good, and slowly Loccard began to relax. He glanced once toward the door of his room. His rifle stood just inside the door.

As though reading his thought, the man in the black suit asked, "Do you always wear a pistol?"

"This country," Duro replied for him, "a

man better. No tellin' what a body'd run
into on the road."

Andrea Ritter smiled. "I am sure there's
noth--" Her voice broke sharply off, for
they all heard it: an eerie cry, heard
faintly but clearly enough during a
momentary lull in the wind.

It was no human cry, nor like any
animal. . . . A bird maybe, but what bird?
What strange sound in the night? Andrea's
eyes went wide; her lips parted as if to
scream, but no sound came. All were
transfixed, all but the man in the black
suit.

"There it is," he said coolly enough, "all
that was needed. It's out there."

They looked at him, staring, nor did any
one of them speak. The cry came again . . .
closer.

"It is coming then," the man in the black
suit said. "It's coming."

COMMENTS: Dad found the Southern California wilderness to be a spooky place. He touched on it in *The Lonesome
Gods* and used that strangeness to a much greater extent in
The Californios. I agree with him. We used to talk about the
feelings we'd get back in the hills and the hot, chaparral-
choked arroyos. It is a haunted landscape, even more so than
a Colorado or Utah canyon full of cliff dwellings. I have no
idea why that should be the case, but we shared the feeling
nonetheless.

The location of this story seems to be very near to

Tehachapi Pass in the area along Highway 58 between Bakersfield and Mojave. The idea of seeing a sandstorm come up from the desert makes complete sense; these days the area is near a giant wind farm. I'm confident in saying this story was written in the early 1970s because Louis mentions a narrow canyon where buckeye trees grow and the Kawaiisu Indians left *pa-haz*, or grinding holes, in the rocks—a description of a piece of property we owned not too far from the pass.

By the time he gets to Chapter 4, it seems Louis had reached a decisive moment in the writing process. The arrival of the odd group of stage passengers suggests that the mystery of the disappearing station agents, and even the existence of some sort of monster, is just the tip of the interdimensional iceberg. The place where Louis stopped writing is probably the place where he was going to have to commit to what the book was going to be about. Dad usually worked

My mother and sister sitting in that narrow canyon at the base of the rocks with the grinding holes.

this sort of thing out unconsciously, but whether it was a conscious or unconscious process, it is obvious to me that he wasn't quite ready to take the next.step. No doubt several of the passengers are in on whatever is happening and it would seem that Jeremy Loccard's amulet will also play a role.

It is amusing to see a moment of Chick Bowdrie–style forensics when Loccard places the smelly hairs in a folded piece of paper. (Bowdrie was a Texas Ranger character Louis wrote about early in his career.) The monster may be a giant sloth, though even as big as they were, I'm not sure they'd be all that aggressive. Perhaps it was a short-faced bear, an extinct carnivore of colossal size ... which would definitely have been something to fear. The bones of both have been found in the La Brea Tar Pits in Los Angeles.

As I mentioned, Dad was working with ideas here that were very similar to ones he experimented with in his novels *The Californios* and *The Haunted Mesa:* strange animals that come from somewhere else, another reality of some sort, and people who know about this other place and, regardless of the danger, wish to exploit it in some way. In his notes on this story Dad mentions checking into Harold Courlander's *The Fourth World of the Hopis* and Frank Waters' *Book of the Hopi.* Both were also inspirations for *Haunted Mesa.* Additionally, Louis considered rereading some of the work of Talbot Mundy, a writer who influenced Dad's more occult-oriented adventure fiction, and Charles Fort, an early collector of unexplained phenomena.

In some ways it seems as if Louis was about to expand on, or even write a sort of sequel to, *The Californios* with this story. His notes mention "a lost city in the desert and the people who lived there." Juan, the old Indian in *The Californios* who can travel between worlds, told the tale of such an Atlantis-like city. Louis jotted down the following bit of dialogue for one of the characters to impart:

"People throw things out of kilter.
The Old Ones knew. Young folks lost a
lot of knowledge. There was a wall in
that town, and on the Wall were
inscriptions. This wall could be read by
the Old Ones, but when the storm came
they were suffocated in the dust, all
but a few who had gone through the
Portals. When they came back all was
gone, their folks, temples, houses
everything gone. They live on the Other
Side now and just return for
pilgrimages, but they don't want folks
in the way. . . . This here is on the
route, the temple is in the mountains
yonder, and the Portals are there. There
were other Openings. . . ."

This idea of portals to other worlds is a significant element in *The Californios* and *Haunted Mesa*. In both there is
another plane of existence that invites exploration and offers
a sense of possibility that our world has been running low on
recently. Louis grew up in a time when the ends of the earth
had yet to be completely explored, but by the time he wrote
these chapters, the likelihood of discovering *King Kong*'s
Skull Island or *Lost Horizon*'s Shangri-La had been reduced
to nearly zero. A parallel universe was the next step for a
writer of the frontier.

Dad also jotted down one final note, possibly of what was
intended to be the last scene in this story:

A vanishing stagecoach? A Lurch of the
stage, a jolt, a cloud of dust, then a
trail the driver has never seen before.
A shining city in the distance. Stage

picks up Loccard, he warns them to turn
around and drive fast, before the
Opening closes. They escape--"Still,
that city now. I'd like to have seen
it."

———————————————

TRAIL OF TEARS

The First Seven Chapters of a Historical Novel

CHAPTER 1

She stood poised and naked upon a point of
rock, caught in a beam of light that fell
through clouds rifted by some far wind.

For an instant she stood upon her ledge
beyond the trees, and upon the high trail
where he rode his horse, Miles Tolan drew up
sharply, astonished by the sudden glimpse of
beauty . . . and then he reached for his
glass.

Yet even as the glass found her figure she
sprang out into the still air, arms flung
wide, and vanished from sight beyond the
trees.

The minutes marched, but he did not ride
on. Far from any settlement, riding through
a mountain wilderness, what he had just seen
was clearly impossible. Yet he had seen her.
How far away had she been? Was it four
hundred yards or a bit less? The clear
mountain air made the distance deceptive.

The sky was overcast with lowering gray

clouds, and the shaft of sunlight where the
girl had stood was the last, anywhere. Now
it, too, was gone. A few scattered drops
fell, and he went to his saddlebags for his
slicker. Huge drops spattered and rattled on
the leaves of the forest, and from afar he
heard the coming of the cold battalions of
rain.

Lieutenant Miles Tolan rode through wild
country upon dim trails known only to wild
game and the Cherokees themselves. He had
chosen this route to Atlanta in making his
change of station, for he loved the wild and
lonely mountains and now it was late summer
with the nights carrying a promise of early
autumn. It had been three days since he had
seen anyone at all, and to see such a girl
in such a place . . . It was preposterous.

Slowly, he walked his horse forward. In
the last ten miles he could remember no
trail that turned off in her direction, but
he searched for one as he rode. The trail he
followed was a narrow passage between two
walls of towering forest, and under the
trees there was a thick tangle of
undergrowth and brush. Then, when he had
traveled more than a mile, he dipped down
from the rise into a wide green meadow where
a mountain stream tumbled over rocks and
beside it ran the thread of a rarely used
path. Despite the impending storm, he turned
the black horse in that direction and rode
swiftly along.

Almost at once the trail left the meadow
and went up into the trees. With mounting

excitement he knew he was riding toward the
rock on which he had seen the girl.

The trail seemed unused, yet suddenly he
emerged from the brush into a small parklike
space, and here at the base of a huge rock
was a pool. Deep, clear, shadowed by
surrounding trees, it was a place of eerie
enchantment, but it was empty.

Arrested by the strange stillness, he sat
his horse in absolute silence, listening.
There was another swift patter of rain upon
the leaves, and somewhere beyond the pool
and cloaked by the trees he could hear a
trickle of running water. Turning his horse,
he rode around the pool's edge to the
towering mass of rock. The ledge from which
the girl dived was at least fifteen feet
above the water, but due to a rise in
elevation, it was all of a hundred feet
above the trail where he had been riding
when he had glimpsed her.

On the far side, near a small stretch of
sandy shore, he found natural steps and a
path leading upward. In the sand at the base
of a rock was a small, smudged print like
that of a moccasin.

Dismounting, he climbed the rock and
looked all about him. The land was deserted,
empty, still.

Turning slowly, he surveyed the entire
scene, and for the first time saw another
trail leading westward. It must have been
this path the girl had taken. Reluctantly
he turned to go, then wedged between the
rocks he saw a book.

Apparently the book had fallen there and been forgotten, perhaps by the girl who had only just left the ledge, for the book showed no mildew or dampness. Careful not to damage the covers, he extracted it from the crack. It was an almost new copy of Thomas Moore's Lalla Rookh. There was no name on the flyleaf.

Glancing around for some sheltered place where the book might be left, he found none. After a moment's hesitation he thrust it into his pocket.

The rain came across the forest with a rush of strength that belied the preliminary showers, and Miles Tolan scrambled down from the rocks and into the saddle. Reluctantly, he rode back to the trail he had been following. There would be adventure enough waiting for him in Atlanta; what he wanted now was an inn where he might get a hot meal and a bed.

Six feet and two inches tall, Miles Tolan was a lean and powerful one hundred and ninety pounds with a dark, Hamlet-like face and green eyes, and he was riding toward an assignment he did not want and had not requested.

It was beautiful land, this country of the Cherokees. He did not blame them for wanting to stay, yet the government had decreed they must move, and move they would. It was the last job he would have asked for, and was definitely not an assignment he had expected after his service in the field, but an Army

officer did not question his orders, he
merely obeyed.

The rain fell steadily. His thoughts
returned to the diver. . . . What would a
woman, especially one familiar with the
writings of Thomas Moore, be doing in such a
place? From all indications there was no
plantation or house within miles, and yet
there she had been.

The smashing sound of a shot cut across
the day like the crack of a teamster's whip,
and then, just ahead of him, Tolan heard a
high-pitched scream.

Leaping the gelding into a run, Tolan
raced down the trail to swing around a bend
into a small clearing. Beyond the clearing
and facing him was a long, low house built
of logs.

A girl was running toward him, a child
half-blind with fear. Only a few steps
behind and rapidly overtaking her was a
lean, rawboned man whose features were
filled with a savage exultation that
revolted Tolan. Even as his horse pounded
toward them, the man overtook the girl and
threw her to the ground, grasping her dress
at the shoulder to rip it away.

The black covered the ground in a breath
and Tolan's hand dropped to the scruff of
the man's neck and seized him by the collar.
The horse had not slowed and the man was
jerked from the girl, and Tolan dragged him
a dozen feet before he let go.

Beyond the shed Tolan heard the report of
another shot and a crackle of flames.

The man got shakily to his feet, fell, then got up more slowly. "What right you got, buttin' in here?" he yelled. His lean jaws were covered with a coarse stubble of mixed-gray beard and he was almost frothing in his fury. "She's nothin' but a damn Cherokee! The state says they got no rights, so what's to stop a man?"

"I am. I'm stopping you."

His eyes ugly with malice, the tall man rubbed hard palms on his coarse jeans. "Are you now? I reckon Hallett will have something to say about that."

Tolan reined his horse around. "Walk ahead of me." He indicated an opening between the shed and a corral. "Walk out there into the open."

He turned to speak to the girl, but she had chosen the moment to disappear into the trees. Girl? A child rather; she could have been no more than fourteen.

There was a pile of loot in the clearing, and nearby an old Indian woman sat on the ground staring dumbly at the flames that consumed her home, her face seamed with age and grief. A man was stretched upon the ground, a patch of blood covering most of his back. Standing nearby superintending the rounding up of horses and cattle was a big man in high boots, carrying a blacksnake whip.

"Mr. Hallett"--the man Tolan had interrupted in his attempted rape was, Tolan noticed, both respectful and fearful of

Hallett--"this here sojer says we got to leave them Cher'kee gals alone."

The big man turned sharply around, his face hard-set, ready to command. He had a strong-boned face with the skin drawn taut over the bones. His eyes were intensely black, his mustache was black, and it was obvious he was a man accustomed to command. Yet as he saw Tolan's uniform and recognized his rank, his manner changed. "How are you, Lieutenant? I am sorry you came up when you did, but we have to let the men have their fun. This is disagreeable duty."

"Since when did looting and rape become a duty?"

Hallett's features stiffened. "Obviously, Lieutenant, you are a stranger to Georgia. It is our business to root these people out, and that's what we'll do. I will be obliged if you would not interfere."

Tolan's expression did not change. "I have interfered." He sat straight in the saddle. "I am sure you can do what must be done without murder and rape. Now call off your men and get out of here."

For an instant Tolan believed Hallett intended to strike him with the whip. All the planes of Hallett's face seemed to flatten out and the skin around his eyes tightened. "I take no orders from you," he said, "nor from nobody else but my boss and the state of Georgia."

"You will take these orders." Tolan's tone was crisp. "I have been directed to report here by General Winfield Scott, and my orders are to see the Cherokees are moved with every care to their comfort and security. My orders do not condone rape."

Hallett hesitated. It was obvious to Tolan, and the fact surprised him, that the big man cared not a whit for Tolan's orders; but Hallett apparently was not sure exactly how far he might go in such a case. Miles Tolan, who had estimated many a man's potential before this, knew now that Hallett was not only a dangerous man but a capable, intelligent one as well.

"Very well, Lieutenant," Hallett said finally, "we will move along, as you suggest. This is a matter that can wait, and we can always return when we see fit. We will simply have to see that you are put right by your superiors."

"I have my orders."

"Ah? From General Scott, I believe you said? General Scott is not in Georgia, sir, and your orders here will be very different. You are to report to Colonel Loren White, I presume?"

"I am."

"You will learn, Lieutenant, that Colonel White is in command here, and your future orders will be from him. And one of those will be to refrain from molesting or inter-fering with citizens in pursuit of their business."

Miles Tolan was suddenly angry. He did not relish being told off by a civilian, nor did he like the implication that rape and murder would be tolerated by the American Army. "Be that as it may," he repeated coolly, "you will now get your men together and move along. The Indians will be brought in by the Army, and all in good time."

Hallett's smile was equally cold. "And if I choose to ignore that order, Lieutenant? What then?"

"I should be obliged to enforce it, sir."

Hallett made a great show of looking around and behind Tolan. "You are alone, I see. Doesn't it strike you that enforcing such an order might be difficult?"

"I should require no assistance, nor should I request it."

"You're very sure of yourself, Lieutenant. Too sure for an officer in a bright new uniform. One day I may decide to find out what is behind those shining buttons . . . if anything."

"I shall look forward to the moment, Mr. Hallett. And just so you will not be deceived by this bright new uniform, I might say it replaces a number of them worn out in service during and since the Black Hawk War."

He sat his horse as if on parade, watching Hallett get his men together. They came grudgingly, and one of them started to drive the small herd of gathered stock.

"Leave them," Tolan ordered.

When the drover hesitated, Hallett spoke to him in a low voice. Reluctantly, they mounted their horses. The man whom Tolan had interrupted had a rifle across his saddle. "Got a notion to bury me a sojer," he said.

Tolan was looking at Hallett, although
every man in the group was under his gaze.
"Mr. Hallett, if that man moves that rifle
muzzle I am going to kill you."

Hallett's shock was evident. Tolan's
holster flap was unbuttoned and the pistol
butt was near his hand. Hallett's eyes
lifted from the gun to Tolan's eyes and he
knew that Tolan would do just as he warned.

Hallett's rage was evident. "Turn around
and get out of here, you fool!"

Watching them ride reluctantly from the
clearing, Miles Tolan was profoundly
irritated with himself. Why had he made such
a point of letting Hallett know that he was
no desk soldier? Explanation to such a man
was a weakness. Still, it might have averted
a fight. When the riders had disappeared
from sight, Tolan looked slowly around.

He was alone but for the aged woman and
the dead man. For he was dead; no man could
lose so much blood and live. Dismounting,
Miles Tolan crossed to the dead man and
turned him over. It was the face of a
middle-aged man, careworn and tired, yet a
face possessing that innate dignity he had
seen in many an Indian before this. The dead
man's clothing was clean; his hair had been
neatly combed.

His pockets had been turned out and
everything of value stolen.

Tolan drove the small herd of stock into
the corral and put up the bars. During all
this time the old woman had neither moved

nor spoken, and the girl he had rescued
seemed nowhere about.

The house was burning and nothing could be
done about that. Tolan walked toward it,
disturbed by something here that he could
not quite fathom. The swept yard, the
carefully constructed buildings . . . This
was evidently the farm of an Indian of some
consequence. Too many Indians he had known
previously, those who had taken to the white
man's ways, had often been lazy, drunken, or
indifferent.

Not so the warriors he had met in battle.
Tall, splendidly built men, many of them,
and they could fight like so many cougars.

Sudden hoofbeats sounded on the trail down
which he had lately come, and from the trees
rode a small cavalcade of Indians. Several
of them were young men, stripped to the
waist and in buckskin leggings, but the two
men who rode at the head of the group were
dressed as prosperous planters might dress.
The oldest of them, a short, powerfully
built man obviously their leader, wore a
black hat, and although his clothing showed
wear, it was also neatly brushed. The young
man beside him wore a cabin-spun shirt, open
to the belt. He had a ragged scar across his
cheek.

This man glanced from the dead man to the
old woman, and then to Miles Tolan. "Does
the white man's army now make war upon old
women? What would he do if he faced
warriors?"

"I have faced warriors," Tolan replied

brusquely. "I have faced the fighting men of
the Sac and Fox, Sioux, and Kiowa. What
warriors have you faced?"

"My people are at peace." The young man
spoke haughtily, but Tolan realized he had
touched a sensitive spot.

"It is of no importance whom we have
faced," Tolan replied quickly. "We are not
at war here, and what has been done was not
of my doing. I am sorry for it."

"He speaks true." The girl he had saved
from being raped slipped from behind the
saddle of one of the riders.

She had repaired the tear in her dress,
and now she came up to the older man and
spoke rapidly in what Tolan believed to be
Cherokee. When she had completed what was
obviously an explanation the older Cherokee
said, "We thank you, Lieutenant, for what
you have done, but we must warn you also.
The man Hallett is a dangerous enemy, and he
will not quickly forget. We have come to
know him well."

"Won't the law protect you?"

"The law!" The young Cherokee's fury
exploded into words. "There is a law for the
white man, but there is no law for the
Indian! The law here is a club to beat us
down and rob us of all we possess!"

"It has been arranged for you to migrate,"
Tolan suggested mildly. "If you are
dissatisfied, why don't you go?"

"A man does not willingly leave his home,
Lieutenant," the older man said. "This is
the land of our fathers, and of their

fathers before them. The dust of Cherokee
bodies has helped to build high the
mountains, his blood flows in the sap of the
trees, and his stories have grown into these
rocks. This is our home."

"It is a good land in the West."

"So we have heard. But the Cherokee have
lived here since the memory of our oldest
men. These hills have been our hunting
ground, and these valleys have known our
crops.

"Now we are asked to go . . . to live
among alien spirits and the ghosts of
strange peoples. We are asked to abandon the
graves of our fathers, the fields we cut
from the forest, the homes we built with our
hands. I ask you: How can we?"

He gestured toward a huge oak beside the
clearing. "Beneath that oak my grandfather
died fighting the Creeks, and my mother is
buried beside him. Here I played as a child,
and by this stream I killed my first deer.

"The Cherokee, White Man, is born of these
hills. He was not a homeless people. Here he
was born, here he has lived, and here, God
willing, he shall die."

Miles Tolan was profoundly moved. What
reply had he to such a statement?

"You have been kind," the old man added,
"and because of us you have made an enemy.
Moreover, the man who employs him will
become your enemy as he is ours."

"Who is this man?"

"His name is Rounce . . . Wilson Rounce."

Miles Tolan was shocked. "<u>Rounce?</u> Did you say . . . <u>Rounce</u>?"

"The name is familiar to you?"

They stared at him as he absorbed the information . . . and remembering Will Rounce he felt, for the first time, something of apprehension.

"We were children together," Tolan replied. "Yes . . . yes, I know him."

CHAPTER 2

"He is the worst of our enemies."

"I shall speak to him."

"Tell him," the old man said proudly, "that it is I, Tsali, who call him enemy. If he will come among us I will repeat it, and stand before him when I do so."

Miles Tolan sat very still, watching them go to the old woman and help her from the ground, but he was remembering Wilson Rounce.

Seventeen years had gone by since they had parted. Had they ever been friends? Had Will, beneath his friendly exterior, ever been anything but an enemy? As boys they had hunted and fished together, and they had fought side by side against other boys. Everyone else had considered them friends. Everyone, Miles remembered, but old Elias Rounce, Will's grandfather. But then, nobody ever outwitted old Elias. Not even Will.

And now Will Rounce was here. . . . What

could have happened to Rounceville, the town old Elias had founded, and which should have been Will's?

Why would any sane man leave those broad planted and forested acres? Why would someone give up ownership of the mills, plants, and factories that Elias Rounce had broken from the wilderness? With such an inheritance a man of Will's intelligence and training could have built a great financial empire.

The sense of apprehension returned to him. Will Rounce was the only man who had ever beaten him . . . and he was the only one who had ever beaten Will.

Suddenly, he thought of the girl who had dived into the pool. He swung the black horse over to the old Indian. "Tsali, back up the road I thought I saw a woman dive into a pool. It was west of the road."

Tsali's face was expressionless. "I know of no one in that area."

Tolan had a feeling the Indian was lying. "Is there a pool up there? Or a lake of some kind?"

"I know of none."

"Thank you." Miles Tolan turned his horse into the trail and cantered away. Now he knew he had been lied to . . . and if Tsali would lie about the pool he might also lie about the girl. But why should he lie? What was the secret there?

Tolan shrugged. It was unlikely that he would ever know, and even more unlikely that he would ever come into these mountains

again. His way led westward, guiding the
Cherokee to the new lands beyond the
Mississippi, and there would be no time for
searching the mountains. Anyway, he
reflected philosophically, she was probably
unattractive, married, or both.

It was very still. The clouds hung dark
and low and secretive sounds stirred in the
forest. The trail widened now, and
occasionally smaller trails turned off
into the green, mist-shrouded hills. Here
and there great crags jutted from the
forest, thrusting their serrated edges
against the sky. It was a lovely land. There
were running streams and small meadows,
parklike stretches of forest and occasionally
now fenced fields where corn grew.

His thoughts reverted to the woman on the
rock. It was an unexpected place for anyone
to be at such a time. The Cherokee Removal
was far advanced and many had already taken
the westward route. With their going the
land was, as he had just witnessed, filling
with renegades ready to profit by what the
Indians had been forced to leave behind.

Miles Tolan had no feeling one way or the
other about the Removal. In a vague sort of
way he had been aware of the discussion for
some time, and aware of the violent
animosities that had arisen from it. He knew
that Clay, Calhoun, and Webster had all
spoken against it, but that Jackson himself
was for it, all the more surprising because
he had heard many of his brother officers

speak of the excellent service rendered by
the Cherokees in the Creek War . . . and
they had been led by Jackson during that
war.

Knowing nothing of the arguments pro or
con, Tolan recalled only that Davy Crockett
had made excellent speeches in the halls of
Congress for the Cherokees. For an Indian
fighter this was unexpected, but Davy had
the reputation of being a fair man, and he
had fought both against and beside the
Cherokees. He had, in fact, sacrificed his
political future by taking a course in
opposition to that of the Jackson party with
which he was affiliated.

Politics was not a soldier's business.
Miles Tolan had been given a task to perform
and he would carry it out to the best of his
ability and leave the arguments to the
civilians.

Of one thing he was certain. Indians could
not hope to survive by their old way of
life. They represented a hunting and food-
gathering society in conflict with an
agricultural and industrial society, and
when two such diverse cultures opposed each
other the less productive was sure to fall
by the way. Right and wrong might be
debated, but the outcome was certain.

Yet the farms he had lately seen,
including the one where the trouble had
taken place, had been well-tilled farms,
with compact buildings and an atmosphere of
productivity and well-being about them. If
these farms were examples of Cherokee

industry, then the picture had to be far
from one-sided. But of course they must be
the exceptions. They had to be.

The presence here of Will Rounce was a
disturbing fact. Since the day when Elias
Rounce had called Miles Tolan into his
office and told him he must leave Rounceville, he had known a sort of freedom such
as he had only dreamed of before. Only the
fact that he owed a debt to the old man, who
had taken him in and educated him, had kept
him in Rounceville so long. What the others
saw as ignominious dismissal he saw only as
a door being opened.

Before him the trail dipped into a wide,
shallow valley and in the bottom of the
valley lay the post road. Further along he
could see a stage station. Slow smoke rose
from the chimney and a private carriage had
only just drawn up at the entrance.

Two women, one young, one elderly, were
getting down from the carriage. As the
younger turned to wait for her companion,
their eyes met.

They were wide, lovely eyes, either blue
or gray, and nothing in his training as an
officer hinted that he should be laggard.
"How do you do?" He swept off his hat and
bowed. "I am Lieutenant Miles Tolan."

"And I," she replied sweetly, "am not
interested." With that she was through the
door and into the station.

From behind him he heard an unpleasant
laugh. "You sure didn't make no hit, Sojer!
An' just as well, too. Will Rounce wouldn't

stand for nobody sparkin' around his
woman . . . even if she ain't nothin' but a
'nother Cherokee!"

It was Hallett's man, the one who had
attempted the rape. He was loafing near the
corner of the building, and now he grinned
broadly in appreciation of Tolan's
discomfiture.

Ignoring him, Tolan turned his horse over
to the Negro stable boy.

Will Rounce's woman.

Was it to be Will Rounce wherever he
turned? How would it be between them after
seventeen years? What had Will become? And
if it came to a struggle between them, who
now would win when old Elias was no longer
in the background? Slapping his hat against
his thigh, Miles knocked dust from it and
from his clothing. Then he opened the door
and stepped within.

The long room served the functions of
office, waiting room, dining room, and
saloon. Its floors were of hand-hewn plank,
the furniture of rough homemade
construction, including four tables with
four chairs at each. When Miles entered the
room the girl and her companion were already
seated. Only one other table was
occupied . . . by a group of card players,
and there were several rough-looking men at
the bar.

As he seated himself at a table not far
from the girl and the elderly woman who was
her companion, a young man, clad as befitted
a gentleman of fashion, entered from the

rear door and joined them. Rounce's man had
called her a Cherokee, which was obviously a
mistake. He had also called her Rounce's
woman. . . . Was that another mistake?

He thought she glanced toward him, but
when he looked toward her she was busily in
conversation with her friends. She was, he
decided, even more attractive than he had at
first believed. Almost, in fact,
uncomfortably beautiful.

There are women, he reflected, so
beautiful that men are awed by them, and
many a man who might otherwise be interested
is inclined to stand off, doubting that such
a girl would be interested. He grinned at
his hands, reflecting that no such
inhibition had ever held him back.

A man had come from behind the bar wiping
his big hands on his apron. From the
deference in his manner, Tolan decided he
both knew and respected the newcomers.

"Sam," the young man was saying, "we'd
like some of that home-cured ham of yours.
Whatever else you have . . . we'll trust
your judgment."

"Leave it to me, Mr. McCrae."

Sam crossed to Tolan's table and hit the
boards a swipe with his cloth. "I'll have
the same as the people at the next table,"
Tolan said. "They seem to know your food."

"You'd do better not to wear that uniform
hereabouts," Sam advised, low-voiced.
"There's some around as don't care for it."

"It's our country's uniform," Miles
replied quietly. "I wear it with pride."

Sam's face changed. "Comes to that," he said, "I've worn it myself. Only there's some, the Cherokees and their friends, who don't care much for it."

"From what I've heard," Miles replied, "it is less the Army that makes the trouble, and more some of your Georgia politicians."

Sam glanced toward the men at the bar. "That's right enough. And those are some of their friends. What they're doing is a rotten shame."

Sam left for the kitchen and Miles Tolan carefully avoided looking at the men at the bar. They were drinking, and as they drank they grew progressively more noisy, and such men were inclined to become quarrelsome.

Moreover, Hallett's man had come into the room and from the glances cast his way, Miles was sure he had been telling them the events of the morning. From words overheard Miles learned the man's name was Adam Couch.

When the food arrived Miles realized for the first time how really hungry he was. The long ride in the mountain air had been invigorating, but strenuous, too, and the ham had proved all that McCrae had implied. He ate hungrily, aware that the loud voices from the crowd at the bar had dropped to a conspiratorial mumble. From what he could hear the women at the next table were growing increasingly apprehensive. McCrae was stubborn, and refused to be hurried.

Suddenly a pockmarked man with a tough swagger detached himself from the group and strode to the table where the women sat.

Leaning over, he put his big palms flat on
the table. "You got the on'y woman here,
fella," he said, grinning at McCrae, "I
think we ought to give you some comp'ny."

"The lady you refer to is my sister."

"Is she now?" Grinning insolently, the man
pulled up a chair and sat down. He was,
Miles observed, just drunk enough to be both
mean and dangerous.

McCrae got to his feet. "Shall we go? It
is quite late."

The man in the chair grinned up at him.
"You can go anytime you like," he said, "but
she stays."

One of the men from the bar was strolling
casually across the room, his intent to get
behind McCrae. Another man moved to the
table where Miles Tolan sat.

Miles continued to eat, alert to every
shift of position. The man behind McCrae
could seize him if he offered any opposition, and the third man was obviously
supposed to keep Miles from interfering, but
Miles had already planned to shove a chair
into that man before he could move, and a
pistol would cover the others. Such affairs
were far from new to him, and though he
savored the coming action he was worried for
the sake of the women. His dislike for the
men at the bar was surpassed only by his
dislike for Adam Couch.

"We will go," McCrae said quietly. "I
advise you not to interfere."

"You'll have the law on us, I suppose?"
The man at the table grinned insolently.

"There ain't no law for Injuns, so we can do what we want. You've no comeback, not none a-tall." Outside there was the sound of hooves and harness.

Miles put down his cup and thought of an alternative that was equally pleasing and less physical. From his waistband he took a pistol and placed it on the table, and as he did so the man watching him spoke quickly. "The sojer's got a pistol, Stanky."

Stanky's head turned sharply around, glancing from the pistol on the table to Miles Tolan quietly sipping his coffee. His cup was rather obviously held in his left hand. He had said nothing. Only the cold steel of the pistol lay there, more eloquent than words.

"Your carriage has just drawn up, Mr. McCrae," Miles said then, "and you have some distance to go, I believe."

McCrae's poise did him credit. "Of course . . . Will you join us?"

"No." Miles Tolan looked over at Stanky as he spoke. "I am sure these gentlemen would like to arrange some entertainment for me here, and I would dislike to miss it."

"We would enjoy having you for our guest," McCrae insisted politely, "and our accommodations, begging Sam's pardon, are somewhat more satisfactory than his. It would be a privilege to have you, sir."

Miles Tolan got to his feet and picked up the pistol. "In that case, I shall accept. I am sure these gentlemen will understand and postpone whatever plans they had until a later time."

Stanky's face was set in ugly lines. His drunkenness seemed to have disappeared. "I think," he said coolly, "I think I'll make you use that pistol."

CHAPTER 3

"I would not advise it."

The voice came from the doorway, and Miles was irritated with himself for hearing no sound from the opening door. "I would not advise it, Stanky. Mr. Tolan was always a most excellent shot . . . one of the best I have ever seen."

Miles Tolan did not turn his eyes from the man he was watching, but said quietly, "It has been a long time, Will."

Stanky backed off hurriedly. "We didn't mean nothing, Mr. Rounce. We was just havin' some fun."

"Get out."

Will Rounce did not lift his voice, but there was something in its tone that could not be missed. "Get out . . . and if you ever speak to Miss McCrae again, or trouble her in any way at all, I'll kill you."

Thrusting the pistol back into his waistband, Miles turned to meet Will's outstretched hand. "Miles! Man, but it is good to see you!"

Rounce turned. "Laura, I want you to meet Miles Tolan. We were boys together."

Her acknowledgment was brief. "Will! Why did you not tell us you were coming? We had no idea!"

"It was a surprise, Laura. I was on my way to visit and hoped to surprise you, and now it is you who surprised me."

Miles Tolan knew Rounce was lying. He had no idea why he was lying, but this advantage he always possessed over Will. He had always known even though old Elias, for all his shrewdness and judgment of people, seemed never to be aware of it. Miles, with better judgment than he had normally shown, knew, but had never let on that he knew.

Will had been a handsome boy, and he had grown into an even more handsome man. He possessed a noble head, finely carved features, and was even bigger than Miles, at least an inch taller and probably thirty pounds heavier. He had a shock of golden hair above a fine brow, and blue-white eyes, piercing and shrewd. He looked like a younger and much more handsome Andrew Jackson.

Standing to one side, Miles watched Will talking to Laura and her brother. Laura's eyes glowed with excitement, and if she were not already Will's woman, Miles reflected, she well could be, for she was obviously infatuated.

As always, Will dominated the room. All eyes were on him, and all hung on his words. With a curious sense of relief, Miles Tolan

realized that he did not. Was it because he
remembered Will from old? Or was it
something else--something new and different?
In any event, he felt that there was
something shallow and false about the entire
scene. For seventeen years Miles Tolan had
dealt with the harshest kind of reality, and
in those years he had known many men, but he
was realizing that he had never liked Will.
They had been thrown together by
circumstances and others believed them
inseparable friends, but such had never been
the case. Under the apparent friendship they
had always been rivals, but that rivalry had,
on Miles' part, always been tempered by the
debt he owed to Will's grandfather.

"Come!" Will caught Miles' arm. "We will
go on to Brignole."

Outside, once he had helped Laura into her
carriage, Will swung astride a fine-looking
sorrel and cast an admiring glance at
Tolan's black, which the stable boy led out.

"Still a taste for horses, I see." He met
Miles' eyes with a smile. "It's good to see
you," he said sincerely. "We should never
have lost track of each other. Believe me,
I've needed a man I could trust, and often
wondered what had become of you."

The McCraes' carriage clattered off and
Will gestured widely. "This is a growing
country, Miles. Look what's happened in
Texas, and then look at what is happening
here. Within the next few months the last of
the Cherokees will be out of Georgia.
Believe me, Miles, I am very close to the

men behind this, and when that land is re-
divided I expect the best of it. You should
give up your commission and join me."

"I'd have to think about that." Miles
remembered that Will Rounce had always been
full of plans, large plans. There was no
denying his intelligence, and Miles knew the
training they had both been given was such
as to place them in an advantageous position
in any bargaining that would be done. Too
many times in the past men had underrated
Will Rounce. To outward appearances he was a
stalwart and handsome man who looked the
soul of honor; only long familiarity allowed
one to realize the devious cunning that lay
beneath the surface.

Yet the offer was tempting. Will was a man
who might go far, particularly as he was
devoid of the scruples that might hold
others back or make a more honorable man
somewhat cautious.

"You'll report to Lorin, I suppose. We're
very close, he and I, and you'll do very
well if you listen to me and work with me."
He was silent for a few minutes. "For the
time it would be better for you to stay in
the Army. I can use a man like you."

Miles Tolan shifted his seat impatiently.
It irked him that Rounce should so readily
assume that he was not doing well, and that
he would so readily fall in with whatever
schemes Rounce had in mind. He was about to
say as much, but restrained himself. Nothing
was to be gained by starting trouble.

Rounce lowered his voice. "There's gold

here, Miles. Have you heard of that?
Gold . . . and better than that, there is
fertile soil. Once the Indians are out of
here we'll have a chance to get rich fast.
Much of the land is already cleared and
planted to crop.

"Reap the crops and sell, cut the
marketable timber and sell, take the cream
off the gold mines and sell . . . then move
west. This is a big country, Miles, and all
of it open to development."

"If you go west you'll be coming up
against the Cherokees again. They may be
tired of moving."

Will Rounce chuckled. "They're Indians,
Miles. They had this country to themselves
for thousands of years and did nothing with
it except hunt, fish, and plant corn. We're
building a country, Miles, a big country.
Nobody can stand in the way of that."

Miles switched the conversation. "This
place to which we're going tonight . . .
what's it like?"

"Brignole? It's the country home of the
McCraes, and a lovely place, a very lovely
place. I would hate to see it fall into the
wrong hands."

"There was some reference to the McCraes
being Indian. That's nonsense, of course."

"It was not. . . . You must realize, these
are by no means the wild Indians of which
you've heard. They have gone the white man's
way, or tried to. They've something like
their own legislature, their own newspaper,
and even their own courts.

"Some of these Indians are planters and businessmen, Miles, and not a few of them are very well-off. Some, like the McCraes, are truly wealthy."

"But if they are moved west, what happens to that wealth?"

Will Rounce smiled into the dark. "That, my friend, is something to which we must give our attention. It would be a pity, a great pity, to have all that fall into the wrong hands."

Brignole stood upon a tree-clad knoll well back from the high road, and was a long manor house of two stories with wings running back from either end. Across the front was a broad veranda and six columns. The house was painted white, and made a lovely sight surrounded by the huge old trees and fine expanse of lawn and garden that surrounded it. A drive surfaced with gravel swung in an easy half-circle from the high road to the door and back again to the road. The house possessed all the quiet dignity and elegance Miles had come to associate with the Virginia homes where he had often been a guest.

The slaves who met the carriage were tastefully dressed in dark livery and conducted themselves with pride and deference.

Inside, the house was tastefully and beautifully done in a style much less cluttered than was usual, and the room which he was shown had wide windows that opened

upon a hillside. It was dark, but he could
appreciate what the view must be. When he
had bathed and changed into fresh linen and
a carefully brushed uniform, he descended
the stairs and found his way to the library.

A man of slightly more than medium height
got up from his chair to greet him. He had
black eyes and a faintly olive skin topped
by pure white hair. "Lieutenant Tolan? I am
John McCrae. Welcome to our home, sir.
Please consider it your own."

"Thank you, sir."

"And may I present John Ross?"

Miles Tolan turned with quick interest.
John Ross, a chief of the Cherokees, was a
man of medium height, rather squarely built
with a shock of graying hair and keen blue
eyes. He was, as Miles had heard long
before, only one-eighth Cherokee, yet having
grown up among them he considered himself
one of them. Both his father, Daniel Ross,
and his maternal grandfather, John McDonald,
had come among the Cherokees as traders.

"How do you do, Lieutenant? Yours is a
familiar name."

"Mine, sir?"

"A friend of mine served with you during
the Black Hawk War. He had much to say of
your gallantry . . . and your marksmanship."

"He was exaggerating, sir, I'm sure."
Miles hesitated. "Are you among the
Cherokees who are migrating, sir?"

Ross chuckled. "I doubt it, Captain. I
doubt it very much. Tell me: You rode down

through the mountains, did you not? What did you think of them?"

"What is there to say? They are beautiful, sir, beautiful beyond belief."

"Then you can understand why we do not wish to leave. This is our home. . . . We have grown up here, lived here, and we wish to die here."

"That was what Tsali told me."

Ross glanced at him sharply. "You have met Tsali?"

Miles accepted a glass of sherry and sketched briefly the circumstances. "It is a pity," he said at last, "that violence could happen, but I have no doubt it was a rare occurrence."

"We wish it were. . . . Unfortunately, Georgia passed a law denying the right of any Cherokee to institute a suit against a white citizen, or to appear as a witness against him. The rougher element have taken this as giving them the right to rape, plunder, and murder."

Laura McCrae came into the room, and John Ross turned to her at once. "My dear," he said, "I've never seen you look more lovely than tonight."

She smiled at him, then her eyes swept the room, searching for Will Rounce, no doubt. Miles felt a little twinge of irritation, and was amused at himself for the feeling. Yet there was no question that Laura McCrae was a girl of singular beauty. Her black hair was parted on the side and combed back, several carefully composed ringlets dangling

in front of her ears. The long hair was
built into loops on the crown of her head,
and her eyes, he noticed, were gray . . .
gray and very beautiful.

The gown she wore was one that left her
lovely shoulders bare, and the tight bodice
tapered down to a small waist and a loose
gown that flowed to the tips of her toes.
With surprise, Miles realized it was the
first gown he had seen in America that
followed the new Paris fashion where the
ankles were no longer visible. The material
was of tulle over satin, and of a soft green
that emphasized the color of her skin.

Miles felt uncomfortable, and hated
himself for the feeling. It was not as if he
were a stranger to good society, for he had
traveled some in those seventeen years since
he had last seen Will Rounce, but he was not
accustomed to being ignored by pretty women,
or any women at all, and he was vain enough
to be irritated by it.

He turned to the bookshelves, drawn by
curiosity as well as a genuine love for
books. He could never leave them alone, and
until he had scanned the books in a house he
was never completely at ease.

Whatever else John McCrae might be--and
from all the evidence he was a very
successful planter--he was also a man who
knew and appreciated good books. For these
were not only well chosen, but all showed
evidence of use. Out of curiosity he looked
to see what poetry there was, but found only
the Greeks. Of the contemporary poets such

as Byron, Keats, Shelley, and Moore, he
found no sign.

Could the girl who dove from the rock have
been Laura McCrae?

The thought came unexpectedly. It was odd,
Miles decided, that the idea had not
occurred to him before. She had come from
that direction, the timing was about
right. . . . He turned to look at her. . . .
No . . . there was something, some scarcely
definable difference.

She turned at that minute and their eyes
met. Excusing herself from her father and
Ross, she crossed the room to him.

"That was a strange expression,
Lieutenant. Do you usually look at girls
that way?"

"No . . . probably not about you." He
looked down at the book in his hands, a copy
of the odes of Horace. "Do you read poetry,
Miss McCrae?"

She glanced down. "Horace? No, that is
Father's."

"I mean . . . do you read the contemporary
poets? Thomas Moore, for instance? In
particular, have you read Lalla Rookh?"

She was startled; he recognized that at
once. When she lifted her eyes to his they
were innocent and her expression was bland.
"No . . . I can't say that I have read
anything of his. Of course, I've heard of
him. Why do you ask?"

"It is a beautiful poem. It is natural to
think of beauty when one speaks to you."

"You are gallant, Lieutenant." She looked

directly into his eyes. "I appreciate the compliment, of course, but that was not at all why you asked. You had a reason, Lieutenant, and I am curious."

"And if you talk to Miles any longer, I shall be quite jealous."

Will Rounce had come up to them, and he was smiling. At the same time Miles noticed that there was irritation present, too, and he liked the feeling that Will could be irritated. He was always so sure of himself, so perfectly possessed.

"We were talking about poetry," Miles commented. He recalled very clearly how disdainful Rounce had been toward anything related to the arts.

"Oh . . . then I came just in time to rescue you, Laura," Will said. "Miles reads too much. I was hoping he had gotten out of the habit over the years. Perhaps he is incurable."

"No, really," she protested, "we were talking about Lalla Rookh."

Will Rounce turned slowly and looked searchingly into Miles' eyes. It was an utterly cold, probing stare.

Miles felt a queer, leaping excitement. For some reason the title had some special meaning for Will, and whatever the meaning was, Will was not pleased that Miles might know of it.

"Why that poem?" Will inquired abruptly.

"It is one of Moore's." Miles brushed the comment away as if no longer interested. "We were talking of Moore and Byron."

"I am not interested in poetry," Will replied abruptly. "Poetry is for women."

"Many of us in the Army," Miles replied quietly, "found poetry very interesting. It is easy to recall, and sometimes on the long marches one can remember it with real pleasure. You might be interested to know, Will, that every war brings on a new interest in poetry . . . and it is the soldiers who are interested."

During the meal that followed Miles found it difficult to believe that the people among whom he sat were mostly of Cherokee extraction, and that at least two of them were full-bloods. Yet they had been in contact with Europeans for upward of three hundred years, some say from the time of de Soto and his conquistadors. After the Spanish had come Frenchmen, and then the Scots, Irish, and English traders.

Will Rounce was in great form. Always an easy, graceful conversationalist, he was at his best tonight, turning from topic to topic with ease. Strange, that with his admitted attitude toward the Cherokees he should be here. Miles' thoughts returned to Will's queer reaction to the title of the poem. Obviously it meant something more to him than just the title of a book . . . but what?

Laura's laughter drew his attention and he found all eyes on him. "Will was telling us about the time you were thrown from the black horse."

"Did he tell you," Miles replied dryly,
"that it was because he'd put a burr under
the saddle blanket?"

"Will!" Laura protested. "Did you do that?"

Rounce looked up, laughing.
"Probably . . . Miles was growing too sure
of himself, and I thought the fall would do
him good."

As he spoke the last words he looked down
the table, but his expression was cold,
almost threatening.

So here it was again, Miles thought: They
sometimes worked together but they always
fought . . . and who would win this time?

CHAPTER 4

Yes, that was the way of it. Will had put
the burr beneath his saddle to give him a
fall. What Miles neglected to tell his
dinner companions was that it was a contest
with a gold guinea as the prize, offered by
Elias Rounce.

Trust Will to pull a stunt like that with
a prize at stake. It was a good thing to
remember, Miles told himself, and helpful
to have recalled it just now. He would
remain with the Army and let Will make his
money with whatever scheme he had planned.

There were other stories Will Rounce could
have told, like the time the four Dutch boys
had set upon them. It was four to two, but
unequal at that, for the two had been

trained at fighting, well taught in boxing,
wrestling, and the quarterstaff by that man
of many wisdoms, Phineas Cronkite.

The first thing Phineas had taught them
was that most such fights are won by the
first blow, so to strike first and strike
hard . . . and strike hard they did, and
from then on it was two and two, and a fair
fight except that the remaining two Dutch
boys had seen what had happened to the first
two. Victory had been complete.

There had been a subsequent occasion when
two rough-looking men had set upon them in
Philadelphia. Neither boy was yet sixteen,
and the two men had followed them up a dark
street and demanded their money.

Miles struck first. He was quick with his
fists and the two men were expecting no
trouble, and Miles' blow had been an
underhanded blow to the belly, and in the
darkness the man had not seen it coming. As
he doubled over with pain, his face made a
perfect target for Miles' jerked-up knee,
and as he fell, Miles hit him again. It took
Will Rounce little longer to finish off his
man.

It was a time when little was known of
boxing and wrestling beyond the usual
frontier sort of back-heel and hip-lock, a
strong back type of gripping and throwing
with relatively no science to it. Phineas
Cronkite was a master at Cornish-style
wrestling and while in England he had picked
up a fancy bit of fist work, which he taught
them. No doubt about it, the school directed

by Elias Rounce had been an odd one, but
efficient.

It was seventeen years since then, and
Will a man of importance now, far more than
any mere lieutenant of cavalry who owned a
few blocks of land out west, land of so
little value that a neighbor traded off
three square miles of it for a pair of red-
top boots.

Yet it was good to be here, dining in the
candlelight on the fine old silver and
crystal, with the soft movements of Negro
servants and a distant sound of music to
lend background to their talk. It was a long
way from the campfires of the Comanche or
the Sac and Fox, and farther still from the
fo'c'sle of a windjammer beating up to Vigo
Bay.

Seventeen years . . . What a lot could
happen to a man in that time! And what a
lot had happened to him. He was a different
man now than he had been when he left
Rounceville to go out into the world by
himself.

Later, alone in the library, Laura found
him. He was looking over the books again, a
glass of Madeira in his hand.

"Do you find time to read, Lieutenant?"

"There is always time. Those who say they
do not have time for books simply do not
want to read badly enough. Often they have
been my only companions, and their advantage
is that they say the same words to
everyone."

"And people do not?"

"They tell you what you wish to hear . . . or what they believe you wish to hear."

"And what about Will?"

"It is for you to make your own judgment on that score."

"You don't like him?"

"I did not say that, nor did I mean to imply it. How can one judge a man one has not seen in seventeen years?"

"You are quibbling."

"Perhaps."

"But you were his best friend!"

He considered that. "Yes . . . yes, I believe I was."

"Then how can you talk so against your best friend?"

Miles returned the book to its place on the shelf.

"Miss McCrae, they were your words, not mine. I have said that I believed I was his best friend. It does not necessarily follow that he was also my best friend."

She studied him curiously, and without, he suspected, much liking for him. "You make me very curious, Lieutenant. Will has told me of the education you two received, and unless I am mistaken you two were together for twelve years. He said you came to them when you were five."

"Yes."

"Who were your people?"

He hesitated, then he said, "I do not know."

She tilted her head to the side a little. "Do you know, Lieutenant, Will told me the

same thing, and I believe he told me the
truth, but I do not believe you have told
the truth. I believe there is something you
knew that you never told them, not Will, nor
your Phineas nor Elias Rounce."

He smiled, listening to the drum of
horses' hooves upon the road outside.

"What would it matter?" he asked.

"I don't know." She was puzzled. "But I _am_
curious."

Several people came into the library and
Miles walked toward the door. He was in time
to see a horseman arrive, the same he had
heard approaching.

The rider was a uniformed soldier who
swung alongside the veranda, dismounted, and
tendered him a letter. "You are Lieutenant
Tolan, sir? The Colonel's orders, sir. You
are to go to him at once!"

"You mean I must leave tonight?"

"Tonight, sir. The Colonel was most
explicit."

Miles ripped open the envelope.

Report to me at once. This station.
I will accept neither delay nor excuses.

Miles spoke to a waiting slave. "Have my
horse saddled and brought around."

He went hurriedly to his room and gathered
his few possessions together. He was
hurrying down the steps when he met McCrae.
Laura was right behind him.

"Here! What's this? You're not leaving?"

"Sorry, sir. Orders from Colonel White."

John McCrae was serious. "I hope you are
in no trouble. Colonel Lorin White has the
reputation of being a very difficult man."

Laura walked with him to the door. She
looked up at him, her expression showing her
curious indecision. "I can't make up my mind
about you," she said.

"Is it necessary?"

"I don't know. Somehow I feel that it is.
I want to thank you for helping us tonight.
I am afraid there would have been trouble.
James . . . my brother . . . is not very
coolheaded at times."

"It was nothing."

"I was rude to you, too. I could at least
have been polite."

He chuckled. "It was nothing."

It was very late and he was bone-tired. He
walked to the horse, who looked at him
reproachfully. "Nothing for it, old fellow,"
he whispered. "Believe me, I'd rather you
rested."

There was a step on the porch behind him
and he looked around to see Will Rounce
standing there, and he was smiling.

"You see, Miles? This comes of interfering
with my men. You will find it much simpler
to keep out of things that do not concern
you."

Anger choked him. For an instant he felt
like striking Rounce, and then he asked
calmly, "So this is your doing?"

Will grinned at him, a taunting,
challenging grin. "If you want to work for

me, Miles, I could use a man of your
training. It is hard to find good men . . .
who know how to take orders."

"Go to hell, will you?"

He stepped into the saddle and reined the
black horse around. As the horse leaped into
a run, Will's sardonic voice came to him.

"Good-bye, Miles," Will said.

And then it began to rain again, a soft,
drizzling, soaking rain.

Laura McCrae awakened to the sound of
rain, and for a long time she lay still,
listening to the drops pattering on the roof
and looking out her window at the far-off
hills, veiled now with streamers of moon-
touched cloud.

The old house was silent, for it was very
early. The old stones and timbers slumbered
with their memories of a hundred years of
McCraes who had lived and worked, loved and
dreamed within its walls. It was impossible
they should be forced to move, to leave
their home, the soil they had tilled, the
forests they had used and protected, the
land that meant so much to them all. Wide
awake now, she looked up at the ceiling. All
her memories of childhood and girlhood were
here; the few years she had been away had
been filled with longing for Brignole. . . .
To her it had always been home, and she had
never thought seriously of leaving it.

Angus McCrae had been the first to come
here . . . a lone man with a rifle, ax,
knife, and blankets. He had brought with him

a few odds and ends of trade goods, having
landed from a ship that lay briefly off the
coast and that had put him ashore at his own
request.

He had been a strong man, Angus McCrae,
but a kind man. A fighting Highlander, he
had feared neither man nor devil, and had
the gift of making friends, and from the
first he had found a place among the
Cherokees. He studied their customs, found
much in them to admire, and remained among
them, taking the daughter of a Cherokee
chief to wife. That had been in 1680. For
several years he had been hunter, trapper,
and trader.

That same year he had come upon the site
of Brignole and laid the foundation stones
with his own hands, completing the first
room that first season, and using it for a
one-room cabin. Yet he had never thought of
it as one room, only as the beginning of a
mansion. He built of granite and he built
solidly, as a man would descended from a
long line of working masons.

Three sons had been born of that union,
the first killed fighting the Spanish from
Florida, the second to die in war with the
Creeks. The third son had gone north for a
wife, selling his furs in Virginia and
finding a Devonshire girl there, who took
readily to Cherokee ways. And that same year
they had added a fourth and fifth room to
the house on the hill, and William McCrae
had gone north again to Virginia, this time

to drive back a bull, three cows, a ram, and
seven sheep to Brignole.

It was William who added to the lands
Angus had bought from the Cherokees, and who
began the fur trading business. Old Angus
had already begun farming, planting wheat,
barley, and rye, as well as Indian corn.
William set up a smithy, and brought hand
looms into the area. On that ground the
family had lived for one hundred and fifty-
eight years, and now they were being forced
from their lands, driven out because they
were Cherokee.

They bore the name with pride. How much
Cherokee blood did they have? Nobody knew
exactly; there was no generation or branch
of the family that had not seen inter-
marriage. Regardless, they considered
themselves Cherokees and were so considered
by others.

The Cherokees were a proud people, and a
great nation among the Indians of eastern
America, related although not allied to the
Iroquois, a strong people, vital, energetic,
and filled with love of the land in which
they lived.

They had learned early that the way to
survive was to study the white man's way.
They had fenced their fields, tilled them
carefully, and learned the crafts and the
small arts. But they were still Cherokee,
and now they lived upon land the white men
wanted.

Intelligent and keenly perceptive, the
Cherokee had among them men who not only

understood their old ways, but who grasped
the effect changing times were to have. The
result was that by 1830 great herds of
cattle grazed the Cherokee hills, and their
fields produced corn, tobacco, wheat, oats,
indigo, and potatoes. Their cotton was
exported to New Orleans on their own boats,
apple and peach orchards were common, and
butter and cheese of their own manufacture
was upon their tables.

A printing press and a newspaper were
established. A metalsmith named Sequoyah had
devised an alphabet, one so well designed
that within a short time several thousand
Cherokees had learned to read their own
language. A library and a museum were built,
and the schools increased in number each
year.

Yet each success angered many of the white
citizens of Georgia and each success became
an additional tool for the politicians.
Throughout the state there were many who
found much to admire in Cherokee progress,
and who had done what they could to prevent
encroachments on Cherokee lands. Unhappily,
these men of goodwill were in the minority.

Laura McCrae got up and slipped into her
robe, then went to the window. It was light
now, and the sun would soon be over the
trees that crested the hills in the east.
Yet she never saw the sun first in the east,
but from the west, for the western hills
were higher and the first rays always
brought to them a crown of pale light that

strengthened and grew rose and red with
growing dawn.

How could she leave this? How could she
trek west riding in a wagon or walking
behind one? It was unthinkable! But no, it
would not happen. Will would not let it
happen. He loved Brignole as she did, and he
would do what he could to keep it for them,
and to see that the McCraes did not have
to go.

Was she selfish to think of herself and
her own family now? What of the others? She
had heard her father and John Ross
discussing the arrival of Tsali at the
raided farm on the previous day, and they
had worried for fear something would happen,
some incident that would give the Georgia
militia an excuse to move into the Cherokee
Nation in force. Tsali was a recalcitrant, a
hard old man who loved his hills and would
fight to the death for them. Those who hoped
for a reprieve feared what he might do as
much as they admired his convictions.

Her thoughts returned to Miles Tolan.
There was something disturbing about him,
and he kept coming between her and her
thoughts of Will. Somehow it was hard to
feel the old excitement for Will since she
had seen Miles. Yet there was no reason for
it. He was nothing to her and she was not
interested in him.

She was, she told herself, very sure of
this. She was not interested in Miles Tolan.

He was a striking man . . . not so handsome as Will Rounce, but a fine-looking

figure in his uniform, with such splendid
shoulders. . . . Yes, she admitted it
reluctantly, he was exciting.

She could imagine the girls in Atlanta.
What a fuss they would make over him!

For some reason the thought made her
impatient. After all, he was a friend of
Will's, and she would not like to see them
make a fool of him. Remembering the dark,
clean lines of his face, the quiet amusement
of his eyes, she was suddenly not so sure
the girls of Atlanta would make a fool of
Miles . . . or that any girls would, or
could.

And then she remembered the book. He had
mentioned Lalla Rookh . . . but it must have
been a coincidence. Surely, there could be
no connection.

She must talk to Will . . . but could he
tell her? Would he tell her anything at all?
He had never talked to her about it, had
always brushed off all her questions. Yet
something was going on that she did not
understand.

Books by Thomas Moore were just not very
common in Georgia at the time. He was a
modern poet, and only slightly more
acceptable than Lord Byron. But then Lord
Byron was quite shocking and no nice girl
read his poetry . . . at least, not in
public or where it could be seen.

It was impossible that Miles could know
her, and his mention of Lalla Rookh must
have been an accident, although Laura knew

that Will had gotten her a copy of the book
just before she disappeared.

The rain fell steadily. It was a pity
Miles Tolan had to leave in the middle of a
storm . . . it was a long ride to Atlanta.

It would be a longer ride to the lands on
the Arkansas, and so many of her people had
already taken it, marching through forest
and swamp, dying of fever, falling by the
way, pillaged and robbed by those who
pursued them with their hatred. Already
thousands had gone . . . and there was
bitterness among the Cherokee for those who
had not proved loyal, or those who yielded.

Should she go? Should she herself take that
march, take it despite all Will might do?

She knew there were Cherokees who thought
they should--that if _they_ were forced to go,
all should go. Others were already talking
of taking to the remote hills, fighting it
out there and dying rather than leave. She
had no taste for that life either.

Yet Chief Ross still hoped there would be
a chance, despite the growing pressures and
the orders from Washington. He would return
there soon in a last attempt to get Van
Buren to allow them to remain. But even if
he succeeded, there would be trouble if they
stayed, for already many of the Georgians
had come into the Cherokee Nation, had
burned homes, looted crops, even driven off
cattle the Cherokees had hoped to take west.
Others had been robbed on the road west,
robbed in Alabama and in Tennessee by bands
that had followed the march from Georgia.

Let them go. She would stay. Will would arrange that. They would keep Brignole; after all, they had a Scottish name and a well-known ancestor. They could stay on. She would marry Will, and in a few years this would all be forgotten.

She bathed, dressed quickly, and went down the stairs. Her father had just seated himself at breakfast, and he looked up with a smile. She was suddenly aware those smiles were all too rare these days.

"Laura! You're up early."

"I could not sleep."

He nodded. "Few of us can, these days."

"What does Uncle John think?"

"He's going to try again. He never gives up, that man. I don't know what we could have done without him. He has given most of his life to the Cherokee Nation, and few people appreciate it."

She paused. "Father . . . what do you think of Will?"

He chuckled. "What does it matter? When a man has a headstrong daughter and she decides what man she wants, what can a mere father do?"

"Do you like him?"

John McCrae hesitated. Will Rounce had been a guest in their home many times. The fact that they were so far unmolested was due entirely to the fact that Will stood between them and potential depredations. He was a strong and capable man with excellent connections. He was very close to the military command, and even closer to the

governor. That he had influence in
Washington was undoubted. Chief Ross frankly
admitted that doors closed to him had opened
as a result of Will's influence . . . not
that it had done Ross much good. But then,
nothing much did, nowadays.

"Yes," he said after a minute, "I like
him."

Even as he said it, he had a disturbing
thought that maybe he did not like Will
Rounce. . . . But if he did not, why should
he dislike him? Certainly Will had been a
good friend, and he was an affable,
agreeable companion.

"He's a very able man," he added. "I think
Will Rounce will go far. I should not be
surprised to see him a United States senator
one of these days."

"Not if he befriends the Cherokee much
longer." Laura realized suddenly that she
had never considered it in that light. "We
may be the cause of him making enemies."

McCrae smiled. "Not us. I know we consider
ourselves Cherokee, but I doubt many others
do. Not in Washington, anyway."

James came down the steps and joined them
at breakfast. He was still excited over the
events of the evening before. "He was so
calm," he told his father. "I never saw a
man like him. He was calm, yet he seemed
perfectly sure of himself, as though it were
something that had happened many times
before and he knew just how it would go."

"He's a soldier. John tells me he made a

fine name for himself in the Black Hawk War, and that he's been into the far west."

"Fighting Indians," Laura said.

Her father looked up. "Yes, Indians," he said. "If we go west we may have to fight them ourselves."

They were silent. The thought of going west hung heavily above them all. So many had been forced to go, and now the threat faced them every morning when they awakened; yet despite the number who had already gone, the idea that they, too, might go was unreal to them. Angus had been the first McCrae to cross the ocean to the New World, and this had been the only McCrae home since the day he had first come upon the knoll where the house stood.

True, members of the McCrae family had gone out to other parts of the Cherokee Nation and established places of their own, but to them all, Brignole was home. It had been named for the ship Angus McCrae's father had long sailed in trade to the West Indies.

McCrae looked up. "James . . . I wish you would not go to Atlanta this week. You may be needed here."

"You think there might be trouble?"

"I hope not. But stay here."

Laura went to the door again, and stood looking down the road. Will was still asleep in the guest's quarters, and she wanted to talk to him. She was becoming frightened, more frightened than she had ever been, and

it was because her father was worried. Only
Will could protect them; he had constantly
assured them there was nothing to be
concerned about.

Only a few weeks before, her father had
suggested they might still sell out for a
good price, but Will had laughed at the
thought, and they had wanted to be
reassured. Sell Brignole? It was unthinkable . . . but suppose they lost everything?

It was then, and for no reason, that she
remembered what Miles Tolan had said. That
he might have been Will's best friend, but
Will was not his best friend.

What had he meant? She felt the remark was
somehow disparaging of Will, and was nettled
by it. Yet as she turned back inside the
house the remark stayed with her, irritating
and troublesome . . . like a burr under the
saddle.

CHAPTER 5

Colonel Lorin White stood with his feet
solidly apart, his fists resting on his wide
hips. His round, fat face was set in hard
lines. "Lieutenant Tolan"--his voice was
high, but its tone showed his peevish
anger--"you are not a Moravian missionary,
but an officer of the Army of the United
States sent here for escort duty! Your
orders give you no right to interfere with

private citizens going about their legitimate business!"

"General Scott's orders were--"

"He placed you under _my_ orders! I will
tolerate no interference with civilians! You
are to escort a group of Indians that I
shall designate, and nothing more!"

"Am I to understand rape and murder are
licensed by this command?"

White's face stiffened; he took a step
away from the window and his voice lowered.
"Lieutenant, I will not tolerate impudence
from you. I have given you your orders. You
are to take what men you need and ride
through the backcountry and make a thorough
search for all Indians that may be hiding
out. These Indians are to be brought in to
the camps and to be held until they can
be taken west.

"You will observe there is nothing in
those orders that will allow you to interfere with civilians in any way. You are
especially to refrain from interfering with
Mr. Hallett."

"Or Wilson Rounce?"

Colonel White came around his desk. "I did
not mention that name. Nor is it to be
mentioned."

Miles relaxed a little. "But Mr. Rounce is
an old friend. I might say, a very old
friend."

White stared at him doubtfully. "I did not
understand that you knew him."

"I know him very well." Pleased that White
was no longer so sure of himself, Tolan

gathered his gloves and turned to go. "I know him well enough to know that those associated with him usually find themselves in trouble . . . but Will Rounce gets off scot-free."

"That is none of your business," White said firmly. "You will follow your orders."

Miles Tolan walked outside and stopped on the steps of the building. Inwardly, he was furious. Obviously, White was playing it cozy with the local politicians, and certainly Will had wasted no time in demonstrating his influence.

Well . . . they were right, of course. It was none of his business. A law had been passed and a treaty signed, and it was not his position to ask questions, but only to obey. Yet Will Rounce's position here intrigued him, and whatever else might happen Miles knew very well that he was not through with Will. There was that in Will that would never leave well enough alone.

It had begun long ago, in Pennsylvania. Miles Tolan had been five years old when he fell under the supervision of Elias Rounce of Rounceville, and despite his mixed feelings for Will, Miles could never feel anything but affection and respect for that stern, just, and eccentric man who for twelve years had been guardian, foster father, and mentor to him.

He had never been addressed by any name other than "Mister Elias." He ruled his household as he ruled his varied businesses, with a firm hand. Never in his presence did anyone laugh or speak loudly, nor did anyone who worked for him ever idle at a task. Not only would such a man have been dismissed at once, but he would have found it difficult to find work of any other kind in the community. Despite this, Elias Rounce was a man not only feared, but admired by many and respected by all.

His family were reported to have been fisherfolk, although it was rumored there had been shipbuilders among them too. He rarely spoke of himself, and Miles could recall only three occasions when he had made any reference to his past.

It was Mister Elias's firm belief that education was for the purpose of building character. He did not believe in the way schools were traditionally managed; he maintained his own school for his grand-children and for the children of a few of his immediate associates. Their teacher was a man imported for the purpose by Mister Elias.

Phineas Cronkite was tall, almost as tall as Mister Elias, who himself stood six feet and four inches in his size-fourteen boots. Whereas Mister Elias was a solid man of broad chest and shoulders, Phineas Cronkite was lean, hollow-cheeked, and sparse of hair. His skull was long rather than broad like Mister Elias's, and what little hair he did possess was thin and pale. His nose was long and busy as a ferret's while his thin lips were tightly compressed, as though he feared to say something extraordinary.

Phineas Cronkite, who was the only teacher
Miles could remember, possessed an amazing
fund of knowledge on a peculiar variety of
subjects, but Miles had never been able to
discover where or how he had come by such
knowledge or the skills he had at hand.

When he instructed his few students he did
so in a dry monotone that yet held some
strange quality of fascination, for Miles
could never recall finding him either dull
or uninteresting. Somehow, the moment he
began to speak one's attention was captured,
and from that instant no one in class ever
thought of anything else.

His instruction would have been considered
radically unorthodox in any other school,
but Miles did not believe that Phineas saw
it in that light at all, or even gave any
serious thought to the opinions of others.

Miles would never forget those classes.
There were six students, ranging in age from
ten to fifteen during the years Miles
remembered them best. Phineas would look
past them with his yellow eyes and begin to
talk, and from that moment their attention
was captured. Yet looking back, Miles could
never remember Phineas showing excitement,
pleasure, or sadness.

No matter what he taught, his manner
remained the same. He instructed them in
cheating at cards with the same dry, empty-
faced manner in which he taught the Psalms,
and he taught them how to kill a man with a
knife in exactly the manner in which he
instructed them in Thucydides. If he was

able to distinguish one pupil from another, Miles could recall no indication of it.

Mister Elias was a successful man. It was impossible that he could have been anything else, being the sort of man he was. Miles never knew all the details of Mister Elias's business, but Rounceville was Mister Elias, and vice versa. He owned and operated the tannery, blacksmith shop, carriage shop, and a gunsmithy. He operated a provision store, and employed cobblers, tailors, and dressmakers. Rounceville was an economy complete in itself.

Yet all this was but a small part of his business, for Mister Elias bought things. It was said of him that Elias Rounce would buy anything, and it was also noted that he sold everything he bought, and invariably at a substantial profit. If no profit was immediately available, he waited. As a result there were warehouses of amazing odds and ends, through which Miles and the others had rummaged and searched for things to excite their interest or with which to play.

Mister Elias's orders were that each child was to be out of bed at four a.m. and after a cold bath to breakfast at four-thirty. They were to be employed by five o'clock. Each Saturday morning the boys were called to the desk by Phineas and each was given a rifle and six loads of powder and ball. By sundown they were expected to report to him with at least five rabbits, squirrels, or game birds.

On this day the boys were not allowed to

carry a lunch, so if they ate at all, it
must be from food found in the forest or
fields. These rules were laid down by Mister
Elias and given to Phineas Cronkite for our
instruction, and remarkable as it might
seem, Miles could not recall that after the
first few months any of them ever went
hungry.

Once each month Mister Elias would receive
each of the students alone in his study, and
at that time questioned them on topics
connected with their work, study, or
hunting. Each of them might be called upon
to speak extemporaneously upon a topic
selected by him from their field of
activities. These meetings with Mister Elias
began when they were ten and proceeded, with
rare interruptions, until they were freed
from their education.

Never during the twelve years at Rounceville could Miles recall any evidence of
favoritism, despite the fact that two of the
students were his own grandsons and one a
granddaughter. Mister Elias had been strict
with them all, yet perceptive of their
individual traits, attributes, and talents.
Later, Miles realized Mister Elias knew more
of their faults than he had suspected, and
that he was prepared to deal with them.

When Miles was sixteen Mister Elias came
to the room where Phineas held class and
placed on the desk before Phineas a volume
of Blackstone. "Miles Tolan will read this,"
he said, "and he will report to me after

examination by you. Every man should know the rudiments of law."

At intervals, following Miles' fourteenth birthday he was given a horse, a small wagon, and a load, usually not large, of trade goods. With this he was expected to go out and trade, and he was expected to show a profit; if such a profit did appear it was put into Miles' account in Mister Elias's bank. It was the same for each of the boys.

At the trading he had been moderately successful, but never so successful as Will, who had concluded some rather fabulous deals.

All that had ended rather suddenly when Miles was seventeen.

On the morning that Mister Elias sent for him, Miles had been surprised, because during the year that had just passed these visits had grown increasingly less frequent. Mister Elias was seated behind his huge desk, and he had surprised Miles still more by suggesting he be seated. Mister Elias not only kept most standing at attention during their recitations and examinations, but he would tolerate nothing slovenly nor lacking in respect in his charges' conduct.

He had been occupied with some figures when Miles entered, and seated in the high-backed chair, Miles watched him. How old he was Miles had never known, but at the time he must have been nearing seventy, although still a powerful man, physically active and showing no more evidence of the passing years than a huge old oak tree. His square-cut

beard was streaked with gray, but so it had
been when Miles first saw him, and his face
seemed unchanged.

Mister Elias looked up suddenly. "Miles,
you are no relation of mine."

Of this Miles was aware, but he sat
awaiting what might follow, and his
curiosity was keen.

"When I die I shall leave you nothing, nor
do I believe you have expected it, so the
time has come for you to act for yourself.

"I have never felt that advice was
important. Men of my years are far too ready
with their advice, and it is rarely worth
the bother. All too rarely they have thought
out the advice they offer, and the further
you go in life the more you will realize
that few people think. They follow lines of
least resistance or take advantage of
opportunities that occur. If you think,
Miles, the world can be yours."

He paused. "I now have something to say to
you that I know you will not repeat. I have
observed you carefully, and have found many
qualities in you to admire, and one of them
is that you invariably keep your own
counsel. I like this, and I know there are
many things you might have discussed of
which you have said nothing.

"I want you to leave here, Miles, and I
want you to go far away. I ask you to do
this because one of the things I have
observed is the unhealthy rivalry that has
developed between you and Will.

"No." Mister Elias lifted a hand. "Do not

explain or protest. I know the rivalry is
mostly on Will's side. Will is a boy who has
to win--he cannot take second place, and
will not. You are aware of this, and in a
number of cases you have deliberately
allowed him to win because, I believe, you
feel you owe a debt to me."

Miles started to object.

"Please! I have thought this out, and I
know the character of each of you. You have
no reluctance to let Will win because
winning is important to you only when the
issue is itself important. Regardless of
that, Will has lately taken a new course.
For some reason, through some insecurity I
cannot fathom, competing with you and
winning has become more important to him
than anything else in the world.

"During these past few years he has lied,
cheated, and stolen. His 'successful'
trading was not successful, Miles. He was
selling his goods and then stealing because
of his need to be absolutely sure he bested
you.

"I want you to go away, Miles. Go far from
here, and stay away from Will if you can
possibly do so. Will has great ability, but
you have qualities he will never have. You
have character and you have persistence. If
you remain in the same area, sooner or later
a time will come when an issue or a woman
would become so important to you that you
would not allow him to win. I fear then that
he would try to kill you. He would try;
whether he could succeed or not I have no

idea . . . but whatever the result, it would
be disastrous.

"I am not a foolish old man, Miles. There
is something lacking in my grandson, some
moral sense that I have been unable to
provide. I have watched you both grow, and I
could wish, Miles, that you were my
grandson. I would admit that to no one else.
I am proud of you, and wherever you go, I
know you will survive and you will achieve
whatever it is you wish to achieve."

"That will be due to you, sir."

"In part, perhaps. The education I have
given here is different. Many believe it is
severe, but life is not mild. Many believe I
have concentrated too much on some aspects,
but I do not think so. Here we try to build
character first--self-respect, independence
of spirit, self-reliance--and to offer the
equipment for survival and for citizenship."

Mister Elias got to his feet. "No one has
been told of your going and I would prefer
you to tell no one. You will ride Ambrose,
my Irish stallion; he is now yours. Your
clothing has been packed, you have a bill of
sale for the stallion, and your money is
here. You will find on your saddle a new
rifle and a brace of pistols. You are to go
as if on a business dealing for me. You are
not to come back."

Miles remembered how he had gotten to his
feet. He looked across the table at Mister
Elias with a lump in his throat. "Thank you,
sir. Thank you for everything. You have been

more than a father to me, and I shall try to
follow your advice."

Elias held out his hand, and Miles
suddenly realized that it was the first time
they had ever touched. Then the boy turned
toward the door.

"Miles?" Something in Elias's voice had
turned cold. "I send you away in hopes that
by being apart each of you may grow
naturally, and my grandson will live out his
days. But I would do you no favor to leave
you unwarned. If ever you and Will meet
again, do not think of what I have done for
you, but simply protect yourself. You are my
son also, in my feelings if not in blood."

And now what Mister Elias had feared had
come to pass. They were together again . . .
and the Army had ordered him here, and the
Army would not permit him to leave.

Already battle had been joined, mildly so
far, but joined nonetheless.

There was only one thing to do. Avoid
Will. Avoid Hallett, avoid Adam Couch, avoid
anyone or anything that led to him or was
close to him.

Avoid Laura.

CHAPTER 6

During the days that followed there was
little time for thinking of Will Rounce, nor
of Laura McCrae. Oddly though, it was the
girl in the forest to whom his thoughts

reverted again and again; the mystery of her presence there and her sudden disappearance haunted him.

Not less did he wonder about the peculiar reactions of both Will and Laura to his mention of Moore's _Lalla Rookh_. Certainly, there was nothing in the contents of the book that could create such an effect. It was simply a rather charming and romantic love poem with some interesting overtones.

However, it was Mister Elias's admonition that remained most in his mind, and he took care to avoid any further meeting with Will Rounce. For the moment Miles' duties were more than sufficient to keep him busy, and it would not be long before he would again be going west, and this time with a party of Cherokees. Once west he would contrive that he not come east again, one way or another.

How could a man dedicated to pushing the Cherokees from their land still remain a friend to the McCraes? Especially when that man was an avowed enemy of Tsali's?

More and more he found himself puzzled by Will's presence here at all. What had become of Rounceville? Mister Elias must certainly have divided among his three grandchildren a sizable fortune, if all had survived until his death. Will would have been a fool to leave a going business in a community where he could assume the mantle of his grandfather's prestige and be immediately a personage of some importance, in every sense.

What had happened?

* * *

As the weeks passed, bitterness increased among the Cherokees who remained in the mountains at the corner of Georgia, North Carolina, and Tennessee. The Treaty of New Echota, signed by fewer than five hundred of a tribe of more than sixteen thousand, required the Cherokees to surrender their lands in Georgia and move to Indian country beyond the Mississippi.

The Cherokee Nation was to be given five million dollars, an equal amount of land in the new Indian Territory, an educational fund of half a million dollars, and compensation for abandoned property in the East. But there was open talk of bribery, and the known fact that many of the Cherokees present at the treaty signing had been made drunk and were in no condition to know what they were signing. The situation was made even more complex by the passions involved, passions that led to several of those in favor of the treaty having been assassinated and what amounted to a Cherokee government in exile being established over the state line in Tennessee.

Reports of a gold discovery in the Cherokee country increased the cupidity of those politicians who were exerting pressure on Washington and Atlanta, but the rougher element were not inclined to wait upon the Removal. Rushing in, they tore down Cherokee fences, ruined their crops, and defiled the pure waters of their streams. Ignoring both the tribal government and the federal

treaties, the state of Georgia passed laws
extending her jurisdiction over the Cherokee
country, and even went so far as to forbid
any Cherokee to hold office in the tribe, or
any white man to live in Cherokee territory
without swearing allegiance to the state of
Georgia. The Georgia Legislature, eager to
preserve the gold for the white man, even
made it illegal for any Cherokee to dig for
gold on his own land.

Rarely, Miles Tolan thought, had the
legislative right been so abused. It was at
a time when throughout the United States
there was strong sympathy for the Greeks in
their war for Independence, yet only a few
went so far as to speak out for the
Cherokees in their own land.

Detachments of soldiers were sent out to
scour the fields and the mountains with
rifle and bayonet, to search every cabin
hidden away in the coves of the hills or the
deeper valleys, and to seize and bring in
Cherokees wherever found. From dawn to dusk
they were in the field, rounding up the
Indians and escorting them to stockades,
where they were concentrated prior to their
movement westward. It was cruel work, and
few in the Army liked it.

Resistance was rare. The Cherokees had
been worn out by the long struggle to keep
their hills and by the continual inroads of
white men seeking gold, stealing stock, or
merely searching out land they wished to
claim. More than once the people had

scarcely been moved from their cabins before looters had them in flames.

In all of this, Miles Tolan was a part. He had been given a job to do and he did it, acting with speed, efficiency, and with whatever kindness was possible. With care, he managed to avoid the parties of looters, or bands he suspected might be directed by Will Rounce.

In the fifth week he again met Laura McCrae.

They recognized each other at the same instant, and she rode up to him at once. "Have you seen Will?" He thought there was a note of anxiety in her tone. "He has not been to Brignole."

He hesitated, and despite himself he was worried, worried for this quiet, attractive girl who seemed to have placed her faith in Will Rounce. "No," he said finally, "I haven't seen him . . . but then I have been very busy."

"My father is worried. We have received orders to vacate."

Miles glanced down at the reins in his hands. "It is the law," he said. "All Cherokees must move."

"We won't be forced to." He thought there was a shadow of doubt in her voice. "Will assured us we had no reason to worry."

"I think he was wrong." He heard himself speak the words almost without volition. "I don't believe it is a good policy but I _do_ believe you will be forced to move. No word

has been given to me to provide for any
exceptions . . . and there are other factors
to be considered."

"Will is very close to the governor," she
replied, "and to Colonel White. He told us
just to stay where we were, that everything
would be all right."

"He has given you false hope."

She was not convinced. "I do not know what
you think is wrong, but I assure you, you
are mistaken. Will is a fine man, a very
fine man. My father admires him very much,
and so does James."

"And John Ross?"

"No," she admitted, "I do not believe they
like each other."

"And Tsali?"

"Tsali?" She was surprised. "Why, Tsali is
nobody. Just an old mountain farmer."

"But a Cherokee," Miles interposed, "Tsali
told me to tell Will that he was his enemy.
And the men whom I stopped from looting that
farm were under Will's orders."

"I do not believe that. Oh," she added
quickly, "he may claim some of the land now
that people are forced to leave, the same as
many others. But he would not allow such
things as you saw there. I know he
wouldn't."

Miles did not like the way the
conversation was tending, and gathered his
reins. "My only advice to you is to place
your trust in no one concerned with this
movement. Listen to Ross if you will. He is
trying to do something."

"That is strange talk from a soldier," Laura said, "advising me to place no faith in anyone concerned with the movement."

"A soldier does what he is told, but that does not mean he does not have his own opinions. I only know that what has to be done, will be done, so far as I can arrange it, without hardship to those involved." He spoke stiffly, feeling an antagonism from her he could not quite understand. Unless she was resenting his attitude toward Will Rounce. "I believe no one is in any position now to promise anything, and I have no faith in Will's promises."

"You hate him, don't you?"

"No," he said honestly, "I do not hate him. I really do not even dislike him. I simply do not trust him, and my lack of trust is based on past experience."

"I think you hate him more than you suspect because he was always better than you in everything you two did."

Miles laughed. "Did Will tell you that? Well, sometimes I know he was better than I. He could jump farther and higher than I could, but he could not run or walk as far. He was always a little better in shooting at targets, but I usually came in with the most game. I just think Will was born lacking some other quality the majority of us have."

There was no warmth in her eyes. "I do not like you, Lieutenant Tolan. I believe you have no right to talk of Will that way. Someday he may thrash you for it."

Miles chuckled. "He may, at that." Then he

added more gently, "But it will take some doing."

Both were prepared to ride on, yet neither moved. The sun dappled the trail with leaf shadow, and somewhere off under the trees they could hear birds scratching and rustling among the leaves.

"Miss McCrae," he asked suddenly, "did Will ever tell you what happened to Rounceville?"

"No. So far as I can recall he's never mentioned it. When you appeared he did tell me something of your early life there."

"It should have been his. I believe Mister Elias had planned it so, and he was a man who thought things through. Often I've wondered what happened to Phineas Cronkite, our teacher."

"Will never discusses it." Her curiosity was aroused. "What was it like?"

"Mister Elias . . . he was Will's grandfather . . . was a man of original mind. I never did hear how he started it all, except that the first time he came through the valley where he built Rounce- ville he was a wagon-peddler. He traded with the Indians, fought them on occasion, then bought cattle, horses, and hogs. When the country began to settle up he was the main source of supply, and he invested in shoemaking, tanning, and a blacksmith shop. It developed for thirty years until he owned an entire community, and had put by a good bit of money."

"Will told me you left when you were seventeen."

"By invitation. I mean, Mister Elias educated me, cared for me, and at seventeen I was old enough to fend for myself."

"What did you do then?" Laura asked curiously.

"Saw some country . . . went down the river to New Orleans . . . joined up with the Missouri Fur Company."

"You were a trapper?"

"Trapper, hunter, trader. I came back to St. Louis and then made a trip over the Santa Fe Trail to the Spanish settlements there. I did pretty well."

Laura watched his eyes curiously. "You're a strange man, Lieutenant. I don't quite know what to think of you."

"We're all much alike." He made a move to start again, and said, "You could tell me something, however. . . ."

"What?"

"Who is the Beloved Woman?"

CHAPTER 7

Laura had evaded his question--that was Miles' first thought upon opening his eyes. He lay very still with his hands clasped behind his head, knowing it was time to get up, yet wanting to think.

It was Sunday morning, he was without

orders, and for this one brief day he was
once again his own man.

For more than a week he had been hearing
references to the Beloved Woman, and his
curiosity had been excited. She was without
a doubt a personage of some importance, but to
questions asked of the Cherokees he received
only evasive replies, replies that had
whetted his interest. In general he had
found the Cherokees a courteous people, and
usually willing to explain any of their own
customs that aroused interest.

Among the Georgians themselves he found
few who knew anything about the Cherokees,
and most of them doubted they were
interesting. Here and there he found a
degree of sympathy for their plight, but
these people felt that decisions had been
based upon much that had gone on before
their time--and seemed less aware of the
role played by a few self-seekers and
politicians who wanted the vote. There was
also a hard core of people who saw the
Cherokees prospering and believed it was
something in the land they owned rather than
their own energy that brought them such
prosperity. These shiftless ones wished to
drive the Cherokees from the land so that
they might have it.

There was also, deep-seated within all
peoples, the desire to seek out anything
different from themselves and destroy it.
That desire was not exhibiting itself for
the first time, nor would it be for the

last. It was blind, unreasoning hatred of
all that was different.

Miles sat up in bed, then swung his feet
to the floor, staring irritably across the
room. He wanted a transfer. He wanted to get
out of this situation, to get away from what
was happening here. Uncle Elias had done
much to shape his thinking, and had fostered
within him, among other things, an appreciation for industrious people; and now,
everywhere his eyes turned, he saw clear
evidence of the sort of work he understood
best.

No craftsman, whether blacksmith, weaver,
carpenter, or leather-worker, had been
allowed to live among the Cherokees unless
he had taken Cherokee youths as apprentices.
No missionary was allowed in the territory
of the Cherokees unless he also conducted a
school. All he could learn of this people
indicated a keen appreciation of the
necessity for change and the best way to go
about it. True, some had taken to drink, and
there were laggards among them, but they
were few. Fewer, Miles reluctantly admitted,
than among his own people.

As he shaved, bathed, and dressed, Miles
grew annoyed with himself for pondering a
problem beyond his control. What could he,
Lieutenant Miles Tolan, do? He had
authority, but limited authority only. He
was subject to orders from his government,
from any superior officer, and, it seemed,
from Will Rounce. At least, that is, if they
came via Colonel White.

Already, Miles knew he had overstepped his orders to a degree. Wherever possible he was careful to inflict no additional hardship upon the Cherokees who were to be moved. Fortunately, the rank and file of the Army were men from the frontier or farms, and they understood what had been done here and how much work it entailed. As a result they had little but sympathy for the Indian.

Only yesterday a man had struck an old Cherokee with a whip, and Miles had coolly walked his horse between them as the Indian got to his feet. The man had attempted to walk around Miles' horse, but seemingly without a glance at him, Miles kept his horse between them. And the Cherokee, seeing his chance, walked away.

Angrily, the white man demanded, "What's the matter? You sidin' with these Injuns?"

"What?" Miles Tolan asked as if noticing the man for the first time. "You were speaking to me?"

Disconcerted, the man protested, "I was givin' that Injun what he had comin' when you come between us."

"I did?" Miles had looked astonished. "Why, I didn't even see you!" Confidentially, Miles leaned toward him. "They give us a lot to do, these days. Riding all the time, rounding up these Indians. I must have fallen asleep in the saddle."

He rode on, Sergeant Turpenning following. Turpenning had said nothing, for he was a man who held his ideas inside his head, and

rarely ventured opinions unless asked a
direct question. Sergeant Turpenning was
forty-two years old, with thirty of those
years spent on the frontier and most of them
in the Army. He was a man who knew his
place, but he also had his own ideas about
the Indians, for he had fought them.

COMMENTS: Although I remember some work being
done on this novel in the early 1970s, I believe the majority
of the material you have just read was created between 1958
and 1960. *Trail of Tears* was considered a potential move
toward more "serious" work, both the first time (the late
1950s) Louis tried to break out of writing Westerns, and
during his more calculated, and more successful, attempt in
the 1970s.

Dad often joked that if a novel was written about the
nineteenth century and set west of the Mississippi, it was
labeled a Western and deemed inconsequential by the critics,
yet if it was set east of the Mississippi, it might be thought
of as a historical novel, and be taken more seriously.

Not only is *Trail of Tears* set firmly in the historical novel
territory of the East, but its time period is earlier than most
consider appropriate for a traditional Western. Better yet, it
deals with themes and moments in history that both Easterners and Westerners would consider highly significant
culturally and historically.

Prior to its completion, Louis wrote a proposal in order
to sell this book. It was offered to both a publisher and a
movie studio, though, ultimately, he did not conclude either
deal. Hardcover publishers were a quandary for Louis. They

got books reviewed. They got respect. They earned you a bit of extra money if your book sold well, because they cost more . . . but they also took part of your paperback earnings (for having promoted the book, and for brokering the deal), they weren't really available at a price appropriate for the common man (something Louis cared about deeply), and they wanted a piece of the movie rights. With the exception of critical recognition, for a popular writer like Louis L'Amour there weren't many advantages in those days to publishing in hardcover.

Once Louis knew he could earn a good living selling directly to the paperback publishers, the only reason to try for a hardcover sale was prestige—but prestige was an important goal for Louis in the early 1970s. He knew he could knock the ball out of the park in the paperback arena, but he wanted to win over the critics, too.

While none of the proposal drafts took the story through to its completion, they do reveal a few additional details.

The inclusion of the intriguing, sylphlike Woman on the Rock, the girl who turns out to be the Beloved Woman of the Cherokee, was made late in the process. I can remember Dad talking about having discovered the concept of the Beloved Woman while he was doing research for one of his later attempts. He was excited by the opportunity it posed for the creation of a fascinating character. At times she seemed almost a Native American Joan of Arc, and would have been an interesting addition to a tragic story of this scope.

For the longest time, Westerns and science fiction were the two genres where anything but the most superficial love interest was a taboo. Not so the historical novel, which often showed a tendency to cross over into romance territory. In his proposals, Louis made sure publishers knew he would be playing by the rules of historical novels:

> There is a strong love story, and in
> certain phases of the story, a good bit
> of sex, tastefully handled but
> definitely present. Aside from the
> action, the love story will be, I
> believe, one of the most entertainingly
> developed of recent years. With proper
> promotion I believe this book will have
> a great sale, of which we can all be
> proud.

Louis intended to play on the hypocrisy that surrounded the Cherokee Removal, showing that the prejudice of the white men did not need a target as obvious as the Western genre's typical Indians.

> . . . these Indians were, in many
> cases, educated, well-informed men and
> women who lived in the same sort of
> houses as white men and who wore the
> same sort of clothing as the white man
> from preference. Their differences from
> white society were few; they were not a
> group of "outsiders." Many were at least
> as well educated as the average white
> man of his time, and several had
> qualities of genius.

Not only was he exploring the fact that many Cherokee did not look or act differently from their white neighbors (many were even Christian), but some of his characters among the Cherokee elite were meant to be pathetically tone-deaf to the catastrophe that was bearing down on them. To add irony upon irony, there are some indications that he also intended to add major characters who were the black slaves of those same Cherokee elites, slaves who traveled and died on the Trail of Tears.

Although, for Louis, being an entertainer came first and a historian a more distant second, he did quote some of his sources for research on this book, and mentioned a few of what I'm guessing are actual episodes that he intended to use in the narrative:

Material for this book has been culled from the Library of Congress, War Department records, the Peabody Library in Baltimore, the Enoch Pratt Library in the same city; from family records of descendants of Indians who made the march, and many other sources.

Some of the episodes likely to be included in the novel are the following:

The massacre of Tsali and his family;

The burial of Chief Whitepath;

Gen. Scott's thwarting of the Georgia militia's efforts to publicly horsewhip sixteen Cherokees;

The separation of the Indian, Epenetus, from his son while helping a missionary administer sacraments;

The lashing of a Cherokee for striking a soldier who had goaded the Indian's wife;

The attempt of the Cherokees to put to death members of the treaty party who betrayed them;

The sinking of the overloaded ferry in mid-Mississippi and the drowning of hundreds on it.

A quote included in some of Louis's notes sums up the attitude of many of the military men involved (throughout the frontier period the US Army, while being the blunt tool of government policy, was, in my slight experience, often vastly more sympathetic to Native Americans than the private citizens who were their neighbors):

> General Wool, in command in the area, asked to be relieved rather than carry out the distasteful mission. In the majority of cases the Army was sympathetic, and before the end of the march, almost to a man they were helping the Indians. General Wool is quoted as saying, "The whole scene since I have been in this country has been nothing but a heart rending one. . . . I could not do them a greater kindness than to remove every Indian beyond the reach of the white men who, like vultures, are waiting to pounce upon their prey and strip them of everything they have or expect from the government of the United States."

The final pieces of the narrative that lurk in the fragmentary proposal drafts are set out here:

> Meanwhile, Miles is rounding up Cherokees and bringing them to the stockades to be held pending movement to the west. He is disturbed to find them totally unlike the Indians he had known. They are a prosperous and successful

people farming their own land, running
their own mills, in almost no way
different from their white neighbors. It
is a fact that causes him to ask
questions of himself and others. It is a
fact that causes him to reconsider his
attitude, which has been positive yet
patronizing, toward the Indians he once
fought in the far west.

. . . Laura is confident they will not
have to go, for Will has constantly
assured them not to worry. Through
beauty, wealth, and education, she is
able to straddle the divide between
worlds and is unaware of the depth of the
prejudice she faces. She dismisses Miles'
warnings as jealousy because Miles
doubts the honesty of Will's intentions.
On one side Will is seemingly friendly
to the Cherokees, on the other he is
working with those who are looting them.

. . . Miles meets the girl he has seen
diving into the pool. She will tell him
nothing of herself, but they arrange
several meetings in the deep woods. She
is hiding from someone. He becomes aware
that that someone is Will Rounce, and
the powers that he represents. She is,
he later discovers, the Beloved Woman, a
personage of real influence in the tribe,
an influence even greater than that of

many chieftains, and to whom they all
must listen with respect, a leader
they might rally around in time of war
or trouble.

During one of their meetings Miles
hears a faint sound and learns they have
been watched. Following the watcher to
prevent him from telling what he has
seen, he comes suddenly on the body of
the man. He has been killed. Later, he
sees one of the sons of Tsali leaving
the area. He is a Cherokee Miles has met
before.

Miles himself is subjected to
searching inquiry, for it is realized
that he has won friends among the
Cherokee. It is believed the Beloved
Woman knows the location of a vast
deposit of gold, for the gold
discoveries on the Cherokee lands so far
have been limited and the interlopers
are unwilling to believe there is no
more.

Miles meets Hallett again, and this
time in a fight. Hallett attempts to
strike him with a whip. Miles gives
Hallett a severe beating and is
arrested.

Orders are issued for the McCraes to
go west. Shocked, Laura tries to reach
Will, but she cannot. They are driven
from their home, and escaping, she
returns to find Will and some of his

```
friends holding court in her home, and
for the first time she realizes that
this was what he had always intended,
that he had pretended friendship to have
first chance at one of the best places
in the Cherokee Nation.
```

The above would suggest that Will's short-term goal is to keep the McCraes from selling their land so that he can grab it without having to buy it ... but who his mysterious connections are and what the long game is remains a mystery, as does what happened to Will's inheritance from Uncle Elias.

Louis was interested in the many utopian, often experimentally socialist communities that sprung up on the American frontier, like the Shakers and New Harmony. I know he had many more intriguing details up his sleeve about the community of Rounceville and the characters of Elias Rounce and Phineas Cronkite.

Here's a short breakdown that was done somewhere along the way. It's the only indication we have of the shape of the entire plot. It's important to realize that Louis rarely referred to outlines like this once he started writing, so he might have gone on to do something completely different. The "FIRST," "SECOND," "THIRD," and "FOURTH" he is writing about are acts or the major sections of the story.

FIRST:

```
Story opens, protagonists meet,
problem is unfolded. Hero's character is
revealed, also that of heavy and girl.
Situation is revealed, conflict begins.
```

SECOND:

Conflict increases, characters
revealed still more, problem develops,
and the whole condition and state of
affairs is revealed and made clear. Hero
begins coping with problem, meets with
failure. His love for girl is revealed
to him suddenly.

THIRD:

Removal begins: a long, bitter, brutal
trek. Take much time with this, and with
individual characters who have been
developed in early sections, now meet
with trouble, death, bereavement. Hero
is recalled to Atlanta; refuses to abide
by orders; attempt at assassination.
Plans are revealed whereby heavies will
cut off a small band of Indians and rob
them. Heavy reveals his true attitude
toward girl: He despises her as an
Indian.

FOURTH:

Removal continues. After terrible
trials, hero returns to girl finding
much death, pity, and fatigue along the
way, and afraid she will be dead or
lost. He comes to her, but is pursued by
hatred of heavy until final fight in the
swamps or on the river's edge or on the
plains of Oklahoma.

> Begin writing tomorrow and do 1,000
> words of the beginning. Do them over.
> Begin with action, poetry, power. Create
> a character worth reading about.

I love that last bit. Louis was always writing himself these sorts of affirmations. They are another facet of his lifelong motivation to keep moving, think positively, and improve himself. Below is the most interesting set of notes on this story, because they are written in first person, as if he, Louis, was the actual narrator. I don't know of another case of him doing this, even for a story that was ultimately written in first person.

OUTLINE: TRAIL OF TEARS

1. I arrive in Georgia, and meet girl and [illegible]; I meet old friend; develop acquaintance with girl, find doubts of friend. Become friends with some Cherokees. Told off by [illegible] in Atlanta.
2. Trouble develops, affair with girl, acquaintance develops with friend's girl. My girlfriend's father also involved. Old friend plots against me. Break becomes definite. Fight at Cherokee town.
3. The Removal Begins: Harassed, betrayed, the first fight, herds driven off, murder.

Finally, there is this cryptic passage from some of the *Trail of Tears* materials:

1. Meetings and development:
I arrive in Georgia, and meet girl and Trali; I meet old friend; develop acquaintance with girl, find doubts of friend. Become friends well some Cherokees. Told off by com. in Atlanta.

2. Trouble develops, affair with girl, acq. dev. with friends girl. My girl friend's father also involved. Old friend plots against me Break becomes definite. Fight at Cherokee town.

3. The Removal Begins: Harass, Astray, I'll ain't fight; Leads driven off, murder.

A different, handwritten version of the first-person notes.

```
1st section: in love but don't know it.
2nd in love but won't say it.
3rd in love but can't do anything about it.
4th can say, can do, no future
```

I'm not sure why this book wasn't eventually completed; possibly it was because of changing priorities in Louis's career. The struggle to break into the hardcover business may have become less important as his success replaced the need to be well reviewed. He also became more focused on planning his "three family" (Sackett, Chantry, Talon) series and recognized that sooner or later, because of changes in the book business, he was going to be able to publish in hardback without changing genres. While Louis very much wanted to write other kinds of material, he also wanted to win widespread acceptance for his Westerns, and as much as he liked a challenge, he preferred to succeed without having to accommodate others. It was a tension that ran like a subtle stream throughout his later life.

A WOMAN WORTH HAVING

A Treatment for an Adventure Story

COMMENTS: A "treatment" like the following document is the description of a story rather than the story itself. It is used as a sales tool when an author is attempting to present an idea for which he wishes to be paid, by a publisher or a movie studio, to write. In Louis's case, treatments were almost never intended to be an exact description of the finished work; they were much more like a very early rough draft where he experimented with the potential of different structures and ideas.

"A woman worth having must be fought for or stolen."

--Arab proverb

Hot and dusty were the crowded streets of Mosul on that afternoon in 1845, but the tall, erect young Englishman who made his way through the crowd was aware of something

more than the dust, smells, and flies of the
Near East. He was aware of a subtle
undercurrent of revolt, of seething unrest.
And Henry Layard was fully aware of the
reason for that feeling, for during his
short stay in the country he had seen much
and heard more of the sadistic cruelty of
the local governor, Mohammed Pasha.

Layard was a handsome young man, skilled
in the arts of diplomacy, which was his
profession, and knowing in all the languages
and many of the dialects of the Near East.
Yet he was a man ridden by a driving urge to
find the fabled cities of Nineveh, to
uncover the ruins he knew existed in the
valleys of the Tigris and the Euphrates. Nor
was this his first trip to Mesopotamia, for
he had been here before and had scouted the
country carefully while hunting. Near the
rivers he had found several huge mounds that
seemed geologically out of place, and he had
come to believe they were actually heaps of
sand and debris blown up and over the ruins
of the ancient cities mentioned in the Old
Testament.

He was walking now to a meeting with Sir
Stratford Canning, British ambassador to the
government of Turkey, who was visiting in
Mosul from his headquarters in Istanbul.

As he pushed through the crowd, his mind
was fraught with anxiety. He needed money to
finance his project, and he feared he would
neither get it nor receive permission to
remain in the country until conditions
became calmer than they now were. The

slightest wrong move could explode into
revolt, and only fear of the bloody
vengeance of Mohammed Pasha was keeping the
people quiet.

Ahead of him he saw a sedan chair carried
by slaves and preceded by two stalwart
desert tribesmen. It was an unusual sight,
for sedan chairs were rarely seen and almost
never in charge of Bedouins; it betokened a
person of some importance.

As he drew abreast of the sedan chair
there was a sudden outburst in a dark
alleyway and a rush of men. In an instant
the marketplace had exploded into a
fighting, screaming, brawling mob. One of
the bearers was knocked to the pavement and
the chair fell, turning half over and
spilling a very startled, and beautifully
robed young woman into the street.

The Bedouins who were her protectors had
been separated from her by the fighting, and
in an instant, Layard sprang to her side and
stood over her, fighting off the brawling
Arabs. Quickly as it had begun, the fighting
washed past them, and Layard helped the
shaken girl to her feet.

"Are you hurt?" He spoke as he helped her
up, and he found himself looking into a face
covered by a heavy veil but revealing a pair
of large and amazingly lovely dark eyes. For
an instant she was in his arms, then she
stepped back and, to his surprise, thanked
him in English!

Before he could ask a question the
Bedouins had reached her side and she had

moved toward her chair, which had been
righted and was awaiting her. She looked
back once and thanked him again, but
startled out of his lethargy by the prospect
of losing a girl he wanted very much to
know, he started after her, asking who she
was and where she lived.

The girl got into the chair without
seeming to hear and then was borne away,
leaving him standing in the street. This was
not, he remembered unhappily, Paris, London,
or Naples. It was a Moslem city where the
women did not talk to men other than those
of their immediate family and rarely met
foreigners or even set eyes on them.

Disappointed, but excited by her touch and
the memory of her eyes, he hurried on to
keep his appointment with Sir Stratford.

Henry Layard is an Englishman of French
parentage, a brilliant scholar, gifted in
his command of languages, and a skilled
hunter of big game. Yet his greatest
interest is in antiquities. For a long time
many people had believed the great cities
of the ancient east, Babylon and Nineveh,
to be mere fantasies of the imagination,
like the Arabian Nights. Herodotus, who
wrote many of the legends, had also written
of other things too fantastic to be
believed, and most of the scholars of the
time either doubted the cities had ever
existed or doubted their size and
importance. When other students had been
concerned with boating or cricket, young

Layard had been studying Arabic, perfecting himself for just this task. With his dark, strongly boned features and his tall, lean build, Layard could, and in fact had, passed for an Arab himself.

Sir Stratford Canning was a tall, white-haired man of great dignity, and Layard was his personal friend and protégé. Far more than Layard realized, Sir Stratford shared his enthusiasm, but he doubted the time was favorable for such an endeavor as Layard had in mind. He knew this was reputed to be the home of the oldest civilizations on earth, older even than Egypt. The idea that fantastic cities, filled with the treasures of centuries, might lie beneath the sands had been rumored since the discoveries of Botta, but these wild theories were not discussed by sober men of science. Still, Sir Stratford knew Layard's enthusiasms and what to expect of this conference, though he had not made up his mind as to his reply.

He was torn between what he considered sane and sober reasoning, his duty to his young friend, and his friend's interests, as well as his own. Diplomat he might be, but beneath it, as with many of the greatest diplomats, there was a romantic strain, and had he been a few years younger . . .

Layard talked of the mounds, of the broken bits of marble mingled with the sands, of the fragments of pottery. He drew upon the stories of Daniel, of the Tower of Babel, of the conquests of Alexander.

"Fables!" Sir Stratford objected. "It is all too indefinite! If the cities had ever existed they would still be occupied!"

"Some things remain." Layard was positive. He had crossed the area, and he told of what he had seen and heard: the legends of cities buried in the sands; a great image of white stone, winged and mighty.

Finally, Sir Stratford agrees to finance him to a limited degree, deliberately making the amount a mere sixty pounds in hopes Layard would give up. Layard accepts eagerly and Sir Stratford admits himself defeated. Then Layard tells him of his exciting meeting in the bazaar.

The ambassador laughs. "I'm surprised she didn't agree to meet you. That must have been old Hakim's daughter, and from all I hear there's not a conventional bone in her body."

Layard learns the girl was probably Alissa, the only child of Hakim, of the Hadida tribe, from the wild deserts of southern Arabia, the land reputed to have been the home of the Queen of Sheba. Old Hakim was sheik of one of the most powerful desert tribes in Arabia, the master of ten thousand horsemen. Without a son, Hakim had reared his daughter with an amount of freedom considered disgraceful by other Moslems. She had ridden to battle with him as a child, had hunted with him, and she went about Arabia and the Near East, guarded by a handful of tribesmen and the knowledge of her father's power.

Layard leaves Sir Stratford with a parting warning from the older man that he must at all costs avoid the attention of Mohammed Pasha. If the governor learned of Layard's presence he would most certainly forbid any digging and might imprison him on some pretext. Stratford further warns him of the troubled state of political affairs.

All this Layard knows only too well. He has not mingled with the camel drivers and merchants for nothing. He knows the gossip, and knows that the Pasha has spies everywhere.

Mohammed Pasha was a short, squat man, possessed of a macabre sense of humor and a sadistic streak that made him relish the utmost in cruelty. If he suspects a man _might_ begin plotting against him, that man could at any time be condemned to torture and death. Pockmarked, with an ear missing, and with queer, jerky movements and a hoarse, bellowing voice, the Pasha is as repulsive in person as his policies are to the populace.

Not satisfied with burdening his people with taxes to an extent almost unimaginable, even in the Near East, Mohammed Pasha had his own spies incite his people to riot or rebellion so these could be put down with cruelty and bloodshed. This retinue of spies, forming a network all over the country, allowed almost any conversation to be reported to him at once.

Layard knew this, so when he went again to

the Tigris he went as a hunter of wild boar,
a casual British sportsman, armed with
several heavy rifles and a pig spear. And so
he returns to the area of his interest, and
makes an inspection of the mound where he
has chosen to dig.

Here he finds himself blocked, not by
Mohammed Pasha, but by Sheik Awad, the half-
brigand, half-friendly sheik who controls
the area. Awad flatly refuses to allow
digging. Layard is stalemated, and suddenly
a new factor enters the situation. A lavish
caravan appears, tents are spread, the black
tents of the desert Bedouins, the tents of
the daughter of Hakim!

Unknown to him, Alissa has him spied upon
by one of his own men, and she has followed
him here. He tries to see her, and is
refused admittance, yet when he sees Awad
again, the way is suddenly opened for him,
and he is permitted to hire laborers. Alissa
has interceded for him without his
knowledge.

Although he has seen her but twice (she
passes near him riding a magnificent
stallion) he is half in love with her.
He wishes to meet her, but she refuses.
Disconsolate, he seeks the advice of the
slave girls at the well, but they will
not talk to him. Yet on the following night
there is another girl among them, and as she
turns away with her jar of water she gives
him a long, slow look. He follows and talks
to her, she flirts with him, teases him, but
assures him that if she, the slave of a

powerful princess, is not supposed to talk
to him, how can he expect to see Alissa the
daughter of Hakim?

She taunts him with being an infidel, an
eater of pig meat, and they meet again, and
then again. She taunts him with being
fickle. Who is it he is in love with? The
daughter of the Hadida? Or the slave girl?

Layard is himself in a state of utter
confusion. He will not admit he is in love
with the slave girl, but he finds himself
making excuses to see her. Meanwhile, the
digging goes on.

A wall is uncovered and on it are amazing
reliefs, and some pottery is found: a small
jar covered with gold leaf, some broken
tablets. All are dusted and preserved with
the greatest of care.

Meanwhile, the spies of Mohammed Pasha
have reported the digging by the strange
Englishman. The Pasha believes he is
searching for treasure. He sends soldiers,
and Layard is ordered to stop. Yet the Pasha
knows now that the young man is the friend
of the ambassador, and that he will have
other friends in Istanbul. To protect
himself he tells Layard that he is digging
in a Moslem cemetery, that he is desecrating
graves.

While Layard sleeps the soldiers carry
stones and place them about to make it
appear that the words of the Pasha are true:
that this is, indeed, a graveyard.

Again, hopeful of assistance, Layard goes
to see the daughter of Hakim, but again

Alissa refuses to meet with him. So he
leaves and goes to Mosul, determined to face
the Pasha and demand an explanation, and
also to get, if it is at all possible,
permission to continue his digging.

At Mosul he finds the city wildly excited.
A rumor is out that the Pasha is dying, that
he left the palace in his carriage and was
stricken suddenly, then rushed back to the
palace, and now word is out that he is
either dying or dead. Soon the wails of the
mourners are heard, and a friend of Layard's
rushes to him, overjoyed at the news. Layard
is suspicious and holds back.

A huge crowd has gathered outside the
palace and they are dancing and laughing,
shouting for joy at the death of the tyrant.
Suddenly, the Pasha appears on a balcony. He
begins to roar with laughter as his soldiers
rise suddenly and fire into the mob. Men
fall, screaming and dying, and then other
soldiers rush forward and those men still
alive are made prisoners, their property to
be confiscated, themselves to be tortured
and killed.

Revolted at the bloody spectacle, Layard
nevertheless persists in his purpose. He
goes to the palace, and the Pasha, in a vast
good humor, admits him. The Pasha is
suddenly sly. This man may have powerful
friends--he suggests that if Layard is
searching for gold, that he can tell him and
that something can be arranged.

The Pasha is by turns tyrannical and
obsequious. Layard suggests he will have

nothing to do but return to Istanbul and
report to his friends there that the Pasha
will not allow him to continue. Disturbed,
the Pasha finally allows him to return and
continue digging. Secretly, he plans to let
Layard find the gold he believes he is
searching for, and then to murder him.

On his return Alissa arranges a meeting
for him with a Turkish official from the
Ottoman capital who is traveling incognito.
Layard explains the situation, and takes the
Turk through the ruins he has uncovered. An
educated, cultured man, the Turk is
entranced, and Layard gives him several
presents, a vase and some polished tile, to
take back to the sultan in Istanbul.

Attempting to thank Alissa, Layard is cut
coldly off. Her act was mere courtesy, such
as would be extended to any honest man. She
understands what he is about, and wants to
help; that does not mean that she can permit
any friendly overtures from an infidel.

Furthermore, she advises him, she
understands he is carrying on an affair with
one of her slave girls, that he is arranging
clandestine meetings. Just what are his
intentions toward this girl? Does he not
know that he is upsetting her? Disturbing
her heart?

She tricks him and teases him, asks him
if he believes any slave girl is as
beautiful as she? He hesitates, flounders,
then says he cannot say, he has never seen
her with her veil off. She seizes upon this:
Then he has seen the slave girl's face? She

has removed her veil for him? He defends the
girl, says it was his fault, and she leads
him on, berates him, and finally sends him
away, angry and confused. She knows how he
feels and is vastly amused.

Then the stone carving of a huge Winged
Bull is discovered with great excitement by
the diggers. They rush to him, and the
spies, believing the treasure discovered,
and that only gold could induce such
excitement, report to the Pasha. Soldiers
appear from nowhere and both he and the girl
(the slave girl, as she seems to be) are
made prisoners. They are to be tortured to
reveal the hiding place of the gold that the
Pasha cannot find.

In the nick of time he escapes with the
girl and they get away into the desert. At a
lonely oasis they hide, and when they
return, accompanied by Bedouins of her
tribe, they kill the Pasha's brutal soldiers
and take the Pasha prisoner.

Istanbul appoints a new Pasha who gives
Layard permission to excavate as much as he
wishes, and Layard visits the old Pasha in a
filthy, leaking cell where the onetime
tyrant is now cringing and bemoaning his
fate.

Layard is summoned then to the black tent
of the daughter of Hakim. She accuses him of
infidelity again, of pretending to be in
love with her and all the while carrying on
with the slave girl. She forces him to admit
that he has found the girl lovely, that she

is exciting. She accuses him of loving two
women--he says he can love but one. She
demands that he leave and see neither of
them again. He refuses and, angered, he
seizes her. Her veil comes loose and he sees
the princess and the slave are as one.

Furious, she sends him away.

That night the great Winged Bull, the
statue that he is sending back to the
British Museum (where it can be seen today),
is at last taken from the hole. Upon a huge
wooden cart surrounded by workmen, the
Winged Bull starts to move away.

And then a slave girl comes to him
and, kneeling, hands him a note. It is
from Alissa. The girl speaks in a low voice.
"Alissa sends to her master a message of
love."

"Love?" He is angry now. "Why, that--!"

The girl on her knee giggles, and he
wheels around to stare at her. She stands
erect and throws off the dark cloak,
revealing herself as the daughter of Hakim--
truly a woman worth having.

They stand together, watching the Winged
Bull drawn away to the chanting of the
workmen and the creaking of the great cart.

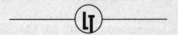

COMMENTS: Although modern, scientific archeology has
both merit and morality in the real world, the swashbuck-
ling adventurers/grave robbers of the late nineteenth and
early twentieth centuries have great appeal as the heroes of

stories. Austen Henry Layard was a real person, a world traveler, archeologist, and diplomat who published nearly a dozen accounts of his discoveries and expeditions. Here is Louis's introduction to the character taken from some of the notes pertaining to this project:

> Layard was a member of a French family that settled in England. He was born in Paris in 1817, lived in Italy for a short time with his father. Studied law. As a young man, an adventurer at heart, he traveled in the Near East, where he became impressed by the vast mounds which seemed geologically incongruous. He believed they covered ancient buried cities, known at that time only through the Old Testament and Herodotus. After long efforts he convinced Sir Stratford Canning and received limited financing, and at twenty-eight, in 1845, he began the excavations that were to write new chapters in world history.
>
> Like those other archaeologists Lawrence of Arabia (later famed as soldier and author) and Belzoni (who was a strongman in a London music hall before going to Egypt), Layard was first and always an adventurer of romantic nature.

A highly abbreviated and romanticized version of Layard's adventures in the Near and Middle East, this treatment, I believe, dates back to the 1950s. The subject matter and style suggest it might have been intended as a potential sale to a motion-picture company, but since we have no contract to back up that suspicion, it is impossible to be sure. The following character breakdown offers a bit more detail about how some of the characters might be used:

CAST OF CHARACTERS

HENRY LAYARD. . . . .
Englishman of French ancestry. Tall, handsome, energetic. Skilled linguist, amateur archaeologist destined to become one of the great names in the field. Obsessed with the idea of excavating the mounds along the Tigris, he refuses to be delayed by either the machinations of the local governor or the civil unrest prevailing. Sharp, intelligent, and courageous, he doesn't allow his interest in the dead past to interfere with his interest in the living female.

ALISSA. . . . .
The daughter of Hakim, sheik of the powerful Hadida clan of southern Arabia. A girl with a mind of her own, who knows what she wants and how to get it but not above having some fun in the process. A beautiful and sexy wench with brains and education and more freedom than Moslem women are usually allowed. The kind of a girl to walk beside a man, not behind him.

MOHAMMED PASHA. . . . .
The kind of a man who would pull the legs off flies in private. One ear and

one eye missing, pockmarked face, short,
jerky, ugly, sly, cunning, tyrannical,
and obsequious. His main interest is
sadistic cruelty--and money.

SHEIK AWAD. . . . .
A soiled, thieving brigand with a sense
of humor, plenty of courage, no
conscience, but he catches some of
Layard's enthusiasm for uncovering the
buried city of Nimrud. Willing to take
orders from Alissa because he knows
where his bread is buttered and the
Hadida clan are notoriously lacking in
sympathy for opposition to the daughter
of Hakim.

SIR STRATFORD CANNING. . . . .
Layard's friend and superior. Dignified,
and shrewd. Interested as Layard is in
the antiquities of the land between the
rivers.

IDRISI PASHA. . . . .
Turkish official who comes incognito to
camp of Alissa. A man of intelligence
and enthusiasm, secretive yet the
counterpoint to the depravity of
Mohammed Pasha.

ISMET & MAHMOUD. . . . .
Gun-bearers and assistants of Layard.
Ismet a conniving boy, Mahmoud a giant
in strength.

RAMIS. . . . .
The name Alissa assumes when she poses
as the slave girl of her own retinue. So
she can see Layard more often.

While some of these characters are fictional and typical of Hollywood stereotypes of that era, Mohammed Keritli Oglu, Pasha of Mosul, is actually reported to have been even more odious than the way he is presented here. When traveling, he was known to tax villagers for the wear and tear their simple food caused his teeth and there are stories that he actually did, on occasion, allow his death to be reported, and then confiscated the property of all who celebrated his passing!

The Winged Bull was a colossal relief, carved on the sides of a block of stone, rather than an actual three-dimensional statue. It depicted a winged bull with a human head, and it was one of two protecting the palace of Ashurnasirpal II, an Assyrian king.

Whatever this treatment's intended market, it is unlikely that Louis considered it finished. As a careful read shows, its tense is somewhat unstable. He was used to writing fiction in past tense, but movie treatments are nearly always written in the present. A shorter version was also produced, possibly to coincide with the brief attention span of studio executives. Neither was edited well enough to have been ready for presentation.

True Louis L'Amour fans will note that the title *A Woman Worth Having* is also a title that Louis considered for one of the sequels to his novel *The Walking Drum*. This is a single case out of many where Louis switched titles from one project to another when the need arose.

JOHNNY BANTA

Several Beginnings to a Western Novel

COMMENTS: Here are three attempts at starting a Western novel. As you read, you can track the changes Louis made as he figured out what he wanted the story to be, how he wanted to set up the characters, and the differences between them and the threats they would have to face. It's a nice, quick example of how a story would develop.

VERSION ONE

When we came up the valley of the Sweet-water the frost was white on the lowlands and upon the far slope of the mountain the aspens were clouded gold. At nineteen I was the youngest of the lot, although for seven years I had done a man's work, and proud of it.

Only there was a searching in me, for I had found nothing I wanted very much, nor any place I cared to stop, but the soft look on my face was only the softness of being young, and reflected little that was inside me. When a boy is left alone at twelve he becomes a man or he becomes nothing at all.

Yet it was a hard land in which I had come to manhood, and the way I had found for myself was never easy. When a boy takes a man's place he is expected to be a man and not a boy, so it was stand up to a man's work and a man's responsibilities, and I did that, although it gave me difficult moments.

There were seven of us riding east, and until what seemed but a few days before we had been strangers. And now we were still strangers, but we rode together, shared our grub and our watchfulness and our awareness of danger.

East of us, a distance of hundreds of miles, was St. Louis, our destination, and we were seven armed and belted men, riding with our rifles ready, for we had passed the Pai-ute country and were heading into the land of the Sioux.

There was the Sailor Swede, Coyle the gambler, Harran who had been a trapper, and Seagrave, the only one of us who had done well in the gold fields.

Fleming had crossed the Plains seven times, he said, and Sheedy had kept a store in the gold country, and there was me, Johnny Banta, born in a west-bound wagon and now going to the States for the first time.

We rode with Fleming at point, the Sailor and Coyle on one flank, Harran and Seagrave

on the other, and bringing up the rear were
Sheedy and myself. In the middle of our
group were our nine pack animals, three of
them belonging to me.

We crossed the Divide short of noon, and
when we crossed it was nothing like the
Sierras, just a rise in an almost flat
area . . . although it was high up, more
than seven thousand feet where we crossed
over. We found the Sweetwater and rode along
it, riding loose in the saddle and ready for
trouble, for we had been lucky so far and
were worried by it.

We stopped for the night in a hollow among
the low hills near the Sweetwater and
Fleming got down from his saddle and turned
his eyes on me. "You'll cook tonight," he
said.

"I'll not," I told him straight. "Three
times this week I've cooked and no
complaint. We're seven here, so we share and
share alike."

Coyle had begun a fire, and he looked up,
mildly amused but interested. I think he had
been expecting this.

"You talking back to me?" Fleming stared
at me, but I'd been stared at before.

"Telling you," I said, "and not only for
today. It's turn and turn about."

Fleming put down the pack he held in his
hands and looked at me. "I don't want to
give you a whuppin', so do as you're told."

"Anywhere we go," I said, "I'll make
tracks as big as you."

Coyle's pleasant voice intervened. "The

boy's right. From the beginning he's done his share, and more than his share."

"You buttin' in?" Fleming was a man ready for trouble. He had an arrogant way about him that raised my hackles, but he was unsure of Coyle, who might be a man to leave alone.

"Trying to save your life," Coyle replied quietly, and from the way Fleming took it I knew he figured it was a threat from Coyle himself.

"I'll cook," Sheedy interrupted hastily. "I don't mind."

Sheedy cooked, and I almost wished I had, it was that bad, but I rustled wood for the fire before finding a place to bed down with a natural hammock of earth to give me shelter from the wind, and from bullets, if it came to that. With my hunting knife I cut blocks of sod and forted up a little.

"You expectin' a fight?" Harran asked me. "Ever' night you build yourself a hole to hide in. How long you gonna keep it up?"

"Until we're in St. Louis," I said, and meant it.

Coyle awakened me two hours before dawn to take over the sentry duty, and I slid out of my blankets and rolled them up for traveling.

"All quiet," Coyle told me, and then he went to his blankets for a little sleep before daybreak.

It was almighty still . . . the sky was touched up with stars, and along the

Sweetwater the trees and brush were a black
snake winding among the low hills. This was
almost the hour when Indians liked to
attack . . . in the gray hour of first dawn.

Trouble was shaping for me among my own
crowd, but it was trouble I would have to
handle my own way, and I was set for it,
believe me. None of this bunch knew anything
of me, and I was almighty sure they had let
me join up because I had horses and they
needed pack animals. Horses, those days,
were bringing a fair price and hard to come
by even when a man had the money. And maybe
because Fleming figured me for a camp
flunky.

Fleming was a bullying man. He had wide
shoulders and was muscled like a wrestler,
and he liked to throw his weight around.
Harran was of the same stripe, dark and
surly with an ingrown streak of meanness in
him. Sheedy . . . well, Sheedy was living
in Fleming's shadow. Figuring Fleming for
the strong man, Sheedy latched onto him
for the trip.

Maybe I was young, but I was taking no
pushing around. If they wanted to drive this
hoss they'd best get set for trouble.

There was gray in the sky now. Individual
trees were standing out now, and the grass
moved under the long wind. My rifle lay easy
in my hands and I kept my head turning,
trying to see everywhere at once. That rifle
was a Deane, Adams & Deane five-shot
revolving-cylinder rifle. An Englishman
who was on his uppers in Frisco had sold it

to me, and I'd never seen a faster-shooting gun.

There was dew on the grass, and suddenly I saw a gray streak in the grass . . . a difference, but it was there. Reaching down, I picked up a stone and chucked it back into the middle of camp and it hit near Fleming's foot. He sat up and I lifted my rifle and pointed into the grass where the streak stopped; somebody was crawling there, and had brushed the dew from the grass as he moved. There was no taking aim, I just squeezed off my shot into the head of that wide streak.

There was a sharp movement there, and then the Sioux came out of the gray morning, running low and running fast. My second shot went wide, the Sioux was moving too fast, but my third, held low down, dropped an Indian in his tracks. On the other side of camp a rifle opened fire and then still another from beside me. Sudden as it had begun, the attack stopped.

Only the grass moved, rippling under the gray skies, and leaves of the aspen whispered and chattered along the hillside. Fleming crawled over to me. "How many did you see?" he asked.

Reloading my Deane, Adams I laid out five extra paper cartridges on a flat rock. If I got that many shots during the next rush I'd be mighty lucky.

"Maybe four," I said, "but if they're like Modocs there might be fifty out there."

"You fought Modocs?" Fleming glanced at me.

"These here are Sioux," I said, "maybe
they're different."

With my Bowie I dug out under my body and
got deeper into the ground. The others were
doing the same, settling down for

VERSION TWO

When we came up the valley of the
Sweetwater the frost was white on
the lowlands and upon the far slope of the
mountains the aspens were clouded gold. At
nineteen I was the youngest of the lot,
although for seven years past I had done a
man's work, and proud of it.

Only there was a searching in me, for I
had found nothing I wanted very much, nor
any place I cared to stop, but the softness
of my face was only the softness of being
young, not of anything inside me, for when a
boy is left alone at twelve he becomes a man
or he becomes nothing at all.

Yet it was a hard land in which I'd come
to manhood, and the way I had found had
never been easy, and with the hardness this
gave me there was a truculence, too, for I
had some of the urge to prove myself that is
in every boy.

There were but seven of us, and until a
week or two before we had been strangers.
A week? It was more than that, but on the
trail there is a small sense of time, and
only distance by which to measure.

We were seven armed and belted men riding

east from the gold country with St. Louis a
long way off. There was the Sailor Swede and
Coyle the gambler, there was Harran who had
been a trapper and Seagrave who had struck
it rich on the Feather River.

There was Fleming who had crossed the
Plains seven times, and Sheedy who had kept
a store in the gold country, and there was
me, Johnny Banta, born in a west-bound
wagon, now going east for the first time.

We rode with Fleming at point, the Sailor
and Coyle on one flank, Harran and Seagrave
on the other and bringing up the rear were
Sheedy and myself, and in the middle of us
were the nine pack horses, three of the nine
belonging to me.

We crossed the Divide short of noon and
after that found the Sweetwater starting
from the low hills and we rode along it,
riding loose in the saddle and ready for
trouble, for we'd been lucky this far and
were worried by it. Too much good luck is a
danger, for a man knows it must change. Back
along the Humboldt we'd had a brush with the
Pai-ute, but they had no stomach for what we
gave them.

There was a hollow where a creek flowed
down to the Sweetwater and there Fleming got
down from his saddle. "We'll stop the night
here," he said, and turned his eyes on me.
I'd no liking for the man and knew what was
coming before he opened his lips to speak.
"You'll cook tonight," he said.

"I'll not," I told him straight. "Three
times this week I've cooked and no complaint.

We've seven here, so we share and share alike."

Coyle looked up from the fire where he was poking sticks into the new flame. He looked interested, and mildly amused.

"You talking back to me?" Fleming stared at me, but I'd been stared at before.

"Telling you," I said, "and not only for now. It's turn and turn about."

Fleming put down the pack he held in his hands and looked across the camp at me. "Now look, boy, I don't want to give you a whuppin', so do as you're told."

"Anywhere we go," I said, "I'll make tracks as big as you."

Coyle's pleasant voice intervened. "The boy's right. From the beginning he's done his share and more than his share."

"You buttin' in?" Fleming was ready for trouble but he was unsure of Coyle. He might be a man to leave alone; a gambler had to be tough to live.

"Trying to save your life," Coyle replied quietly, and from the way Fleming looked at him I knew Fleming was taking it for a warning and a threat.

"I'll cook," Sheedy interrupted hastily. "I don't mind."

Sheedy cooked, and I wished I had, it was that poor to eat, but I rustled wood for the fire and found a place to bed down with a natural hammock of earth to give me protection from the wind or bullets. With my hunting knife I cut sod and forted up a little.

"You expectin' a fight, kid?" Harran asked me. "Ever' night you build yourself a little hole to hide in. How long you gonna keep it up?"

"Until we're in St. Louis," I said, and meant it.

That night there was talk around the fire but little was said to me and none of it by Fleming. He had me marked for trouble, that much I knew, but it was no different than it had always been for me.

At daybreak I was out and around before any of them, and had killed a white-tailed deer, an easy shot at a hundred yards, and I was skinning him out when Coyle rode up. "Figured there might be trouble," he said. "I came running."

"Thanks." Rising from beside the deer, I gathered the hide around the best cuts. "Seemed a chance for some fresh meat, and as for trouble, I'm likely to find as much of that in camp as away from it."

"Fleming won't rest."

We rode back toward camp, riding side by each, and I said to Coyle, "He'll have you marked. . . . It will be trouble for you if you're seen with me."

"I'll accept that," he said, "and Seagrave will too, I think."

"Ah," I said, "now there's a thing. He's carrying plenty, I've an idea. Fleming has been watching him."

We rode on, but there was a difference now, for the unity that had been with us was

gone; we were drawing apart. Coyle and
Seagrave took flank together, and it might
have seemed an accident, although Sailor
Swede merely took the place alongside Harran
and we rode east along the Sweetwater.

Our nooning was near a grassy bank,
outcropped with ledges, and we built our
fire close under the bank, of buffalo chips
and a few scattered sticks.

We made coffee there and chewed on some
jerky and gave ourselves talk about the
trail behind and what lay ahead. This was
Sioux country, and I'd heard a sight about
the Sioux from my folks before they died,
and from others in California. The Sioux
were a lot of Indian . . . every one a
fighting man from the high timber. At that,
everything might have gone all right if
Harran hadn't found that squaw.

She was young and she was walking. She was
also a mighty pretty girl of maybe seventeen
or a year younger. Hard to tell the age of
an Indian.

She was carrying a small pack on her back
and she came on us as we sat there eating,
but the only one who saw her right then was
me and I could see she was alone and scared,
so I said nothing at all. Then Harran went
down to the creek and the next thing we hear
a fight.

All of us went down and Harran had caught
him a squaw, and he was grinning. He looked
around at Fleming and said, "Lookit here.
Lookit what I found."

"Leave her alone," I said.

Harran looked at me like he hadn't heard me or couldn't understand, but Fleming knew, all right.

"Why, now," Fleming said, "finders is keepers. Ain't that right?" He looked around. "I reckon we found her, and we'll keep her, and if you want to leave her alone, Banta, you do just that. Fact of the matter is, we'll see that you do."

"Let her go," I said. "This is Sioux country. That's a Sioux squaw. You want to get us all killed?"

Nobody had said anything, although I had an idea that Coyle

VERSION THREE

When we came up the valley of the Sweetwater the frost was white on the lowlands and upon the far slope of the mountains the aspens were clouded gold. At nineteen I was the youngest of the lot, although for seven years I had done a man's work, and proud of it.

Only there was a searching in me, for I belonged nowhere and had found nothing that I wanted very much, nor any place I cared to call home. It was a hard land in which I had come alone to manhood, and the way I found for myself was never easy. When a boy takes a man's place he is expected to be a man, and not a boy, so it was stand up to a man's work and a man's responsibilities, and that

I did, although it caused me some bad times
and some difficult hours.

There were seven of us riding east,
seven who until a few days before had
been strangers to one another. We were still
strangers, although we rode together, shared
our grub and our watchfulness, our awareness
of danger.

East of us, hundreds of miles away, was
St. Louis . . . a distance not to be
measured in miles but in hours of danger,
for the land we rode through was the land
of the Indian who wanted no such interlopers
as we.

We were seven armed and belted men, riding
with rifles across our saddles. There was
the Sailor Swede, Coyle the gambler, Harran,
who had been a trapper, and there was
Seagrave, the only one of us who had done
well in the gold fields.

Fleming had crossed the Plains seven
times, and Sheedy had kept a store in the
gold country, and of course, and last of
all, there was me, Johnny Banta, born in a
west-bound wagon and now going to the States
for the first time.

We rode armed for trouble, with Fleming at
point, the Sailor and Coyle upon one flank,
Harran and Seagrave on the other. Bringing
up the rear were Sheedy and myself. In our
midst were our nine pack animals, three of
them belonging to me.

We crossed the Divide just short of noon,
and it was nothing akin to the Sierras,
which is a fine, tall range, but only a long

roll in almost flat land . . . although it was nigh to eight thousand feet, they said, where we crossed over.

The Sweetwater was where we expected it would be and for the night we camped in a hollow among sand hills. Getting down from his saddle Fleming turned his eyes upon me. "You'll cook tonight," he said.

"I'll not." I told him straight out. "Three times this week I've cooked and no complaint, but we're seven here, so we share and share alike. I'll be flunky to no man."

Coyle had begun a fire, and there was a sparking interest and some amusement in his eyes when he looked up. He was a pleasant man but a cynical one who derived a wry pleasure from many a thing that would get most men's nerves on edge. But this, I believe, he had been expecting.

"You talking back to me?" Fleming stared at me, but I'd been stared at before when I was more of a boy than I was now.

"Not talking back," I said, "but telling you. From this point on it will be turn and turn about."

Fleming put down the pack he had taken from the horse and looked at me. "If you don't want a whuppin', you do as you're told."

Now, I was not as big a man as Fleming by forty pounds, nor as tall by inches, but there is a time for all things, and one thing I'd learned was, not to be put upon.

"Anywhere we go," I said, "I'll make tracks as big as you."

"The boy's right." Coyle spoke casually, working his fire to build a bed of coals. "He's done his share and more."

"You buttin' in?" Fleming was a big man and one with an arrogant way about him that raised my hackles, but he was not too sure of Coyle, who might be a man to leave alone.

"Trying to save your life," Coyle told him, but Fleming took it as a threat from Coyle and not a warning.

"I'll cook," Sheedy spoke hastily. "I don't mind."

Sheedy cooked, and it was that bad I almost wished I'd not forced the situation, but I rustled wood for the fire before choosing a place to bed down beside a hammock of earth and grass that gave me some extra shelter from the wind, or might, if need be, stop a bullet. With my hunting knife I cut blocks of sod and forted up a mite, being of cautious nature and not my first time in Indian country.

"You scared?" Harran looked at me with a look in his eyes I cared little for. "Ever' night you build yourself a hole to hide in. How long you gonna keep it up?"

"Until St. Louis," I said, and meant it.

Trouble was shaping among my own crowd, for it was Fleming considered himself our leader, knowing the Plains as he did, and Fleming was a bullying man. Harran was like him, and Sheedy a shadow for Fleming in all he did. None of this lot knew anything of me, and I'd been thinking the only reason I was invited along was because they had need

of my horses, for horses at that time were
hard to come by.

It was curiosity taking me east, and maybe
something more, for it was in me to find a
place for myself and as yet I'd had none.
There was nothing behind me but drifting and
working, wherever a job could be had. A time
or two I'd tried panning gold, with no
amount of luck, but I'd saved a bit, bought
myself some horses, and done some packing
for other owners of claims who worked deep
in the hills.

Coyle awakened me two hours before dawn to
take over the sentry duty, so I slid out of
my blankets and rolled them for traveling.

"All quiet," Coyle whispered, and crawled
away toward his blankets for a nap before
daybreak.

It was almighty still . . . the sky
touched up with stars, and along the Sweetwater the trees and brush lying like a
winding black snake among the low hills.
Soon it would be growing light.

The night had a waiting in it, a sort of
stillness like something was set to happen.
My rifle lay easy in my hands. It was a
Deane, Adams & Deane five-shot revolving-
cylinder rifle. I'd picked it up from an
Englishman who was on his uppers in Frisco,
and I'd never want a better gun.

Individual trees began to stand out from
the dark, and there was dew on the
grass . . . then I saw a gray streak there
where it should not be. Picking up a small

pebble, I chucked it into the middle of
camp, where it hit near Fleming's foot. He
sat up, looking at me, and I lifted my rifle
and sighted into the grass where that streak
in the grass ended. Somebody had been
crawling, brushing the dew from the grass
where he crawled, so I just squeezed off my
shot into the end of that streak.

There was a movement down there, and then
the Indians came out of the grass, out of the
gray morning, running low and fast. My
second shot was too quick and a miss, but
the third, held lower, dropped a Sioux in
his tracks. Beside me another rifle opened
up and from the far side of camp, another.
And then no Indian could be seen, anywhere.

A faint dawn breeze stirred the grass;
nothing else moved. Reloading the Deane,
Adams I laid out five extra paper cartridges
on a flat rock. If I got off half that many
shots during the next rush I'd be
lucky . . . if there was a rush.

Aspen leaves whispered. Fleming was beside
me, and Coyle off to my left. We waited
through long minutes and then Seagrave
calmly slipped back into the hollow, just a
few yards behind us, and stirred up the fire
and put on the coffeepot. If a man was going
to fight, he had to eat. That was Seagrave's
thinking and for my mind it was right.

How many had we got? Studying the
situation, it looked like the two I'd nailed
were the only ones, although the Swede
thought he might have barked one. Their
surprise had failed and by now it was full

light although the sun wasn't over the eastern ridge.

Our situation was good. We had a fine field of fire in every direction and some shelter for ourselves. In the bottom of the hollow a man could stand almost upright without being seen and we had both grub and water, so if the fight continued we wouldn't run short for several days. Our horses were in the hollow with us, as safe as we were ourselves. So far, after that first attack we had seen no Indians anywhere, but I didn't like the look of it.

Harran wanted to go on.

"They've gone, so we'd best push on before they bring help."

"If these were Modocs," I said, "they'd still be out there. I don't figure Sioux are much different."

Waiting gets a man. It works on him, and nobody knows that better than an Indian. He also knows that most white men are the get-up-and-get-at-it type who have no patience. Therefore an Indian usually figures if he waits a white man will move and give him a chance. That was what Harran was all for doing, and Sheedy and the Swede were right with him.

Not me. Not Johnny Banta. One time I nearly got my fool head shot off like that, and nobody needs to show me twice. In this sort of fighting, a man doesn't get many mistakes. Mostly he gets a chance to make only one.

"You want to move," I said, "you go ahead. But you leave my horses here."

"Suppose we decide to take them?" Harran was a mean one, a most trying man.

"Why, anytime you get your mind made up," I said, "you just try. Only there's two Indians out there with my mark on them who offered a slight less target than you do right now."

Harran, he didn't know what to make of me. He figured me for a kid who wasn't dry behind the ears yet, but he had seen me shoot, a time or two. He just wasn't sure.

"I believe Johnny is right," Seagrave said. "I believe there are still Indians out there."

So nobody went anywhere right then. The wind stirred the grass out front and the sun came up and when the sun was over the hill in our eyes, they came out of the grass again, running swiftly, and shooting as they came. Fleming was quick; he shot fast and an Indian fell, and then the rest of us were shooting and the attack stopped again.

Harran had nothing to say about that, nor anybody, all of them realizing how some would have been dead had they tried to leave. It wasn't that I was smarter than anybody, I had fought Indians before, was all, and maybe I was more scared. Nobody wants to die at nineteen.

They pulled out then. The Sioux weren't a big party and they decided there was easier hunting. They pulled out, so a short time

after, we left, riding away in the same
formation as before.

Only there was friction among us. Fleming
didn't like me, nor did Harran. Coyle had
nothing to say; a watching man like him
couldn't be expected to take sides until the
last minute, if at all. Seagrave rode up to
me and said something that had been on my
mind.

"Johnny, I think you're my friend, and I'm
a man who needs friends."

"Well, now."

"I mean it. I need friends, boy and you
know why."

Fleming, Harran, Sheedy, and the Swede,
they were going back empty. Sheedy might have
had a little put by, but mighty little, and
this was a lonesome country where a man might
die and no questions asked. Seagrave might
be just realizing that, but I'd had it in
mind for some time now, ever since I began
to get windward of Harran.

He was a hungry man . . . hungry for all
the things he thought he deserved. A hungry
man and one eaten by envy and dislike is a
dangerous man when opportunity offers, and
here with us was Seagrave carrying gold home
to the States, and a lot of gold at that.

The Sailor Swede was a hard man. Big,
powerful, and sullen, he was a man with a
violent temper and unless I was mistaken,
killing lay behind him. He was a fit one to
walk beside Harran, and Sheedy would follow
the two of them.

Fleming? The man did not like me, and he

was a man big with his own sense of importance, and little enough reason for it. I
did not know about Fleming, nor about Coyle,
for that matter. It was beginning to look
as if it might be Seagrave and me against
the lot.

For I'd seen what he saw. Fleming staring
into the fire of a night, remembering that
he was returning from gold fields with
nothing to show, and no answer to the
questions he would be getting except the
admission of failure. It comes hard for any
man, but harder still for one like Fleming.
And there was Harran, hating and full of
envy, the Swede wanting gold for women and
liquor, and there was Sheedy, a coyote ready
to snatch at the wolves' leavings.

That I was one with Seagrave was a natural
thing. First, I was disliked, and secondly I
owned some of the horses, which were
themselves worth a price. And they had seen
me friendly with Seagrave.

It was a far-off place, the California we
had left behind, where we had all been
friendly enough, joining together for the
long trek across the Plains, and shaking
hands around, or eating together. Now that
trouble had come on us there were divisions
obvious to us that had not been so easily
seen before.

We rode on, and after a time Seagrave
dropped back and offered to take the place
of Sheedy, who gave up willingly, not liking
me, nor the dust we both had to eat. So
Seagrave rode beside me, and not another

word was said about what might come, only he
talked of his family in Vermont and what
would come to them if anything happened to
him.

There was nobody anywhere who gave a
thought to me, but I'd no wish to feed the
buzzards or the coyotes out on a grassy
hillside somewhere, so we made it up between
us that one of us would always be awake and
watchful. And that was the way it was right
up until we came upon the woman.

Only she was no woman, only a girl. A
scared girl of sixteen or so . . . there in
the middle of nowhere.

Fleming was well out in front and when he
saw her running along the grassy slope he
drew up his horse, and we all bunched, a bad
thing to do, and stared at that girl in the
gray dress running like a frightened deer
along the slope.

At first we thought she was chased by
Indians, but there were no Indians in sight.
We waited, wanting to rush into nothing but
what we could handle.

"Must be a wagon train close by," Sheedy
suggested.

"Off the trail," Fleming objected. "They
hold farther south where there's fewer
hills."

"Let's go," Coyle said. "That girl needs
help."

COMMENTS: This is how many of L'Amour novels got started. A number of tries, getting the tone or the particulars of the first scene or first few chapters set up. Sometimes the differences between the different versions were very minor, sometimes radically different. Then something would click and the narrative would take off ... or it wouldn't. Quite a few of the story fragments in this book are pieced together from a number of parallel attempts such as these. Cutting and pasting them together I have tried to present a version that shows off the most complete vision or most interesting aspects of what Dad was trying to create.

These three attempts contain a favored plot of Louis's: a tough group of guys and a stash of money that isn't going to be big enough for the ones who steal it to share. What role the girl was going to play and why she was changed from Indian to white is anyone's guess.

Louis experimented many times with "the tough guys and a bunch of money" concept ... to the point where I've wondered if it was something he'd actually confronted in real life. The idea shows up in a couple of other places here in *Louis L'Amour's Lost Treasures*. In fact, we'll see it again and I'll discuss it a bit more thoroughly before we get to the end of this book.

JAVA DIX

The Beginning of a Crime Story

When I woke up that morning I was broke.
Not even coffee money. Out on the street
there was a slow rain falling and I walked
along, wondering what to do. I was two days
back in town from the Far East and I didn't
know anybody.

Finally I stopped on a corner and was just
standing there when this Buick convertible
drove by. There was a girl in it with auburn
hair. She was lovely . . . so lovely it made
a guy catch his breath and start to hurt
down inside. I watched the car until it
turned the corner. Then, just as I was
starting across the street, the convertible
came up again and this girl stopped the car
and looked at me.

She was young. Not more than twenty. Only
the way she looked at me wasn't young . . .
she looked me over.

"Want to make some quick money?"

"Sure," I said, and she opened the car
door and I got in.

This babe I didn't figure. She was no
tramp. Every line of her breathed class. Nor
could I figure the youth of her along with
that wise way in which she examined me. The
two things just didn't go together.

We drove on for a couple of minutes and
neither of us said anything. She had good
legs, but I tried not to think of that. This
babe wasn't on the make and she wasn't
likely to go for a busted drifter.

"You," she said, not looking at me, "you
haven't had breakfast, have you?"

"No." I switched to the far side of the
seat where I could look at her. "How'd you
figure that?"

"It's nine o'clock," she said, "and you
just came out on the street. You walked past
a diner and you walked past a good
restaurant. They wouldn't let you make
coffee in that hotel where you stayed.
Then you stopped on the corner looking
around. You didn't know where you were
going. I'll bet you're broke."

"You're a smart kid."

"And you're a stranger in town."

"How'd you figure that one?"

"The way you look at the signs, the
way you walked. The way you hesitated on
the street like you weren't sure about the
traffic."

"You do a lot of figuring. What's the
gimmick? What d'you want?"

"I want a man," she said quietly, "with

nerve enough to tackle hell with a bucket of
water."

That about floored me. Somehow it didn't
figure, not this girl needing help, and not
the way she asked for it. She swung the car
around a corner and pulled up at a small
restaurant. "They don't know me in here,"
she said, "and it won't be busy now. We'll
go to that booth almost to the back. We can
talk while you eat."

We got out of the car and went in. She was
wearing a green raincoat and she walked
quickly, not minding the rain on her hair.
We took a table and she watched me eat. And
then over her coffee she started to talk.
But not until after she had pumped me for
plenty.

Me? I'm a big guy, not heavy. I weigh only
one-seventy, but I'm six-two. I can do a
lot of things, none of them usual and not
many of them legitimate.

Name? They call me Java, and my last name
is Dix. Merchant seaman, lumberjack, placer
miner in New Guinea, and pearl poacher. I was
with the OSS during the war and afterwards a
freelance journalist. . . . That's the quick
version. Fights? I've won and I've lost, but
I won more than I lost and got off the floor
a few times to win.

I can talk nine languages like I was born
to them. I'm proud of that.

"I need a man," she said, "who has nerve
and brains. I'm in trouble, real trouble."

"Somebody else is in trouble," I said,
"not you."

She smiled a little, hesitated, then
nodded. "Yes, you're right. It's my mother."

"If your mother is in trouble," I said,
"then it would be your father you took
after."

She smiled again, only this time it was
not just a mechanical smile, it was warm and
beautiful. "You're right," she said, "but my
father is dead. If he were here I'd never
have stopped you. I wouldn't have been
looking for you."

"He must have been quite a guy."

"Dad was wonderful," she said quietly. "He
was honest, and he had nerve. You would have
liked him," she said, and suddenly she
looked at me, a little surprised, "and he
would have liked you."

"Fathers don't like seeing drifters with
their daughters. Drifters without money."

"He would understand. He had been a
drifter himself. Only he was rich when he
died. He made it in the oil fields. He was a
big man," she said, "with red-gray hair,
and--"

"Slasher Hannegan," I said, "he was
Slasher Hannegan, of Spindletop, of
Seminole, of Tampico and Balikpapan."

She stared at me, and tears came into her
eyes. "You knew him? It . . . it's
unbelievable!"

"Worked for him, kid. I worked for him in
Tampico. I was a tool-dresser. I worked on a
tower for him in Borneo. That was ten years
ago. And I remember you now, all freckles
and knees, living in a house on the bluff

above the road that wound around from the
port to the Dutch Club."

It was crazy, but there it was. She had
picked up a tough-looking drifter off the
street when she needed help, and I had
worked for her old man. Only it wasn't so
strange, in some ways. A lot of tough men
had worked for her father during the wild
days of the oil booms.

We were both quiet then, and after a while
she said, "It's almost like he led me to
you. I was desperate. I knew what he would
have done, and knew I could not do it, so I
started looking for the right sort of man.
Yesterday I looked. I went to bar rooms, I
rode along the docks, I looked
everywhere . . . and then I saw you."

She opened her purse and took out five
twenties. She handed them across the table.
"That's a stake, Java. That's for nothing.
That's what Dad would have given any man of
his old crew if he was broke. You take it
from Dad, and pay it back when you can."

Once the money was in my pocket she did
not waste any more time.

"My mother drinks," she told me. "She
drinks too much. She never drank when Dad
was alive, and she never had reason to." She
looked me right in the eye and said quietly,
"My mother needs a man. When Dad was around,
she was all right. She was happy. . . .
Now she isn't happy anymore and she drinks.
And sometimes when she is drinking she goes
out."

This was tough for her. I could see how

tough, only this kid was game. She must have been living with this for a long time, and it had not been easy.

"Usually she went out of town, but once it was the wrong man."

"Blackmail?"

"Yes . . . but not just a little blackmail. He wants it all . . . everything."

"You've talked to him?"

"Yes"--she looked up from her coffee--"he includes me."

Something in me started to get mad then. It was bad enough to take advantage of a woman's weakness, but to get this girl into it . . . "He's got evidence?"

"Yes."

"You said he wanted all of it? There's a lot?"

"There's eleven million, more or less," she said quietly. "But it isn't the money. It's mother, and it's Dave."

"Dave?"

"My brother. He's to be married soon, a girl from--a very prissy family."

I grinned. "I take it your brother doesn't take after your dad."

Little by little the story shaped itself. But there was something about it that did not quite fit. Her mother, I gathered, was just forty, a lush and lovely woman. She had been closemouthed, however, even when drinking, but somehow this one particular man had found out exactly who she was, and he had come to town, looked the situation over, and then moved in with his demands.

"She's already given him money?"

"Several times . . . about four thousand dollars."

She waited while the waitress filled our cups, then she said, "He's not in it alone. There's somebody else."

"What did you want me to do?"

"Find out all who are involved. Get the evidence. Prints, proof, everything."

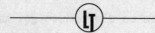

COMMENTS: There is a nice reference to some of Louis's personal travels hiding in this story. When he writes

Louis Lamoore in Balikpapan, Netherlands' East Indies.

. . . a house on the bluff above the
road that wound around from the port to
the Dutch Club.

Louis is talking about Balikpapan, a town on the Borneo
coast, now part of Kalimantan, Indonesia. He visited there
while working on a tramp freighter in the 1920s. Seeing that
it was part of the Netherlands' East Indies at the time, it was
literally a club for the local Dutch residents. Louis claimed
that, on certain evenings, they ran movies that, back in the
States, would have been considered very out-of-date . . . seeing that this was still in the period before sound, I have always wondered exactly how old these films were!

INVESTMENT IN CHARACTER

A Treatment for a Western Story

Bill Ryan, carrying ten thousand dollars, is en route west to meet his future bride and her father. The money is to be paid for a partnership in a going business that promises well, and Bill is enthusiastic over his prospects. His girl's father has never approved of Bill, but has resigned himself to the inevitable--but Bill must produce the ten thousand to prove he is able to care for the girl and to provide a good living for her. The money is Bill's entire savings, combined with a small inheritance he has had since he was a child.

On the train he meets a kindly old gentleman who is both interested and sympathetic. He kids Bill about losing his freedom, and quotes frequently, among others the quote from Kipling,

"Pleasant the snaffle of courtship, improving

the manners and carriage.
But the colt who is wise will abstain
from the terrible thorn-bit of
marriage."

At the hotel Bill finds his girl and her
father will not arrive until the following
day and he is restless, with time on his
hands. His kindly old friend introduces Bill
to a tall, polished man who is "in the mining
business" and the three have dinner together
and Bill hears much talk of "leads,"
"drifts," and "ore bodies" and is impressed.
The mining man picks up the check. Later,
with time hanging heavy on their hands, the
mining man suggests a poker game to the old
man. Both advise Bill to stay out of it, but
he decides to play a few hands. He feels that
his luck is in--that he can't lose.

And he wins, wins again--three straight
pots. Then he loses, wins again, loses, and
wins twice more. Now well ahead of the game,
he is feeling good. He gets an excellent
hand, and the betting runs high. Before he
realizes it he is out of his winnings and
deep into the ten thousand--and he loses.
Then he wins and loses again. Soon he is
winning only small, occasional pots, but
losing the big ones.

Disgusted, most of his money gone, he
suggests they call it off, and the others
agree--though they all know he still has
well over two thousand dollars.

They leave the room and he sits there,

then gets up and paces around the room.
Worried and restless. He drops into the
chair where the mining man had been seated,
starts to get up, but his fingertips brush
something pushed down between the side of
the chair and the cushion. He reaches back
and draws out--an ace of spades! Then the
ace of hearts, and then the other two aces
follow!

He has been cheated!

Then it all adds up: the old man on the
train, his own free talk about what he was
going to do, his plans, etc. The arrival in
town, introduction, and the game. He is
enraged, but suddenly, he has a plan. Most
of all, the old man's continual quotations
irritate him. He had believed them an
amusing quirk; now that the man has been
revealed as a card shark, Bill's attitude is
less tolerant.

At breakfast he meets the men, comments on
the fact that he is down to his last two
thousand, and says he might as well go for
all or nothing.

Bill now knows their pattern. They will
let him win a couple of small pots, then get
into a big one--and they will see that he
has what he thinks is a good hand--and then
they will take him. He doubts if they will
delay long.

As expected, he rakes in a couple of small
pots. He has carefully watched the mining
man and noticed that his hands have not been
off the table. Bill Ryan is dealt two queens

and two kings. He discards the fifth card
and draws--another king!

A full house.

He acts--shows excitement--digs out
another wad of bills (actually, it is a
Kansas City bankroll: newspaper wrapped in a
few bills), and gambling on their belief in
his gullibility, he ups the ante until
everything he has is in the pot, and all the
money they have won from him. He sees the
gambler's hand drop from the table as if to
ease his position a little, and Bill Ryan
calls--and spreads his cards on the table:
queen and four aces!

The mining man and his companion stare
blankly at the aces and Bill places a pistol
on the table. "Brought it along for rattle-
snakes," he comments, and rakes in the pot,
stuffing the money into his pockets, and
easing from the room.

The two crooks sit staring at each other,
then the old man explodes with anger. "You
had those aces!" he shouts. "You had them in
the chair!"

The mining man springs up, and the two
lift the cushion. A neat white typewritten
card is in the position where they had left
the cards, on it the words:

"Lie to a liar, for lies are his coin;
steal from a thief, for that is easy;
lay a trap for the trickster and catch
him at the first attempt, but beware of
an honest man!"

COMMENTS: This feels like a treatment for a half-hour TV episode, but I have no idea if it was intended for any particular show. From the late forties until the sixties, there were dozens of "anthology series" on the air, shows where every episode was a different story with different characters. Some of these were exclusively Western and many others would accept Western genre materials. In the 1950s, other short stories and treatments of Louis's were purchased for shows like *Rebound, Fireside Theater, Ford Television Theatre, Climax!, Schlitz Playhouse,* and *Chevron Hall of Stars.* Selling quickly sketched out ideas like this one or repurposing old short stories was an additional way for Dad to scrape together some money. He also sold or created episode concepts for reoccurring character series like *Tales of Wells Fargo, Maverick, The Texan, Sugarfoot, City Detective,* and *Cowboy G-Men.*

Dad's relationship with Hollywood was as much a relationship with the TV industry as it was with feature films. *Cowboy G-Men* was produced as early as 1952, and he also wrote the pilot for 1956's *Hart of Honolulu,* which, if picked up, might have been TV's first "private detective in Hawaii" crime drama.

THE GOLDEN TAPESTRY

The Beginning of an Adventure Novel, and a Treatment

CHAPTER I

He lay upon his face in the wet sand, a
tall old man in shabby clothes, and looking
down at the body, Ballantyne knew it had
begun again, but this time he did not know
why.

It was an austere face, judging by the
side of it he could see, with a high-bridged
nose and prominent cheekbones, a face worn
and old, but strong with lines of character
and determination. Poor, he might have
been, but this man had been proud also.

Glancing swiftly to right and left, then
along the rim of the cliff above, and seeing
no one, Ballantyne lifted the edge of the
worn coat and checked the pockets. . . .
They were empty. The coat, no doubt
purchased secondhand years before, bore no
label.

Gently, Ballantyne lifted the old man's
hands, for the hands of a man are revealing,
and often tell more than his face or the few

odds and ends his pockets may contain. These
were strong hands, calloused but agile.
Ballantyne had seen those callouses before.
These were the hands of a weaver, a weaver
of rugs.

The dead man was unknown to Ballantyne,
but the three stab wounds in the kidney
indicated the hand of Mustafa Bem. In
Samarkand, Damascus, and Kashgar, Ballantyne
had seen similar wounds, and he needed no
autopsy to know the blade had been long and
thin, the blows hard-driven and slanted
sharply upward.

Yet Bem took no action without orders.
Somehow this old man had incurred the
displeasure of Leon Decebilus, and soon so
might Villette Mallory unless Ballantyne
moved with extreme care.

Villette Mallory was alone, and unaware
the man she had so recently met, Leon
Decebilus, was one of the most ruthless
criminals in the Near East. No matter the
mask of refinement and culture he might have
assumed, Decebilus was a ruthless and
violent man, intolerant of interference and
utterly without scruples.

Ballantyne stood up, and then walked
quickly away from the body and mounted the
cliff by a rarely used path. The last thing
he wished was to become involved in an
investigation by provincial authorities.

When his eyes cleared the edge of the
cliff, Ballantyne paused and swept the area
with a swift, practiced attention. Assured
that he was unobserved, he went up quickly,

and proceeded to stroll carelessly along the ancient path that skirted the cliff's edge.

The narrow beach where the body lay was on the shore of the Gulf of Izmit, known in classical times as the Gulf of Nicomedia, in Asiatic Turkey. Some fifty miles from Istanbul, the former capital of the once-great Byzantine empire, the Gulf was off the beaten track.

Whatever the reason for this man's death, it had to be big, for Leon Decebilus no longer involved himself in petty crimes--the thief, spy, panderer, blackmailer, and murderer had come into wealth and power.

Even the law moved warily where he was concerned, for he was an international figure with friends in high places, and he had been shrewd enough to implicate or involve them in his own dealings, involve them to such a degree that their fortunes depended upon the success of his.

The dead man obviously had been unaware of the risks involved in dealing with Decebilus, a fatal disadvantage in such affairs. That certainly could not be said of Ballantyne, but what of Villette Mallory? Did she recognize the manner of man Decebilus was? Could she?

Ballantyne swore bitterly and impatiently, and he was not an impatient or bitter man. He knew why he was getting involved, but he did not understand what was behind the curious chain of events that had led him to this place.

He was involved because of Villette. You

are, he told himself, a silly romantic fool.
No, a guilty fool. And guilt is never a good
reason to dig yourself in deeper.

He was a man who lived by his wits, he
told himself. He liked this explanation
better. Wherever Decebilus showed his hand
there was a profit to be made and where there
was a profit he could make it as easily as
Decebilus. Well, almost.

Turning from the track along the cliffs,
Ballantyne walked through the short grass
and up the slight slope to the ruins. The
area was known as Eski Hissar, Turkish for
"old castle," but the Byzantine tower for
which it was named was only one among the
many ruins along the Gulf of Izmit.

They were unimpressive ruins, without
boldness or beauty: a few crumbling walls,
scattered stones, and grass-covered mounds.
The walls that remained were often
constructed of stones from still older
walls; even the most ancient ruins in
sight had been built from the stones of
others.

On the crest of the hill not far away,
tall cypresses marked the tomb of Hannibal,
and from that vantage point one could look
over the slope below and see an incredible
maze, design interwoven with design, the
outlines of walls invisible on the ground
itself.

Seating himself among the ruins where he
could observe without being observed,
Ballantyne took the camera strap from his

shoulder and placed the camera beside him on the grass.

A camera, he had discovered, automatically marked one as a tourist, and tourists were apt to be regarded as harmless, somewhat blundering and gullible creatures inclined to go almost anywhere. The camera was a visible passport to almost anywhere but a military zone.

To Ballantyne all ruins were interesting, and from time to time he emerged from such ruins with a stone tablet, an ancient vase, or even a fine stone head. Discreetly removed and even more discreetly disposed of, such odds and ends had solved his financial difficulties on more than one occasion. But today he was not scouting such a midnight dig--there was larger game afoot. The dead man had affirmed that suspicion.

Ballantyne settled back to wait. Warm and lazy under the sun, the slope from where he waited was freshened by a gentle breeze from off the Sea of Marmara and the Gulf. If life had taught him nothing else, it had taught him patience.

Yet when the gray car appeared, he felt a premonitory chill. It left the village and came slowly along the goat track, a track rarely used by carts, never by cars. The Renault grumbled cautiously along the crumbling edge of the cliff toward the ruins.

That they returned at all to where the body had been left was evidence of their concern. The track they followed led only

from the nearby village to the pastures
beyond. Yet it might be possible, if one
were a skillful driver, to follow the track
along the shore, over the ridge, and then by
a woodcutter's trail through the dark patch
of forest beyond. A dirt road somewhere over
there connected with the highway from Ankara
to Istanbul. No car had made the trip but in
years past it had occasionally been done by
carts.

He watched the gray car coming slowly
along the track; his own position concealed
him and he had chosen it for that reason. He
was known to both Barbaro and Mustafa Bem.

Across the blue waters of the Gulf he
could see the thickly wooded shores that
ended in the promontory known as Boz Burun,
and at the farthest point on the southern
horizon he could just make out the peak of
the Bithynian Mount Olympus. The closest
town was the fishing village Gebze, but, as
with many places in this corner of the
world, history complicated the simplest of
things. Gebze had once been Libyssa, the
spot where Hannibal had spent his last
years, hiding from the power of Rome. It was
there, in 183 B.C., he had taken poison to
avoid capture.

Yet, he had fooled them at last, in one
respect at least, for the vast treasure he
was known to have with him disappeared when
he died. Vanished also were the hollow
bronze statues, gods sacred to Phoenicia and
Carthage, which he had brought with him from
Crete to Nicomedia.

More than one adventurer, wandering
soldier, goatherd or peasant had entertained
himself with the thought of what he could do
if he found that treasure, yet the story was
but one of many told along this coast. War
and trouble lead men to conceal their
riches, always with a plan to return and
recover them, but slavery, imprisonment, or
death have a way of intervening. How many
such treasures might lie buried within a
hundred miles of Istanbul? Or even within
the city itself?

The gray car had stopped some forty yards
off, near the ragged boy who tended a flock
of goats that grazed among the ruins.
Mustafa Bem got out of the car, looking as
lean and savage as ever, and called to the
boy.

"Have you seen a blue Maserati? A blue car
driven by a woman?"

The boy walked toward them, accompanied by
his sheepdog. "There may have been a car. I
was far up the hillside."

"Where does this road go?"

"It does not go. It is always here. For
twelve years I have been coming here and the
road is always as it is."

"Where does it _end_, boy?"

"The road has an end? Each road leads to
another, yes? So all the roads of the world
begin here at our feet."

Mustafa Bem grew impatient. "Do people
come here? Strangers, I mean?"

The boy shrugged. "Why should they come?
Here there are only the grass and my goats."

"The blue car . . . did it go on?"

"There are only pastures and forest beyond. I was with the goats. Perhaps the blue car went back when it discovered this was not a road for cars." Mustafa Bem returned to the Renault and talked to someone within.

The air was clear and their voices could be heard, but Ballantyne could no longer distinguish the words. He had not heard the woman's car or seen it, but neither would have been possible during the time he had spent on the beach. Had he missed his chance . . . ?

Mustafa Bem got into the Renault and drove on, but no great distance, for where the track ran past the base of the ruined tower the cliff's edge was of crumbling rock. Only a fool would try to go further unless on foot, and for a minute or two the issue was in doubt and Ballantyne watched them in amusement. At last they backed up, turned around, and started back.

There was a route through the ruins, a route Ballantyne had himself located when he scouted the area on his first visit. Ballantyne had the tactician's distaste for a cul-de-sac. Was it not Plautus who said that not even a mouse trusted himself to one hole only?

The goatherd seemed concerned only with his flock, but Ballantyne was sure the boy also watched the car. He was a thin boy of something around twelve years, with large, expressive eyes and an olive skin. Yet he

wore his rags with a savoir faire that went
beyond mere assurance. Ballantyne had seen
the boy on each of his previous visits and
they had nodded to one another in passing
but they had not talked.

When the gray Renault disappeared in the
direction of Istanbul, the boy walked to
where Ballantyne sat among the ruins.
Squatting upon his heels, the boy looked
where Ballantyne was looking.

"You see something?"

"I look at the sea . . . sometimes at the
ruins."

"The sea?"

"I find it beautiful. The ruins, also."

The goatherd scarcely glanced at the time-
blackened stones. "The ruins are no good,
even for goats. The roofs have fallen in."

The boy glanced again at Ballantyne. "Why
do you look at the sea and not at the goats?
I think the goats are more beautiful than
the sea. Look at them!"

To please the boy, Ballantyne turned to
look at the goats. Some two dozen of them
browsed or reclined upon the hillside. The
boy seemed pleased that Ballantyne appeared
to agree.

"They are not my goats," he explained,
"but someday I shall own goats. Perhaps as
many as these. Then you shall see beauty!
They shall be as white clouds upon the green
sky of the hillside."

He glanced at the camera, leaning over it,
curiously. "You have a machine. What is it
for?"

"To make pictures. I shall want some pictures of the sea and of the ruins."

"Of the goats, too?"

To please him, Ballantyne agreed. "Yes, and of the goats, too."

The reply seemed to satisfy the goatherd on that score, but he still seemed restless and puzzled. Gravely, they exchanged introductions. The boy's name was Rashid. Ballantyne waited, aware of the boy's curiosity, and aware that in some way he himself was undergoing examination.

There was something here the goatherd failed to comprehend. He broached the subject to Ballantyne as one gentleman to another. "You make pictures of the sea, the sky, and the ruins. Of the goats, too. Why do you do this?"

"To catch their beauty, and to hold it. Then I can look whenever I like."

"But why a picture? They are here! You can see them without a picture."

"For you they are here, for you they will remain, but I shall go away and it is good to have something with which to remember. I shall look many times at the picture and will see all this as I knew it today."

"You need a picture for this?" The boy was astonished. "I remember without a machine. I can remember the goats, each one of them." He considered the problem, and suddenly his expression brightened. "Ah, then! The machine is your memory! It is very strange to remember with a machine."

Neither of them spoke for several minutes,

each in his own way marveling at the wonders of the world. "I have heard men speak of this," the boy said, "that you have machines for everything. I should not like that."

Ballantyne watched the changing light on the sea and the shore. If the Maserati had come and gone it was not his plan to remain longer, but the conversation left him dissatisfied. He had an amusing feeling that he had, somehow, been bested.

He offered the boy a cigarette, which was accepted gravely.

"You have been here before," the boy said.

"Several times."

"Not many come to the ruins. Most who do merely look and go away." The boy lit his cigarette and puffed shrewdly, cupping it in his hand as do those who smoke much in the wind. "I think you come for a reason, and I do not think it is because of the machine or the pictures."

The kid was observant and he had something to say that he hadn't gotten around to yet. Ballantyne watched the white puffballs of cloud over the far, wooded shore.

"You have a woman?" the boy asked, finally.

"No."

"No woman? It is good for a man to have a woman."

"No doubt." It was a conclusion Ballantyne had no wish to debate. "And you? Do you have a woman?" He asked the question in all seriousness.

It was accepted in the same manner. "No, I

am young for a woman and they can be much trouble."

The comment seemed to explain much. The boy smoked in silence and Ballantyne waited for him to speak.

"Do you have goats at home?"

"No," Ballantyne confessed, "I have no goats."

"A camel, perhaps?" Rashid was giving him every chance to prove himself a man of substance.

"No, I have no camel." Inspiration came to him. "Once I owned two horses."

Rashid pondered the matter. "It is good to have horses, but a horse is like a woman. It is unproductive. If you have a horse or a woman you must also have goats."

"I think you come here for a reason and I do not think it is because of the machine." Rashid repeated himself. Ballantyne said nothing but the boy seemed to be arriving at a decision. "There is a woman who comes to this hillside," Rashid said. Then glancing at Ballantyne as if to challenge his disbelief, he added, "A woman with a rug."

When the quarry is sighted the hunter moves with caution. Ballantyne waited for several moments before he asked, "She sits on a rug?"

"She <u>looks</u> at a rug. She sits on the grass, or sometimes on the stones. She is very beautiful," he added, "and not old." Then reluctantly, "She is more beautiful than the goats."

It was a compliment of the highest order.

"That cannot be," Ballantyne said positively. "How could a woman be more beautiful than goats?"

"It is difficult to believe," Rashid admitted.

A dead weaver . . . a woman with a rug. A pattern was emerging.

"She comes often?"

"She is here now." Rashid got to his feet. "She has much trouble, this woman, and she has no man."

"You protected her from the men in the gray car," Ballantyne suggested. "I know them, and they are evil men."

Rashid looked at Ballantyne with interest. "You speak Turkish then?"

"I am a man of many tongues." Ballantyne paused, and then he took the plunge, knowing what icy depths lay before him. "I will help her if I can."

"Come, I will show you."

The woman was Villette Mallory.

The magazines called her "The Incomparable Villette," and whether it was modeling the latest design from Christian Dior or Jacques Fath or dropping a playful wink while presenting a cut-glass bottle of perfume, the term suited her.

On this day she wore a gray suit and a blouse of pale blue, and her hair, a dark auburn, was tied with a scarf of the same shade as the blouse. Her eyes were green and her cheekbones high, the bone structure of her face delicate yet strong.

This moment was what Ballantyne had come

for. And, he feared, so had the old man on the beach.

"My friend Rashid has come to me with the story of a beautiful woman who sits among the ruins and looks at a rug. Being a romanticist, naturally, I came."

"A romanticist?"

"A romanticist when I think of women, Madame, a realist when I deal with them."

She measured him with cool eyes. He was a tall, athletic-looking man, something more than thirty. He was tailored well, if casually, but there was something indefinably down-at-heel about him, the sense that his fortunes had ebbed and flowed like the tides.

"Who are you?"

Rashid squatted upon his thin, bare heels and looked upon Ballantyne with dispassionate eyes, as if to say, "You know nothing of goats, let us see how you do with a woman."

"It is a question I have often asked of myself, Madame, but who can reply to such a question? Born of woman, I am a man . . . possessing no fortune and no family; it has been left to me to live by knowing, and if I have no wit, Madame, I have at least wits, and I live by them."

She wore no makeup today and was even more beautiful than he remembered, but it was not a cool classical beauty. There was some humor that showed in her eyes, but there was sadness too.

"One more thing I have, that is curiosity,

and curiosity opens windows upon the world.
And . . . I know something of rugs."

Something happened then, for her eyes were
suddenly no longer green, but hazel, almost
yellow, like the eyes of a leopard in the
jungle.

"Do you know me, then?"

"Let us say that I have seen you several
times before this. . . . Madame was in
Honfleur, at the Auberge du Cheval Blanc.
You were motoring along the coast and you
had stopped for lunch. The food there is
quite good."

"And there have been other times?"

"Twice in the Mouski marketplace in Cairo.
The first time I sat at an adjoining table
listening to your voice and enjoying your
profile. The Marquis was quite annoyed."

"And the second?"

"I sold you an antique ring . . . a lovely
green stone."

Her eyes were cold. "I remember the stone.
It was fake."

"It was, Madame, and I regret it, but at
the moment I had nothing else to sell. I
would make it up to you if you would let me."

"I think you are a thief, if not worse."

"One lives as one can."

Ballantyne seated himself on the wall
facing her. He was, she reflected, a
graceful man for one so lean and tall. He
handled himself like a fencer or a boxer.

"For example," he said, "by this time
Madame has guessed that my being here is no
accident. I came to meet you."

"That's absurd. How could you know I would be here? Or that having been here, I would come again?"

"It was a slight gamble, but there are few secrets in the East, Madame, and as I have said, I am a curious man.

"For example, your husband, the late Maharajah of Kasur, was an ardent sportsman. Suddenly, on the eve of an important polo match, he withdraws. His withdrawal was a serious blow to the chances of his team, and he was known as an honorable man. Nothing but a matter of life and death could cause such a last-minute withdrawal.

"Then came the news of his death in a plane crash while en route to Istanbul. Why the sudden flight? Why Istanbul?

"These questions sharpened my curiosity, and as I have said, there are no secrets in the East. I heard rumors, made discreet inquiries.

"Your late husband, like many others, had lost his estates when India and Pakistan were divided. He settled large sums of money on old family retainers . . . he was forced to modify his way of living . . . and still he owed many debts.

"Then a most curious thing. This Maharajah who had only a small income by his former standards recently assured his creditors that all would be paid . . . within a month."

"So?"

"So one could only assume that he expected, somehow, to come into a quite

large sum of money from some hitherto
undisclosed source. Then the unexplained
flight to Istanbul, so I asked myself . . .
was the money here?

"There was also a disturbing story. That
in deciding to fly here the Maharajah knew
that he caused his own death. The whisper
was that had he not died in the plane crash
he would have died in another way, and
soon."

"Why would anyone wish to kill him?"

"That was what I asked myself. But behind
many murders there is a matter of money.
Somehow, in some way, he was coming into
money and somebody else wanted it. It is as
simple as that."

She was thoughtful, but finally she asked,
"Do you have a name?"

"I am called Ballantyne."

"Merely Ballantyne? Nothing else?"

"If you must have more, I am Michael
Surendranath Ballantyne. My mother was of a
Rajput family of an ancient line. She named
me for a great teacher, a scholar. I fear I
have not lived up to her hopes."

"My husband was a Rajput."

"I know. . . . That is among the reasons I
am here today, along with the ring." He
paused. "Ballantyne is enough. Throughout
Asia they know that name."

"I am impressed."

"You need not be. I am a dealer in chance,
a liaison man, a go-between, an arranger of
meetings. I said that I live by my wits, but

it is equally true that I live by whom, and
what, I know."

Her handbag, a large one, lay open on the
rock before her, the open side within easy
reach of her hand.

"For example, you have a gun in your bag.
You will not need that for me, but keep it
close. Today you lunched with Leon
Decebilus."

"So?"

"He is a thief, and a master of thieves."

"I doubt if he would spy on me so
obviously as you have done."

Ballantyne turned to the goatherd. "A gray
car came along the track a short time ago.
What did they wish to know?"

"They asked if I had seen a blue car with
a woman driving it."

"You see? The men in that Renault were
Mustafa Bem and Barbaro, and where they are,
Decebilus is. They are his men."

Her eyes were cold. "I am sure you are
mistaken. We have mutual friends. Mr.
Decebilus is a financier, a respected man."

"If you said 'feared' rather than
'respected' I would accept that." He nodded
toward the cliffs. "Walk down to the shore
and you will find a tall old man in shabby
clothes lying dead upon the sand. He was
killed by Mustafa Bem. You are in greater
danger than you realize."

She looked startled. "A dead man? Down
there?"

"Do you know this old man?"

"With a scarred jaw?" She was thoughtful. "About sixty? In a worn black suit?

"He came to my hotel the day I arrived and wished to buy a rug from me. He said it was for sentimental reasons, that an ancestor of his was the weaver."

He looked at her seriously. "Madame? How many rugs have you sold in your lifetime?"

"Rugs? Why, none of course."

"You do not think it strange that immediately after you arrive in town a man comes to your hotel room and wishes to buy a rug from you?"

"Strange? Of course I thought it strange. But my husband--everyone wants something and many think he is still wealthy."

"You did not agree to sell the rug?"

"I refused. He started to argue so I closed the door in his face."

"But you did see him again?"

"He must have followed me. He was outside the Abdullah where we went for dinner."

"And you mentioned it to Decebilus?"

"I may have. In fact, I am sure that I did. After all, the man had followed me. Decebilus was amused."

"No doubt. But now the man is dead. You see no coincidence in all this?"

She was silent, and Ballantyne glanced at the ridge and the cypresses at Hannibal's tomb. From the track they were hidden, but an observer up there on the ridge, especially if he had field glasses, could see anyone here. In fact, he could see the three of them even without glasses . . . and no doubt the blue car was close by.

"Whatever it is," Ballantyne continued, "that your husband knew, you may be sure Decebilus knows also, or some of it. And you may also be sure that the knowledge concerns money, for Decebilus is interested in little else."

Villette looked away from him toward a wedge of blue sea visible through a notch in the ruined wall. Her husband's sudden trip . . . without explanation . . . it was so unlike him. And the rug? It was possible that Ballantyne was right, but what, then, of Leon?

She had known the name of Leon Decebilus for years, it seemed. Friends returning from Monte Carlo, St. Tropez, and Paris had mentioned his name as they mentioned the names of Onassis, Pignatelli, or King Farouk.

When they met . . . quite by accident . . . they had talked briefly. Then they had lunched together, and last evening there had been dinner.

He was a brute. Instinctively, she knew that, but a fascinating brute. He dressed with extreme care . . . with too much care. His manners were perfect, too perfect again . . . as they are apt to be when acquired late in life and not from childhood. Yet there was also a bizarre touch: the rings on his fingers, one huge one on his left hand, two slightly smaller rings on his right.

He had been gracious. He had offered his car, even a chauffeur, anything she might require. He offered his sympathy for her loss; he had not known the Maharajah, but had known of him.

Who had not heard of Dhyan Jai Rathore? She had known of him for several years before they met. Their pictures were often in the same magazines, he gambling in Monte Carlo . . . attending the movie festival at Cannes . . . fishing in the Bahamas. He was exotic, a Rajput, educated at Cambridge, a man with a gift for friendships and for sports. If "Jay," as his friends called him, was known for something in particular, it was making the most demanding feats like climbing mountains, blazing across the finish line at Le Mans, or leading a champion polo team look easy and fun. After her first year in New York it was almost fated they would meet.

Her success had been spectacular. A farm girl from Oklahoma, she had started modeling for Neiman Marcus in Dallas but quickly moved into the world of New York and Paris fashion. She photographed well from any angle and wore clothes with an easy grace. The ready wit for which she had become famous was rather a gift for quick, deft characterizations, a quality inherited from her father. Though never an actress, her ability to banter and poke fun at herself had made her a favorite on TV variety programs.

She had never been sure whether she really loved Jay. From the first they had fitted into each other's lives easily and naturally. They liked each other and liked many of the same things, and he was at home anywhere. She had been happy with him, he seemed to love her, and when he had proposed she accepted.

Ballantyne interrupted her thoughts. "Your husband gave you no clue to his secret? Could it have something to do with the rug?"

"The rug that the man wanted to buy? It is a prayer rug . . . but what could a rug mean? I think it was just a talisman, a good-luck piece. I know it had been in Jay's family for years."

"A prayer rug, a rare one, can be worth as much as a valuable painting. And, believe me, I'd rather have one. I could talk for a year on the subject of rugs. But . . ."

Ballantyne was thoughtful. All he had said of rugs was true, yet somehow it did not make the kind of sense he was seeking. If Decebilus wanted something it would be worth millions, not thousands. Was it then the prayer rug of some religious leader? Something of importance in the Moslem world? He could think of no story of that sort, but such a rug might exist.

"Do you have the rug with you?"

She paused, still suspicious. "Not today. Jay asked me to keep it for him in Paris. When he wired me to meet him in Istanbul, he asked me to bring the rug . . . not under any circumstances to forget it."

Villette turned to him suddenly. "What do you expect to get out of this, Ballantyne? You have admitted you sold me a stone that was not genuine--why should I trust you?"

"You need not trust me. Go to the police. Ask for Hamid Yalcinkaya, only him. Tell him what has happened, tell him of me, of the man on the beach, then get on the first plane and fly back to the United States."

All Ballantyne could do was make his play. "Or you can see this through," he said. "See it through with me . . . or with Decebilus. You will choose one of us, because he will give you no alternative and I will try to take it from him . . . whatever it is. I, however, will accept any deal you think is fair--a bargain, if you ask me."

She arose suddenly. "I must go." She extended her hand.

He took it, touching the fingers lightly with his lips. "Do you know the Pandeli?" he asked. "In the old town? Lunch with me there tomorrow . . . at twelve?"

She studied him coolly, then assented. "Very well, Ballantyne. At twelve."

"And in the meantime . . . be careful."

She started away, then hesitated. "Do not forget that I have a pistol."

"Your eyes, Madame, are the greater danger." He bowed, smiling a little.

She laughed. "Ballantyne, I think you're a nineteen-karat phony. You would lie in your teeth for money or a woman."

"Madame . . . let me assure you. Your

money is safe with me. Until tomorrow,
then?"

The blue Maserati had been hidden in an
angle of the wall. She pulled the car from
its place of concealment and, with a rasp of
exhaust, started slowly back toward the
track.

Rashid moved up beside Ballantyne, and
there was no childishness in his face.
"Treat her well. She is my friend. If
not"--he drew a dagger from among his
rags--"I shall have your heart."

The words were theatrical, the gesture
boyish, borrowed no doubt from some story
heard in the marketplace. But some stories
are not to be taken lightly, for they form
the instruction and discipline of a people,
and the goatherd, boy though he was, meant
what he said.

"And do you take care," Ballantyne warned,
"if you are questioned, to know neither
of us."

A man could walk almost as fast as a car
could be driven along the goat track, so he
reached the village only a few minutes
behind the Maserati. His battered Land Rover
awaited him, hidden in a ruined camel shed.

The Maharajah . . . or Jay, as Villette
called him . . . was dead. And it appeared
the only one who might keep Decebilus from
attaining what he wanted was Villette
herself.

Nor had she taken Ballantyne's warning

seriously enough. There are some who will
believe nothing ill of those they meet
socially . . . and there are many who will
accept anyone who has the money to put up a
good appearance and be introduced by the
right people. Leon Decebilus appeared to be
what he wished people to see him as: the
operator of a number of freighters and
tankers, of a small airline, and, through
various associations, several nightclubs and
restaurants in Cairo, Alexandria, Athens,
and Aleppo.

That Villette knew and understood men,
Ballantyne had no doubt. A beautiful woman
becomes habituated to using her beauty,
learns subconsciously, at least, that men
are not only willing but eager to serve her.
Her smile, her frown, her graciousness--all
these can be used, almost without thinking,
on all ages and types of men. None of this
would have any effect on Decebilus.

Prostitution had long been one of the
sources of his income . . . the first stable
source. Refugees were his stock in trade and
with the shifting of borders, wars and civil
wars, supply was never an issue. His orders
shipped women, like so many head of cattle,
from Marseilles to Genoa, Cairo to Tangier,
Alexandria. He had no desire that could not
be satisfied merely for the promise, or the
threat, of a transfer from one better or
worse brothel to another. There was no
experience he could not have, or had not
already had, for safe passage for a family

or one more dose of heroin or hashish.
Villette Mallory was a beautiful woman, but
she would need to rely on other qualities
if she was to defeat Decebilus.

Ballantyne drove swiftly and with the
knowledge of many roads, and as he drove he
worried over the problem as a dog worries a
bone. He had too little, all too little with
which to work.

The sudden, unexplained flight of the
Maharajah and his subsequent crash. The
arrival of Villette in Istanbul, and
the quickly arranged meeting with Decebilus.
The man who came to Villette to buy a rug
and was immediately murdered. It all meant
something, yet what it was he could not
guess.

To put a period to the matter, Mustafa Bem
and Barbaro had followed Villette to the
ruin, inquired about her. Had they followed
her to kill? Or merely to watch?

Until he knew more, Ballantyne would
assume that Villette's rug was the joker in
the deck. He had to get a look at it, one
way or another.

By the time the outskirts of Istanbul were
reached, Ballantyne was close behind the
Maserati. Or rather, he was close behind the
car that followed the Maserati.

The battered Volkswagen had appeared
from nowhere in the vicinity of Kartal,
falling in behind the blue car, but clinging

too close for a man experienced at his job.

Ballantyne had been watching for the Renault, not a Volkswagen, and when he realized it was following Villette, he drew up during a crush of traffic and studied the driver.

He was a stranger, yet hauntingly familiar. A narrow face, badly pocked, with a pointed beard and a trimmed mustache. The man's shirt collar was greasy, the upholstering of the car torn and old. At the instant Ballantyne came abreast of him, the man's coat gaped somewhat, revealing the butt of a heavy pistol.

Falling back to a discreet distance, Ballantyne watched the Volkswagen trail Villette into the sweeping drive that led up to the looming modernist rectangle of the Istanbul Hilton.

The stranger locked the Volkswagen, then almost ran to catch up as Villette went through the doors.

Parking alongside the car, Ballantyne took time for a quick glance inside. An ancient cardboard valise, a few old newspapers, and a paperbacked American novel. Whoever the man was, he apparently could read English.

Walking swiftly toward the hotel, Ballantyne stopped just in time to keep from being run down by the gray Renault. Behind the wheel was Barbaro, beside him Mustafa Bem.

They drew up, and Mustafa Bem darted for the doors. Neither had paid any attention to Ballantyne.

CHAPTER II

Following Mustafa Bem inside, it became immediately obvious that although Bem knew the stranger, the stranger did not know him.

The driver of the Volkswagen turned to glance back toward the entrance at the moment Mustafa Bem stepped through, and although the latter turned sharply away, the Volkswagen driver paid him no attention. In turning away, Mustafa Bem came face-to-face with Ballantyne.

"So!" His eyes flared. "The wolves gather!"

Indicating the driver of the Volkswagen, Ballantyne replied, "Decebilus must be hard up to bother with such as that."

"He is no business of yours! Stay out of this!"

"Tell Dice that I'm in town, will you? He will be pleased, I am sure."

"He wishes nothing to do with you, Ballantyne, and consider yourself fortunate, for the next time he gives the word I shall kill you." And then he added, "And do not call him Dice. You know he doesn't like it."

Ballantyne strolled away and going to a booth, bought a newspaper. The dark-eyed girl who took his money scarcely moved her lips as she said, "Leon Decebilus is staying here."

Ballantyne's face revealed nothing, but he

was startled. For years Decebilus had stayed
nowhere but at the Parc Oteli, formerly the
town's leading hostelry. Could the sudden
change mean that he wished to be near
Villette?

"No," the girl whispered when he asked if
Decebilus' arrival was unexpected, "he
reserved a suite just one week ago today."

The same day the Maharajah of Kasur
reserved his rooms. "Thanks." He glanced at
the paper. "Tell Johann I wish to see him."

"He expected you. He is in the barber-
shop."

The fact that Decebilus had reserved his
suite on the same day as the Maharajah might
be pure coincidence, but Ballantyne did not
believe it for a moment. It was another
small link in the chain of evidence tying
Decebilus to the visit of the Maharajah and
Villette.

Suddenly a man was beside him, a slender
blond man with a saturnine expression,
neatly dressed in a dark suit and a snap
brim hat. The man paused to light a
cigarette, but as he lifted the match it
served to cover the words he spoke from the
corner of his mouth. "The Scylax is lying in
the port of Galata."

"Thanks, Johann."

"Arrived last night . . . in ballast."

The blond man walked away and Ballantyne
stared at his newspaper with unseeing eyes.
The Scylax, named for an ancient Greek
navigator of the Indian Ocean, was a
freighter of Decebilus' Green Star Line. To

bring the freighter in ballast to Istanbul
represented a contradiction for a shipping
man as shrewd as Decebilus; it would not pay
to sail empty unless some very valuable
cargo was expected.

There were many pieces of the jigsaw, but
fit them together as he might, they refused
to represent any intelligible picture. And
here in the lobby of the Istanbul Hilton
were several of the pieces.

Obviously the man in the Volkswagen wanted
to watch or speak to Villette Mallory . . .
and just as obviously, Mustafa Bem was here
to watch for her . . . or for the Volkswagen
man.

Ballantyne had a theory that the way to
defeat a careful enemy was to keep his plans
from developing, and Leon Decebilus was a
planner, a conniver. Shrewd, careful, and
unemotional during the early stages of
planning, Decebilus left little to chance.
Yet if his plans became disturbed or
frustrated, he was inclined to become
enraged. And when aroused he gave way to
fits of fury and brutality that could be
shocking, a fact known to but few of those
who now surrounded him. Ballantyne knew it,
of old, and it was a gap in Decebilus' armor
that could be exploited. It was a very
dangerous gap, however.

Ballantyne had succeeded in outmaneuvering
Decebilus on two previous occasions, each
time by forcing him to move before he was
ready. When such men move hastily they make
mistakes, and the mistakes of others belong

to the man prepared to seize what opportunity has offered.

Now Ballantyne made such a move. Crossing
the room, he walked directly up to the
driver of the Volkswagen, and as he did so,
he saw Mustafa Bem turn sharply toward him,
a hand half-lifted as though to prevent the
meeting.

"My friend," Ballantyne said quietly, "you
are in great danger. Unless you are very
careful you will be killed as was"--suddenly
Ballantyne knew he was right--"as was your
brother."

"Brother?" The Volkswagen man stared
blankly at Ballantyne. "I have no brother."

"Perhaps your father, then? A tall old man
in a black suit?"

The man grabbed his sleeve. "What are you
saying? Where is he?" The voice echoed in
the glass and marble lobby.

Heads turned. Mustafa Bem, his face pale
with shock, had headed toward the exit. He
had, however, to pass them in reaching it.

"He lies dead on the sands below Eski
Hissar," Ballantyne said, speaking so only
the Volkswagen man could hear, "of three
knife thrusts in the back."

The man's face was yellow and sick. "You
are lying!" he gasped hoarsely. "It cannot
be true!"

"You may see for yourself."

"The woman! That foul--!"

"She had nothing to do with it. He was
killed by a man sent by Decebilus."

"Decebilus!" Again people turned to look.

"It was he who gave the order," Ballantyne
said. Then, turning, he pointed at Mustafa
Bem, who had just edged past them, and said,
"But <u>there</u> is the man who actually killed
your father!"

Mustafa Bem sprang for the entrance and
the Volkswagen man leaped after him.

There was a wild scramble at the door as
people rushed to either get out of the way
or to see what was happening. Ballantyne
stepped back, watching.

Behind him a cool voice said, "You are a
fool, Ballantyne, a pitiful fool."

Turning, Ballantyne looked into the eyes
of the one man he really had reason to fear.

It was Leon Decebilus.

He was three inches over six feet with
black hair and intensely black, piercing
eyes. His cheekbones were high, the bone
structure of his face massive. He wore a
dark suit of excellent tailoring and
material.

"You could stay out of this," Decebilus
suggested, "and we could forget the past."

"You might forget it, Dice. I would not."

Ballantyne saw a dark flush of anger under
the swarthy skin at Ballantyne's use of the
old nickname.

"I never liked you, Ballantyne. You
interfere with me and I shall have you
killed."

"Again?"

"You were lucky before. I could have you
taken away, then drowned or burned."

"Aboard the <u>Scylax</u>?"

Ballantyne saw the jump of fury in Decebilus' eyes, and for an instant he thought the man would strike him. Instead, Decebilus hissed, "Stay out of this!" and turned sharply away.

Ballantyne went out into the night, stopping under the portico, the roof of which was the architect's interpretation of a flying carpet. He shook a cigarette out of the pack in his shirt pocket.

Suddenly he saw the Volkswagen man coming back up the drive. He was perspiring freely and Ballantyne stopped him before he could reenter the hotel.

"I would stay out of there if I were you. They will have you arrested."

The man stared at him from great, anguished eyes. "You are my friend, I think. . . . Why?"

"You have given me no cause to be otherwise, and Decebilus is my enemy. It is as simple as that." He paused, then added, "Look, you are in trouble. Your father died because of the rug."

The man showed no surprise at the mention of a rug, accepting the connection without comment. "You are sure he is dead?"

"Three stab wounds in the back. It is the method of Mustafa Bem."

"I shall kill them all," the man said gloomily. "My father was a good man." He looked up at Ballantyne. "He knew nothing of the rug until I told him. But for me he would still be alive."

"Do not blame yourself--we are all in God's hands." After an instant and keeping his manner casual, Ballantyne said, "Tell me about it."

He held his breath, expecting anger, suspicion, or that the man would walk away from him, but the Volkswagen driver was preoccupied with his own grief. "It was a dream. An impossible dream." He turned large, sad eyes upon Ballantyne. "Ours is a poor family; it has always been a poor family.

"We are weavers, and weavers have their own tales, whispered among themselves, stories half-real, half-fantasy, stories of rugs and magic and legend. To tell a tale comes naturally to a weaver, you understand?"

"It was the story of a rug?"

"Yes, and a story of my family and a knot, a knot that only we know how to use."

"A knot? You mean a weaver's knot for a rug?"

The man started to speak, then stopped abruptly, seeming to realize what he was about to do. He turned sharply and stared at Ballantyne, his eyes hard with suspicion. "You are not my friend! You want the secret for yourself!"

"I can tell what you wish Madame to know. I can speak to her for you."

"No! I will tell nobody!"

"Decebilus knows."

"It is impossible! Only a weaver could know! Only a weaver from--!"

He broke off and strode away, his skinny
legs covering the ground in long strides.

Ballantyne swore softly. He had been
close, very close . . . to what he had no
idea, but it might have supplied him with
part of what he needed to know.

The sun had gone down beyond the Sea of
Marmara, beyond the crumbled ruins of
ancient Troy. He stood where he was,
enjoying the cool air and the pleasant
evening, trying to imagine what the story
might be. He thought of the storytellers in
the Old City, not far from where he himself
lived. Which would be most likely to know
and which the most likely to tell a
foreigner if he did?

He must move with extreme caution, for
every step he took now was a danger. Leon
Decebilus had never liked him, but for the
past few years he had actively hated
Ballantyne, hated him because of all the men
Decebilus had known, Ballantyne was the only
one ever to have seen him weak and frightened. Had it not been for Ballantyne,
Decebilus would now lie dead under the
searing desert sun.

"Ah, Mr. Ballantyne!"

Ballantyne turned to face Hamid
Yalcinkaya. He was a man of medium height,
extremely well built, with fine shoulders
and a strongly made face. An officer of the
police, he was also much more than that, for
he acted as a liaison man between the
highest powers in the government and the
police. Whenever he took an interest in a

case, it was sure to have international or
political overtones.

"Hello, Hamid. Late for you to be out,
isn't it? I mean, a growing boy and all
that."

"I could go to sleep earlier, Ballantyne,
if I was sure of just what you were doing.
Not that I enjoy being suspicious of an old
friend, but I know you too well."

Ballantyne hesitated. Hamid might have
just the information he needed, but the man
was shrewd and from anything Ballantyne
might say he could construct some idea of
what was involved. Ballantyne had no wish to
cause an old friend trouble; nor did he wish
to be troubled by him.

At this stage he was not altogether sure
whether he was thinking of Villette first,
or of himself. To protect her from harm was
a debt he owed: The few dollars he had
bilked from her in Egypt had literally saved
his life . . . but when it came to a
treasure or a new source of profit, if such
existed, he would have to do some thinking.

"Now how do I keep you from sleep? I am
out here only for a bit of fresh air."

"You should have found the air at Eski
Hissar invigorating enough."

Ballantyne straightened his tie. So they
knew about that? A little frankness
then . . . just a little.

"Well, she didn't say no."

"Did she say yes?"

"No."

Hamid chuckled. "The lady is very

beautiful, and very expensive, no doubt. I
mean no disrespect in saying that, only her
friends spend freely, I believe."

"You mean Leon Decebilus?"

"Old friends, aren't you? You and
Decebilus?"

"Neither of us would use the term."

"And yet, you carried him out of the Empty
Quarter. Three days, I believe, on your
back."

"I should have left him there."

"You should have been a Turk. A Turk would
have left him right where he was."

Hamid glanced at the tip of his cigarette.
"What was all that inside just now? That
business with Mustafa Bem?"

"Keep the enemy worried, keep them afraid
of what you know, of what you might do."

"It is a philosophy of which we Turks
approve, though perhaps not in our best
hotels. . . . But why Decebilus? And just at
this moment? Is it only because of the
beautiful lady from America? Or is there
something more? Something of which I should
know?" Hamid paused. "How, for example, does
it connect with a certain plane crash in
Iran and the death of the lady's husband?"

"What do you know about that?"

Hamid shrugged a shoulder. "It was no
accident, if that is what you mean. Someone
planted a bomb in the tail. Very accurately
timed to explode over one of the wildest
regions in the Elburz Mountains."

"And you tied it to Leon Decebilus?"

"If we could connect it to him he would be

under arrest. To you, my friend, I shall admit this much, no more. There were indications."

"There was a shift of hotels, and a suite taken near that reserved by the Maharajah, is that what you mean?"

"More than that. Tell me, Ballantyne, did you know the Maharajah of Kasur?"

"Only by reputation."

"Would you say he was an impulsive man? A dreamer? I mean, was he impractical?"

"No . . . I saw films of him driving in the Le Mans race, and I've read of him playing golf and polo. A realist, I would say, a very cool, hardheaded man, but with imagination."

"I see."

Ballantyne was watching the place where his car was parked. Was that a moving shadow? Or a trick of the eyes?

"What is she like?"

"Intelligent. She's been courted around Paris and Cannes by a lot of playboys, but she's more levelheaded than you might suspect."

"She was a model?"

"I'm guessing she could go back to it. She has something a girl is born with if she has it at all. Women always look to see what she is wearing that gives her that look, but it's the lady, not the clothes. She traveled a good bit following her business as a model, but she invested a little money in Broadway shows and a couple of them did very well. Being a beautiful girl, she meets

everybody sooner or later. That's about the
size of it."

"Did she tell you all this?"

"We met only today. We were introduced by
a goatherd."

"Rashid?"

Hamid never missed a trick. Ballantyne's
surprise must have shown in his face because
Hamid smiled with obvious satisfaction. "Oh,
yes! I know Rashid. In fact, he reported a
murder. A weaver named Yacub . . . stabbed
to death, out at Eski Hissar."

Like the Ottomans of old, Hamid must have
informers everywhere. Ballantyne made his
decision suddenly: When in doubt, be frank.

He explained in detail his visits to Eski
Hissar, hoping to meet Villette, his
discovery of the body, his recognition of
the wounds. And then he repeated what
Villette had told him, that the dead man had
followed her to the Abdullah. He did not
mention the rug.

"Have you any idea why?"

"You're joking. Men always follow
Villette. Only . . . she mentioned his
following her to Decebilus."

"You're not suggesting he was killed
because of that?"

"I suggest nothing. I comment, that is
all."

He glanced toward his car once more, but
saw no movement there. "Can I drop you
somewhere, Hamid?"

"I have my own car." Yet Hamid made no
move to go; he lingered, as if about to say

something, then at last when he dropped his cigarette to the pavement he said only, "He has not changed, Ballantyne. Decebilus is the same."

"They tell me his fingers reach even into the government, to the police."

"If they do, I should like to know it." Hamid glanced at Ballantyne. "They do not reach to me."

"If it was shown to me in black and white, I still would not believe it," Ballantyne said.

"Thank you. Thank you, my friend." Hamid turned and walked away. He looked hard, capable, and tough. Hamid was a true Turk, and it would never do to underestimate him.

Ballantyne started for his Land Rover. He was thinking of what might be done before morning, for whatever was to be done must be done quickly. Decebilus was not one to waste time.

The VW had been replaced by another, larger car. Ballantyne dug out his key, his eyes sweeping the other vehicles, searching for that movement he had seen. He heard the whisper of clothing behind him . . . too late.

A knife-point pricked his back, and a car door opened behind him, the car parked directly alongside his own. The knife must have been put against his back through the window of the car. If that was so, when the door opened for the man to emerge the knife must be for a moment withdrawn while he moved it around the window frame.

Ballantyne stood very still, trying to judge from where the knife-blade was how tall the man might be. It was not Mustafa Bem, but a shorter man.

"Don't move!" the voice growled, in English. The pressure of the knife-point slackened and Ballantyne spun swiftly, hands shoulder high, knocking the knife-hand aside.

His attacker lunged out of the car but Ballantyne jerked a knee into his groin and knocked him back into the car seat. Then he slammed the door on the man's leg.

The man screamed.

People around the hotel stopped, staring toward the parking lot. Ballantyne climbed into the Land Rover and backed out, taking his time. He could hear his attacker moaning and cursing, but he ignored it. Turning his car, he drove unhurriedly away.

When Villette Mallory closed the door behind her, she stood for long minutes with her back against it, her eyes closed. No matter how desperately she fought the feeling, she was frightened.

The poise that was so distinctly a part of her was endangered by the frightening realization that she was broke . . . and in a foreign country where she had no friends.

She had always earned a good living, but she had lived too well and there had seemed no end to the money or the opportunities. Planning for the future, saving, had seemed something she could put off for a

while. Despite her reputation as a glamor
girl, despite how easy it had been to accept
the attention and the pay, she had never
been truly comfortable in that world. There
was a darkness at its core, a corruption
that made her uneasy.

When Jay had come along she was at a low
ebb, emotionally. She had almost despaired
of finding the sort of man she wanted, the
sort toward whom she was naturally
attracted.

Like many another girl who becomes a
success in the world of fashion, motion
pictures, or the theater, she had not
realized how much it would limit her choice
of men. Instead of meeting more men when she
became famous, she met fewer . . . fewer
she actually trusted, at least.

Too many were alcoholic playboys, veterans
of a handful of unsuccessful marriages;
still others were simply not interested in
women at all, or were those who pretended an
interest for protective coloration. Many men
merely thought she was unapproachable,
others assumed she was too approachable, but
among them she found no men of character.

Not, at least, until she met Jay. His
fortunes had been up and down so many times
that he had no illusions left. Born into
fabulous wealth in one of the poorest
countries in the world, when India was torn
asunder he had rebuilt what was left of his
inheritance, enough to allow him a
comfortable living. More than money, it was
his dominance on the polo field and in the

Team Lotus cars at Le Mans and Monaco that
had kept him in the public eye. He had a
love of life and a great trust in himself
and the hand of fate.

When his investments in Cuba had been lost
to the revolution, he found himself on the
verge of going broke again. Villette was
concerned--she had passed up another
contract when they married. She made
arrangements to fly to Paris to see what
work was available.

But Jay had laughed. "There's nothing to
worry about," he had said. "I've still got
the rug."

"The rug?"

"It's a long story. And it will be quite
the adventure for us."

Later he had commented on it again.
"There's millions in it, but it will take
some doing."

He was excited by whatever plan he was
making, but then he was off with the team
and their ponies to India . . . and while
there something had gone terribly wrong.

Now Jay was gone, and if she was to
believe Ballantyne, he had been murdered.

She moved away from the door, and as she
undressed and prepared for a shower, she
considered the situation as coolly as she
could.

Jay dead . . . He had been so filled with
energy and the desire to do things that it
was hard to conceive of the idea that he was
gone.

COMMENTS: Dad left behind a bewildering array of revisions of this particular story. In trying to create a single coherent vision of his best ideas, I have combined the most complete material from five of the nine or ten drafts into the version that you have just read.

All of these drafts appear to originate from a very short short story, one that seems like an autobiographical vignette, called "By the Ruins of El Walariah," first published in *Yondering, The Revised Edition*. It is merely an amusing conversation between a Moroccan boy and a young traveler, a man like Louis might once have been. It contains no hint that it ever could or would attempt to transform itself into a thriller.

I can only assume that was this story's original incarnation. It is the simplest version, and stylistically it feels like a part of the *"Yondering* era," stories that Louis wrote in the 1930s and '40s before his mainstream career took off. At some point later on, he evidently got the strange idea to turn that particular story into a treasure-hunt adventure.

The next step in the evolution of this narrative seems to be the following concept, one that does not use either the Moroccan (El Walariah) or Turkish (Istanbul) locations. These notes read:

    Ali Brogan is a bit of the flotsam of
    the Middle East. He lives by his wits,
    and usually lives well, but occasionally
    he fails to come upon the needed
    opportunity.
    He knows a multitude of things. Most
    of it is highly useless knowledge, and
    he has a horror of work. Wherever he is,

he gets along, and always with a weather
eye for the chance.

In Samarkand he overhears a conversation about a rug . . . a very rare
rug, indeed, and woven into it is a map
indicating the presence of a buried
treasure.

Let's say Ali sees a man killed and
finds the rug. He carries it off, then
an attempt is made to buy the rug from
him. He studies the rug with great care,
can find nothing, only the design in the
center strikes him as a bit off pattern
(in one corner, rather) and has a
faintly familiar appearance.

He goes to a woman who knows most
things and discovers to whom the rug
belonged, and gets some of the story
from her, an old lady. One thing she
says rings a bell.

The elderly lady with whom he deals
was once married to a nobleman of
Turkish or Arabic background. . . . She
was an adventuress, but a shrewd and
beautiful woman in her youth. Now an old
lady with little money left she is still
the grand dame, and still as gifted in
her way as always. Ali has an admiration
for her which he cannot keep secret, and
he gives up his own profit for her.

Perhaps the design on the rug gives a
map of a ruined building outside
Samarkand. He is a crook who is
outsmarted by his own sentimentality.

That idea led to a draft of the story that is much more like the chapters of *The Golden Tapestry* that you have just read. It included the characters of the shepherd boy, the mysterious and beautiful young woman, and some Bad Guys who want something she has. This draft was, like "By the Ruins of El Walariah," set in Morocco. Subsequent versions, however, make the jump to Turkey and incorporate Hannibal's treasure and the whole cast of characters; in fact, there is very little difference between the next nine drafts. Dad made small adjustments, the timing of some of the events, figuring out how to best establish certain bits of information, and that is about it. In one draft, Ballantyne is named Baliran and he experimented with some different names for Jay, the Maharajah of Kasur.

He wrote one of these drafts in the first person from Ballantyne's point of view . . . then realized that was a mistake, that he needed to allow his audience to witness a number of scenes where Ballantyne could not be present. The first-person perspective made the delivery of that information difficult, and led to some extremely awkward expositional dialogue.

There were so many rewrites that I could see the storytelling begin to deteriorate; even as he got certain aspects of the plot nailed down, he began to take others so much for granted that he glossed over them, probably because he knew them too well by then. Louis did not like rewriting for this exact reason—unless a writer truly enjoys revision (and he did not), too many drafts can suck the life out of a story before it ever gets going.

It is very rare to see Louis sweating a bunch of little details like he did in these drafts. Usually, he was very self-assured about what he was doing and forged ahead with certainty. Even though he gave up on *The Golden Tapestry*, it seems like this is a pretty solid concept. Ultimately, he did get all those troublesome details nailed down in one version or another, and as you will see, he had a version of the entire story mapped out. Possibly Louis's biggest issue when it came to rewrites was that he didn't bother to do a careful analysis of the strengths and weaknesses of each draft. That, combined with the lack of a secretary (or a word processor!) to quickly shuffle all the good bits together, may have caused some of these story concepts to be left behind.

The bulk of these "Istanbul drafts" seem to have been written in 1960 and '61, the same era when he wrote the first version of *The Walking Drum* and tried to develop several other ideas to break out of the Western genre. Only one novel, *Sackett*, was published in 1961, and it ended up being a lean year. That was also the year I came along, and Mom and Dad were forced to move because their apartment building didn't allow children.

Eventually, they bought a house, and it's my guess that the financial pressure of the failed attempts to broaden his style, then my being born, plus the down payment on the house was what pushed him to accept the deal to write the novelization of the movie *How the West Was Won*, which came out in 1962.

At some point it seems Louis tried to sell *The Golden Tapestry* as a motion picture, no doubt feeling he could afford to go back to it if he had a buyer set up. No deal was ever made, but at least we will get the benefit of being able to read a treatment that suggests how the story might have developed and then ended if he had written the full novel.

As you read through the treatment below you may notice slight differences from the chapters of prose Louis wrote. Although the outline allows us to see what the overall structure of the story would have been like, I believe it was written fairly early in the process; the outline gives us the best overview, but the two chapters of prose you have just read are an indication of how he would have continued to work out the details in a more complete and sophisticated fashion.

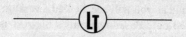

THE GOLDEN TAPESTRY

Outline of a Novel

CAST OF CHARACTERS:

BALLANTYNE: He knows who is bribing who from Delhi to Istanbul, from Cairo to Samarkand . . . he knows where the power and influence lie, and who to see about getting things done.

His father was an Irish-American adventurer who came out to the Middle East with a bridge construction company and stayed on as an oil prospector. His mother was a Eurasian girl of good family, and Ballantyne, except for a few short periods in the States and in Europe, has grown up in the East.

His experience has been varied and colorful; he speaks a dozen languages, most of them fluently; he knows the argot of the beggars and the thieves; and he has wires out to all parts of the East where the only secrets that exist are the ancient ones. The bazaars, the coffee shops and wine shops teem with gossip.

At thirty-three he is good-looking, rugged, quick to make a fast buck or a fast lady, and is a good man in a fight, but a

better one at talking himself out of
them.

He makes his living by acting as liaison
man for oil companies in their dealings with
Arab sheiks and other tribesmen, as a local
contact for motion-picture companies, for
archaeologists, etc. Occasionally, when he
noses about old ruins he comes up with a
fine head, a plaque, or a vase . . . and he
knows who will pay best for what he has
found.

He speaks fluent Turkish, Arabic, Hebrew,
Hindi, Persian, English, and French; he
speaks a smattering of Russian, Chinese,
Bengali, German, and Greek.

They know him in Aleppo and Isfahan, in
Kashgar, Srinagar, Damascus, and Bagdad as a
fast operator, but one whose word is good,
whose courage is unquestioned.

He has had frequent dealings with LEON
DECEBILUS.

VILLETTE MALLORY: Born in Pawhuska,
Oklahoma, on a ranch, she was singing on
various radio stations in the vicinity when
only fourteen; at sixteen, passing as older,
she was a model for Neiman Marcus in Dallas;
at seventeen she had gone to New York and
had become within a few months one of the
best-paid models in the country, her income
had moved up to five figures, and she was
known as "The Incomparable Villette."

She is beautiful, bright, and quick in
conversation, and she knows how to take care
of herself. Even with all her glamor and the

romance that has become attached to her name she is a very regular gal who has never forgotten where she came from.

She has been courted without much success by an assortment of international playboys, visiting nobility, Texas millionaires, and the usual names that make up cafe society.

She had met the Maharajah of Kasur, a sportsman noted for his polo playing, race driving, etc., but a very regular guy who lost most of what he had when Pakistan split with India, and who divided much of what remained among relatives and some old family retainers.

Villette is not in love with him, but she does like him very much and they have become engaged. He has told her, and at first she believed he was joking, that he was not worried about money. He said he had a rug that would make his fortune . . . a prayer rug.

Villette knows a good deal about the world and about men, but she has never encountered the kind of trouble represented by LEON DECEBILUS.

LEON DECEBILUS: Tall, strong, and with a superficial polish that quickly disappears when he grows angry. His voice grows rough, his language changes.

"Decebilus" is a name he uses; his own name is unknown, and he himself may never have known it. His nationality is equally indefinite, except that he comes from the Levantine coast.

He has been a thief and a pimp, a smuggler and a runner of guns and other contraband. He has but one loyalty, to himself, is egocentric and cunning. He has the shrewdness developed from practice and from the peoples who live in the marketplace. He is a completely ruthless man, totally unimpressed by beauty. He still operates a chain of whorehouses throughout the ports of the Eastern Mediterranean, and women mean nothing to him. He takes them when he wants them, discards them when he wishes.

Villette, accustomed to coping with men without too much trouble, finds herself completely at a loss with him, a thing she does not sense at first.

Decebilus is interested only in money, and over the years, through murder, blackmail, and a series of fast operations he has become a financial leader in the Near East. He owns a line of decrepit freighters and tankers, a small airline operating in the Middle East, and various other enterprises.

He uses bribery, threats, and blackmail to get what he wants, but being absolutely ruthless and willing to kill or destroy anything in his way, he is a man feared wherever he appears.

He is handsome, dresses with great care in suits tailored in London. His outward manners and good taste are visible everywhere except that he constantly wears three large rings on his right hand, two on his left. His good taste in clothes is an acquired thing. . . . Personally he would prefer something more garish, but he has learned. Only in the rings is this aspect visible. Yet the veneer is thin. When angry the change is shocking.

RASHID: A goatherd who is twelve years old going on forty; young in one sense, he was never young in another; he has listened well over his few years, and has observed the comings and goings of men. He will have more to do in the story than the brief outline of the action indicates.

MUSTAFA BEM and BARBARO: Sharp tools for the cutting hand of Decebilus, they supply his "muscle" when he does not wish to be involved.

YUSUF: An old man who has lived long in Istanbul and for whom life holds no mysteries. He knows much of rugs, the rugs of Persia, Turkey, Bokhara, India, and China . . . he knows the myths and legends woven into the rugs, even some of their origins, for each rug is itself a puzzle, and the motifs may be borrowed from China that appear in a Persian or Turkish rug, or vice versa. Long ago his family were retainers of the Maharajah of Kasur, and like him, he is a Moslem.

HAMID: A cool, hard-bitten, and thoroughly honest police officer; formerly of the Army, he knew Ballantyne in Korea, where the latter functioned as an intelligence officer

and liaison man because of his command of
languages. They mutually respect each other,
but Hamid has always been a little
suspicious of his friend. Hamid has a
complete dossier on Decebilus but no opening
for an arrest. Hamid is, however, more than
a mere officer of the police . . . he is a
liaison man between the police and the
national government.

YACUB & KHALID: Father and son, who know
the secret of the rug and have searched for
it as have their fathers and grandfathers
before them.

ZAIDA: Who has her own ideas about
Ballantyne, Decebilus, and the rug. She is
dark, slender, exotic, and is brought into
the picture by Decebilus but decides to
double-cross him and get the rug for
herself.

LOCALE:

Algiers, Casablanca, and Hong Kong have
been the subject of successful motion
pictures, but Istanbul, formerly Constan-
tinople, has never been used as it should
have been. The harbor, the Golden Horn, the
Bosporus, are indescribably beautiful and
photogenic. The Old City, with its ancient
walls which still stand, its mosques and
minarets, is romantic and exciting.

During spring, summer, and fall the air is usually startlingly clear and the sky blue as it only is in the Greek islands, southern Italy, or Istanbul's vicinity. The average temperature in July and August is 72 degrees. Istanbul is 16 hrs. by air from New York, 5 hrs. from Paris.

The best view of the Golden Horn, long famed as one of the most beautiful harbors in the world, is from the cemetery at the end of the bay.

The city is divided into three parts: the Old City, and then across the famed Galata Bridge over the Golden Horn is the modern city, and some old suburbs. Across the Bosporus (the fare across by ferry is about five cents) lies Asia.

Pop. about 1,200,000, and a mixture of all nationalities in the world. The city was founded in the 9th century B.C.

The Istanbul Hilton is the city's luxury hotel, new, bright, and smart. The Parc used to be the lushest spot in Europe and was a hangout for correspondents and adventurers. In the Chez Afrique, a subterranean nightclub off the Street of Spices, von Papen used to meet his secret agents. Every street has its own story; many of them have thousands of stories.

The Seraglio Palace, which used to be the harem of the sultans of Turkey and the Ottoman Empire, is now a museum. It is a maze of rooms and passages, and part of the chase sequence in this story takes place there. It covers acres and acres of parks and buildings, is picturesque and exciting.

The Sunken Palace is one of the ancient cisterns built beneath the city (miles of these still exist, most of them forgotten long ago) to supply the city with water in time of siege. This one looks more like a vast cathedral than a cistern, and has 12 rows of 28 columns to hold the vaulted roof, 336 columns in all. But this is only one of the cisterns. It still contains water, and part of the chase takes place there, by boat and torchlight.

The Grand Bazaar has 92 streets and thousands of shops selling everything in the world. Not so mysterious-looking since the fire of some years back, but still an interesting place, always crowded and busy.

The Tin Village is a collection of shacks and huts built of old sheet metal, oil barrels, packing cases, etc. Gypsies live there.

The Gulf of Izmit and Eski Hissar is roughly fifty miles from Istanbul by a good road.

The Pandeli, mentioned in the story, is a romantic place in the Old Town, and the best food of the Turkish variety. There are a lot of good eating places in town. The Abdullah, also mentioned, is very good and considered the best in town.

Istanbul is a hotbed of intrigue, and visitors are there from every country in the world. The Turks are a hardy, rugged people who have fought the Russians many times in their history and any Turk believes he can whip any four Russians and is quite ready to prove it. Their government is friendly to ours and has been so for a long time.

The Istanbul Hilton is located in the heart of the city in a lovely park, and alongside the lobby is a promenade overlooking a garden terrace, a reflecting pool, swimming pool, cabanas, tennis courts, and the gardens.

There are a lot of theaters, good music, etc. The city has nearly 500 mosques, some of them extremely beautiful. There are miles of good beaches, and the place has a romantic flavor all its own.

BRIEF OUTLINE OF ACTION:

BALLANTYNE discovers the body of an old man in a worn black suit on the shore near Eski Hissar, and the man has been murdered by three knife wounds in the kidney. This use of the knife is a trademark of MUSTAFA BEM, the right-hand man of LEON DECEBILUS, formerly known as "Dice," a name he would like to forget. Decebilus has in the past been a thief, a panderer, and a murderer. . . . He is now a shipping magnate and financier.

Few recall his criminal background, or that his success was founded more upon blackmail and murder than upon financial cunning. The few who do remember prefer to keep silent.

Ballantyne waits among the ruins and sees a Renault come along the goat track. Mustafa Bem gets out and talks to RASHID, the goatherd, asking about a blue car with a woman in it. Rashid professes to know nothing, and they leave.

The boy comes over and after some talk with Ballantyne, introduces him to VILLETTE MALLORY.

VILLETTE was to have met her fiancé, the Maharajah of Kasur, in Istanbul, but he was killed in a plane crash en route. She has beautiful clothes, and almost no money. She is living on her jewelry, which she has pawned bit by bit, and other than that has only a rug, a prayer rug given her by the Maharajah, who told her to keep it at all costs, that it would make them rich. She had thought of the rug as more of a good-luck piece than anything else but there have been several attempts to take it from her and she is no longer so sure it is only that.

The only person she knows is an old man who keeps a shop in the Grand Bazaar, known as YUSUF, and her fiancé has assured her that he is trustworthy. She has no one to turn to except him, and he is a relatively poor man.

Ballantyne, a fast operator where a buck is concerned, has arrived at some conclusions of his own, which explains his presence among the ruins at Eski Hissar. Actually, he knows nothing of what is going on except that something is happening. He

has learned a few things and drawn some
conclusions.

The Maharajah, an internationally famous
sportsman, suddenly canceled, without
explanation, an all-important polo game on
the eve of the game, and took a flight for
Istanbul.

The plane exploded in midair over Iran and
the Maharajah is killed. There is some doubt
about how the plane came to explode.

Leon Decebilus, long known to Ballantyne,
arrives suddenly in Istanbul and occupies a
suite opposite that of Villette Mallory.
Heretofore Decebilus has always stayed at
the Parc.

A beat-up old freighter, owned by
Decebilus, has come from Greece in ballast
and is anchored in the Golden Horn; it is
not attempting to load a cargo but is
instead waiting. . . . Why?

The Maharajah, who lost his estates during
the split between Pakistan and India, is
nearing bankruptcy, but before flying for
Istanbul assured his creditors they would
all be paid in full within the month.

It is obvious that the Maharajah expects
to come into money in Istanbul and that
Decebilus is aware of it.

Rumors are coming through on the
grapevine, but nothing tangible. Not until
Rashid spoke of it had Ballantyne heard of
the rug.

Always keenly aware of any opportunity to
turn his hand to making a fast buck,
Ballantyne discovers that Villette is

driving to Eski Hissar each day, and begins
to haunt the place to meet her, and to
discover what she is doing there. It is an
unlikely place for such a girl to be.

Villette has lunched and dined with
Decebilus, and Ballantyne warns her about
him. He asks if she does not think it
strange that he was so quick to arrange a
meeting on arrival. She replies that men
always meet her when she arrives anywhere,
and if they did not she would change her
perfume . . . or her coiffure.

She doubts his warnings until she hears
him mention the dead man on the shore. She
recognizes the description as that of a man
who had come to the hotel and tried to buy
the rug from her . . . a fact she had
mentioned to Decebilus when the man followed
her to her meeting with Decebilus at the
Abdullah.

She had mentioned it . . . and now the man
was dead.

She doubts the connection but she is
uneasy. She agrees to lunch with Ballantyne
but she will also see Yusuf . . . whom
Ballantyne also knows.

Ballantyne observes that Villette is
followed to Istanbul and to the hotel by a
man in a battered Volkswagen whom Ballantyne
later recognizes as having a strong
resemblance to the murdered man.

Following his policy of pushing the
opposition until they make mistakes,
Ballantyne promotes trouble between Mustafa
Bem and the man in the Volkswagen, whom he

correctly supposes is son to the murdered
man.

Villette meets Decebilus for dinner, but
though she's discounted Ballantyne's
suspicions she is wary when the subject of
the rug arises and Decebilus suggests that
to avoid future trouble she dispose of it.
In fact, he would buy it himself.

When she refuses, he drops the matter.
Later, speaking as a "friend," he warns her.

Ballantyne, meanwhile, has been visited by
Hamid, the police officer. It turns into a
fencing match. Hamid likes Ballantyne but
does not altogether trust him. Hamid also
has received the rumors Ballantyne has been
getting. He is alert to something going on.

Villette returns to find her suite
ransacked.

Hamid then appears to ask about the death
of the Maharajah. They are cooperating with
the Iranian authorities in the
investigation. Hamid inquires about her
association with Decebilus.

She meets Ballantyne at the Pandeli and
she is followed to that place. Evading their
pursuers they go to Yusuf's shop and find
him murdered, the shop a shambles.

As Ballantyne and Villette are about to
leave the shop, Mustafa Bem and Barbaro
appear. Ballantyne keeps them occupied while
Villette escapes with the rug, which the
searchers had failed to find.

Thoroughly frightened, she narrowly eludes
a man who grabs at her, escapes down an
alley, and hiding in a doorway, sees three

men consult, then dash off in separate
directions.

She is stalked along the Step Street, and
people seem to be watching her or pursuing
her everywhere. At last, frantic with fear,
she runs into the Tin Village. Around her
are people who look at her with utterly
emotionless eyes, strange faces, savage
faces, empty faces. At last she falls, and
is helped up . . . by Ballantyne.

They are stalked through the cisterns,
through the Sunken Palace, and then by a
secret way under the Seraglio Palace itself.
Coming up inside, they manage to join a
party of tourists and file out with them.
They get to Ballantyne's car and escape into
the country, driving to Eski Hissar.

From a point near Hannibal's tomb they
stop, take the rug, and open it for study.
It is late afternoon.

The secret of Hannibal's treasure is woven
into the rug. Ballantyne studies the
pattern, explains something of the symbols,
many of them very ancient, as he goes along.
Yet he cannot solve the problem. Somewhere
here there is a key.

Villette recalls that Yusuf's hand lay on
the rug, which he had simply spread on the
floor amongst many others instead of hiding
it, as he lay dying. Was it accident that
his hand lay at a certain position? Or had
he, in dying, tried to tell them something?

His hand had lain upon the lamp hanging in
the prayer arch of the rug.

Carefully, they examine it. The treasure,

they know, is the treasure of Hannibal, and
that it is somehow connected with his tomb
at Eski Hissar. . . .

And then they see. The design woven into
the rug, the design of the lamp, is also the
key to the treasure, for it is the design
of the ruined walls that lay scattered below
them!

And plainly indicated is the place of the
treasure.

Excited by their discovery, they start
running down the slope toward the ruins.

Rashid is gathering his goats, but he
ignores them. They call to him, but he walks
on, never turning his head.

Warned by the boy's actions, they stop. It
is too late.

Having lost them in town, Decebilus and
his men returned to where the old weaver had
tried to contact her. They step from the
ruins, and they have guns.

Ballantyne tries to bargain. Let them go
and they will give up the rug. Decebilus is
too shrewd. He knows the rug holds the
secret, woven into it long ago, and if he
is willing to forfeit the rug, Ballantyne
must have solved the mystery of the weaving.

Decebilus has no intention of struggling
to solve a problem when a man who has the
solution is in his hands. He has a counter
offer: their lives for the treasure. Suppose
they found it, he argues. What could they
possibly do with it? How would they move it?
How could they dispose of it without

exciting the cupidity of those with whom
they dealt or corrupt officials?

Gold is very heavy, and people are
curious. Decebilus offers here some comments
on treasure-finding that are rarely
considered. Most people at one time or
another have thought of finding a treasure,
yet few of them have gone beyond that to
decide what they would do if they found it.

The government of most countries would
take half; some countries would confiscate
it all. They would have to transfer a large
amount of gold and gems into Istanbul, and
like any large city, it is filled with
thieves. What then?

On the other hand, Decebilus explains, he
is equipped to cope with the problem. He has
underworld means of disposing of the loot;
he has the force necessary to guard and
protect it; he can use methods they as
reasonably legitimate people dare not use.
He has a ship and a crew prepared to handle
it. He has a truck nearby to take it to the
loading dock in a fishing village, and he
has means of persuading the curious to be
less so.

Ballantyne, realizing that Villette is in
worse danger than he himself, tells them
where to dig. They dig, uncover a stone
slab, remove it, enter an underground
chamber.

It is an ancient temple, prepared for
worship. A Phoenician god faces them from a
dais. In niches in the wall are four
slightly smaller replicas. In the center of

the room there are twelve large amphorae
lying piled in a bunch.

Mustafa Bem calls to Decebilus.

They go to the opening and look. It is not
yet dark, although the sun is down. Standing
on the slope are forty or fifty people. They
are the villagers, the friends of Rashid,
and they stand very silently, watching.

Decebilus is furious. He demands of
Ballantyne who they are, and Ballantyne can
only guess. "They are my friends," he said,
"and they want no trouble, but they are
prepared for it."

It is a Mexican standoff, and Decebilus
knows it. If he starts shooting he will kill
some of them, but he will also raise such a
turmoil that troops will be rushing down
from Istanbul, his ship stopped, the
treasure confiscated.

He bargains. Ballantyne will let him take
half. They argue. Finally to save the
villagers from a fight that is not their
own, he agrees to let Decebilus go with
eight of the amphorae, if he goes at once.

Decebilus departs and Rashid comes.

Villette comments that they have some of
it, anyway, but Ballantyne replies that they
actually have it all!

THE TREASURE:

After his defeat by the Romans, while they
sought him everywhere, Hannibal escaped to
the island of Crete. He brought with him

some large jars that were heavy and were kept sealed and guarded. These were believed to contain his treasure.

When the Romans discovered his hiding place he slipped away from Crete to the Gulf of Nicomedia, where he lived in a fishing village. Discovered again by the Romans in 183 B.C., he killed himself rather than face capture, and his treasure was never found.

For our story purposes, the treasure could have always been kept inside some hollow Phoenician idols (also the gods of Hannibal's Carthage) outside his door.

A weaver of rugs, following a legend handed down in his family for generations, found the treasure room at Eski Hissar, but took only a few pieces away with him.

Arrested in trying to sell a gem, he was imprisoned and after a while, because he was a weaver, was put to work. He refused to tell the whole story, claiming he had found only a few things buried in a ruin miles from Istanbul. After a while, he was believed, but he was kept busy weaving rugs for the Ottoman Turks. Into one of the rugs he wove the secret of the treasure, and into four other rugs he wove a key that only his own family would understand.

He died without knowing his son had died before him, and his daughter had been sold into slavery in India. A beautiful girl, she was taken into the harem of one of the Maharajah's family. With her she took the secret of the rug and a bracelet that had once belonged to Hannibal.

The Maharajah of Kasur's great-grandfather had finally found what the rug was, but not until Jay had they found anyone who could read the secret, and he read it too late.

COMMENTS: I believe that, had Louis continued on with this novel, he would have improved it considerably. The treatment you have just read seems to have been a fairly "quick and dirty" attempt to make a sale to a movie studio. If Dad had pressed on with this project, there would have been more development of the backstory between Decebilus and Ballantyne, and certainly some sort of mano a mano final fight between them. The arrival of the villagers at the finale feels like a cop-out intended to wrap up the treatment so he could get on to the next project. It is not the sort of thing that Louis ultimately would have gone on to actually write in a book.

Given that Decebilus discusses the difficulty of unloading a treasure, I suspect that Louis would have realized that Jay, being a fairly wise man, had worked out how to transport and dispose of whatever he finally discovered. Perhaps Jay had even been intending to use Decebilus in this capacity but Decebilus double-crossed him by planting the bomb in his plane once he decided (erroneously!) all he had to do was grab the rug from Villette. It is also clear that, unless Louis was planning to rewrite the beginning yet again, Villette knows more than she is letting on. The story starts with her spending part of several days at Eski Hissar. That indicates she already has a general sense of where the treasure is buried.

Louis left behind notes that suggest part of the secret is

how the ruins look as the light changes toward the end of the day. It's not just that the pattern of walls is woven into the rug; the shadows they cast are also a part of the weaving. He also included a good deal of information on rug-weavers' knots, so much that I began to think that the ultimate trick in a story like this would be to have a certain thread that could be picked out of the rug and then pulled. This would unravel the section around the rug's archway lamp, leaving behind a different design ... the one that showed the location of the treasure. I became so enamored with this idea that I added the line where the weaver mentions his family's secret knot. I may not be done with this story. We'll have to see.

At another point in his notes, Louis seemed to consider the idea that two different groups might be searching for the treasure, one a bunch of crooks, the other with political motives. ... I believe this idea came before he conceived of the Decebilus character. The "political" group might have created a way of using the treasure for a higher purpose, as well as a method of unloading all that precious metal in a world that was still on the gold-exchange standard.

As was his way, Louis included a pep talk for himself in his notes:

Make this a suspense story in line of The Maltese Falcon, but make it deeper, better, a fine love story, a story of background and suspense, a sexy story.

Make the love affair gay, lighthearted, two people at an outpost of the world, both skating on thin ice.

Make this a definitely superlative book, something completely out of the ordinary. Discuss books, politics,

```
painting, jewels, beliefs, folklore,
magic, etc.
    Make this something really fine. With
a great suspense yarn and a beautiful
love story. Make the writing something
very special.
```

A final comment on the one thing about this story that I have never been able to figure out. It is this piece of the opening line:

```
He lay on his face in the wet sand, a
tall old man in shabby clothes, and
looking down at the body, Ballantyne
knew that it had begun again but this
time he did not know why.
```

"... *knew that it had begun again* ..." It's a great opening and Louis definitely had something particular in mind. Initially, I thought "again" referred to the bombing of Jay's plane—chronologically, that is the first death related to the plot—but now I'm not so sure. At a guess, taking other drafts and notes into consideration, "again" may imply Ballantyne suspects that those who got too close to the treasure were being bumped off by someone guarding it ... maybe an individual, maybe a secret group, who didn't even really know what they were guarding. Perhaps Dad realized later on that having the hero know too much in the beginning of the story wasn't going to work all that well and started to pull back from that concept, or at least from Ballantyne's knowledge of an ongoing plot or series of murders.

LOUIS RIEL

The First Three Chapters of a Historical Novel

CHAPTER 1

He stood upon the street in St. Paul and
watched the people go by. Here he was a
stranger, a lonely man with an aching in his
heart that he did not understand. He wanted
the nearness of people, but something within
held aloof, feeling the difference within
himself.

This was Minnesota, and off to the north
lay his own land. Yet even here he glimpsed
the blanket-coats of the métis, the half-
breeds from the northern prairies and
rivers, his own people.

For years they had been coming south to
St. Paul or St. Cloud for their trading.
This was the United States, and the cities
of Canada lay far to the east over some
rough country that made crossing a struggle.
It was so much easier just to come south, to
travel with the Red River cart caravans or
to take the steamboat on the Red.

People brushed by him. He shifted his

valise to the other hand and walked up
to the door of the Merchants Hotel. He
opened the door, catching the old familiar
smell of the place: the stale cigar smoke,
the warm, close air of the lobby.

This, at least, remained the same. The
worn leather settees, the brass cuspidors,
the buffalo head upon the wall. As a child
he had once come to this place. To a boy
from the vast plains this seemed a
mysterious and somehow magical place.

He paused inside the door, letting his
eyes grow accustomed to the change of light.

"Louis? Is it you? Mon dieu, but how long
it has been?" It was Ambroise Lepine, a
welcome face in a city of strangers.

"Ten years."

"Well, you have your father's look. More
handsome, I think, and broader in the
shoulder. He was a man, your father."

They sat down at a table and stared at
each other, amused and curious, Lepine the
woodsman and Riel the scholar. Lepine wore a
coat made from a Hudson Bay blanket, typical
of the country, Riel a plain, black, neatly
cut suit.

"You are not a priest, then?" Lepine said.
"Not a priest after ten years of study?"

"I am a religious man, Ambroise, but
toward the last I believe the good fathers
were worried. I doubt if it is in me to
become a priest."

"Was it money? We could have found it. For
a son of your father, nothing would be too
much."

"My mother needs me. You know that better than I, for you have been here. I have done little for her, and there are the girls, my sisters. I worked for a lawyer in Montreal but the pay was very poor. Besides . . ."

"Besides what?"

Riel was embarrassed. "I was homesick."

Lepine nodded. "I know. A man cannot go far wrong when he is close to the trees, the rivers, and the plains. After all, Louis, we are a part Indian, you and I."

Riel's smile was twisted. "I have had cause to remember that, Ambroise."

Lepine put down his pipe and reached for his glass. "It is better that you have come back, Louis, and better that you are not a priest. We need you."

"Is Mother well? She never writes of herself."

"She is well, I think." Lepine shook his head in awe. "She is a woman, your mother. But she does need you; it has not been easy for your mother, and now with the surveyors--"

"Surveyors?"

"Have you heard nothing? Men have come from Ontario who survey right across our lines. They say we own nothing, that the whole land must be resurveyed and reallotted.

"They say this to us! Three, four generations we have lived on this land. We have built our homes, cut hay in our meadows, fished in the streams, and trapped for fur. Old men have died here and young men have had sons.

"I reached out and touched a tree and it is mine, it has grown with me, as has the grass beneath our feet. I drink from a cold stream, smell the pines and the grass warmed by the summer sun. I turn the sod and see the corn grow where the seeds fell. . . . And now they say the land is not ours, that we are only métis, we are nobody."

"You have spoken to the Company?"

"The Company is no more. The Company is selling out, it is leaving us. The Hudson Bay Company was our father and our mother and now it goes from us."

"But who is to govern? The Company administered the land. It has been the government. What will be done?"

"Who knows?" Lepine spread his hands helplessly. "Some say the Queen does not want Prince Rupert's Land, that Canada does not want it, but Louis . . . those men from Ontario . . . I think they want it. I think they mean to have it, and that is why we need you."

"Me?"

Lepine looked down at his huge hands. "I can lift anything, Louis, anything I can take hold of, but words do not come to me. You are your father's son, and when in the old times there was trouble, we went to your father, the miller. It was he who led our fight for free trade. It was he who went to Ottawa to speak for us. He was a man of words, as you are."

"You have spoken to the governor?"

"Mactavish is an old man, and he is ill. He is tired now, and soon will leave us. I do not believe he likes what is happening, for he has always been a just man. A stern man, but just."

Louis Riel was silent. The love of his people for the land was no small thing. They had not come to get rich and get out. They knew nothing of politics or land speculation, for they were a people of the earth, of the forest, the lake, and the stream. They walked where the grizzly walked, and hunted the elk for meat on its own pastures. They knew the whistle of the marmot and where the beaver built his dams.

When the Company first sent its men west to trade with the Indians, many of them, French, English, and Scottish, married with the Indian girls, and from them came a different people, a fine, strong people. They were woodsmen and canoemen by birth, natural horsemen, confident hunters.

Louis Riel was himself one-eighth Indian; the rest was French, Irish, and Scandinavian. Yet he was considered a métis, a half-breed. He had borne the designation with pride, never really thinking of what it meant to some until . . .

"We must talk of this, Ambroise. I have been gone too long and have missed much. In Montreal there are rumors, sometimes, but to Montreal this is a far and savage land. They know nothing of us, and care less."

"They know of us in Ontario. They hunger

for our land." Lepine got to his feet. "I have much to do, Louis. You are going home now?"

"I have no money, Ambroise, and cannot go empty-handed. To have an education is one thing, to have money, another. In Montreal I could save little, then like a fool I stayed overlong with friends in Chicago. I was like a child. My money just seemed to melt away, while I dined and talked with friends."

Lepine chuckled. "It is the way of money. They make the coins round so they can roll. But when did a métis save money?"

"I kept hoping a way would open for me, Ambroise. Out here there is little need for educated men."

"Bah! You can do anything, Louis! At St. Boniface you were the brightest of the lot."

"I had too many questions, Ambroise. There were books to read, and I read them, but it worried the fathers that what I saw in the books was not always what they saw, so I did not become a priest; but what is a man to become who studies to become a priest and then is not a priest?"

Lepine chuckled. "He becomes a politician, Louis. Come home; help us. You know them, these men of the cities. You know their minds."

The big man scowled, but it was worry, not anger. "Louis, men come among us and say disturbing things. You will meet them in Pembina, when you go north. One of them is an American who has no legs."

"No legs?"

"From the waist up, he is magnificent. He has a special saddle, this one, and you should see him ride. It is a miracle that he rides, but he does."

"What about him?"

"He wishes to see Rupert's Land a part of the United States. He wishes us to sign a paper to the United States asking them to govern us."

"We are Canadians," Riel objected. "We are not Americans."

"Agreed. But do we not have more in common with the men of Dakota and Minnesota than with Ottawa? When we ride north from here, where is the line between us? The color of the grass does not change, nor does the air have a different smell, or the wind blow in a way other than it does here. God made no line upon the earth; it exists only in the mind."

"We are British subjects," Riel objected. "We should remain so."

Lepine nodded unhappily. "So I believe. I believe it in my belly, but I have no words to answer the men from Pembina. They say the Queen does not know we are here, and they say the men in Ottawa wish to please the voters in Ontario, so they will give our lands to them, and who are we to object? They say Ottawa will not listen."

"They will listen, Ambroise. We must send somebody to talk to them."

Riel was silent, thinking of what had been said. "You spoke of men who would resurvey the land? Who are they?"

"They come from Ontario, most of them. They are Protestants."

"There are many Protestants, Ambroise. The Company was Protestant, and we got along with the Company."

"I do not believe the Company had any religion but fur. They treated us fairly . . . most of the time." Lepine grinned cheerfully. "And we treated them fairly . . . enough of the time. These men are not the same."

"They have a leader?"

"A man named Schultz. He is a Swiss, I believe. A very big man, very strong . . . but not so strong as me, I think." Lepine hesitated, no longer joking. "There is MacDougall who says he will be a king out here. And there is Dennis."

"MacDougall I know of. There are others?"

"There is Scott . . . Thomas Scott. He is a loudmouth and a troublemaker. He gets along with no one, but he hates Catholics, Indians, and métis. He says we are dogs."

"He said that to _you_?"

"Not to me, nor does he say it where I am. If he did I would squeeze him . . . so," and he closed his huge fist.

When Lepine had gone, Louis Riel stayed at the table. Only a few men remained in the lobby. Two were talking in a desultory fashion of the wheat crop, and across the room a big man was telling of a cattle drive he expected to meet in Rapid City.

"Longhorns," he was saying. "They're big

and they're mean, but they could walk across
the world. These come from Texas. Last year,
in '68, nearly three hundred thousand head
came over the trail from Texas to Kansas!"

Riel was scarcely listening, for his
thoughts had gone back to his last meeting
with his father, who had been returning from
a business trip as Louis left for school in
the East. They met on the trail, and none of
the words they had to say to each other had
anything to do with what they were thinking.

The bond between them had been strong, but
unspoken. Why had he not told his father he
loved him? Why had he never said it aloud?
Yet his father had not said the words to
him, either.

How could he guess the father he loved
would die while he was away at school?

Yet when the news came it was his mother
of whom he thought. She had always been
strong, original, and with a great
appreciation of the amusing. Never while
her husband was alive had she had to exert
her strength or her will, for Louis Riel the
elder had been a forceful man, although
quiet, lifting his voice rarely, his hand
never. He had given off a feeling of
strength, of quiet assurance, and his mother
had drawn upon that, and been all the more
warm and loving because of it, there being
no need to expend elsewhere the strength she
herself possessed.

His was a strong heritage. Was he worthy
of it? Was he half the man his father was?

Or a quarter the person his mother was known to be?

The Merchants Hotel was old, born with almost the first breath of St. Paul, and over the years it had become a hodgepodge of logs, lumber, bricks, and stone with all the various repairs and additions. During the late summer and fall rooms were scarce, but Louis Riel went to the desk and asked for John Dodge, the clerk.

"I would like a room," he said, "and I should like to stay for a while."

Dodge hesitated, puzzled by the half-familiar features. "Have we met before, Mr. . . . . ?"

"Riel . . . Louis Riel."

"Of course. I knew your father. Knew him well." He glanced over the register. "Yes, yes. I think we can find something for you."

"Thank you, sir. I will be also looking for employment. If you hear of anything I would appreciate it."

"Of course. Yes, I have a room for you, and Mr. Riel? Do make yourself at home. Your father was very helpful on many occasions and your people have been coming here for years."

"Thank you."

He went up the stairs to the room. A bed, a dresser, a white bowl, and a pitcher filled with water. Two towels, a washcloth, and a bath at the end of the hall.

He put his valise on the bed and removed his coat, hanging it over the back of a chair. When he turned about he found himself

looking into the mirror above the dresser,
at a reflection which regarded him
seriously.

Wavy hair, a high forehead . . . He had
been called handsome, which he was not. Five
feet ten inches with shoulders so broad that
he appeared shorter. He was physically
powerful without wanting or trying to be.
He had always been strong, yet curiously, he
had never been healthy.

He shrugged. A man could not dwell on such
things, but must get along with what was to
be done.

In this almost bilingual town--for so it
was at the moment--there should be a job for
him. At this season of the year the influx
of French-speaking trappers and traders was
great. Each year the great caravans of Red
River carts came down from the north, and
after unloading their freight, prepared to
load up again for the trip back.

Many Indians came as well, but he spoke
several dialects so they would present no
problem.

He stared at his reflection. At St.
Boniface he had been considered a brilliant
scholar, and so attracted the attention of
Archbishop Taché. Because of him he won his
chance to attend school in Montreal.

There he had done well despite the greater
competition, first in his class many times,
often second or third, rarely fourth.

What had gone wrong? At what point had he
lost his desire to become a priest? Or had
he ever desired it? Was it not simply that

it offered the only road he knew to an education?

Reluctantly, he admitted to himself that he had never considered himself priestly material. There was too much in him that was impatient, restless, demanding.

Was he ambitious?

He walked to the window and stared out at the gathering darkness. No, he decided after a few minutes, he was not really ambitious. He did not want wealth. Security for his mother and sisters he did want, and his own lot sufficient enough that he was himself not a case for charity. Searching himself, he found no need for luxury or power.

Yet he did want something.

He had come from a land where all things were useful. A man had an ax to cut wood, a plow to break the soil, a canoe with which to travel lakes and rivers, traps to take fur, a pole or a net for the catching of fish.

Everything must be useful, so it followed that he himself must be so. A priest was a useful man, a necessary man. So, if not a priest, somehow he must become useful and necessary.

He removed his vest and hung it over his coat, then taking off his shoes he lay down on the bed, clasping his hands behind his head. Then he prayed.

Prayer had been his custom since childhood, but he did not always kneel or bow his head. He prayed when he felt like prayer . . . yet that, too, left him uneasy.

Was he actually talking to God through prayer? Or only to his better self? Did it matter?

That was always his problem: He questioned all things, even his own decisions, his own plans.

He did not lack faith. He had never lacked faith. He was, and had always been, a deeply religious man, yet he was a reasoning man as well, with a naturally cautious, judicious, measuring attitude of mind.

His eyes remained closed when his prayer ended, but his thoughts drifted like a soft wind toward his northern land. The land he loved, the land that was home.

His eyes opened to reality. He must find work. He must have something to take home, even if it was ever so little.

Tomorrow he would look. He knew a few people by name, and had friends from the north who had traded here. He would find something.

He sat up on the edge of the bed, suddenly worried. What right had anyone to survey land the métis had held for generations? What was happening up there?

If the Hudson Bay Company was leaving, and no other government stood by to take its place, what would happen to his people?

The métis numbered only a few thousand, and if The Bay no longer controlled Prince Rupert's Land, which was virtually all that lay between Hudson Bay and Lake Superior west to British Columbia, then hordes of people from the east or from the United

States could rush in and deluge his own people, taking their land, their privileges, their all.

Lepine, he realized, had been more than merely worried. The big man had been frightened.

CHAPTER 2

It was wet and cold in the morning streets. A late storm had blown down from the north, pouring rain upon the town, but he turned up his coat collar and walked along, unminding of the rain. He walked slowly down to the river and looked at the swollen waters.

This was the Mississippi, flowing away from here to the south, toward a sunny land he would never know, for it was not his river. His river was the Red River of the north, flowing out of the United States into Canada, flowing through one of the most fertile valleys on earth.

When he returned home it would be along that river by steamboat, for the Red River carts would soon be a thing of the past. He remembered those great caravans and the wild, screeching, caterwauling sounds that had come from those wooden, ungreased axles. . . . One of the caravans had numbered as many as five hundred carts, and the sound of them could be heard for miles.

He must go home. He must hear the troubles

of his people, and if necessary he must
speak for them. As his father had been
before him, he would be their voice.

First . . . a job.

When he found one it was in a store
selling dry goods and hardware, a store to
which the métis came, and to which more of
them came when they discovered he was
working there. They brought not only their
trade but gossip as well, and he needed the
one as much as the other.

Again, several times in fact, he heard
the story of the surveyors, and always they
spoke of Schultz . . . John Christian
Schultz. Not a surveyor, but one who
cooperated with them, possibly even invited
them to make their surveys.

He was a doctor, a storekeeper, and a
Swiss. He detested Indians, Catholics, and
the métis. "Bastards," he supposedly called
them, "the misbegotten sons of riffraff and
savages."

Whether Schultz actually said such a thing
Riel did not know, but it was widely quoted
and widely believed.

He had been behind the counter but three
days when a lean, dark man came in and stood
about, waiting until Riel was alone. "You
are Louis Riel?"

"I am."

The man glanced quickly right and left.
"Come across a man from up your way. He was
buyin' rifles."

"It is a country where all men are
hunters," Riel replied mildly.

"This man wanted a hundred rifles for delivery at Pembina. He was gettin' them through some of them whiskey-peddlers at Fort Whoop-Up. He said somethin' about showin' a bunch of breeds who was boss."

"Why do you tell me?"

"Heard you was a breed, although you surely don't look it. I'm half-Sioux myself, an' just figured you should know."

"Thank you," Riel said, and the man left.

One hundred rifles . . . It was a lot, yet the métis could muster several thousand if need be. If there was someone to call them out and to direct their actions.

There had always been rough characters along the border, men who would lend themselves to any action if the price was right or if there was a chance of loot. The Fenians, too, had been talking of invading Canada again. They were an Irish organization inspired by hatred of all that was British.

Of course, they had been talking for years, threatening and blowing off steam, yet there were hotheads among them prepared for any desperate action, and if there was an invasion there would be violence . . . and his mother and sisters were there.

The thought disturbed him. What if some such an attempt were made? Who was there to stop it? If the Bay Company was stepping down, who would act? Who could act?

There was no one.

The métis were men accustomed to the quick, iron discipline of the buffalo hunt

and the fur brigade. Such groups could move
like a well-oiled machine, but so far as he
knew they had no leader, nor any plan of
action.

Such lawlessness as was known in the
mining and cattle towns of the American West
had never existed in Prince Rupert's Land
because of the Hudson Bay Company. From the
beginning The Bay had complete authority,
and it was there first, firmly established
and in command before there was any
possibility of others coming into the
country.

Their authority had been complete, and
from their decision there was no appeal.
Without The Bay no supplies were to be had,
no ammunition, food, or liquor available.
Access to these things depended on
conformity to a pattern of behavior that
suited the Bay officials. They also offered
the only market for furs west of Montreal.

Any westward movement had been held in
check by that desolate wilderness that lay
between Hudson's Bay on the north and the
Great Lakes on the south, and particularly
that area north of Lake Superior.

If one wished to migrate westward it was
far easier to go to America, as many were
doing. The Ohio, the Missouri, and the
Platte offered easy access to the heart of
the plains country and the mountains that
lay beyond.

There was talk of a railroad that would
join British Columbia to eastern Canada, but
thus far it was no more than talk, and most

of those who knew the land ridiculed the
idea. The easiest way to go west, or even to
Rupert's Land, was to take the Grand Trunk
Railway from Toronto to Detroit, then
westward to Chicago and La Crosse,
Wisconsin. From there it was a short ride by
steamer to St. Paul.

He shook his head irritably. It was
madness. All men needed some restraint, for
few could restrain themselves. If there was
no government there would be anarchy, and he
was a man who believed in order.

If Rupert's Land was abandoned by the Bay
Company and no other government existed,
settlers might rush in, and he could see
fighting and confusion, for none of the
inhabitants of Rupert's Land would
relinquish their lands without a fight. Yet
if the area was to become a part of Canada,
it should be as a province, with its own
government and proper representation at
Ottawa.

Several days passed. He was paid, and
carefully put aside all but what was needed
for the bare necessities. He was doing well
at his job. His quiet dignity and reserve
were perfectly suited to selling to the
métis, Indians, or settlers. They came
seldom to town, but one and all they loved
shopping, fingering the materials, wandering
through the stores and trading posts to see
what was available.

He knew his people, and he let them look,
offering suggestions only when asked or when

there seemed some hesitation; at other times
he simply listened to them talk.

Between the store, the hotel, and a
boardinghouse where he ate most of his
meals, he was gradually coming to understand
what had happened in his homeland, and what
seemed about to happen.

The fur trade was no longer as bountiful
as it had been, and although there were
buffalo, even they seemed to be thinning
out. The great profits the Hudson Bay
Company had once known no longer existed,
and the problems were increasing. The Bay,
wisely, was stepping out to avoid an
impossible situation.

Lepine came around to the hotel when
several weeks had gone by. The big leather
chair creaked when he dropped into it.
"Louis? When do you come home?"

"Soon, Ambroise." Riel leaned his forearms
on the table. "Have you heard any talk of
rifles? A lot of rifles?"

The big man looked up. "I have heard such
talk."

"Who would want so many rifles? Who do
they plan to shoot?"

Lepine leaned forward. "Look, my friend,
you must have forgotten your homeland.
Think, man, is it not a prize worth taking?
Do you think those who talk of confederation
are thinking of anything but our land?

"Who cares about us? We have no voice in
Ottawa! We are scattered people on a far
frontier, and those who would take our land

from us have voices to speak for them. I
think you had better come home, Louis, and
see what can be done."

"Do you think there will be fighting?"

"Louis, they have sent surveyors, and we
have stopped the surveyors. I do not think
they intend to be interfered with again."

"I want no fighting."

"There need be none. But we must have
someone to speak for us. There is enough
land for all, but we wish to keep that land
we have. . . . Let them take other land.

"However, there are some who threaten
violence. That Orangeman named Thomas Scott
is a troublemaker. He had trouble when he
worked for Snow on the road they are
building, and he threatened Snow. He is
forever starting fights and threatening to
kill people."

"He is a leader?"

"Only of a few like himself. He has no
intelligence. He is a child. He worries me
because he could start trouble. He could
begin trouble where there need be none.

"Then there is Schultz. Schultz uses
Scott, and Scott follows him as much as he
will anyone, but Schultz is no fool. He is
very intelligent, but I think he has no
scruples. . . . I think he would stop at
nothing, but that is only my idea."

Riel was silent and worried. If there was
trouble--and certainly all the ingredients
were there--his mother and the girls might
suffer. Also, his people were regarded by
many Easterners as people of no account.

They had had a great hand in building the
country, in gathering the furs, laying out
the trails. Without them there would have
been no Hudson Bay Company, and no opening
of the West for many years. But in Canada,
as in the United States, the Indian was
regarded as an obstacle to be brushed aside,
with only a slight claim to the land on
which he lived. He had heard such arguments
in Montreal.

The white man was taking the land, using
it. Just as the Indian had taken the land
from those he found when he came, other
varieties of Indians or aborigines of some
kind. From the beginning of time it had been
so, a weaker people displaced by a stronger.

In England the Celts had pushed back the
Picts, the Angles and the Saxons pushed in
their turn, and then there was the Norman
invasion.

Yet this was not conquest. Rupert's Land--
for so it had been called for many years--
was being sold by the Hudson Bay Company
without any thought for the rights of those
who lived there.

There was no question of fighting for what
was theirs--it was simply being sold out
from under them. Of the open lands, well and
good . . . but what of their homesteads?
Their villages?

"I will want a place to stay, Ambroise. My
mother will be crowded, with the girls
growing up. I would not be a trouble to
them."

"I will speak to Schmidt. I think he has
room enough to spare. He is a good man."

"He is. And I would like that."

He remembered Schmidt. They had been in
school together and he was an easy man to be
around, one who did not intrude upon another
man's thoughts.

Mentally, he counted his money. The sum
was small, but soon he would be paid again,
and he owed very little.

He would go north. He would take the
steamer.

"Tell me about Schultz," he asked.

Lepine hesitated, then said, "You will
have to meet him, to hear him. He used to
operate a newspaper, The Nor'wester. Ran it
four years, from '64 to '68. He's anti-
métis, he's for annexation, and he thinks
we've nothing to say about it. Near as I can
get it, he was born around 1840 and started
to practice medicine when he was twenty, but
he's been so busy with his store and the
newspaper that he's had little time for
medicine except what he prescribes over the
counter.

"He was thrown into jail when he refused
to pay a judgment the court declared against
him, and he simply broke out and stayed out,
defying them to move against him.

"Whatever he says, Louis, do not take him
lightly. He is an ambitious man and he
refuses to be balked by law, custom, or
anything that gets in his way.

"There's a man named Mair who is or was
living in his home who is a very able

journalist. Some of his writings about this part of the country have been getting into the Toronto papers. Of course, he's preaching the Schultz side of things."

Lepine hunched his shoulders and folded his hands before him. "He is one of a small group," he explained, "who wish to set themselves above all others. They would like to bring to us again what our fathers escaped in coming to America. They want a small aristocracy, Schultz and his friends, to be the ruling class. He has frankly said that when Rupert's Land, or Assiniboia as it is called, becomes a part of Canada, he will rule."

"He and MacDougall?" Riel said wryly. "I think we will have too many kings, when all we want are citizens."

He sat silent, brooding. There were too many complications, and he wanted simplicity. He wanted only to be home, to see his mother and sisters, and to find a place for himself.

"It is all right, Ambroise," he said, finally. "I shall come home now."

CHAPTER 3

He stood on the street before the Hayward Hotel in St. Cloud and waited for the stage. A dozen others waited beside him, one of them a fat, amiable man with an elk's tooth on his watch-chain.

"The Northwest'll be part of the United States soon," he was saying, "and that will solve problems for them as well as us."

A lean, sour-faced young man glanced at him. "Where'd you get an idea like that? Do you suppose the British would let all that country slip through their fingers? Besides, you don't know how the people feel about it. It is their decision."

Riel glanced at him. The man was perhaps thirty, or even younger. In the hotel lobby he had seen him reading Vico, a writer on the philosophy of history too little known.

"Sure it's their decision!" The fat man waved a hand. "But how else could they decide? Most of their trade is with us; lots of them have relatives this side of the line. You just wait until the U.S. government moves in--"

"It will not 'move in,' as you say." The young man was impatient. "Do not be misled by such windbags as Alexander Ramsey and his like. Grant will have no part of it, nor will any of the others. There will be a lot of hot air over it, and then nothing will happen."

"Nothing will happen?" The fat man's tone became shrill. "You just bet something will happen! Those French Indians up there will rise up! They'll want to be American citizens! Why shouldn't they?"

"Perhaps they will wish to remain British subjects," the young man said mildly, "and there is no reason why they should not."

"You a Canadian?" the fat man demanded suspiciously.

"I'm a Vermonter," the young man replied, "and in Vermont we tend to look at realities. There will be fears north of the line and a lot of shouting south of the line, but nothing will happen, believe me.

"I have talked to several senators, and they do not want it. We have had our share of trouble with the war, and we want none with England. We would rather have a friend north of the line than a suspicious enemy, and we have enough to do with what we have."

"You just wait and see! I happen to know there's a movement up there to join up with us, and then there's the Fenians--"

"A bunch of hotheads," the Vermonter said.

"They'd better join up," the fat man argued. "I happen to know there's some as expect to get rich up there when Canada takes over the government. The only chance those folks have is to join us.

"This outfit I'm talking about, they figure to grab title to most of that farmland, and if there's trouble they'll have support from the Army--"

"I doubt it," the Vermonter said. "Anyway, that's no hide off my nose as long as we're not involved."

"You'll be involved. You take them métis, they're mighty fine rifle shots, and they can outwalk, outride, and outshoot anybody around. They'll stop anybody tryin' to take over, but then they'll come to us for help. You'll see."

Riel was irritated. They talked like children, at least the fat man did, but he supposed there were many who felt as he did. Yet how right was the Vermonter? He glanced at him thoughtfully, and the Vermonter caught the glance and winked.

"How about you?" he said, with an amused glance at Riel, but speaking to the fat man. "Will you shoulder a rifle and get into a fight for Rupert's Land?"

"Me?" The fat man was startled. "I am not a fighter, I'm a lover. I'm just telling you what will happen. I happen to know--"

"Nothing . . . just nothing at all." The Vermonter's smile took the sting from the words. "You make a mistake, sir. Those who talk of Rupert's Land becoming a part of the United States are indulging in fantasy. No sober, serious student of affairs would have anything to do with it, and most of the citizens are well pleased to have the late war ended and to get down to business again without going off on tangents.

"Grant is a serious man. Despite his cronies, he is no fool. He will lead us into no foreign adventures. You will see that all this talk of annexation is so much wind."

The fat man was not persuaded, but Riel had not expected him to be. Personally, his opinion was that of the Vermonter. If some of the border Americans and promoters wished to indulge in foolish dreaming, that was their affair. He was sure neither the government in Washington nor the rank and file of citizens had any such idea.

He wanted no part in the discussion. He
simply wanted to be seated in the stage and
moving toward home. He waited, shivering a
little in the predawn chill, and when the
stage finally drew up he was the first
aboard, taking a seat on the far side, where
he relaxed and closed his eyes.

Despite the fact that he was at last on
the road home, he was uneasy. What would he
find there? What would he do himself?

When the stage stopped at Sauk Centre he
got down to stretch his legs. He had been
very young when he had come this way
before . . . or had it been exactly this way?
He scowled, trying to remember.

Whether or not he had come exactly this
way, the town had a flour mill, obviously
new. There was a blacksmith shop, a lumber
mill, a store, and a saloon. When they left
Sauk Centre their way took them over rolling
prairies dotted with clumps of oak and
poplar, with occasional lakes or sloughs.

From Lake Osakis they took a road cut
through the Big Woods to Alexander, and
then on to a night station with a log
stockade, called Pomme de Terre.

"Riel?" the stage driver said confidentially. "Better sleep in your clothes. The
bugs will eat you alive."

It was good advice, and he took it, but
even so the bugs did their best, and their
best was far too good.

They crossed the Otter Tail River above
its junction with the Bois de Sioux and

turned west to avoid the alkali and came at
last to the Red River and halted at McCauley-
ville, opposite the fort.

There was no room in Nolan's Hotel, but
Nolan advised he sleep in the hay-barn.
"Damn sight better, anyway," he admitted
frankly. "They're sleepin' four an' five in
a bed, and some of them snore something
fierce. If it were me, I'd take the hay."

Riel shrugged. Why not? He had slept in
hay before this, and enjoyed it.

The restaurant was crowded with a rough,
casual crowd of would-be settlers, farmers,
drifters, and trappers. He found a place at
the table and helped himself to the trays of
food that were continually refilled. The
meat was good, the gravy and potatoes even
better.

"You goin' north?" his neighbor asked.

"Yes . . . to Fort Garry."

"Me, too." The man was a burly, affable
sort, roughly dressed. "I want a piece of
that land. They say the soil is deep, rich,
and black."

"Are you a farmer?" Riel asked politely.

"Hell no! I'll just grab onto a piece of
it an' sell it to the first one offers me a
good price."

"How do you propose to get a piece of
land?"

"How? Just take it. How else?"

"What of the people who live there?"

"You mean the Indians? Hell, they don't
own any land! They just drift across it. A
few years from now they'll all be settled

down to farming. At least, the smart ones
will."

"They probably enjoy the life they are
living," Riel suggested.

"So would I. That there's a good life, but
it isn't practical anymore. Times are
changing, and a man, Indian or white, who
won't change with them just doesn't have a
chance.

"Look, there ain't no way to avoid it.
Folks want land, and one way or another,
they'll get it. Down here in the States, for
example. How's the Army going to stop
people? Tell them they can't go any further?
They'll slip by at nighttime. Shoot them?
The public wouldn't stand for it.

"Sure, the Indians kill a few here, and a
few there, but there's always more a-coming.
Look at the Little Crow massacre. The
Indians rose up when the Army was away
fighting in the Civil War, and they killed
nigh onto a thousand men, women, and
children; now there's twice as many living
there. They just keep comin'. It's land
hunger; folks want homes, a chance to
improve their lot.

"I like the Indian way, myself, but it
surely isn't practical. The Indian lives off
wild game, wild seeds and roots, and in the
same area that it takes to feed a hundred
Indians, you can be plowing and planting and
feed fifty thousand by the white man's way."

"I hear much of that land is lived on by
the métis," Riel offered mildly.

"The half-breeds? It don't make no

difference. From what I hear they are a shiftless lot."

"But good with their rifles. Most of them have been hunting all their lives, and are dead shots."

"Well, that's another kind of thing. Me, I don't want any land that belongs to somebody else. There's plenty that stands empty. But I'm only one, and there's men right in this camp who don't care who they ride over. They aren't much worried about the breeds, because they're scattered and they won't stand together. They've got no leader."

"Americans?"

"Some of them. A good many are likely Canadians. Most of them don't care if the American government takes over or the Canadian, just so they get in, and get in they will.

"But, hell . . . look around you. See the big black-bearded one by the end of the bar? He's a Russky, and that man next to him is a Swede. Used to be a sailor. There must be fifty Scotsmen in this crowd, and twice as many English. . . . You can't just call them one thing or another.

"They tell me that once you've seen that land--"

"I have seen it."

"You have?" The man's interest quickened. "Is it as pretty as they say, or is that all talk?"

"It is one of the most beautiful lands under the sun," Riel said quietly, "and it has everything--deep soil, good grass, timber, lots of running water, lakes, ponds, game . . . especially game—and that's why I think the métis will fight."

"Look," the man protested, "maybe they will, but whether it is the Canadians or the Americans in charge, they stand to lose. The Hudson Bay Company sold out and nobody could care less about the breeds. The Bay owned the land. The breeds just lived on it, so what title can they have?"

"They have lived on the land for generations," Riel replied. "It is theirs by right of possession. In many cases The Bay upheld their right of ownership."

"Maybe . . . maybe." The man shoved back and got up. "Nice talkin' to you. My name's Graham."

"Mine is Riel . . . Louis Riel."

"French?"

Riel smiled gently. "Yes, it is, Mr. Graham. I am a métis."

The _International_ was lying a hundred miles from Fort Abercrombie at Frog Point.

At breakfast Graham came around and straddled the bench beside Riel. "You catchin' the boat? If you are you're welcome to ride with me. I got one of those Red River carts and I'll be pullin' out in maybe thirty minutes."

"Thank you. I will appreciate the ride."

Graham glanced around. "Can't carry more than you and one more. Get your bag and slip away. Meet me down the road maybe two hundred yards into them trees. All right?"

Riel glanced after Graham as he walked away. For a moment, he hesitated, then shrugged. The man seemed honest enough, and probably was. He wanted no trouble, but if attacked, he felt himself strong enough to handle any one man.

Borrowing a cord, Riel hung his bag from his shoulder and walked out from the settlement as though starting to hoof it. If anybody noticed, they apparently did not care, for there was no comment. Soon he was lost in the oaks and giant cottonwoods along the river.

He had walked almost three hundred yards and was prepared to give up when a voice called, "Hold up there!"

Glancing quickly to his left he saw a Red River cart drawn by a single horse waiting in the shadows under a tree, but well hidden by brush.

"Climb in." Graham glanced around apprehensively. "If they guessed I had me a cart hid out there'd be fifty men wantin' a ride to Frog Point," he explained, "and some of them I've known for a while. Seemed to me, you going home and all, that you might need the ride most of all."

"Thank you."

Creaking and groaning, they pulled out into the muddy road.

"You've ridden this way before? I mean in a cart?"

"I came down from Fort Garry in one, a whole caravan of them."

The carts, with two giant wheels, were

made entirely of wood cut from the forest.
No oil could be used on the wooden axles,
for it caught the dust and sooner or later
the axle would "freeze" in place. The sound
of such a cart was like what one imagined a
tortured banshee would sound like.

"Been wet," Graham commented. "You being
from this country know what that means."

Riel nodded. It meant mosquitoes . . . and
mosquitoes in such clouds they had been
known to kill a horse or an ox that was left
tied and unable to escape. Mosquitoes so
thick they drove both men and animals wild
in their efforts to escape.

"Got an oilcloth. If it gets too bad we'll
tie the horse behind and cover cart and all
with the oilcloth. It won't keep 'em out,
but it will help some."

Prairie chickens flew up and away. Within
the first mile after leaving the forest they
started a dozen coveys. The groaning and
screaming from the wheels was such that it
precluded conversation, and Riel was just as
pleased. He wanted time to think, time to
get the feel of the country once again.

They met no one. Once, off in the
distance, they glimpsed a buffalo . . .
perhaps two.

"Don't see many this far east," Graham
commented. "Getting mighty scarce."

They stopped to eat at Georgetown, then
moved on, then camped alongside the road,
but it was just a brief rest, and then they
were moving once more. The steamboat would

not remain long, nor would there be another
for some time.

Graham seemed tireless. Twice, for brief
periods he handed the reins to Riel and
dozed, but the horse needed little guidance,
and just a slap of the reins every now and
then to keep him moving. The trail wound in
and out of the brush, allowing glimpses of
the river from time to time through the
willow, chokecherry, and cottonwood that
lined the stream.

Finally, they caught a glimpse of white
through the green. It was the steamboat. The
International was tied to the bank, moored
to a couple of large trees, and already
crowded with passengers.

To Riel's surprise, Lepine was one of
them. The big man moved to him at once. "Got
to talk to you," he said, low-voiced.
"Trouble's brewing."

They stood together in the stern near the
huge paddle-wheel.

"What is it, Ambroise?"

"Some of this crowd are landing at
Pembina. Listen to them when you get a
chance. They're all going north after
land . . . our land."

The International backed slowly out of her
berth along the bank and swung into the
current. The big stern-wheel reversed itself
and slowly the steamboat began to edge
upriver, gaining speed.

One hundred and thirty feet long, the
International drew but two feet of water.

Already a veteran of seven or eight years upon the river, she showed the harshness of hot summers and the bitter cold of winter when she lay idle.

The green banks slipped away behind them, now and then permitting a glimpse of the prairie beyond. There were many twists and turns in the river, so actual progress in miles amounted to very little.

Riel walked aft and stood watching the great wheel turning, crystal drops falling back into the water. For two hundred years the Hudson Bay Company, under a charter granted in 1670 to Prince Rupert and his associates, had ruled the vast territory known as Rupert's Land which lay east of the Rockies to the shores of Hudson Bay.

Not that their control had been unlimited, for in 1783 a group of "free-traders" had combined to form the North West Fur Company, and there had followed for nearly forty years a bloody rivalry.

In 1812 the Earl of Selkirk planted a colony upon the Red River, a colony of Highlanders displaced from their own land in Scotland. They were viciously attacked, and many, including the governor of the Hudson Bay Company, were shot down.

Later, the earl imported portions of two bodies of foreign troops, marched them west, and took possession of Fort Douglas. They in turn were attacked, and peace was not finally resolved until the two companies merged to leave only the Hudson Bay Company in the field.

The inhabitants of what was called Assiniboia were not all métis. Many were retired Hudson Bay Company factors and servants, others their descendants, often of mixed blood. Aside from occasional disputes over religious matters the colony was singularly peaceful, considering the time and the place. Now all that was to change, and Louis Riel paced the deck, hands clasped behind his back, considering what might be done.

Graham found him on the top deck. "Looking for you," he said mildly. "You'd better go ashore at Pembina. That's my advice for whatever it's worth. You listen a mite. There's talk to be heard there that'll teach you more about your country than weeks of living in it."

"Where do you stand, Mr. Graham?"

For a moment, he seemed to be thinking about it. Then he said, "I'm not a well-off man, Riel, not at all well-off. I'm an American, but there's little choice, seems to me, whichever side of the border a man decides on.

"I'm looking for land, and I'll be looking there, I imagine." He paused a moment. "But I'll look for unsettled land, and that's more than most of them expect to do."

COMMENTS: Louis Riel went on to lead two resistance movements in Canada, seeking to preserve the rights of the métis people. He was elected three times to the Canadian House of Commons, though he was never able to attend due to being forced to live in exile in the United States. One of the most controversial figures in Canadian history, he was executed by the Canadian government for high treason in 1885.

Growing up in North Dakota with a father who had spent a good deal of his life in Canada, Louis L'Amour was raised on stories of Louis Riel, debates on his sanity, and discussions of French versus British and Catholic versus Protestant Canadian identities.

The idea for this book was suggested to Louis by Governor William L. Guy of North Dakota in 1972, and fairly quickly a motion-picture production company jumped on board, taking an option on Louis's yet-to-be-written novel. Dad went and did something like this every once in a while, and it nearly always got him into trouble.

He loved making the deal, or the idea that he *could* make the deal (he'd struggled for so many years), and there was that part of him that always figured it would be easy. And often it was easy, when he'd had time to get the whole story settled enough so he could write with a minimum of conscious thought. In this case, he seems to have optimistically assumed that he could research, plan, and write this book just about as fast as he might have written a story he'd had in mind for years. The further he got into the research, the more interesting yet more demanding the story became, and the more he realized that the schedule was simply not going to work. Almost as soon as he started writing he was offering to return the option money. In a letter to his movie agent he wrote:

I have to take my time on these
projects. I have worked very hard and
given a lot of time to this one and look

forward to completing it, but I simply
can't work with demands being made on me
for pages or such things. I am sorry. I
would like to have completed it in the
time specified, but new materials kept
developing and new aspects of the story
that deserve consideration.

The story is a very involved one, with
many political ramifications and many
characters. I have turned up a manuscript written by one of the major
participants, and some letters, that
have been permitted to my view in
confidence by a Canadian reader. It has
made it necessary for me to backtrack
and revise some of what I have written,
and make it essential for me to rewrite
several portions of what I have done.
There is no doubt as to their historical
accuracy and they permit a greater
understanding of the material.

However, that is beside the case. This
is a book that in many ways resembles a
jigsaw puzzle with bits and pieces that
need to be fitted with care. It is not a
simple, straight-line story, and cannot
be written as such. It is utterly
fascinating material and the characters
are remarkable, and of course, the
events led at least to the formation of
the province of Manitoba, and to other
wider effects.

If I am wanted at all it is because I
approach my work with a feeling for
history and a sense of its overall

meaning. I would be contemptuous of my
readers and of the history of Canada if
I were to hurry this through.

I insist on returning the complete
$5,000 myself. I want no strings
attached.

By "the complete $5,000" he means that he did not ex-
pect his agent, Mauri Grashin, to return his 10 percent of
the fee. Louis would pay it all back himself.

Some unknown element, however, seems to have kept this
deal puttering along, because these comments start showing
up in Louis's journal two months later:

October 11 1973--I am working on LOUIS
RIEL, and occasionally the first
Sackett, to take place in Shakespeare's
time. The Riel book is an irritation. I
want very much to do it, but Kathy
[Kathy L'Amour, Louis's wife and my
mother] is right and I should never take
on such jobs. I agreed to do this, and I
prefer to write on what excites me at
the moment. This does not . . . at the
moment.

November 7 1973--Working on the Riel
book; I want to write it, but not now
and because of the commitment, I must. I
like to write what takes my mind at the
moment, and to write swiftly upon what
excites me.

On the third of December he finally returned the option
money, writing:

> I want to write the book but to be
> free of deadlines. Kathy happy, and I
> also.

Louis eventually did end up using Riel in a more limited
way in his novel *Lonely on the Mountain*.
Here are a few more notes:

> Open with action.
> RIEL - suffered from the handicap of
> being a fair man. His loyalty to the
> Queen and to his people did not waver.
> He wished to do the best for the latter
> without in any way failing in loyalty to
> the Queen.
> Had he been a fanatic he would have
> had no decision to make. Rebellion would
> have been his course; he could have been
> more dynamic, he could have given
> unlimited scope to his speaking, he
> could have and would have resisted the
> Canadian Army, and might have stopped
> their advance.
> His fault lay, if fault it is, in
> being a reasonable man. He hesitated at
> points where a fanatic would not. Yet,
> considering the situation, his end was
> inevitable.
> His vision of lost opportunities
> brought him back to seek a victory when
> the time was past.

LLANO ESTACADO

The Beginning of a Western Novel

CHAPTER I

As they say in that song, my hat was
throwed back and my spurs was a jinglin'. I
was sittin' up in the middle of that old
paint pony of mine and headin' for the same
horizon I'd been riding for these past two
weeks, with nothing changed.

That country was so flat out yonder I seen
a prairie dog come out of his hole against
the horizon and he looked so big I thought
he was a bear. It seemed like an awful
lot of nowhere and I was fresh out of grub
and down to my last couple of swallows of
water.

Supposedly, somewheres up ahead there was
a buffalo wallow where after rains the water
gathered, and that was supposed to tide me
and my horse over until we could find us a
water hole.

Nevertheless I was young enough so's
trouble didn't seem like nothing more than
sweat off my neck, and I was riding free and

lonesome with the world all to myself. Or so
I thought.

Next thing I knew something hit me spang,
and I heard a shot. I went off my horse a
rolling into the dust and somehow I'd had
the good sense to grab for my Winchester
when I left the saddle. Maybe it wasn't no
good sense a-tall. It was pure-dee luck or
some kind of instinct. Anyway I hit the dirt
and by the time I quit rollin' I seen some
dude come from behind a little throwed-up
dirt and leggin' it for my horse.

Well, I wasn't about to see somebody ride
off on my horse and leave me out here. A man
caught afoot where I was would be a sure-
enough dead man, so I rolled over again,
come up on my elbows, and got off a shot
just as that gent hit leather on my saddle.

My shot missed him but burned the pony's
neck and he went buckin' off across the
prairie with this man not down in the saddle
yet, and believe me, that paint could buck!
He done a good job and throwed that hombre
sky-high and when he came down he was
settin' and the horse was gone a-flyin' off
across-country and there we was, both afoot
and miles from anywhere.

My hand just naturally worked the lever on
my rifle and she spat an empty shell and
taken another one in the chamber. I looked
at him settin' there cussin' and I held that
rifle on him and said, "I never shot no man
cold turkey afore, but I'm about to."

"You fly at it," he yelled. "We ain't got
nothin' but a little time, anyways. You damn

fool. Had you left me alone on that horse
one of us could of had it, anyway. Now we're
both dead!"

"That was my horse," I said. "I was alive
and headin' for more days of living. You was
afoot out here and as good as dead."

He got up off the ground and I seen he
didn't even have him a six-gun. His holster
was as empty as my belly. Right then I
should have started using what good sense I
had, allowing as how I had any a-tall, but
I never paid it no mind. I was sore, and I
was fixing to shoot that man.

"You say that was your horse," he said.
"How do you figure?"

"I ketched him myself right out of the
wild bunch and broke him to carry," I said.
"That makes him my horse."

"Well, I say you just had him prisoner. He
was his own horse. You had no more right to
him than me. He was runnin' wild when you
caught him, and he was runnin' wild when I
jumped him. I say he was my horse."

Such a boneheaded reasoning just throwed
me there for a bit and then he said, "You
goin' to shoot or just stand there? I'm
gettin' tired of waitin' for it."

"Oh, shut up!" I said, disgusted. "You
talk too much!"

"If you ain't goin' to shoot me," he said,
"we'd better start pickin' 'em up an'
puttin' 'em down. I mean, we ain't gettin'
no closer to grub or water just standing
here while you run off at the head. Let's
walk."

"What the hell?" I said, disgusted. I fell in alongside him and started to walk. He kept looking at my rifle. I also had a six-shooter.

"Rifle gettin' heavy? Want I should carry it for you?"

"Are you crazy? I'll carry my own piece."

"It's goin' to get mighty heavy, give you a mile or two," he said cheerfully. "You'll be glad to let me tote it afore sundown."

Well, we hung up our jaws and took to walking, which no cowboy ever likes very much. By the time we'd gone a couple of miles that rifle was getting heavy but I wasn't about to let him have it. If ever I saw a man who was a coyote this was him, right here alongside me.

We walked maybe six miles before we stopped to look around. I don't know what for. That West Texas Panhandle country they call the Llano Estacado or the Staked Plain was just about the flattest country on earth, and there was an awful lot of it.

I was commencing to spit cotton and he was already past that, but he was so mean and contrary that I didn't seem to make him no mind. He just didn't care. All he wanted was me dead and my rifle and gun-belt, and I was dedicated to the proposition that he would get neither.

Finally, the sun went down. Darkness comes almighty soon in that country but there were stars coming out and unless I was much mistook there would be a moon somewheres further along, so we just kept puttin' one

foot ahead of the other right on into the
night.

The stars faded and the moon did come up
and out yonder where it was good and black
the coyotes began to howl the moon, talking
it up across that flat country. A time or
two this gent kind of eased over toward me
like he had it in mind to jump me, but I
laid it down to him.

"You ain't much comp'ny and without you,
I'd have been puttin' my feet under a table
right down with a pot of coffee to drink, so
you just step back an' keep your distance or
I'll be walkin' alone."

"You scared!" he sneered. "You're as big
as me. What do you say we fight, winner take
the guns?"

"I got the guns. You want to fight you
just take off into the night and wrastle
with evil or your conscience," I said,
"admittin' you have one, which I doubt."

"I was Christian-raised," he protested. "I
was a gospel-shoutin' Methodist from the
south. Methodists going to rule the world
someday. They believe!"

"You sayin' Baptists don't? I'll have you
know, I am a Baptist, least I was raised
one, an' proud of it."

"Don't take much to make some folks
proud," he said, and I lifted a hand at him,
but he stood his ground. "You Baptists ain't
got a chance out here," he sneered. "You say
to get baptized you got to go down into the
water." He waved a hand. "Where's the water
you can get into? You ain't got a chance to

baptize nobody so there's not going to be
any Baptists in West Texas or anywhere this
side of the Pecos."

"What d'you know about the Pecos?" I
demanded, trying to get away from a losing
battle. I surely didn't know how the
Baptists figured to work it and didn't feel
up to speaking for my church, not having
enough know-how. Truth was I hadn't been to
a church but once in three, four years since
I left home and that time was because I seen
a yellow-haired girl goin' up the steps.
Turned out she was meetin' some gent in a
store-bought suit with his hair slicked down
and no chance for a dusty cowpoke like me.

"I know it ain't but two or three times a
year you'll get water enough to baptize
anybody, even there," he sneers, and I can't
argue with him because I never seen no
Pecos. All I know is it's there, somewheres
yonder across the horizon.

"I seen the Pecos," he said, "and the time
I seen it last I was fetchin' for it and up
ahead I seen a cloud of dust. I figured it
for Indians, maybe, or a herd of cows, but
when I came up to the river I seen it
wasn't."

"What was it?"

"Fish," he said, "swimmin' upriver,
huntin' for water."

After that we didn't talk much and it came
to be mighty tirin' out there. He kept
falling back and I kept urging him on as he
seemed to be gettin' weaker and weaker by
the minute. Finally I was so dry I couldn't

talk and I left off yellin' at him. I just
kept slogging along and next time I looked
back he was nowhere in sight, but it was
still moonlight and I could see a little
way. I stopped and tried to yell but
couldn't make a sound above a whisper. I
walked on, into the night, more than half-
asleep, right on my feet. I stumbled a time
or two, but it was the need for sleep more
than anything else, and I was fairly walking
in my sleep when suddenly there was a
whisper of something behind me and I made
to turn. Something crashed down on my skull
and the last thing I recalled was dust in my
throat, which was already dry enough.

It was the sun brought me out of it. The
hot sun on my back.
I rolled over; the sun hit me in the eyes
and it hurt. I struggled up, my skull
throbbing, and slowly it all came back
to me.
My rifle was gone. My gun-belt and
holster were gone. Even the few coins in my
pocket were gone and a letter I had offering
me a job on a ranch near Wagon Mound, that
was gone.
Worst of all, he'd taken my boots.
Those boots didn't come up to much. They
were old and about wore out, but they were
all I had, and he knowed it, and a man
without boots wasn't going to get far.
Only I was.
Right about then I was mad enough to spit
had I anything to spit with. I seen his

tracks plain enough, and started after him. What I figured to do, him having the rifle and six-gun, I didn't know.

Suddenly I seen something. I seen a man on a horse. At first I thought I was dreaming, for a body could stand in one place and look off across the country for three days and still see nothing, but there he was, maybe two miles off, setting easy in the saddle. I yelled, whooped, and hollered, and nothing come of it.

Anyway, all my whooping was in my mind because I couldn't raise a sound above a whisper.

He disappeared and then maybe ten minutes after, I heard a shot. It was afar off, but I knowed what it was. That skunk who knocked me in the head now had him a horse.

I fell down, I got up, then fell again. Somewhere along there I got kind of light-headed but I kept walking. Something sobered me whilst I was lying on the ground one time and when I got up I seen some tracks.

They were buffalo tracks . . . old ones, leading off to the southwest.

For a moment I studied them, then walked on. Few minutes later I come on some other tracks, looked like wild horse tracks, three or four of them, and they too led southwest.

Now in that country one direction is as good as another unless there's water. I turned around halfway and started off. I walked on, following those tracks, and then they turned west again and all of a sudden the earth split wide open in front of me and

there was a canyon the like of which I'd
never seen, and in the bottom of it was
green grass, even a few cottonwoods and
willows. Trouble was, the side was sheer for
maybe thirty feet and there looked to be
nowhere to get down. Now that didn't make
sense, because those buffaloes and wild
horses couldn't fly. I scouted for their
tracks, found them, and found a break in the
cliff.

A half hour later I was sprawled on my
belly, drinking water.

CHAPTER II

Altogether that canyon was hundreds of
feet deep, just the first thirty was sheer
rimrock, and after that a steep talus slope,
partly grass-covered, to the bottom.

When I had drunk a little water I splashed
more on my face and chest and sat up and
looked around. From where I sat there was a
little mesquite and a few willows, further
along some cottonwoods.

Getting up, I started following the creek
bed, only I ran out of water within about
thirty yards, so I stopped and walked back.
This here canyon was a hidden place,
although how far it ran, I had no idea.
There were horse droppings around, and
plenty of buffalo tracks. The horses were
mostly unshod, although there were two or
three wearing shoes; all of them, and I

could tell by their tracks, were running
loose now.

If a horse is ridden, or even with a herd,
they keep to a direction, but these were
just wandering, grazing, taking a bit here
and there.

From where I stood I could see maybe a
quarter of a mile of the canyon, up and
down. I had taken another drink and then
walked on down the canyon. Knowing where
the water was, I could always come back.

Rounding a bend helped none at all. From
that point I could see almost a half-mile
further, but there was nothing in sight.
What I needed most was a weapon, something
more than my belt-knife, which was all I
had. Luckily, that had been fastened to my
pants-belt, not the gun-belt. That polecat
had not taken the time to undo two buckles.

First off, I was right glad to have come
upon water, but I was sorry to lose my horse
and my arms. Somehow or other I was going to
have to rig something to carry water in,
because this place I'd come upon seemed to
be plumb lost and alone and maybe nobody
even knew of it but me and some Indians.

Suddenly, I seen movement!

In one step I was out of sight in the
brush, but watching. What I saw was horses,
three or four mustangs that came out of the
willows, where they'd probably had a drink
at some pool. One was a kind of dusty-gray,
fine-looking horse, maybe three or four
years old. Although it was some distance off
it seemed to have a brand on it, so it might

have been saddle-broke sometime. Now if I
could just get my hands on that horse . . .

Two or three more showed up. Likely it was
safe enough for them down here, and
certainly there was plenty of water and
grass, both scarce items up on the cap-rock
at this time of year.

Kind of easing myself out from cover, I
just stood there and let them see me. One of
those mustangs pulled up sharp when she
spotted me and she blew through her nostrils
and just stared, ears pricked. Me, I stood
rock-still, letting them get used to me.

The wind was gentle, from me toward them,
so they'd caught a whiff of me too. I
thought that branded horse stood a little
longer than the others, and seemed
interested. "Hiya, boy!" I called, and I
walked out a few steps. The others had
started drifting off, not spooked, but being
careful, yet the one still lingered.

"I think somebody treated you pretty good
sometime or other," I said aloud, "somebody
you're missing, maybe. Well, I'm friendly."

Moving a couple of more steps, I just
stood there, and that horse actually walked
toward me a little, stretching its nose in
my direction. Putting out a hand, I walked
toward it, although I was still a good
hundred yards off. It turned and walked,
then trotted away.

"Given time," I said, "we could get
together."

The trouble was, there wasn't going to be
time. Water I had, but I'd no food, and if I

didn't starve to death then some Indian
would come along and take my hair.

Among the willows and close to a cluster
of big old cottonwoods I found a place to
bed down. It was smooth grass, there was
water close by, and plenty of firewood
around. Gathering sticks for a fire I
startled a rabbit, but it was gone and away
in an instant. I also saw some deer tracks.
Somehow I'd have to rig some snares, or
starve to death.

All the while I kept a sharp eye out for
people tracks, but found no sign. Of course,
moccasin tracks do not make much impression
and rarely last long. A boot heel can cut
deep and sharp and the track may last for
weeks, even months if in a sheltered place.

There wasn't much point in my making a
fire even if I could manage it. I'd nothing
to cook and doubted the night would be that
cold. Also, it might attract unwelcome
visitors. Still, what visit would be
unwelcome?

Something else came to mind. If that horse
yonder had known and liked a man or woman
before this, he must be familiar with
campfires, and much as horses like the wild,
some of them were people-horses, they just
naturally liked to be with people as many a
dog likes it.

Not that I was fooling myself. The chances
of me catching myself a horse was about one
in a hundred. With any horse but that one,
one in a thousand. Yet I had it to think
about and I'd done some mustangin' as a

youngster and knew something of how to trap
wild horses.

If I did catch one I'd need a rope. If I
could find an old campsite there was just a
chance I might find a piece of cast-off
rope. Maybe a dozen times I'd come on such
things where somebody threw out a busted
rope and just let it lay, or left a piece of
it tied to a tree.

One thing I knew. If I got out of here at
all, I'd have to use my head. There wasn't
any kind of settlement within a hundred
miles in any direction, and in some
directions, like north or south, it was more
likely two to three hundred. Not that I knew
for sure, but I knew enough to know I wasn't
going to walk out of here and make it.

Things surely didn't shape up so good for
me. Here I was twenty-two years old, worked
hard all my life punchin' cows around
Beeville and then down Uvalde way, going up
the trail from Texas to Abilene with a herd
of mean steers and just short of town by two
days' drive I tangled with an ornery old
Mossy Horn from down in the brush country
and he hooked me in the side, tore me up
some, and busted a couple of ribs and a
collarbone. By the time I was up and around
again my outfit had gone back to Texas and I
was broke.

All I had was my saddle and a sore-backed
bronc the boss left me. Whilst I was mending
its back healed so when I got on the street
I had a horse, anyway. A cattle buyer taken
me on to ride herd on some stock he was

holding on grass about twenty miles west of
Abilene. When he sold his steers I had
twenty dollars coming.

Standing on the street with that twenty
dollars in my pocket I saw a young woman
come into town riding a neat little filly
and they surely did make a picture. She was
settin' sidesaddle, the way women-folks
rode, and she had a gray riding outfit on.

Right alongside me a girl about fourteen
stopped. She was walking with her pa, a
gray-haired man with a white hat and a neat
black suit. I heard this girl say, "Oh, Pa!
Isn't she beautiful! I wish I had a horse
like that!"

"She is beautiful," her father agreed,
"and if we stay here I'll buy a horse for
you."

That woman on the horse rode up and got
down right close by and the old gentleman
stepped over to her and said, "Ma'am, I will
give you a hundred dollars for your horse."

"Oh, no! I'd never sell her!"

"Two hundred?"

"I am sorry, sir. She is not for sale."

Well, it seemed to me like opportunity was
knocking. I had taken off my hat. "Sir,"
I said, "an' Miss? For two hundred dollars
I'll find a more beautiful horse than that
one and break him gentle."

The man looked at me out of cool blue
eyes. "There are very few horses I have seen
west of the Mississippi for which I'd pay
two hundred dollars," he said, "and that

horse wasn't worth it, but my daughter
wanted it."

Now I looked like pretty much of nothing.
I was wearing a pair of striped store-bought
pants with a blue wool shirt, a buckskin
vest I'd made myself, boots with run-down
heels, and a .44 Colt on my hip. My hat was
battered and had been stitched with rawhide
along the crown to hold it together.
Moreover, I was just nineteen then, and
looked it.

"Sir, I been holding some cattle out
yonder on the plains, and a time or two I
had to ride out west huntin' strays. Well, I
seen the prettiest little horse out yonder
you ever did see, proud, high-headed, and
built like a dream. You should see that
horse move! I started them a time or two
just to see him run."

"What color was he?"

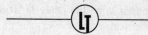

COMMENTS: The Llano Estacado, sometimes called the
Staked Plain, is a high plains area covering a good deal of
western Texas and eastern New Mexico. One theory about
the name was that it was so flat that early travelers used
stakes driven into the ground to navigate across its expanse
and to find water. Though cairns (piles of rock or debris)
and possibly stakes may have been used as guideposts, it is
more likely that the name came from the look of the mesa-
like edges of the plateau, which resembled palisades or a
stockade.

It's very likely that the canyon that our narrator discovers is Palo Duro Canyon, in which the JA Ranch was established in the 1870s. Louis's early experience with this general area came when he got a job skinning dead cattle on the Elwell Ranch, near Lubbock, Texas, in the mid-1920s. Later, his family traveled across the Staked Plain to reach eastern New Mexico, where they worked for some time.

The line about how the "polecat" took the letter containing the job offer near Wagon Mound suggests how and where the two men may eventually meet up again. It seems utterly in character for this conniver to take advantage of that particular opportunity. It's also amusing to see Louis write an exchange about Methodists and Baptists. Dad was raised Methodist, though "gospel-shoutin'" was the last thing his family seemed to be!

I'm not sure what the "polecat" used to shoot our hero out of the saddle. Certainly the next time we see him he does not have a firearm and the narrator doesn't seem to have been shot. Maybe he dropped the gun later when the horse was bucking, or maybe Louis or a good editor would have gone in and changed that section to make it a thrown rock. Obviously, the hero isn't terribly injured, and I think it would have been funnier that way; his pride is wounded, not his body.

SHELBY TUCKER

The Beginning of a Western Novel

We hadn't seen them for a long time, but
we knew they were out there. We were belly
down in the grass on top of a knoll and the
sun was hot. We could smell the dusty grass,
we could almost taste it, and above us was
the wide sky, brassy with sun and heat.

It was mid-afternoon and the earth had the
smell of death, because in all the world
there was no help to come for us, nor
anybody to ask after us or know that we had
gone.

We were four men and a girl, all that was
left of Mellin's wagon train, we five
surrounded on a hilltop, and around us were
vast and empty plains as we lay waiting with
the taste of fear in our mouths.

There was Tuthill, Constanatus, Pike, and
me, Shelby Tucker. And there was Laurie
Connor, seventeen and pretty, already a wife
and already a widow, her tall young husband

dead on the charred earth of the wagon circle.

Out there in the grass were thirty Kiowas, wanting our hair, and some of them fixing to die.

Twenty miles east of us the wagon train lay scattered and burned, a dead thing that had moved with life, its voices stilled, its heart no longer beating. The low rumble of wagon wheels and the creak of saddle leather were gone, and without them the world was empty, for these had been the song of our days.

Fifty-six men and women gone, and more than twenty children, their blood emptied to the grass, their homes to go unbuilt . . . and we, the last of them, pursued to this place of ending, to this hot and lonely hillside in the long grass.

We settled ourselves down, nothing to see but the wind, nothing to feel but the sun. The rifle was hot in my hands.

Nine of us had made a break for it when the last charge came, but four had died before they reached the draw. It had been Pike spotted that draw--Pike, who never went into a place without knowing a way out--and in the rush of the Kiowas after loot and scalps, we got away.

Until they found our trail.

"Hold low, kid." Pike looked over to me. "An' take your time. They'll be comin' soon."

"I'll be all right," I told him, and I would. Pike, he was a great one for giving

advice, but a good fighting man. I was glad
he was with us.

The four of us squared to the compass in
an old buffalo wallow, with Laurie under the
high edge and out of harm's way. When I took
my hand off the rifle to wipe it dry of
sweat on my shirtfront, Laurie was looking
at me, her eyes big and dark, so I smiled at
her to keep her gumption up. After a moment,
she smiled back.

Goes tough on a girl to lose her man that
way, although to my thinking Lafe Connor was
no catch. The Connors were a feuding outfit
from the high hills, West Virginia
folks . . . and Lafe a trouble-hunting man.
If that Kiowa brave hadn't taken him it was
like to have been Pike or me, for he was
pushing us, time to time.

Laurie was folks . . . mighty sweet girl,
liked by all. Pike, he had been giving her
the eye when Lafe wasn't around, but she
paid him no mind.

They came then, just a whisper in the
grass, crouching low and running. My Spencer
took the first, hitting him in the notch
below the throat.

They were coming from all around and I
could hear the others firing. An Indian
loomed suddenly, scarcely beyond the muzzle,
and I felt the gun jump in my hands but had
no memory of squeezing off. The heavy slug
went into his head over his eye and he was
dead before he hit the grass.

Then they were gone, and there was an
acrid smell of gunpowder. One suddenly came

out of the grass trying to get further away, and my bullet split his tailbone. He went down . . . a bloody hand flew up, and I heard a low sobbing in the grass down there, then nothing more.

Pike turned his face around. There was blood on his temple. "Get any?"

"Three."

"Two," he said, "I got two."

"One," Tuthill said, "and maybe another."

"Four," the Greek spoke quietly, "all dead."

Pike looked at him. "Figured you were new to this."

Constanatus shrugged. "They are like Turks. I have killed Turks and Russkies since I was a boy."

We waited then, not thinking of water, not thinking of anything. We had hurt them . . . worse than expected, no doubt. They would be arguing now, planning another attack. But ten down . . . that was shooting.

A cool breeze moved in the grass, and high near the sun a buzzard swung in wide, slow circles. Of us all, he was the one sure to win.

We had two horses when we slipped away during that final attack at the wagon train. Laurie rode, and the others of us took turns. We made fast time, but not fast enough. The Kiowas had stampeded our horses first thing, and even if we drove them off we were footloose in the midst of everything and nothing.

My mouth was dry and my head ached with a

slow, dull throb. Lying there close to the
ground I watched an ant working, felt a dry
blade of grass brushing my cheek. When I
looked around, Pike was watching Laurie and
I could see the woman-hunger in his eyes.

Pike was a blond, lean-waisted, tough-
walking man with scars to his hide. He wore
one gun in sight and a hideout gun under his
shirt. We met in Natchez-Under-the-Hill, him
nigh to thirty, me just pushing nineteen. We
teamed up, neither of us talking much.

Men walked shy of him, all but Lafe
Connor. There was trouble coming between
them, and we all knew it. Pike fancied
himself with a handgun . . . and in Ash
Hollow, on the way west, he had killed a
man.

The sun declined and a low wind stirred
the grass. The Kiowas came suddenly out
of the sun moving with the wind, and they
came shooting.

My first shot laid along the grass tops
into a big, dark-skinned man. He went down,
and I came up, shooting the Spencer from the
hip. A Kiowa screamed . . . another fell.
Behind me there was a thud of a bullet
striking flesh, and I met the last Kiowa
with an empty gun. But the muzzle jerked up
hard to the soft spot behind his jawbone and
his head jerked back, his scream choking on
blood and dying with the dull thunk of my
rifle butt against his skull.

Then there was quiet upon the grass, wind
stirring and the sun low across the plains.

Tuthill was gone. He took one through the

chest and one high through the shoulder, but
dead. The Greek was kneeling and Laurie
working at a bandage on his right arm. You
could see the shock in his eyes.

Pike sat up and rolled a smoke, looking at
me. "You an' me now, kid." His face looked
gray, but the old hard light was there, and
I was glad again that it was Pike, for he
was a fighting man.

Not talking, I got Tuthill's rifle and
loaded it, took the ammunition off his body.
Then I loaded the Greek's rifle. When I put
them down I took out my Bowie. It was razor-
sharp.

"Watch for me," I said. "I'll be back."

Then I rolled over the rim of the wallow
into the grass. Behind me Laurie called my
name and I heard Pike swear, but I was belly
down on the ground and moving through the
grass.

Pike, he figured himself for an old-timer,
but me, I'd lost my parents when I was
eleven on the Overland Trail, and lived
three years with the Shoshones. At fourteen
I was driving a freight wagon on the Santa
Fe Trail and fighting Apaches in the
Mogollons.

The Kiowas would know we'd lost a
man . . . might figure there was two gone.
And they knew Laurie was there. They
wouldn't be expecting me down among them,
and the Shoshones had taught me how to move
in grass.

Sweating, I was, and the dust from the

grass itched my skin. Flat down I moved, snaking along until I saw brown skin, a startled face, a voice starting to scream. My hand choked it off at his throat and the knife went in twice, fast and slick. In and out, and I held his throat until he was dead. Only sound his heels kicking in the grass.

You can bet they heard it, though, and wondered. Then I was moving on . . . only now I had a bow and the arrows.

The next one I saw was a dozen yards off across a little cut in the slope. The Shoshones had taught me to use a bow, too. The arrow went into his kidney and he screamed, leaping up and dragging at the arrow-shaft. My second went to his throat. . . .

A long time I lay still then. The Kiowas would be trying to figure what had happened. They were superstitious and they would not like this happening among them. One reared up as if to see and Pike's Sharps put him down.

After a while I snaked it back to the wallow and rolled over the rim. Laurie, she looked at me big-eyed but Pike, he said nothing.

Not for a while. Then he said, "I think they've gone."

"I think so, too."

He looked to me again. He had me figured for a kid from the farms. "What happened out there?"

Me, I shrugged. Pike looked at the bow and the quiver of arrows. "Find a dead one?"

"He was dead when I took these off him."

When dark came we started out, walking. Then we found four Indian ponies waiting for riders that would never come. We mounted up and rode west, and Pike, he began sidling up to Laurie.

"Lafe's gone," he said. "You should have you a man."

Laurie said nothing, just looking between her pony's ears at the low stars.

Me, I said nothing either, leading that spare horse. It was no time to be talking to that girl. If she had a lot of love for Lafe Connor it could surprise me, for he was a hard, unfeeling man. Nevertheless, he was a short time dead and she had been his wife.

"We'll make it fine," he said, "you an' me. Good country west of here."

She said nothing at all, only I could see the white of her face, looking to me.

"Leave it lay," I said.

Pike's head came around, sharp. "My business, kid."

"Give it time," I told him.

He said nothing for maybe a hundred steps, and then he agreed, "Maybe you're right." But, he added, "She might's well get used to it."

Darkness lay soft upon the land, coolness on our faces, and miles fell behind us with the turning of the stars and the night-walking moon. We'd no water, nor any food,

and where there was water there might be
Indians. Yet when the sky was gray behind
us, I saw a fringe of darkness in a low
place . . . trees.

Dark trees and the smell of water. We
moved toward them, taking it easy. A dozen
cottonwoods, bunches of willows, and a pool.
We drank, and we filled empty canteens, and
Pike looked at Laurie. "We'll bed down
here," he said.

Her face was pale in the vague light, her
eyes large and frightened. I did not know
what she was thinking. Only I said, "No."

Pike looked at me again, and there was
nothing nice in the look. "You crossin' me,
kid? Once too often."

I just looked at him. He could sling a
gun, all right, but so could I . . . and I
had, an' more than him. Only he knew nothing
of that.

"Ain't safe," I said. "We got to move.
This here place is a Comanche water hole." I
lied then. "I seen their tracks."

He stood silent, not liking it, but not
wanting to fight Comanches, either. Kiowas
were bad enough. Comanches were worse . . .
much worse.

We took out, riding west again, the rising
sun at our backs, holding to the hills just
below the ridges, keeping from being sky-
lined, yet staying where the going was easy.
All morning we rode, and Laurie, she was
dropping in the saddle, she was all in.

"We got to rest, kid." Pike was looking
around. "Comanches or not."

"Place up ahead. Water in a cave."

Pike looked at me again, funny-like. He was puzzled, taking me as he did for a kid green to the West, and I'd never told him different.

First thing I saw was that twisted paloverde. Then the white gash in the caprock. We rode over the lip, the horses taking it easy-like, then down a long path toward the bottom of the canyon, but before we were halfway down we made a sharp double-back amongst some broken chunks of the whitish rock. The cave was there, like I remembered it, half-concealed by brush.

Pike looked at it, big enough for us and horses, too. He walked in, then came back. He looked at me, his hands on his hips. "How'd you know this place?"

"Camped here once. More'n a year ago. This here is border country. Comanches east, Apaches west. Not many ride through here."

Laurie almost fell when she got out of the saddle, and I caught her. "Here!" Pike said. "I'll help her."

"She's already helped," I said, and guided her inside the cave to where she could sit down.

Pike, he was almighty quiet while we unsaddled our blankets and canteens, along with the extra rifles. The horses we staked out on grass near the cave, after letting them water at the pool inside.

Out of the corner of my eye I saw Pike shift his gun a little, and he started over to me. Turning around before he got to me, I

said, "Look." He stopped, squared toward me,
his feet apart. "This girl is tired. She
lost her man. It ain't right to start
pushin' her. Let it go for a while."

"You keep your advice to yourself. She's
done been married. She ain't no baby."

"She's waitin', though. She makes up her
own mind, in her own good time."

"Maybe you think she'd choose you?" he
sneered.

"Might be."

For four long counts I let that stand,
keeping him on edge. Then I said, "Pike,
you're a first-class fightin' man. Without
you, neither Laurie nor me would be here.
But without me, neither you nor Laurie would
be here, either. There's a sight of country
west. I know that country. I like you, an' I
don't want trouble, but if you can't use
your head, an' if you want to die, have at
it."

He didn't like none of it. He stood there,
his eyes cold, trying to figure what was
behind my talk. It was not easy to fit this
into the picture he'd made of me, but he was
no fool.

If we started shooting, one of us would
die, maybe both. And it was me knew the
country. He swore and turned sharp away, but
I knew it was not over, just a sort of a
truce-like.

COMMENTS: Okay, a classic L'Amour beginning, except . . . what happened to the Greek guy? He was kind of a badass and he was just winged. But that's why some of these stories were started over and over again; as Louis discovered where the story was taking him, he would adjust and adjust until it was ready to go all the way to the finish. Or he'd discover that the story just wasn't ready to be told and he'd move on to something else. In the next iteration, the Greek would probably never have been there, or would have died in the fight. As in so many other endeavors, getting the beginning right was critical to the way he worked.

This character Shelby Tucker should not be confused with Edwin Shelvin Tucker. Ed Tucker appears in Louis's novel *Tucker* and the little jewel of a short story that the novel was adapted from, called "Cap-Rock Rancher" . . . one of my all-time favorites.

CITIZEN OF THE DARKER STREETS

The Beginning of an Adventure Story

Bangkok is the place . . . two a.m. the time . . . and across the street in the dark maw of an alley waits a lean wolf of the streets . . . with a knife. He is waiting for me.

It is hot and still and in the fetid air there is a lingering smell of dust, overripe fruit, sweaty bodies, heat, and opium. . . . It is the smell of the tropics, the smell of Bangkok, of Makassar, of Pondicherry. It is the smell of death.

Behind me, drawn back into a shadowed doorway, is a hulking brute with huge hands and powerful shoulders. He has been following me, and like his slat-ribbed comrade across the way, he has slowly been edging me away from the principal streets, readying me for the kill.

My name is Martin Cross, they call me "China" Cross, and my home is anywhere in the world.

Somewhere in town there is a girl, a beautiful, luscious girl, with a golden-tan body like something out of a lonely man's dream of paradise, a girl lost and frightened . . . and in danger.

So here I am, citizen of the darker streets, bystander in the alleys of dingy commerce, spectator in the theater of iniquity, a searcher for things lost . . . a man looking for a girl in a town where girls are a dime a dozen. China Cross, the man who finds things, that's me. Paintings, matched pearls, rare volumes, hidden wills, the rarest of rate stamps, strange wild animals from the deepest jungle, and even lost and frightened girls in Bangkok.

China Cross whose life right now isn't worth a plugged peso or a shot of cut gin. A man whom somebody had spotted for what he was before he had his feet off the dock, a man who is never supposed to see the light of another day.

Sweat trickling down my stomach, sweat trickling between my shoulder blades, sweat greasy on my face, it is two a.m. and the only way open for me is toward the rice mills and the wharves, toward the narrowing streets and the dark slips where sampans bob on the slow swell of the harbor waters.

Out of the doorway I move and behind me moves the one man, across the street the other. Ahead of me there is a narrow and odorous alley and they are pressing me toward it. Somewhere out on the water sounds the deep-throated blast of a steamer, and

then in the alleyway before me there is
movement, a quick rush of bare feet on
paving, and there is no time--knives flash,
and my shoulder hits a door in the wall near
me. The latch gives way and I fall inward
into deeper, more velvety blackness, and as
I fall my hand goes to my shoulder holster
and my .380 automatic jumps, a shell casing
taps the wall then the floor and my ears are
ringing. The door is empty again and I hear
the moaning of a dying man who wished to
kill but did not think to die himself.

This is a sort of warehouse, a dark place
haunted by the ghostlike smells of the
thousand cargoes once stored here. I weave
among the bales, finding and feeling my way,
using my fingers for eyes. Behind there is
movement again. . . . My hand lifts a latch,
the door closes softly behind me. I feel for
a bar and find it. Carefully I place the bar
across the door. A stairway leads into upper
darkness.

The air is close and hot and I climb. My
shirt presses damply against my chest and at
the head of the stairs I pause, aware of
life around me . . . the stirring and
breathing of many bodies, a whisper of
movement, a deep sigh, the sickish-sweet
smell of opium and of long-dead smoke . . .
a smell of living bodies in thick, close
air.

Moving, I stumble over legs. A faint voice
is plaintive with protest. . . . These are
coolies waiting for another day of labor--
the loaders of ships, the carriers of bales,

sodden with opium and working only for a
bowl of rice, a dried fish, and the dark
stuff of the poppy's heart which brings them
escape from hunger, misery, and life.

Behind me there is a splintering. . . .
The door is open for the air stirs faintly.
Trapped.

Through the bodies, over them, stumbling,
suddenly a vacant place among them and an
idea . . . Swiftly I strip, glad that my body
is bronzed by sun and wind. Naked to my
shorts, I tuck the legs up until I have only
what looks to be a breechclout, and then I
lie down among them . . . among the collapsed
bodies and among the insect life that
accompanies them. . . . I lie still,
clutching my pistol beneath my body, waiting.

A light flashes and plays over the room,
over the bodies. There is a stirring and a
growing chorus of complaint. It is a huge
loft and over a hundred men are sprawled
about. A low voice says, "I don't think he
came up here." And a reply in the music of
Malaya, "If he did, he went out. He is not
here now."

The flashlight snapped off; feet murmur on
the stairs. Rising, I listen, then climb
into my clothing. My hand feels for my gun
to be sure it is still with me. . . . On the
floor a man stirs, whimpering softly like a
sick child in the night . . . and then I
move away.

Day was a vague promise over the temple
towers when I was once more in my room.

After a shower I stretched out on the hard
bed of the tropics and stared up at the
ceiling beyond the mosquito netting.

Who had alerted them to the fact that I
was searching for Gwen Moran? Or could these
have been casual thieves? Or someone who
suspected me of being an American agent,
spying on the local Communist allies? Most
of all, I wondered, where was Gwen Moran,
the girl whose lovely face had been living
with me since the pictures arrived a few
hours before?

A friend of my father's had known that I
was in Macao; his cabled offer had reached
me there. Five thousand and all expenses if
I could bring her home safely. Pictures and
details were to go by air and would be
awaiting me in Bangkok.

Gwen Moran had been one of a party of
five. She had come ashore from a world
cruise . . . and had disappeared from her
hotel later, leaving a note that she had
fallen in love and would be married at
once . . . a cable to her father to the same
effect. Not to worry, details later.

Silence, then, and nothing more . . .
silence, until one night an agonized cry for
help over the shortwave . . . A man in Los
Angeles, idling over his set in the
morning's small hours, caught the call . . .
another in Manila picked it up. A frightened
girl begging for help, a call cut quickly
off.

American officials could learn nothing.
Local reports were that she had run off with

a man, perhaps had flown to Singapore. The
following morning my own inquiries began. I
only knew two things--she had access to a
shortwave set and her kidnapper could hire
killers. Both indicated wealth, perhaps
power.

The shortwave clue cooled swiftly--it
could have been no known set in the vicinity
of Bangkok. So I gathered the details. Gwen
had come ashore with her party and they had
stopped at the Oriental, an excellent and
respectable hotel near the river, a cooler
location than my own stopping place. The
party had consisted of a man and wife in
their early fifties and the three girls
in their twenties. They had gone to the Chez
Eve for dinner.

Gwen attracted immediate and appreciative
attention. She danced with a French Colonel,
with the local director of an American firm,
twice with former American flyers. And she
had talked briefly with a man in the shadows
at one side of the floor.

Nobody knew what was said or who he was.
Returning to her table, Gwen made no
comment. Local officials knew nothing
more. . . . I fell asleep mulling over the
few known facts.

At noon I awakened suddenly and swung my
feet to the floor. My tongue was thick and
my brain was foggy. The lethargy left by
sleeping through the hot, still morning
deadened my muscles. By the time I'd shaved

and showered I felt better, so I went around to the Chez Eve and perched on a bar stool.

In Bangkok, this is the place to go. It is a nightclub, a restaurant, an odd combination of the American and Eastern. Seated on one of the chromium bar stools, I ordered a long, cool Myrtle Bank Punch and began to study the situation.

A man walked up and straddled the stool beside mine. He was enormously fat with a tiny mouth and three chins. A waxed mustache perched on his lip and he had a high forehead from which the hair waved back gracefully. He smelled of expensive perfume and his large, intelligent eyes met mine in the mirror back of the bar. He smiled. Because of the perfume I viewed the smile with some skepticism.

From an inside pocket he drew a leather wallet, carefully extracting five neat, new hundred-dollar bills. He placed them carefully on the bar between us, and atop them he placed a plane ticket for Los Angeles.

"California!" His voice held a fluted overtone. "How lovely at this time of year!"

Extracting a long, slim cigarette from a gold case, he offered the case to me and when I declined, returned it to his pocket and signaled for a drink. He fitted the cigarette into an ivory holder. "So much cooler in California, Mr. Cross. Have you been there lately?"

So he knew my name. The bartender came and

spoke with respect as he took the order for a drink.

"Not lately," I said, "and I've no plan to return soon."

He lit his cigarette, smiling wisely. Then he touched the money lightly with his manicured fingers, moving it toward me. "A good-bye to Bangkok, then a quick flight . . . Ah, how I envy you!"

"There's the ticket," I said, "and there's the cash. They are yours, aren't they?"

He shrugged dismally. "They are a present, Mr. Cross. A present from someone who wishes you well. Someone who would like to think of you sunning on the beaches of faraway California instead of encountering the risks of life in our dark and lonely streets. Oh, I'm sure, Mr. Cross, that you would find it so much more healthful if you were there!"

"Pick up the money," I said quietly, "and tell whoever you work for to deliver Gwen Moran to me not later than midnight."

His face stiffened and he put his cigarette down quickly. "I know nothing of this Gwen Moran," he said impatiently, "but you are a fool! A miserable, interfering fool!" He hitched his fat behind off the stool and straightened his coat, but before he could speak again my left hand shot out and the fingers went down inside his collar. Closing my fist I bent my knuckles hard against his Adam's apple. He gagged and gasped, his eyes bulging, his hands fighting wildly to tear my fist away.

Pulling him close I said quietly, "Don't

call me a fool, Fat Boy"--nobody had noticed us; the bartender was deeply engrossed in a flashy brunette down the bar--"just go tell your boss what I said!" I jerked him toward me to get him off balance, then shoved back hard and let go.

He hit the floor on his fat behind. Heads turned and the bartender hurried up toward us. My left hand held my drink and I glanced at the bartender and shook my head gravely. "Think of that! Only one drink, too!"

Fat Boy was rising awkwardly from the floor, and when he straightened up his eyes were ugly with hatred. I gestured toward the money on the bar. "Yours," I said.

"Use it," he told me, low-voiced, "use it, or by the--!" He jerked his coat down and bustled out.

The bartender looked at the money and then at me. I picked up the bills. Who was I to look gift horses in the teeth? Then I held one of the century notes in my fingers and glanced up at the bartender. "That guy," I asked. "Who was he?"

The bartender glanced at the century note. "His name is Siatin," he said. "He's secretary to some big shot. Or right-hand man for him."

"What big shot?"

He hesitated, not liking it much but liking the money more. "Banjak," he said, and he spoke the name in a low voice.

"And who," I asked, "is he?"

He hesitated again. "Everybody knows him," he said. "He's from an old family in

Thailand, but a very unpopular family.
Lately"--he glanced right and left, wiping a
glass--"they say he's dickering with the
Reds. But he's got money, he's got power,
and there's men working for him who'd cut
your throat slick as a whistle."

The century note was folded and slid over
the counter. He palmed it. "You watch your
step," he said warningly.

"Thanks." I got up and straightened my
coat a little. "My name," I said, "is Martin
Cross. I'm looking for Gwen Moran, that
American girl who disappeared. If you hear
anything, let me know."

"Yeah." He put the glass down and picked
up another. "That Banjak," he said softly,
"he's completely nuts over blondes."

Banjak's name was a sure way to ring down
a curtain of silence, I soon discovered. But
here and there a ray of light filtered
through the curtain. He had an importing and
exporting business . . . largely, rumor
said, oil and rubber to Russia and Red
China . . . and tin. He had an estate on the
Mekong on the Indo-Chinese border, plus a
house in town, a huge, ancient, rambling
place. From that estate a man with a launch
could get to Indo-China in five minutes, to
Burma in a matter of two or three hours,
to Red China in but a little more.

It was almost dark when I entered the Chez
Eve again, and when I found a seat at the
crowded bar I ordered a bourbon and soda
from the same bartender. He glanced at me,

nodded slightly, and said, "Nice to see you
again, Mr. Cross. Some men were looking for
you."

"Thanks," I said, catching his expression.
Whoever had been looking for me had been
anything but friendly, I could bank on that.

Over the bourbon and soda I contemplated
the situation. If it was true that Banjak
was active in supplying the Reds, a
shortwave set would be an asset, and it
might be either here or on the Mekong. And
one thing was certain. If Banjak had gone so
far as to kidnap an American girl she was
either out of the city or extremely well
guarded.

A man came into the room and walked across
and slid onto a stool beside me. He was a
sallow man with hollow cheeks and a lank,
unhealthy frame. His eyes were large and
luminous, his features a mixture of Eastern
peoples. He ordered a drink and under his
breath said, "You are Mr. Cross? You search
for the young American lady?"

"That's right." I kept my own voice low.

"I can take you to her," he said softly,
"but quickly, or she will be taken away."

"To the Mekong?"

"Who knows?" He lifted a shoulder. "If you
will come, it is outside the door, and stop
for nothing. You have frightened Banjak, and
a frightened Banjak is dangerous."

It could be a trap or it could be the lead
I wanted. "Your interest is what?" I asked
him.

He lifted his drink and speaking around

the edge of the glass, he said, "Nothing . . . except that the lovely lady
looked very sad, and what I am not strong
enough to do might be done by another, such
as you."

He finished his drink and walked outside
and I followed him after a minute or so. He
was standing near a palm and when he saw me
he started to walk away, going very slowly.
I followed at a reasonable distance, which
he seemed to want. . . . The street was
brightly lit, but not for long. . . . He
turned into a dingy byway between two
buildings and issuing out on the street of
the Bampon Boon Building . . . then he began
to hurry. Soon he paused and lit a cigarette
and I joined him.

"We go faster now," he said, gesturing at
an antique car standing by the curb. It was
something hatched in a remote period
probably not long after the Spanish-American
War, if anybody remembers when that was.
Surprisingly, the motor purred like a
contented tomcat and when I climbed in we
moved smoothly away from the curb and down
the street.

"I am a clerk," he explained, "a seller of
jade in a shop. Miss Moran had come to my
shop to buy jade and she was followed there
by a man I knew. He approached her, and she
was very sharp with him and when she talked
again to me I showed her a bit of jade and
warned her about this fat man . . . that he
worked for a powerful man who served a
country that was very dangerous, that she

should join her friends at once and stay
with them."

"And then?"

"She asked that I escort her to the hotel
with her purchases and my employer permitted
me to go, but we were followed there."

"By whom?"

"It is said you have met Siatin. It was he."

Suddenly the car slowed, driving down a
long avenue lined with trees. This was not
exactly a street, and not exactly a country
lane, but it resembled both. Turning the
car, suddenly he stopped under some trees
and got out. Set well back in a huge garden
was a vast, rambling old mansion.

"It is the house of Banjak?"

"Yes, and what you will do now, I do not
know."

"Watch me," I said.

Stepping into the street I started for the
gate. My idea was to go right up to the
house, demand to see the girl, and if she
wanted to come, take her away. There was a
chance in a hundred it might work or that I
might at least find out if she was still in
Bangkok. If that failed, then I could take
other steps. They had started the rough
stuff, but I would avoid it, if possible.

There was an iron gate between stone
columns and it was standing open just a
little. There was a small hut for a gate
tender but he was, fortunately, nowhere in
sight. I entered and walked swiftly up the
gravel drive.

At the huge double door, I pulled a bell

cord and waited. The doors opened finally, and a tall man in a long coat stood there. He wore a small round cap on his head.

"I want to see Banjak," I said.

"I am sorry. He is not here." The servant started to close the door but I put my shoulder against it and stepped in. He backed away from me, his eyes wary but not frightened. "I have said he is not here. If you persist, you shall have trouble."

"I was born to trouble," I replied shortly. "You will tell him I am here. If not him, tell Siatin. But it's Banjak I want to see."

Siatin stepped into sight from a doorway concealed by curtains. His fat jowls were set and hard now, and there was a light in his eyes that was anything but promising for my future. When I started to step by him the servant put up a hand as if to stop me and I swung him aside. Face to face with Siatin, I said, "Where's that girl? I want her and I want her now!"

Before he could speak, there was a slight movement and on the steps at the end of the hall was a huge man clad in a white silk suit with a green sash. He was built like a Turkish wrestler, and he came slowly down the steps. He paused a dozen feet away, his black eyes utterly cold.

"You wished to see me? I am Banjak."

"I have come for Gwen Moran."

"I have never heard of her." He spoke calmly, his eyes level.

"You're a liar." I said it flatly. I was

in this as deep as I could get now, and my
only chance was to push on through. Anyway,
I hate to take a pushing around. This man
had tried to have me killed, and he had
kidnapped an American girl. In my own way,
I, too, could be ruthless. "Gwen Moran is
here or in some place of which you know. I
want her now. And if I don't get her at
once, I'll take steps."

He smiled, a faintly supercilious smile,
yet impatient, too. "What steps?" he
sneered. "Your government will do nothing.
It would be bad for propaganda. There is
nothing you can do. Nothing at all."

It was coming up in me and I could feel
it. I wanted to take a swing at this big
lug. Stifling the impulse for the moment
in favor of sometime more opportune, I
said, "I've no intention of calling in my
government. They have too many problems
to bother with something I can handle
myself."

"You think well of yourself," he said
shortly. "Now leave, or I'll have you beaten
and thrown out."

"Why don't you try it?" I suggested.
"What's the matter? Are you a yellow rat
aside from being a stealer of women?"

He didn't like it. He didn't like it even
a little, and he liked it less that Siatin
and the servant stood there listening. His
face darkened with angry blood and he took a
catlike step forward, then stopped.
"Siatin," he said, "have him beaten and

thrown out." Deliberately, he turned and started for the stairs.

If I was thrown out now--but I wasn't going to be. Not without a fight.

With a lunge, I started for him. Siatin and the servant both sprang for me, but they were too slow. Head down, I rammed Banjak in the behind and at the same time grabbed his ankles and jerked up, hard. Grabbed in that way, a man can only fall on his face, but he strikes headfirst. Banjak came down hard, only the soft carpeting on the stairs saving him from a cracked skull. I went over him, and up the stairs.

The servant was fast but not eager, and Siatin much too fat and slow. I made the top of the stairs with time to spare and glanced swiftly both ways. Somewhere far off in the huge old building I heard a bell ringing.

Now that I was in the house I meant to stay. That bell was calling help, I knew. But with luck they would not find me. The left side of the house opened onto the garden, so I turned left, but then circled around by a passage that led across the building and ducked into the first door on the right side.

It was a cozy room lined with books. On the stand was a cigarette, still smoking. There was also an open book. Evidently it was from here that Banjak had come. I crossed the room to another door, and opening it, stepped into a bedchamber.

Crossing that, I passed through an
ultramodern bathroom into a larger chamber
that was empty. Behind me somewhere, I heard
a door open.

COMMENTS: The mention in this story of the nightclub
Chez Eve and the fact that Gwen was seen dancing with a
"French Colonel" suggests that it might have been written
prior to the mid-1950s, when the French were forced to
leave Indochina. Chez Eve opened sometime in the 1940s
and was famous as one of the few air-conditioned public
places in Bangkok. Louis's comment about "American flyers"
is probably based on the fact that two of the partners who
owned the Oriental Hotel were pilots from the USA; a number of others in the expatriate community were men who
had been with the wartime OSS. Although I do not believe
that Louis was ever in Thailand, he did make several stops
just to the south, along the Malay Peninsula, prior to World
War II, a somewhat similar environment.

Obviously, Dad was still finding his way with this one;
but it was shaping up to be a fun story and I wish he'd
continued it. I'm especially intrigued by Louis's mention
of his protagonist's father. Heroes with important, and
still living, fathers are somewhat uncommon in L'Amour
fiction. I really wonder what he was planning to do with
that relationship, or if it was just a way to get Martin Cross
involved.

The next story is also set in Bangkok. For a while, I wondered if returning to write about this city was due to the
influence of a pair of Thai brothers my mom and dad met in
the late 1950s. They originally came to Southern California
to go to college, and have since become virtual cousins of

ours. We have now known four generations of this prestigious Thai family. Yet both "Citizen of the Darker Streets" and the next title, "Where Flows the Bangkok," feel more like they come from an earlier period, after World War II, but before 1958 or so.

WHERE FLOWS THE BANGKOK

A Treatment for an Adventure Story

Kip Morgan leaves a tramp steamer in
Bangkok looking more like a beachcomber than
the man he is looking for, the drifting
ne'er-do-well nephew of rich old Miles
Vaughn, who had died leaving several
millions and no relatives but Jim Vaughn.
After several months of drifting from port
to port, Morgan has finally arrived in
Bangkok, aware that this was the last place
Jim Vaughn had headed for--twenty years
before.

After making inquiries around town,
Morgan, unshaven and in battered whites,
drifts into a waterfront nightclub, where he
finds a cool, self-possessed-looking girl
he has been told about. He tells her he is a
detective from the States looking for a man
named Vaughn. She leaves him abruptly.

Following her, an attempt is made to kill
him, and after a street battle, Morgan takes
shelter from his hunters in the loft of a

warehouse, where a hundred or so opium-
drugged coolies lay sprawled, sleeping.
Stripping off his coat and shirt he lies
among them, and is so tanned that he is
passed over in the rather cursory
inspection.

Getting back to his hotel, he falls into
bed, and in the morning, freshly bathed and
shaved, wearing fresh clothes, he starts to
follow his one clue--the girl's peculiar
reaction to his comment.

The girl is one Etta Bryan, an entertainer
in a nightclub, and she has lived in Bangkok
most of her life, coming there as a child
from Gorontalo, in the Celebes. Listening to
her sing, he sees another watcher is one of
his pursuers from the evening before. Now,
Morgan is a tough man himself, and doesn't
relish being shoved around. He starts for
the man, and the fellow ducks out the door.
Following, Morgan finds the man laying for
him and they slug it out. The police come
and the man escapes. Etta Bryan will still
not talk to him.

He waits to follow her but several tough
men with guns close in. Morgan is taken to a
waterfront shack, where a bruised and
battered man awaits him. This, the man with
whom he fought, is Shanghai Charley. He
slaps Morgan across the mouth. "So,
Detective, you are lookin' for me, are you?"

Morgan tells him he has made a mistake,
that the man he is looking for is much
older, a man named Vaughn. Jim Vaughn.

"Jim Vaughn? What you want with him?"

Morgan explains about the estate, and
Shanghai Charley smokes thoughtfully. Then
he apologizes for the slap and the trouble,
explaining that he himself is wanted in the
States, and has no intention of going back
or being taken back. He also tells Morgan
that Vaughn is dead. Then he asks, "This
Vaughn now? If he had a kid, wouldn't the
kid inherit?"

Morgan learns that Vaughn had fathered a
child. That he had settled down at last in
Bangkok, had married the daughter of a
planter, and they had lived for years.
Charley claims he can produce the child. For
a price. Five thousand dollars.

The following day, Morgan does a little
investigating of his own, then comes to meet
Shanghai Charley, who tells him Etta Bryan
is the child. That Vaughn was her father.

At Etta's home, she shows him several
pictures of Jim Vaughn, including one taken
with the dead uncle. She shows him a
marriage license--Jim Vaughn and his wife--
she shows him a watch, a ring, and a few
other possessions to prove her claim.

Still unsatisfied, Morgan goes to a
Sister, who tells him some facts and hands
him several papers. Then going to an old
man, he learns from him that Etta Bryan had
come to Bangkok from Gorontalo, all right,
but that Jim Vaughn had gone after her, and
had brought her back with him.

Shanghai Charley insists she is the child,
but Morgan nevertheless believes Charley is
attempting a fraud . . . that he knows

something about the child but is attempting to substitute a stooge of his own. Despite that, Morgan is attracted to Etta.

Charley is obviously worried. He will not leave the house, tries to hurry the decision through, tries to get money from Morgan, even gets into Morgan's room and attempts to rob him while he is asleep. When caught, he laughs it off, then insists again that Etta is the right child. That it is no trouble for Morgan—why not take her back to claim the estate? He can, he says, furnish depositions to attest to her birth.

As Charley has underworld connections everywhere, Morgan has no doubt of this, but he believes that for personal reasons Shanghai Charley would like to see Etta get the money.

Returning to the house, he accuses them both of fraud, and tells them what he has learned from the Sister at the convent—that the child was not a girl, but a boy!

Then Charley, obviously in a sweat of fear, asks him again for money, offers to forward evidence later as to who the child is, evidence to prove there has been a mistake.

Disgusted, Morgan goes to the door to leave. Two men lunge in, firing. Shanghai Charley goes down, killing one man as he falls, and Morgan gets the other. These are the men Charley has defrauded and the ones he has been trying to escape.

Dying, Charley begs Morgan to take Etta anyway, explains that he had planned to blackmail her into paying him large sums after she got the estate, but to take her-- that she's a good kid, and was the daughter of an old friend of Jim Vaughn's. Much as he would like to, Morgan refuses.

Charley then asks to see Etta. Morgan sends her in, and leaves them together with a mission priest who is a doctor.

Called back, Charley tells Morgan that he has made his point. That he has married Etta, making her <u>his</u> heir. When Morgan wants to know what that means, Charley explains that <u>he</u> was Jim Vaughn's son!

He hands Morgan the papers, birth certificate and a passport, to prove it.

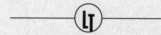

COMMENTS: Kip Morgan was a character Louis first introduced in the somewhat comedic short story "The Dream Fighter." Kip then evolved over the course of several stories from a boxer into a private detective.

Occasionally, Louis would write treatments, like this one, when he was trying to sell ideas or even finished stories to motion-picture or television companies. But because this draft is so roughly sketched out I think it's more likely an example of Louis writing a treatment for his own use, as a trial run for a full-fledged story. He did this very rarely because it was nearly the same amount of work as writing the story itself.

Perhaps this theory explains the origin of some of the other treatments in this volume ... that they were written more as creative experiments than sales tools. I have always hesitated to make that assumption, knowing that Dad disliked having a tale too completely worked out before he really started writing. But he would have had to learn that lesson at some point, so maybe what we are looking at is part of the learning process.

It is also interesting to see both the city of Bangkok and the scene where the hero hides in the opium den show up again. I suspect that this fragment was written before "Citizen of the Darker Streets," but that is only my intuition; I have no evidence.

Certainly "Where Flows the Bangkok" has a lot of aspects that need to be improved, but that is one of the reasons to create a treatment: to allow the writer to confront the story and see where it leads.

VANDERDYKE

The First Three Chapters of a Historical Novel

CHAPTER 1

Icy wind fluttered the small flame and the
firelight danced the shadows on their faces.
The night was bitter cold, and the tiny fire
struggled bravely to put out a warmth that
died almost at the edge of its flame. But
these were men strange to comfort, men grown
harsh in the harshness of the winter
wilderness.

Jeblish Mun, lean and hawk-featured, poked
a small stick into the fire.

"He wants you dead, Van. He was makin'
war-talk, general-like, but when he spoke of
you he was most pa'-tic'lar, and he spoke
clear, with no nonsense to him.

"He said, 'I do not want him taken--I want
him killed. I want to see not his scalp but
his <u>head</u>. I want to look into his dead eyes.
Then I can be sure.'"

"Give any reason why he was favoring me?"

"None that would hold water. He made it
out you were the King's enemy in these here

woods, but it surely seemed like there was
more to it, the way he spoke."

"Jeb?" Vanderdyke looked up from under his
brows from where he lay beside the fire.
"You'd best not go back. I think you've
played out your string around Detroit."

"Kin o' got that idee m'self."

"Did he have a name? Who was he?"

"Never heard no name, an' I didn't waste
around tryin' to find out. Names don't cut
much ice, no way. He was a tall man, on the
thinnish side, but thin like a whip or a
steel blade. Wore one o' them powdered wigs
like they wear down to the settlements.
Described you to a T. Gave me the shivers,
like somebody steppin' on your grave. He
really wants you dead, Van."

Vanderdyke sat up, hunching his shoulders
against the wind. It was cold . . . cold,
cold, cold. Even to him it was cold, and he
had not slept under a roof a dozen nights in
the year.

"Who was there?"

"Couple of dozen Senecas, some Onondagas,
and a Mohawk or two. I seen some Cayuga
around the fort, so if it's Iroquois you
want, they're all there. I could fairly _feel_
those eyes right in the middle of my back. I
taken out. Cold as it was, I never waited
for daybreak. I just up an' skedaddled while
I had my hair."

In the black forest the low wind moaned,
and the river-ice cracked and strained. The
first warm days would break up the ice and

start it downriver. But it would be a late spring.

Vanderdyke was uneasy. For three days he had waited within a mile or two of this place, waiting for Jeblish Mun, Henry Slack, or one of the others to rendezvous here. The longer they stayed in the area the greater the risk, and now that Jeblish had come he wished to move.

"Be war before snow flies again," Jeblish commented. "The Injuns know it, an' I feel it in my bones."

"I will be crossing the mountains, Jeblish. I am going to the settlements."

"What can you tell them they don't already know?"

"I want to see what's happening, and I want to talk to George Mason. He's a canny man, and busy as he is with his plantation he knows all that's happening."

"Comes to fightin', they ain't got a chance back there. Out here on the frontier it's mostly us an' what Injuns they can get to fight for them, but over yonder it'll take an army, which they ain't got.

"Anyway, the Colonies are always wranglin' with each other. Can't agree on anything, so how could they get together to fight?

"Far's that goes, New York, Boston, and Philadelphia are just about as English as the old country. Why, to hear them talk in Detroit there's dances ever' night, and they're dancin' with our girls!"

"Don't worry about it, Jeblish. If trouble comes they will do what needs to be done,

and those girls may like to dance, but when
trouble comes they'll stand with us."

"Who would lead them? Even if those city
fellers could stand up to gunfire, who would
lead them? Who could lead them?"

"There's been some talk of Charles Lee. He
served in the British Army, I think. There's
Montgomery, and of course, Old Put."

"Aye, there's them. Had my choice it would
be that young colonel from Virginny . . .
the one who was with Braddock. Don't recall
as I ever heard his name but he surely
didn't run when the shootin' started. He was
ridin' back and forth, rallyin' the boys to
fight. He didn't scare worth a hoot."

"Washington. He's a planter and a
surveyor. Been out on the frontier a good
bit."

"Injuns still talk about him. They missed
so many shots at him they say he's got a
charmed life. That there's the best excuse
for poor shootin' I ever did hear."

Jeblish took a coal from the fire to light
his pipe. "Him havin' frontier experience
an' all, I can't figure why he didn't tell
Braddock he couldn't fight Injuns the way
you'd fight Frenchmen."

"A colonel of militia," Vanderdyke
explained dryly, "does not tell a general of
regulars what to do or how to do it. He
listens, and speaks when he is spoken
to . . . if ever."

Vanderdyke drew back the ends of several
partly burned sticks to begin killing the

fire. "We'd best move. We've been in one
place too long."

They kicked dirt over the fire, what
little they could find that was unfrozen,
then added snow. The light died and the
shadows took over. Into them the men
vanished as if they had not been. The wind
moaned and blew a few leaves across the
campsite. Where they had been there was
nothing but darkness and the cold.

The forest was thick, then scattered, with
here and there a meadow. Twice they crossed
streams on ice, and finding a place where
the snow had been swept from the ice by the
wind, they traveled downstream where they
would leave no tracks.

Jeblish turned from the ice at a place
where there was no snow and led the way back
through thick forest to a cave under a bank.
Back inside the cave, which had a hole
overhead that had been used in ancient times
to let smoke escape, they built a small
fire.

"Found this place one time. Never seen no
Injun sign around. I laid by some wood a
couple of years ago; nobody never used it.
Either this is one the Injuns missed or they
fight shy of it."

They were not talkative men and now they
were cold. Huddling over the fire, they
gradually warmed, and the small cave grew
less icy.

"You'll be stopping with Lint?" Jeblish
asked.

"Aye. I'll pass the word to him. He's one man alone and he'll need to be watchful."

"That lad of his is coming of size now."

"Aye, and Artemus has a good wife. He's a canny farmer, so they should do well."

Jeblish grunted. "We seen many such, you an' me. Where be they now? Scalps dryin' in some Seneca longhouse."

"But they keep coming, Jeblish. They will never stop coming as long as there's the promise of free land. The French are better traders, and they get along better with the Indians, but trade never settled a land. You need people for that."

In his mind he went over the route he would follow. More and more the people of the frontier were turning to horses, but like the long-hunters, he preferred to travel afoot. By shank's mare, as they put it.

A horse kept a man traveling along a trace while a man afoot could go anywhere. A man left fewer tracks and wearing moccasins as the woodsmen did, their tracks were scarcely to be seen except by a skilled eye. A horse might be faster but day in and day out a walking man could kill a horse, for the man had the greater endurance. A woodsman such as Jeblish or himself could run for hours on end without giving it a thought.

"Figured to scout south," Jeblish commented, after a while. "You figure it's war?"

Vanderdyke shrugged. "Who knows? Most think it can still be worked out, but

there's others, like Sam Adams and Tom
Paine, who think the time for talk is past."

"Figured it might start back there when
the Boston Massacree happened."

"It was nothing but a drunken brawl. Some
idlers on the way home began to pelt the
British soldiers and somebody tired of it
and fired a shot, then they all fired.

"I didn't blame the soldiers one bit.
After all, men were killed with sticks and
stones for thousands of years before a gun
was invented. Anybody who pelts rocks at a
man with a gun is a damned fool and if he
gets shot it is no more than what he should
expect."

"Maybe they thought them guns weren't
loaded," Jeblish commented.

"Then they were doubly fools. I am as
loyal a patriot as any man, and I think the
soldiers were within their rights. So did
John Adams, who helped defend them in
court."

"It'll be war," Jeblish said. "I seen it
comin' for a long time, an' my pa before me,
he seen it. Spoke of it. The King's laws
weren't made for no such land as this, nor
for no such people. They never worked west
of the mountains, and not very well east of
them. Trouble was, Parliament could never
get it through their heads that things were
different over here."

"They've gone against their own laws,"
Vanderdyke agreed.

"Made a nice, neat little package, that
English island did. All the land held by the

King an' a few lords an' gentry. Everybody knowin' his place the day he was born.

"Oh, I ain't sayin' there wasn't some as got out of it! There was . . . one way or t'other. But it would not work over here where there was land forever. If a man doesn't like where he is he just picks up an' fetches hisself west. If folks don't like the government they just move away."

"I know. You and me, Jeblish, we grew up hunting for the table. If we didn't shoot our meat we didn't have any, but over in England only the King and his lords could hunt. Nobody had a gun but the gentry, and no use for one if he did have it. Here everybody has a gun and needs it to live by. If we ever have a country of our own, we can protect it, from foreigners or from rabble alike."

"That's right. If an Injun or somebody comes a-huntin' trouble you might call a constable or the Army. But likely they just get there in time to look at the body and maybe chase who done it. I don't want a government what's going to act without reason, but I don't think I should have to take a chance of dyin' just to give it to them."

Vanderdyke shook his head. "I'm thinking a government that rules an armed people needs be . . . well, polite. I figure that's one way of saying it. They'll learn. Soon enough, the King's men will learn."

Wind guttered the small fire. Vanderdyke drove two stakes into the hard ground and

lay chunks of wood against them to make a
reflector. Rising, he went around the bend
of the cave and out into the cold. Glancing
back, he could see no firelight or moving
shadows. He gathered wood, shivering in the
icy wind, and went back inside.

Jeblish rambled on, suddenly talkative,
but Vanderdyke was thinking of how long it
would take to cross the mountains and return
again, and of what might be gained by
cutting across country. He had learned from
bitter experience that leaving a trail was
always dangerous.

Traces were not where they were by
accident but because long use had proved
them the best routes. Most of them had been
begun by the buffalo; now one never saw a
buffalo east of the mountains, although when
he was a boy there had been buffalo even
there. To deviate from trails meant a man
could get tangled up in swamps, mountains
without passes, and other time-consuming
obstacles. Yet the traces were where the
Indians would be, and where spies would be
watching.

Nobody knew exactly what was taking place
across the mountains. There might be
fighting by this time, and it would be wise
to move with care and approach no settlement
without carefully scouting the area. There
were many Loyalists, men and women who held
to the King and Parliament against all else.
Many of them good people, too.

Most of those living in the Tidewater area
believed things would be worked out and

settled peacefully. As for Vanderdyke, he
was skeptical. With another administration,
perhaps, for there were many in England who
were sympathetic to the Colonies; but
whereas others understood the situation,
George III was both stubborn and ill-
advised.

There were those in England who believed
the Colonies were also striking a blow for
greater freedom at home, but there were
others who wanted the Colonies to pay for
their own defense, and with these Vanderdyke
was inclined to agree. The difference was
that he believed the army to defend the
Colonies should be recruited there, and they
should not have to pay for British Regulars
whom they did not want.

"You comin' back this way?"

"Further south. I may cross by the
Cumberland."

Jeblish added two sections of heavy wood
to the fire. The wind scarcely reached them
here, and there was a chance the fire would
last throughout the night.

"Got no family," Jeblish said, after a
while. "Just as well, times like these." He
banked the fire a little. "Had me an Injun
girl one time. Fine girl. Never was no
better."

"What happened?"

"She was a Huron. Whilst I was off on my
trapline the Iroquois come. Killed her, our
youngster, and half-dozen others. They
taken the hair of her an' the baby." He spat
into the fire. "Taken me two year, but I got

their hair back. Opened up their grave and put it with them."

"No parents?"

"Me?" Jeblish added a small stick to the fire. "I reckon they was good folks. Injuns kilt them, too. That was away back. Neighbor girl, she found me in the bushes an' hid with me. We traveled alone through the woods for eight days, gettin' us to where folks were.

"Eight days in the woods with a baby-child! An' sometimes I figure I done a few things! That damn-fool girl was nigh thirteen when she done it! I tell you, Van, if this here country, with folks like that, don't breed a race of _men_ there's something wrong! Women-folks . . . they can do the damnedest things, if they're of a mind to!"

"What happened to her folks?"

"Kilt. Same time as mine. There was nineteen in the settlement--she told me that when I was older--nineteen, all kilt dead."

Before daybreak, their fire smothered, each went his own way. Vanderdyke started off at an easy trot. The path he followed was little known and rarely used even by Indians, yet it did not pay to take anything for granted. He ran along with long, easy strides. He knew the spring where he hoped to arrive by the time the sun was at mid-sky, and it was some twenty-five miles away. He had often run as far in the morning and an equal distance in the afternoon. The biggest problem was moccasins, for they were constantly wearing out. A fact that enabled a knowing man to identify the tribe of the Indians who had used a camp by the type of moccasins they wore, for each was somewhat different.

He had three hours behind him when he stopped again to look and to listen. Long ago he had learned to trust his instincts and now he found himself uneasy.

Deliberately he turned from the trace and went into the trees. What had alarmed him he did not know, but he realized the senses often perceive things of which a man is not consciously aware. In this case it might have been a faint smell of wood-smoke, a sound, or something distantly glimpsed during one of the moments when he crossed a ridge or hilltop.

He moved now like a ghost, careful to avoid branches or the rustling of leaves. He suspected whatever it was that disturbed him was some distance away, yet he moved warily, pausing often, keeping his eyes and ears alert. He was careful to leave as little sign of his passing as possible, knowing how little an Indian needed.

Again he paused, merging his body with that of a huge old hickory, standing perfectly still, only his eyes moving, seeking, searching. The dampness of fog lay upon the trees and shrubs, an icy fog that had settled all about him. He was some distance from the river now--

A faint <u>clink</u> of metal on metal, but not

close by. In the stillness of the frosty
morning, sounds carried for some distance.

He was well armed, carrying two pistols
for close-range work and his six-shot
carbine. This was a weapon designed by John
Dafte, in London. The six shots were carried
in a cylinder that must be revolved by hand.
The gun had been designed and built in small
numbers more than a hundred years before,
but his was scarcely nine years old, built
by a skilled gunsmith from an ancient weapon
Vanderdyke had inherited from a Dutch
ancestor.

With modifications introduced by the
gunsmith, the weapon had been much improved
and was accurate up to two hundred yards.
After that it became a chancy thing,
although he had scored hits up to three
hundred yards. It was shorter than the long
rifles of the Kentuckians, and much lighter
in weight than the muskets used by the Army.

He waited, listening. For a time he saw
nothing, heard nothing. He was about to step
out when his eyes captured a movement along
the trace, of which he could see only a
little.

Somebody, or something . . . there! Two
men in buckskins, travel-stained and soiled,
behind them a British officer in his red
coat. Then the Indian . . . a Mohawk!

Two more Indians . . . He looked again to
make sure his senses were not deceiving
him. . . . Two women.

Women? White women? Here?

Both women were riding horses and behind

them were several pack mules, then four
redcoats and two more Indians.

The women's hands were free and there was
no evidence they might be prisoners.

Slowly they drew closer, and he stood
rock-still, waiting. To move might be fatal,
for the Mohawks missed nothing.

These were no simple pioneer wives. The
women were dressed for travel, but the
elegance of their costumes could not be
disguised, despite the fact they were far
from civilization, far from any house or
settlement.

Who were they? Where could they be going?

He was no more than thirty yards off the
path and if he was glimpsed they'd be all
around him in seconds.

He held his breath . . . waiting. . . .

CHAPTER 2

A cabin in a moonlit clearing, a barn
adjoining, the skeleton rails of a corral,
and the snow-covered haycocks with the black
wall of forest all around.

A wagon standing alone, the tongue
pointing upward like a finger gesturing for
silence.

Nothing moved but the thin trail of smoke
into the sky, a frail bride for the wagon-
tongue. Nor was there sound, no breath of
wind, only silence and the cold stars. A
smell of wood-smoke on the still air, and

then a shadow that moved under the edging trees.

Inside the cabin a man reclined on a black bearskin before the fire, propped on one elbow to hold his book's face to the firelight, a big man in a rough, homespun shirt, a rifle beside him on the puncheon floor. The man read slowly, moving his lips with the words.

On a bed built into a corner his wife lay sleeping. There was a table, two benches, and a chair made by cutting off one side of a barrel halfway down and building a seat into the barrel's middle.

A candle in a pewter candlestick stood on the table, but it was unlighted. Candles were for visitors, if and when, for stoppers-by were rare. Like the wagon-tongue, it stood straight and listening, for awareness was the price of existence.

In the half-loft where the children slept, young Jacob Lint was awake. He stared up at the rough timbers, thinking of the snow on the roof and of the dark woods beyond the clearing's edge. The Iroquois were on the warpath and revolution was brewing in the Colonies.

He had never seen the Colonies to know them, although he had been born there. He had never seen a schoolhouse and a church but once, nor had he ever seen a store. He thought of these magical, faraway things, often with longing. The only other children of his age he had seen had been the

Elders. . . . That was two summers ago when
they came through, going west.

Pa turned the page and the whisper of it
could be clearly heard. Pa turned half over
to reach for a stick from the wood-box when
they heard the owl hoot.

Jacob saw his father pause in mid-
movement, listening. Very gently then, he
put the book down, marking his place with a
shred of bark. He took up his rifle,
glancing toward his sleeping wife. He got up
in one fluid, easy movement and moved to a
place near the shuttered window. The owl
hooted again, somewhat closer. Jacob Lint
saw his father put the rifle down close to
his hand and draw his knife.

Horrified, the boy stared, his mouth dry.
Indians? Every settler lived in fear of
them, knowing inevitably they would come.
Was this it? Was it now?

They had lived long at peace with the
Indians, but Pa had warned him that Indian
ways were not always the white man's ways,
and they might take offense at something
that seemed insignificant to a white man,
and kill them all. Agreements had been made,
but Artemus Lint knew, and so warned his
son, that such agreements were not
considered binding on those who did not
like them. The old chiefs made agreements,
young warriors broke them, and both were
within their rights. It was a rare chief who
spoke for all his people; as with the white
man, there were always dissenters. Those who

did not wish to accept a treaty simply
ignored it.

At the Lint cabin they had fed Indians,
shared with them what small store they had,
but the Indians took it as their due with no
appreciation of the hard work it took to
grow. The white man was despised for his
planting, for that was squaw's work and only
fit for squaws.

The Indian was inclined to despise the
white man because his traders were always
looking for furs. Obviously the white man
was a poor hunter or trapper or he would
catch his own fur. Artemus, a quiet man with
a quick sense of the feelings of others, had
soon learned several Indian languages and
spoke easily to them. He knew that for the
most part the Indian considered the white
man inferior and looked upon white men with
haughty disdain.

There was a faint scratching at the door.
Jacob saw his father sheathe his knife and
take down the bar and open the door. The bar
itself was a weapon, deadly in the hands of
a man skillful in its use, and Jacob had
seen his father use it on a white renegade.

The latch-string had been drawn in through
its hole so the latch could not be lifted
at night, but when Artemus Lint lifted the
bar, the door swung open and a man glided
swiftly in. The door was closed and the bar
dropped in place. The boy saw only movement
melded into movement and the man was there,
beside the fire.

The newcomer put his rifle down and took

his powder horn off his shoulders and hung it on a peg near the rifle. That rifle had drawn the boy's eye at once, for it was unlike any he had seen before.

"You're welcome. There's meat and bread."

"All's well here?"

"No trouble."

"It will come. I have seen them."

Artemus went to the sideboard. "Milk?"

"It is a good drink."

"Aye, there's many prefer ale, but we've none of it here."

"My father had cows. I grew up on milk."

Jacob's father added fuel to the fire. It was the first comment he had ever heard, from anyone, about the family of Vanderdyke. He was a man of whom no one knew anything, nothing of who he had been, nor of whence he came.

Men who knew said he was the greatest woodsman of them all, and they were not men who were free with compliments. If he had a place he called home no one knew where it lay, nor if he had kinfolk anywhere at all.

Vanderdyke ate his meat and bread, then drank almost a pitcher of the milk before stretching out on the robe before the fire.

He reached over and got his rifle, putting it down beside him. He opened his eyes once. "Seen some Senecas. Six, eight miles back."

He was asleep then, and Jacob Lint looked down from the loft at the long, lean body, the deep chest and powerful shoulders. He looked to be even stronger than Pa, who was considered a mighty man.

Jacob saw his father put the mug on the sideboard and the milk into the cool-hole under the floor. Then his father removed his moccasins and stretched out beside his wife, pulling the buffalo robe over him.

Buffalo were scarce now, and Jacob had seen but three, all at one time. That was over a year ago. The Indians said there once had been a good many and there were still a lot of them south of the Ohio, in Kentucky.

When he awakened in the morning Vanderdyke was squatted by the fire. "Stay close to the cabin," he was advising, speaking to Jacob's mother, "and keep the boy close. He's old enough to keep a good lookout, and to shoot if he has to."

"Artemus will be out in the field," she said.

"Yes," Vanderdyke said. "He came here to build a home, to plant fields, and to make a life for his family and himself. He must get on with it, and you'd have it no other way."

"Times are hard," she said, wistfully.

"They always are," Vanderdyke commented. "There never was a perfect time, and there never will be. You hear of golden ages and glorious times, but they were only so for some people, and even for them it was only some of the time.

"The way to go, ma'am, if you'll take my advice, is to enjoy the minutes and the hours. Enjoy now, not some distant day when things may get better. Maybe they will, but it doesn't really matter. You've a fine son, so watch him grow and become a man. You've a fine husband; enjoy your time with him.

"Maybe if a body works hard enough and keeps a-going, he'll make life easier for himself and his family. Chances are war, taxes, and storm will take a part of it, and maybe all, but those times you have together, those quiet hours, nothing can be better.

"I've known men that wished to be drunk, that wished to have a woman, who wished for this and for that, and all the while, all around them there was so much that was theirs for the taking."

He got up. "I've spoken my piece for the morning, and I reckon I'll drift along now. It is a long way to the settlements."

"The settlements!" She sighed, drying her hands on her apron. "Will I ever see them again?"

He smiled. "More than likely, but you'll find the only difference is there's more to want, more to spend money on. Maybe you live a little more comfortably--"

"I'd just like to sit and talk with another woman." She looked at him, her eyes wide. "It's been two years since I have had a woman to talk to. I don't want to talk about anything particular, just about folks and cloth-materials and how to fix this or that."

"I know." He put a hand on her shoulder. "Folks will be coming by, but pioneering . . . well, ma'am, it's hard on women-folks.

"I'll be back this way . . . maybe next year. I'll fetch you something from a town. Something . . . I don't know what."

"I'd be pleased," she said gently, and watched him away across the field and into the trees.

A moment he was there, and then he was gone, and that was Vanderdyke.

Jacob spoke of it later, to his father. "It's his way. He's a kindly man. A lonely one, I think. Maybe somewhere he lost something . . . somebody."

"He stays nowhere long. He's like a ghost in the woods. He shows up, then he's gone, and never a leaf stirred nor a ripple left behind."

"How does he do it, with the Indians about?"

"He does it. Odd thing about Indians, Jacob, most of them would kill him in a minute and carry his scalp with pride, but they'd miss him. They are warriors and they love a good fighting man. The Iroquois hunt him, and yet they sing songs about his bravery and the things he has done."

Mady Lint stood in the doorway after Vanderdyke was gone. She loved her husband and wished for no other man, yet she sensed the loneliness in Vanderdyke and her heart followed after him.

"He needs someone," she said aloud.

"You speaking of Vanderdyke?" Jacob came close to her.

"Yes. Everybody needs somebody, Jacob. We're lucky, you and I and your pa. We have

each other. Maybe in time you'll have a baby
brother or sister."

"I'd like that, I reckon," he said.

His eyes were on the woods, and he was
remembering what Vanderdyke had said, that
he was old enough to be a good lookout, and
it was something he had already learned. It
was Pa he worried about, out in the field
plowing, and having to give most of his mind
to his work.

Ma had told him the story of how she had
married his father, but he never tired of
hearing it over again. Her father--Jacob had
to remember it was his grandfather--had been
a prosperous man: owner of a store and a
gristmill, a deacon in the church, and
a member of the town council.

She could have married up, as the saying
was, for young men were courting her who
were well-off, but after she met Pa there
was nobody else in her thoughts.

He had come into the store on a day when
she was helping, and he brought furs and
hides to trade. She handled the trading with
him, conscious that he was watching her
always. She was flushed and excited, but not
so much that she did not deal sharply with
him on the furs. They were, she noticed,
beautifully dressed.

"I've come a far piece," he had said,
speaking suddenly and with no preliminaries
or wasted time, "and I'm a woodsy man. I've
neither house, nor land, nor cow, but
there's land aplenty where I ketched my fur,
and a cold spring hard by. I've the hands

and the skill to build a house, if you'll
abide with me."

She looked up at him, right into his eyes,
and her pa said, "Madeline, I--"

She was not listening, although she heard
the words coming to her as from another
time, another age. "I will abide with you,
Artemus. I have been waiting for you to
return."

He just looked at her.

"Three years ago," she said, "in our
church of a Sunday morning. You'd come from
the woods then, too. I tripped on the step
and would have fallen but your hand caught
me. You were so strong, yet so gentle."

"There's a boat going down tomorrow, if
you're of a mind to come."

"What is it like, Artemus?"

"It is sleeping on pine needles and
cooking over a fire. It is trees so large
you cannot believe in them, and lost meadows
with no foot upon them, ever. There are
streams nobody has named, and a far, far
land of beauty that stretches on forever.

"Of a winter the nights are bitter cold,
and time to time there's Indians, some
friendly, some not. It is no easy land in
which to abide, and mayhap you'll grow old
before your time, but there is richness in
it and beauty, and wherever you are, I shall
be close by.

"You will have no fancy clothes and for a
long time there will be no meetinghouse, nor
anybody to attend one. There will be times
you will yearn for the voice of a stranger,

no matter whose, but the soil under your feet will be deep and rich, and you'll have mist rising off the river, the sound of a paddle dipping, and the smell of the forest.

"You will be shaping a new land for those to come after. You will see your own house built and say how you wish it to be, and there will be corn growing where none ever grew before."

"I will come with you, Artemus. Is it to be in the morning, then?"

"Before light," he said.

She took off her apron. "I had best go across to the parson then. He will be wishing to speak his words."

"Madeline?" Her pa was worried now. "It is a hasty thing to do."

"Pa," she explained, her hand upon his sleeve, "I knew three years ago if he came back from the woods and had no woman of his own that he would be the man for me. If you will be telling Mama, I will speak to the Reverend Goslin."

And that had been the way of it. Madeline had never been one to back and fill or flutter her mind over things. She saw what she wanted or knew what she would do and went promptly about it.

She told Jacob later how she had listened to every word she heard spoken about Artemus Lint, and there were words from time to time in those three years while she grew to be a woman and waited for him to come back. There had been talk around the store, for no country is so big that a man is not known

for what he is. They spoke of him as being a
fine hunter and trapper, a good, steady man
who took a drink but did not make a thing of
it, and who saved his money.

She had put by a little of her own,
knowing the man she wanted would probably
never have wealth, although she meant to see
him well-off, in time. She had been sewing
and stitching, too, and no doubt her mother
saw it and wondered somewhat, but Ma was a
woman who kept her own ideas and did not
talk them about.

Jacob liked hearing the story. He knew
this was their third cabin. The first cabin
Artemus sold because he did not like
neighbors crowding him, and the second cabin
was burned by Indians while they were away,
visiting. Artemus had never liked it because
it was too far from the spring.

This, the third cabin, was by far the
best, and with Jacob's help Artemus had put
in five acres of corn, two of barley, and an
acre of vegetables. Hunting had been good
and they'd jerked enough meat for winter.
Soon they would be harvesting corn, but the
root crops were already dug and stored in
the cellar . . . most of them, at least.
Jacob was nine years old now, and worked
beside his father, dawn to dusk on some
days.

On this morning Jacob went to the fields
with his father, driving the old muley cow
his father had trained to draw a cart. They
had begun picking corn; the shucking would

come later. Each walked on a side of the
cart, picking the ears as they went.

At mid-morning they stopped for a breather
and Madeline brought cold water from the
spring and a turnover for each.

"Pa? Who is Vanderdyke?"

Artemus had his mouth full of gooseberry
turnover and he finished chewing before he
answered. "He may be the best long-hunter
there is. Nobody knows how far he has gone
to the westward, to the north or the south.
Folks say he never misses with that rifle,
but he often carries a bow and arrows, too,
and he is equally good with them.

"By name he's a Dutchman, and some say he
came from a Dutch settlement in New York
State. There's Indians who say he's no man
at all, but a 'wind-spirit'. "One story is
that the Senecas killed his family and when
his pa was dyin' he gave Vanderdyke his
rifle-gun and his hatchet and told him to
get away.

"Some Indians say he's always been here,
like the hills and the streams, that he
belongs to the land. One thing seems sure.
He's a loyal man of this country, and will
fight for it.

"He's wary of the Iroquois because he
believes they will join the British against
us if it comes to a fight. They fought
beside the British against the French, and
war will give them an excuse to wipe out
such folks as we are who are moving toward
the frontier.

"One thing is sure. The Iroquois are a

strong, fighting bunch of Indians . . .
conquerors much like the Romans were.

"When the French first came into this
country the fur trade routes were controlled
by the Hurons, enemies to the Iroquois. The
French wanted fur so they naturally sided
with the Hurons, and the Iroquois never
forgave them. At first, because the French
had guns, the Iroquois took a whipping, then
they traded with the Dutch at New Amsterdam
for guns. Then they really started to move.

"They nearly destroyed the Hurons, wiped
out the Neutrals and several other tribes.
For a hundred years they were almost
continually at war, and were feared from the
St. Lawrence to the Tennessee, from the
Atlantic to the Mississippi. What they
haven't subjugated they have destroyed.

"Do not fear them, son. Respect them,
however. They are a shrewd folk, uncommon
fighters, and never to be trusted because
they do not think as we do, nor have the
same standards or beliefs."

Jacob Lint remembered that morning. They
had worked steadily, stripping ears of corn
from the stalks, and from time to time his
father paused, stretched, and took time to
look all about, usually while drinking or
seeming to drink from the water-jug.

That afternoon the cart was not half-full
when suddenly he said, "We will go in now."

"But Pa, the corn--!"

"Can wait." Artemus spoke sternly and
handed the lines to his son. "Drive right to
the barn now, and do not stop."

Artemus picked up his rifle and swung his
powder horn easier to his hand. His face
looked stiff and strange; only his eyes were
alive. "When you get to the house, leave the
cart in the barnyard and go in. Close the
shutters and bar the door."

"Pa?"

"No questions. Move along now, but don't
seem to hurry."

Jacob Lint was scared. He felt his heart
pound with slow, heavy thumps, and his
stomach had gone all hollow. What had Pa
seen? Or heard? Fear choked him, but he kept
his eyes straight ahead while his father
walked alongside the cart.

Often his father had warned him that when
told to do something he should never pause
to ask why or argue, but just to do what he
was told. In an emergency it was best to act
quickly and with intent.

Never had the barnyard seemed so far away,
never had the old cow plodded more slowly.
He wished he had his pa's shotgun. He saw
his mother come to the door to throw out
dishwater, saw her stop and shade her eyes
toward them, then go quickly inside. When
they came into the yard the shutters were
closed and Ma was filling two buckets at the
well.

Turning the cow into the barnyard, Jacob
got down to loosen the traces.

"Don't bother with that. Get into the
house."

There was no sign of anything, no unusual
movement. Taking one of the buckets from his

mother, he followed her into the house. He
took down the shotgun.

His father stood in the barn door. He
caught a movement at the edge of the forest.
Four Indians stood there, in plain sight.
One of them suddenly lifted his bow and
loosed an arrow. It struck, quivering, in
the doorjamb of the barn.

His father did not move. He simply waited,
his rifle in his hands. Another arrow flew,
this one into the casing above his head.

"Why doesn't he shoot?" Jacob cried out.

"That is what they want. If he shoots his
gun would be empty. Once he fires, they will
charge. He could not reload in time."

She was very calm, but her eyes were large
and she was very pale.

Opening the door a crack, Jacob showed the
muzzle of the shotgun, and no more. He
glanced toward his father, and he was there,
his rifle ready and easy in his hands. How
could he be so calm? So steady? He glanced
toward the Indians, and they were gone.

"Why have they gone? Were they afraid?"

"No, Jacob. They are not afraid. Nor do
they wish to die. We were ready for them,
and your father could not be frightened into
firing, and they knew that when he did shoot
he would kill at least one.

"Knowing that, they just went away. They
will come again, and again, hoping to catch
us off guard." She put her hand on his
shoulder. "You did the right thing, Jacob.
You may have made the difference, because
when they saw your gun muzzle they knew two

might die, and if they killed your father, you could still reload and fire again."

"Why do we do it, Ma? Why doesn't Pa take you back to the settlements?"

"He doesn't suggest it because he knows I would not go. This is the life he has chosen and I am his wife."

CHAPTER 3

Vanderdyke's route was south, then east. Deliberately, he avoided the traces, traveling a route roughly parallel to them so as to leave no obvious signs of his passage. It was slower, but safer, and he was never a man to take an unnecessary risk.

This was mingled hardwood and pine forest, and his travel-stained buckskins merged well with the trunks of trees, pine needles, and mottled hillsides, where some snow had melted, leaving patches of gray-brown or yellow grass and leaves.

Crossing a long hillside he came upon an old buffalo trail. The woods buffalo who had frequented the area in the past were somewhat larger than the plains buffalo, and the paths they made were easily followed. Always they held to the contour of the hills and found the best crossings of streams.

By midday he had put thirty miles behind him and found a place on a rocky brush-and-tree-covered hillside where he could rest

and see the country over which he must
travel in the next few hours.

The noonday sun was warm and he had a
sheltered place where he could enjoy the sun
without being seen unless man or beast
approached within a few feet, which was
unlikely as the spot he had chosen was
difficult to approach and far from any
beaten track.

Leaning back against a rock, his rifle
across his knees, he studied the country
before him while he considered the travelers
he had seen the day before. For hours their
presence and probable destination had been
nagging at his consciousness, yet he dared
not let his mind wander in a country so
dangerous.

Two men, obviously women of some
importance, traveling with an escort of
British soldiers and Indians, but traveling
away from any known British fort.

He had back-trailed them for a short
distance in order to establish the
hoofprints of their horses clearly in his
mind. Now he knew he would know those prints
wherever he saw them. All the horses had
been freshly shod, evidently with this trip
in mind.

Had he been less close to the cabin of
Artemus Lint he might have followed them to
see what he could learn; at the same time he
knew how risky that might be, for the
Mohawks were shrewd and cunning woodsmen and
it would not be long before they would
become aware of his presence. It was just as

well he had let them go. Yet their presence
disturbed him.

He broke off a corner of the journey cake
Mady Lint had given him and then a piece of
jerky. He slowly chewed the venison,
enjoying its flavor. The place where he sat
was a hundred feet or more above the floor
of the forest, and he could see the breaks
in the mass of trees that indicated where
streams flowed, and here and there a meadow.
In one of them he could see a deer feeding.

The leaves of the hardwoods had long been
gone, but their gray branches intertwined to
shield the forest floor below that canopy of
boughs. There was a scattering of
evergreens, too, mostly pine.

A slow, lazy hour passed during which he
rested, dozing in the warm sun and storing
energy for the long drive ahead. Such
relatively safe places as that where he now
sat were few and opportunities for rest were
rare.

When he had rested for a little more than
an hour, Vanderdyke started along the slope,
then into the deeper woods. Once under cover
he crouched near a huge old deadfall and
listened. If anybody had seen or heard him
they would come along, hunting him. He
remained unmoving, all his senses alert.
After a brief time, when he heard no sound,
he continued on.

The way he had chosen would take him south
and east across the mountains and into
Virginia. The nearer he came to the mountain
passes, the closer he would come to trouble.

Although there were those who still spoke of the New World, Europeans had been settled along the eastern seaboard for more than one hundred and fifty years. The British colonies expanded slowly but persistently, and those who pushed to the farthest frontiers, building homes in the outer wilderness, developed a sense of independence and self-sufficiency that left them impatient with rulings from the mother country or by the governors of the Colonies appointed from England, rulings that often had little to do with living conditions on the frontier.

Far more important than the ruling powers in the Colonies to the man on the frontier were the Indians. The problem of the Indian was present and immediate, and they met sometimes in friendship, often in hostility. There was right and wrong on both sides-- both white man and Indian had liars, boasters, and outright villains numbered among them; they also had good men, trying hard to achieve a natural and easy relationship.

No two peoples ever met less likely to understand one another than the white man and the Indian, and in those beginning years patterns of behavior were established that were to persist down the years.

Vanderdyke, who had lived with both peoples, had from his first day on the frontier recognized the difficulty. The basic conceptions and beliefs of the two peoples were totally dissimilar.

The word "Indian" is as loose a term as
"European." There were Indians who differed
as much as would a Finn and an Italian. The
Indian was thought to be a stone-age man, but
there were stories of greater civilizations
to the west and south, civilizations that
some white men, with their obsession with
architecture and written language, might have
to take more seriously.

Although the nature of some tribes was
often seen as stoical, the better one knew
the Indian the more one learned to recognize
emotion and expression. He was volatile,
demonstrative, and had a fine sense of
drama. His code of chivalry, while different
from that of the white man, was just as
demanding in its way . . . and, in all
likelihood, the Indian was more faithful
to it.

But only some had anything like the white
man's feelings or traditions regarding the
ownership of land. An Indian rarely thought
of owning land in the usual sense of the
term. Certain areas were regarded by him as
his hunting grounds, but much depended on
the tribe or nation being strong enough to
protect such an area. These areas were often
expanded by war, or were severely contracted
in the same way. The concepts of formal
boundaries and absolute possession were an
alien way of thinking to an Indian.

When the white man first appeared among
them, whether on the first landings or
elsewhere in the country, he was generally
looked down upon by the Indian. Both peoples

were guilty of this, and in this they were
quite similar.

The Europeans' knowledge of the proper
way, the Indian way, of doing things was
either slight or nonexistent. These failures
were seen as weakness and ignorance. Of
course, the white men had weapons that were
superior in certain ways, and their tools
were even better. Yet in other cases
European equipment lacked much. For
traveling rivers and streams the canoe was
superior to the cumbersome boat; for life
upon the prairies the tipi was superior to
any tent the white man owned.

But few Indians understood the source of
the white man's equipment, the technological
progress that it indicated. Few understood
that even the greatest cities in the
Americas were but frontier outposts to the
civilization of Europe. And, as much as
alliances with the American tribes had been
useful to the white men, the larger the
white population grew, the more self-
sufficient it became and the less it needed
the Indian. The days in which the red man
could assume superiority over the whites
were dwindling rapidly.

Vanderdyke came to the path for which he
had been watching. He glanced both ways,
then at the trace itself.

No tracks . . . nothing less than weeks
old, at least. This was an ancient path,
made first by buffalo or perhaps even the
hairy elephants of even older times.

Vanderdyke, who knew a little of many
things, knew such creatures had existed, and
they had been described to him by Indians.
No doubt those Indians had never seen the
creatures, but they had been told of them,
and had shown Vanderdyke some salt licks
where the bones and tusks were to be found.

Vanderdyke had killed his first buffalo
between the Great and Little Kanawha when he
was much younger, and was tolerably familiar
with the country into which he was now
going. There were various Indian trails, all
of them former buffalo paths, and of them
two of the most important led one to the
head of the James, another to the head of
the Potomac.

Before him the valley he had been
following narrowed to a ravine, from which a
small stream issued. He squatted under a
rhododendron and studied the opposite slope
with care, then the slope right below him.
There was a scattering of growth, much of it
only bare branches now. Atop the opposite
ridge he could see a little snow blowing.
The wind was picking up, and if wise he
would be tucked into a new camp well before
sundown.

A fallen log had left a bare space beyond
it where there was no snow and he walked
that way, reaching a cluster of pines where
he stopped again to look around. Although he
had heard no sound, he was uneasy . . .
perhaps because he heard no sound.

He was about to start on again when he

caught a movement from the tail of his eye,
and instantly held himself still.

There was nothing to be seen, yet the
movement had been on the hillside not two
hundred yards off. Even as he looked a chunk
of snow fell from a branch, disturbed by
something that had passed.

He brought up his carbine, holding it
ready in his hands. When he caught the
movement again, it was slight. A shoulder,
or what appeared to be a shoulder.

He waited. Suddenly down the slope he
caught another movement. This was the back
of an Indian, a Mohawk he suspected, who had
just moved into sight. He was on
Vanderdyke's side of the trail, less than
fifty yards away. Both Indians were watching
or waiting for something that was coming
along the creek bed below.

This part of the country was, so far as he
was aware, claimed by no one. The Shawnees
had moved away, the Delawares had been here,
but now it lay empty, although hunted over
by several tribes.

Three Indians appeared suddenly in the
creek bottom. Even as his eyes caught them, he
saw another Mohawk high on the ridge behind
them. Obviously an ambush, and the three
Indians in the creek bed below were the
quarry.

He stood up suddenly and stepped from
the trees, knowing the movement would be
observed. The Indians looked up and he waved
his arms. There was no need to shout.

As instantly as he waved he had stepped

back into the trees. When he looked again
the three Indians in the creek were gone.

Turning swiftly, he darted along the
slope, escaping to a farther clump of pines,
knowing his own life was at stake now. From
below he heard a shot, then another one. He
saw an Indian cross over the ridge, getting
away. In all there had been at least five of
the attackers, and only three Indians in the
creek. Yet the attackers had no desire to
close with their enemies.

Vanderdyke doubted if the Mohawks had seen
him, for their attention had been
concentrated on their quarry, but he dared
take no chances.

Five against three? Vanderdyke was almost
sorry he had warned them, for if the three
were fighters it might have been a battle
worth seeing.

That men might have been killed down below
did not distress him overly much. They had
been lying in wait to take advantage of the
travelers and got no more than they'd
expected to deliver. Men of the wilderness
knew that death was always with them, at
their elbow forever. Men killed and were
killed, just as with the other creatures of
the forest. He had heard it said that only
man killed without need, but that was
untrue. Those who said such things had never
seen a henhouse after it had been invaded by
a weasel. The blood of one chicken might
satisfy his hunger, but it was rare he left
any chicken alive.

Long since, he had come to terms with life

and knew that when death came he would meet
it as might any bear, wolf, or other wild
creature.

The Indian, of whatever tribe, was a wise
fighter. He fought when he believed he could
win, and if he could win without risk to
himself, so much the better. He was none the
less brave because he would kill without
warning, for if challenged to fight he would
almost always do so. His standards were
simply different than those of most white
men; there was no more treachery in him, nor
no less.

Now the three Indians he had warned came
into an open place and stood still, so he
stepped from the trees and did likewise. He
recognized them for what they were . . .
Kickapoos.

A small tribe, but one noted for
fierceness in battle. Now he knew why the
attackers had not wished to continue when
their surprise failed.

The Kickapoos had been relentless in their
resistance to all efforts by white men to
win them over. They had fought the French
consistently, had been attacked by the Sioux
from the west and the Iroquois from the
east, and had resisted both. They had raided
Iroquois towns as far east as Niagara, for
they were noted also for their wandering.
The name "Kickapoo" was derived from an
Algonquian term, Kiwigapawa, meaning "he who
moves about," or "he who wanders."

His rifle was loaded and ready but he

wanted no trouble. "They were Mohawks," he
said. "It was a trap."

"Kickapoo no white man friend," one of
them said. "Why you do this signal?"

"The Kickapoos are great warriors,"
Vanderdyke replied. "I would not see you
killed without a fight."

"You are Vanderdyke."

He was not surprised. He had spent much
time with other tribes; his description
might have gone from village to village,
from tribe to tribe.

"I am Vanderdyke."

"You go?"

He gestured with his free hand. "Beyond
the mountains. I go to warm myself at the
fires of wisdom."

"You find wisdom there?" One of them
sneered.

He shrugged. "As it is with you, some are
wise, some are not."

"You have much enemy."

He smiled grimly. "The Kickapoo has many
enemies, too. A man is known by his enemies,"
he added, "and some enemies of mine are your
enemies also."

"The French?"

He shrugged again. "I do not know the
French. They are not my enemies. The
Iroquois are. I do not seek enemies," he
added. "I wish to be no man's enemy. I am
content to live in the forest, and to hunt."

He lifted his left hand, palm toward them.
"Now I go. I am your friend."

"We do not ask for friend."

Vanderdyke smiled again. "I did not <u>ask</u>
for friend, either. I say I am friend to
Kickapoo."

A step backward put him under the trees,
another step and he was gone. They stood
still, looking after him, and he left them
with no sound, going as a ghost goes, fading
into nothing.

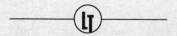

COMMENTS: Below are some of Louis's notes on a story
about the Vanderdyke character. It is likely, however, that
these notes were written years earlier. The story you have
just read seems to be aimed in a different, more sophisticated
direction. As with a number of other entries in this book,
it is written in a form much like a motion-picture treatment with a fairly thin "mid-century Hollywood" plot and
characterizations. Whether he was at one time considering
"Vanderdyke" as a motion-picture sale or not, this treatment
is just the earliest sketch, the bare bones of an idea, which
had not yet developed to the stage where the villain's moti-
vations were completely explored or explained.

VANDERDYKE learns of a mysterious
enemy he has among the British forces;
strange to him, the man obviously has
power and influence, is a strong,
dangerous man. The man is notorious for
his cruelty. His position is uncertain.
Although not an officer, he is seemingly
obeyed by other officers. The sources of
his power are not obvious.

Later, VANDERDYKE visits Gov. Patrick

Henry and meets a young girl there who
is a guest at a neighboring estate, but
often in the Henry home.

VANDERDYKE hears the man who is his
enemy spoken of in most flattering
terms, but expresses his own feelings
frankly. The girl listens to him and is
obviously intrigued by his words, or by
him.

A wealthy woman and her daughter are
also present, and announce their
intention of going to visit a relative
near the frontier. VANDERDYKE advises
against it, but they are indifferent to
his words and plan their trip. They have
a guide and a young man who is going
with them; the latter is very conde-
scending to VANDERDYKE.

He leaves on a further mission and in
the woods encounters the wealthy woman,
her daughter, and the two young men, one
of them an acquaintance of VANDERDYKE's,
as well as a party of Indians accompa-
nying them. The guide invites him to
accompany them, but insists they go to
an Indian village a short distance off
where there will be food. They arrive at
the village and find it deserted, so at
the guide's insistence proceed onward
to a stockade, where they find all gone
but a lone priest and an Indian boy.
They advise the party to escape while
they can, but the wealthy woman insists
she is too tired to go on, and their

guide has assured them there is no danger.

Suddenly a band of Indians led by white men descend upon them; they are taken prisoner, with the exception of VANDERDYKE, who has mysteriously vanished. The leader of the attackers is furious with the guide, but when by questioning he discovers who the woman is, he is somewhat appeased.

When a company of British soldiers invade the area the Indians and bandits mysteriously disappear. Leading this group is VANDERDYKE's enemy, who, posing as the rescuer, is very affable and pleasant. He entertains them all very graciously, and the only skeptic is Van's friend, who sees the whole affair as something of a charade. Yet neither the woman nor her daughter will believe him, and he warns them to say nothing to their guide. The woman does so, however, and the young man is taken prisoner, taken away from them as a "troublemaker." The Enemy then suggests that he will be unable to get them through the Indians around them without help, and he will need from each of them some identification so he can prove to the British they are indeed prisoners. They provide the identification.

Shortly after the renegades and Indians are seen near the stockade by the young man, and the Enemy makes preparations to move out.

The woman and her daughter are convinced VANDERDYKE is the cause of all their misfortune and the girl then says she has seen him near the stockade, talking to the young man.

The other young girl, who had been traveling with them, but who had remained very much in the background, has very little to say, and is not present when a plot is laid to seize VANDERDYKE. Using the girl as bait, they do catch him, and for the first time he comes face to face with his enemy.

VANDERDYKE is to be tortured by the Indians and here the woman and her daughter object. She is refused, and when she angrily objects again, the Enemy knocks her down with a blow from the flat of his hand.

Furious, the daughter threatens what will happen when help comes, and he tells them no help is coming, that he has used the objects they gave him to prove they were dead, and no hope is held out for them.

Horrified, they hear him tell them that when he is through with them they will be given to the Indians, traded into the far west, and if ever found again, they will not be recognized, that the savages have their own way of dealing with such cases.

VANDERDYKE and his friend are to be tortured then burned at the stake.

The other girl gets into the cache of

whiskey left at the fort (its presence
known to her only through a drunken
renegade's babbling) and when the
Indians are drunk, she liberates
VANDERDYKE, and he takes them away with
him.

Under the stockade there is a secret
cache of powder, also, and in leaving,
he explodes it.

An attempt to stop him is made by the
Enemy and there is a fierce hand-to-hand
fight which arouses the Indians and
renegades, but VANDERDYKE'S FRIENDS have
arrived also, and they escape at last.

A few days later, he accompanies
Patrick Henry and some others to a ball
and there he encounters the woman and
her daughter; both cut him dead.

The other girl does not.

VANDERDYKE: a legendary frontiersman,
his exact role uncertain, a mysterious
man who moves through the forest like a
ghost, feared by the Indians, admired by
others, loved by some. He has fed the
hungry, treated the sick, helped the
helpless. He is a dead shot and a
fearless fighting man of great strength
and skills. He seems to have never been
anywhere but the forest, is as much a
part of it as any wild creature. He
appears, then disappears.

A patriot, he carries news to Henry
and his comrades of impending trouble on
the frontier. The Iroquois are being

supplied with ammunition, there is trade
with them going on with the seeming
consent of the British government, and a
shipment of powder, shot, and whiskey
has been attacked by other Indians and
now no one is sure of where it is.

PATRICK HENRY has told VANDERDYKE to
either capture or destroy that powder
and shot as well as the whiskey.

This is a mission, also, to discover
what is happening on the frontier.

There are many stories of his youth,
of his reasons for being where he is,
none of which can be clearly
substantiated.

AUGUSTA GOSLEN: A widow in her
forties, an attractive, opinionated
woman who has always had money, and is
socially ambitious. From a lower-middle-
class family she married into merchant
money. Her husband had invested heavily
in American business and property, so
much against her will, she had come to
America to see what she owned and if
possible to sell it. She has no idea of
conditions on the frontier and insists
on going to the area where her land is.
She has been assured by CHRISTOPHER
SKITTLE that there is nothing to fear,
that he will have adequate help, and
excellent guides.

The plan is to get the widow and her
daughter to a remote place in the woods

and there hold them for ransom while
taking all they possess.

The arrival of VANDERDYKE poses a
problem until they learn that his head
is wanted, and they plan to kill him
also. He senses what is about to happen
and slips away into the forest. His
friend, WILLIAM FOX-FOUNTAIN, is left
behind, which does not dismay him as he
is interested in Augusta Goslin's niece.

One of the aspects of frontier life that this story flirts
with is the differences between the early, colonial-era relationship between Europeans and Native Americans, and
what came later. Early on, there was much more of a balance
of power and a sense of cooperation. Not only did Indians
give some instruction to whites on how to survive in North
America, but they were also important political allies to the

VANDERDYKE: NOT ONLY THE
WOODSMAN BUT A MAN GIVEN
TO CONTEMPLATION.
"OURS IS A DIFFICULT WORLD,
FOR FIRST A MAN MUST DO —
HE MUST BE — WE HAVE NO
TIME, IN MOST CASES, TO CON-
SIDER WHAT WE DO, NOR IF WHAT
WE DO IS WHAT SHOULD BE DONE.
"OURS IS A LIFE OF ACTION.
TO FIRST HAVE A FIRE THAT WE
MAY NOT FREEZE, AND WE HAVE
NO TIME TO THINK OF WHAT
THE FIRE DOES BEYOND GIVE
HEAT, NOR WHAT IT BURNS.
"WE BURN WOOD, BARELY
CONSIDERING WHAT OTHER
USES THERE ARE FOR THE
WOOD — WE BURN COAL ALSO
YET WHAT ELSE MIGHT WE NOT
MAKE FROM COAL?

"YET HE WHO TAKES TIME
TO THINK OF SUCH THINGS
MAY DIE OF OLD BEFORE
EVER HE REACHES A CONCLUSION.

"~~WHAT THE~~
"IF SUDDENLY I AM ATTACKED
BY AN INDIAN, I HAVE NO
TIME TO CONSIDER THE
ETHICS OF THE THING. THE
FIRST CONSIDERATION IS TO
EXIST, TO CONTINUE TO BE.

"PHILOSOPHY IS A PURSUIT
OF LEISURE, AND TO HAVE
LEISURE A MAN MUST
HAVE BOTH SUBSISTENCE
AND PROTECTION.

"VIEWPOINTS DIFFER, HE
WHO VIEWS LIFE FROM AN
ARMCHAIR HAS NOT THE SAME

VIEWS AS HE WHO CROUCHES
BESIDE HIS SMALL FIRE, CLUTCH-
ING HIS WEAPONS.

"WE HAVE DONE HARM TO
THE INDIAN, BUT WE ARE
SIMPLY THE INSTRUMENTS OF
CHANGE.

"HUNTERS HAVE ALWAYS
RESISTED PLANTERS. WHEN TWO
CULTURES COME FACE TO FACE
THE MORE EFFICIENT WILL
INEVITABLY SURVIVE — AND THEY
ARE NOT NECESSARILY EVIL
BECAUSE THEY ARE VICTORIOUS.

"NO MAN NOR ANY RACE
OF MEN CAN BE ISOLATED
AND INSULATED FROM CHANGE.
IDEAS ARE CARRIED ACROSS
SEAS, MOUNTAIN RANGES AND
DESERTS.

Material to be considered for use in "Vanderdyke."

Europeans. As long as European powers fought with one
another over their American possessions, and as long as the
Colonies were not free from their British, Dutch, French,
and Spanish masters, the various tribes were valued for
their ability to side with one group of whites or another.
Though, as is mentioned in this fragment, both Indian and
white did a good deal of looking down on one another, they
could also cooperate in a way that benefited both parties. It
was a situation that did not survive the creation of the
United States without dramatic changes.

In some of the other notes that Louis left behind there is
a slight indication he intended Vanderdyke to be a descen-
dant of his character Barnabas Sackett. However, I am far
from certain that he wrote any of these pages with that in
mind. . . . He may have later decided that would be his direction if he ever returned to finish this story.

MIKE KERLEVEN

Notes for a Crime Story

COMMENTS: This next set of notes shows you what it looked like when Louis was trying to "break" a story. "Breaking a story" is not a term that Dad would have used, but it is how screenwriters refer to the process when they are experimenting with ideas and trying to discover the fundamental building blocks that will allow a concept to become a fully fleshed-out script or movie, or whatever. I've never figured out if the term refers to breaking a story down into acts and scenes, or breaking it open to see what is inside, or even breaking it like it is an untamed horse. . . . My personal experience is that all of these examples are accurate!

Anyway, to discover the pathway into the story Dad would usually use an interesting incident or twist to set it off, then he would try to follow the potential narrative from there. This is a good example because much of the time this sort of work was simply done in his mind.

Mike Kerleven arrives in town; he has lost all his luggage and it is Sunday.

He succeeds in getting some help from
the hotel manager, buying the bag of a
man who ducked his bill.

Mike has bought clothes the evening
before, but had forgotten the traveling
bag. In the bag that he buys he finds
singularly little. There are no clothes,
except that is, for a couple of
neckties, a pair of socks and a dirty
shirt. There are a few other odds and
ends, including a razor (unused) and a
bundle of clippings, all concerned with
fatal accidents and apparently having no
connection. There are several other
clippings and a couple of ticket stubs.

Mike is curious. The various articles
in the bag represent a strange
character, and he becomes obsessed with
the idea, and very little evidence he
has, that the man is in some way
connected with these fatal accidents.
Making an inquiry about the man, he
finds there was a fatal accident in the
hotel on the day he vanished.

Possessed of a little money, he begins
the effort to trace down the owner of
the bag.

Problems: How to bring the killer in
and still keep him a mystery. How to
introduce other characters.

Mike believes in telling about his
belief, hoping in time to attract the
killer to himself, also to make other

people cautious. He finds, after a time,
that the killings center about a certain
area. There are occasional variations,
but it seems the killer has returned
again to certain spots where it is easy
to find someone walking alone and to
dispose of them.

Mike is making friends.

1. The murderer is not known as a "name"
   in the story, not until the very end.
2. The murderer must be tracked by his
   habits, feelings and desires.
3. His character must develop for the
   reader as it does for the investi-
   gator, bit by bit, slowly he pieces
   together a man.
4. In his room, behind a curtain, Mike
   has a jigsaw puzzle of the man. There
   are two charts. One is the figure of a
   man. His size is pieced together by
   various clues. The socks, the shirt.
   His tastes, feelings and reactions are
   placed upon the neighboring chart.

At times changes are made as new
evidence comes in.

Clues: He stayed several days in the
hotel and paid his bill each day.

He stayed several days, yet the razor
is unused. Therefore, he had another
razor or went to barber shops.//
Investigate barber shops.

He likes music, good music.

Bit by bit he forms a physical picture

of the man on one side, and a
psychological picture on the other.

Mike follows down various leads, and
steadily builds up the character of his
man.

And he becomes obsessed with his
figure and does not realize until too
late that one of his new friends fits it
to perfection.

Several friends must be introduced.
The murderer has become aware that he
has someone on his trail. That after
several years of successful killings, he
at last has an antagonist. He draws his
follower near in order to watch him
better. He begins a bloody game. He
tries to trap him into accidents.
He tries to trap him into arrest for a
murder.

The puzzle is first interest. Then the
building of suspense.

The feeling of horror must be brought
in, the helplessness of the victims;
the killer who is not even suspected;
the accidents that no one believes to
be murders; the complete lack of
motives.

Mike must find a man who:

1. Is much alone.
2. Likes good music.
3. Has good taste.
4. Abhors the poor, crippled and
   unpleasant.

5. Who has private income (obviously doesn't work because of times of accidents).
6. He draws nearer and nearer to the criminal. And his danger increases, bit by bit.

Mike goes, in the beginning, to the police. He meets there a detective lieutenant, who scoffs at his ideas. Yet Mike goes to him again, then meets him casually. And the detective begins to wonder, then to believe.

At one time Mike suspects this detective. At one time he even suspects himself. He proves to himself that he could have committed the first crime, and several of the others. His tastes are somewhat similar. He meets the detective at a concert. He begins to wonder. The detective suspects him also.

Then he and the detective work together. The detective gathers material, and they work toward a given end. The detective suggests to Mike that he himself may become a target of the killer. But, if so, the murderer must deviate from his rule. Thus far he has just roamed hither and yon in search of easy victims, off a bridge, under a train.

Decisive clue: a theater stub torn around the edges. In the bag he finds

one curiously torn, then finds another.
The victim has ripped the murderer's
pocket loose in the struggle. Then, in a
theater, he sees the man he has become
friendly with tearing just such a stub!

STAN BRODIE

The First Four Chapters of a Western Novel

CHAPTER 1

His eyes opened upon fear. He lay facedown
on an ill-smelling bed in a small, bare room
with the first edge of daylight showing
around the drawn window-blind. Directly
before his eyes was a boot . . . a boot with
a leg in it.

He lay perfectly still, his eyes open but
his mind empty. Slowly his thoughts gathered
focus.

The leg belonged to a man, and the man was
dead.

How did he know that? Or was he only
surmising? No matter. He did know it. He was
sure of it. Close to his face was a fist,
his fist, and clutched in the fist was a
knife-hilt, the knife gripped for stabbing.
For striking down.

He had not moved and he did not move now,
yet there was a sudden awareness in him, a
realization of danger, a crawling horror of

being trapped, of being caught up in
something he did not understand.

The man whose leg he saw was dead, the
upper part of his body out of sight at the
foot of the bed. Without a doubt he had been
killed by the knife that Stan Brodie now
held, and he was alone in a room with the
body.

He knew he had killed nobody, nor had he
ever wished to kill anyone, but it was
obvious that his good character and good
intentions were not known to the people in
this town and it would be taken for granted
he was the killer.

Murder meant hanging, with or without a
trial.

He sat up quickly, the bed creaking. His
head ached abominably, his mouth tasted
foul, and when he tried to stand his brain
spun. He tiptoed to the window and lifted
the edge of the blind.

An empty alley, gray in the first vague
light of dawn. Western towns were early
towns and in a matter of minutes this one
would be awake and alive.

He looked quickly around: a small, square
room with a bed, a chair, a bureau and
washbasin, a white crockery basin, and a
pitcher of cold water.

He put down the knife. It was bloody.

The hat on the floor was his. No gun-belt,
no rifle. On the bed where he had been lying
in a drunken sleep . . . nothing.

He looked at the dead man. Three narrow

slits in the back of the vest where the knife had entered, very little blood.

One side of the man's face was visible. It was Bud Aylmer.

Bud Aylmer, whom he had met three days ago at a desert water hole, seemingly an easygoing, drifting cowhand who rode in out of nowhere and was going nowhere that he mentioned. Now Bud Aylmer was dead, struck down from behind by the knife that killed him . . . but why?

He had been killed for the gold. They had robbed a stage and the stage had carried twenty thousand dollars. The robbery was supposed to be a lark, simply to scare the stage driver, after which they'd all ride into town and buy him a drink.

Neither Bud nor Stan had known about the gold. At least he had not known about it and did not believe Bud had either. What of the other man, he who proposed the idea? Stan Brodie thought that over and decided the other man had known and that he had planned to kill the stage driver from the first. He and Bud had been suckers, damned fools.

He had a fire going and Bud was making coffee when the stranger rode up to the water hole. He was a tall, high-shouldered man with a swarthy face and a large beak of a nose. His eyes were intensely black and cold.

He had a bottle of whiskey and Bud was ready enough for a drink. As for Stan Brodie, he was no drinker, but as Bud said,

why not one to keep them company? He had
that drink, and then another.

There was no time to think of that now. He
had to get out and get out quickly. He put
on his hat, stepped to the door, and looked
around. An empty hall, an open door a dozen
steps away, and the gray light of dawn on a
dusty street.

Taking one last, quick look about the
room, he stepped into the hall and closed
the door behind him. He had taken three
steps when the door opposite his own opened
and a girl was standing there, wide-eyed and
frightened. He touched a hand to the edge of
his hat to her, and went into the street.

No horses stood at the hitching-rail; the
street was dusty and empty. Wind scurried a
bit of paper into the corner of a building
and somewhere a rooster crowed. Tugging his
hat down he turned toward the livery stable.

Why had that girl stared at him like that?
Had she heard something during the night?
Who was she? What was she doing in that
cheap rooming house for drifters?

He had killed nobody, but how could he
prove that? How did he even know that?
He had known Bud Aylmer but a few hours. He
could not prove that, either.

He saddled his horse in the shadowed
stable. As he reached the stable door there
was a man standing there with his hand out.
"Mister," the man said, "that will be fifty
cents."

He thrust his hand into his pocket, and
his hand stopped. The pocket was stuffed

with coins. His fingers felt among them for
a fifty-cent piece . . . found it. He handed
the half-dollar to the hostler. "There," he
said, "and thanks."

He started to mount and the hostler said,
"Mister?"

Stan Brodie turned, his skin crawling with
apprehension. "You dropped this," the
hostler said, and handed him a gold eagle.

He walked his horse outside, ducking his
head at the door. Turning his mount he rode
down the street at a walk, and his heart
pounded when he realized he had turned the
wrong way, a way that would take him right
down the main street, with all the risk that
implied.

Suppose that girl down the hall had opened
the door of his room and seen what lay
there?

He held the horse to a walk until he
cleared the edge of town, then let it canter
for a half-mile, then a dead run for a
quarter. Seeing where the herd of thirty or
forty head of cattle had crossed the road,
he turned into their trail and followed it
for some distance, heading down into a maze
of ravines.

Of Bud Aylmer he knew nothing but his
name. He had a fire going when Bud rode up.
"Join you?" Bud had asked, and Stan had
said, "Light an' set."

Bud picketed his horse after stripping its
gear, then brought a loaf of bread to the
fire. "Ain't got much," he said. "This an'
some coffee."

"Coffee's on," Stan said. "I've got some bacon."

The third man had come along a few minutes later, made as though to ride by, then swung his horse over to the fire and joined them. He added a can of beans and a fistful of prunes. Then he produced the bottle.

Stan Brodie was no drinker but he knew good whiskey when he saw and tasted it. This was good. Unaccustomed to drinking, Stan took only a sip, but the big stranger smiled at him. "Don't worry, friend. Have at it."

Stan grinned. "Good stuff," he said, and took a hefty swallow. His stomach was empty and he felt the jolt of the whiskey at once.

The stranger got Bud's name, the first time Stan had heard it. He turned to Stan. "Call me Tex," he said.

"Well then, call me Montana," Stan said.

They ate, then they had another drink. Looking back Stan could see how Tex had guided the conversation.

It was not until they had still another drink that Tex suddenly chuckled. "Got a friend drives stage through here. Rides empty most of the time. I've got a notion to give him a scare."

"How's that?" Aylmer asked.

"Oh, I dunno. Maybe put a sheet over my head an' play ghost . . . only I don't have me a sheet. Be fun at that. Tom is sure a scary one. On'y thing he's scared of is ha'nts and holdups, an' I don't reckon he's seen nary one."

"Knew a feller stuck up a stage one time,"

Bud said. "They done it just for the fun of it. For the excitement. You know, they'd been out on the trail pushin' a herd of steers up Kansas way and they was plumb bored, an' they seen this stage . . ."

They ate, drank, and discussed the humor of scares and being scared, each one coming up with a story to tell. Under the influence of the liquor and amused by the idea of a practical joke, they accepted Tex's suggestion.

"What the hell?" Tex said. "Let's do it! Give him a good scare an' then ride into town an' buy him a drink. Be a real lark . . . like Hallowe'en."

The trouble was the stage driver was not scared. He grabbed for his six-shooter.

Tex shot him, grabbed the express-box, and they fled. Half-drunk they raced away, sobering quickly in the chilling awareness of what they had done.

When they pulled up, Aylmer said, "Tex, you shot that driver. You killed him."

"Hell, he was fixin' to kill us! You seen his gun come up!"

"This was s'posed to be a lark, a game, sort of. We didn't bargain for anything like this."

Tex shrugged. "Well, we done it. Might's well divvy up an' skip the country."

"I want no part of it," Aylmer said.

"Me neither," Stan agreed. "I'm no thief."

"You sayin' I am? I wasn't alone back there. But what's done is done." Tex scowled at him.

"I'm only sayin' this was a damn-fool notion and we'd better return the money and light out . . . fast. That man's dead an' that could mean a necktie party."

Tex shrugged. "Well, maybe you're right. It wouldn't do for us to get caught with this stuff. I'll tell you what. We'll ride into town, leave the stuff, have a drink, then get the hell out of the country."

It had made a kind of sense at the time and neither of them had a better idea.

Tex indicated a saloon as they rode in. "Let's have a drink and get the lay of the land," he suggested. "Then we can decide where to leave the gold."

Tex seemed friendly with the bartender and they all had a second drink on him. That last drink evidently carried something special because Stan recalled nothing more until he awakened in the rooming house with Aylmer dead on the floor.

Why had Bud Aylmer been killed? Had he awakened and caught Tex leaving with the loot? Or was there some other reason? The fact remained that whatever the reason, Bud was dead.

Looking back it was easy to see that Tex had planned the whole operation. Obviously he had known about the twenty thousand in gold the stage was carrying, and he had simply picked up a couple of gullible drifters and talked them into helping him. He had then killed Bud and stuffed Stan's

pocket with gold, evidence enough to hang
him for both the killings.

Stan Brodie turned from the trail where
several cows had crossed it and followed
their trail along a ridge until he could
look over the country. He disliked sky-
lining himself but this was not familiar
territory and he needed to put some distance
between himself and town.

He followed a game trail marked with fresh
tracks of a deer. He was no more than five
or six miles from town but well away from
the usual trails.

Nothing was to be gained by riding without
destination, and if he got out of this
predicament it would only be by using his
head. From time to time he glanced down his
back trail and kept aware of the country
around while trying to assay his position.

Nobody back there knew him. He had been
seen by that girl and by the hostler. No
doubt some of those in the saloon the night
before had seen him, but how many would
remember him he could only guess. Nor did he
know how he had gotten into that room where
he had found himself.

Tex had not known his name, nor had Bud
Aylmer, so he had that much going for him.
Yet as soon as Bud's body was found they
would be looking for anyone connected with
him.

Obviously Tex had planned for him to be
found in the room with the dead man, a
knife in his hand and loot from the stage
robbery in his pocket. There could have been

no other reason for stuffing his pocket with a couple of dozen gold coins.

Thinking of that, he counted the money for the first time. Twenty gold coins of twenty dollars each. Four hundred dollars that would buy him a rope necktie if they were found on him.

He had eighteen dollars of his own money and the hostler had seen him drop a gold coin so he would keep the oldest and most worn piece. He began looking for a place to cache the rest.

Rounding a corner of a bluff he saw a huge rock, tall as a three-story building. Momentarily out of sight of any trail, he dismounted and climbed up to the rock, hiding the money under a pack rat's nest in one of the wind-worn hollows.

He climbed down, dusted his pants, and turned to his horse.

A rider was sitting there, holding his horse's reins. He was a tall man with close-set eyes and a coarse face. "What you doin' up yonder?" he asked.

Stan Brodie took the reins from his hands. "Never could pass up one of those honeycomb cliffs," he commented. "Always figured there should be something hid in them. Too obvious, I guess."

"Find anything?" The small eyes probed his.

"Oh, sure! Pack rat's nests, one hawk's nest, and a place where there was fresh bobcat sign. I came down fast. I got no wish to tackle a bobcat on a cliff-face."

He mounted. "One time I did find some
pots, and when I told some Eastern dude
about them he offered to pay me to show him
where they were. He said some folks study
them."

"You mean them ol' clay pots like the
Injuns use?"

"Uh-huh."

"That makes no sense. They're just pots
for storin' water, grain, an' such. Anyway,
what did them Injuns know?"

"Maybe, but he give me twenty dollars to
guide him. Only a few miles, too. Easiest
twenty bucks I ever made."

They rode on, the stranger lagging,
seeming in no hurry. Soon the stranger
pulled up. "I been thinkin'. I've got no
grub for a long trip. You headin' west?"

"Uh-huh."

"I'd better stock up. See you."

The stranger swung his horse and started
back. Stan stared after him, glad to be free
of him yet worried as to what he might say
back in town. He might also stop to look
over that honeycomb cliff, just for luck.

The morning was hot and still. Heat-waves
danced over the bunchgrass levels where the
cattle grazed . . . a few cattle.

A lonely, empty land, and he was unarmed.
Tex had taken both his Winchester and his
Colt. He needed a gun. He had never killed
anyone and did not want to . . . not even
Tex. Gun or no, a man who wanted to kill
could always find a way. Defending yourself,

however, that was often a last-minute thing
and a gun would be good to have.

He had seen too much killing in his time.
All he wanted was a quiet place where he
could work and save a little.

He rode on into the morning, rode until
the sun was high. Sweat trickled down his
face and into his eyes. He looked back.
Nothing . . . nothing yet.

Finding a dim trail leading off to the
east and north, he followed it. When he had
gone a hundred yards he tied his horse to a
clump of brush and taking off his boots
walked back in his sock feet until he
reached his turnoff. The tracks he had left
were vague. He took his hat and fanned the
dust until the tracks showed almost none at
all. Backing up, he did the same thing
further along, then returned to his horse,
brushed off his tracks, pulled on his boots,
and rode away.

Was that a dust-cloud?

He had been a fool to take those drinks.
He had no head for liquor and had never
cared for it. Tex made it all seem like a
joke until suddenly that driver was dead and
it wasn't funny at all. If they caught him
they would hang him.

When that stage driver reached for his gun
Stan knew it was no lark. That driver hadn't
been amused. Then Tex shot and the driver
tumbled into the dust.

Tex had known right where to look for that
box and he had gone right to it, paying no
mind to the driver he had said was his

friend. Of course, that had all been a lie.
Bud and him . . . they were fools. But he
had never heard of anybody escaping hanging
because he had been a fool.

He slowed his horse. No use killing the
poor beast because he was running scared.

Something shadowed the land, far ahead.

Hills? Trees? A ranch? No matter, for
there was apt to be water and he was already
spitting cotton . . . or would have been if
he could spit. The horse needed water.

He glanced at the shadows behind the
brush. Almost two hours past noon. The
shadow ahead began to take shape and it was
all three things he had suspected: low
hills, trees, and a ranch.

When he came up to it the house and barn
proved to be low buildings made of flat
stones taken from a ledge behind the barn.
There were a couple of corrals, no horses or
cattle, but there was a well.

He rode into the ranch-yard and swung
down. There was water in the trough, some
green moss in the bottom of it, and there
was a pump. He trailed the reins and
began pumping. He expected to have to prime
the pump but it was not necessary. Clear,
cold water gushed into the trough. With a
gourd dipper that hung from the pump, he
drank, then drank again.

He pumped the trough full, keeping an eye
on the house. There was neither sound nor
movement. Was it empty?

Stan Brodie pushed his hat back on his
head and, holding the dipper for another

drink, he looked carefully around. No sign of life, no dogs, no stock, yet the pump had been recently used.

The leaves of the cottonwoods rustled and the sound brought him to realization. He was still not far enough away for safety but his horse had been hard ridden and he knew it needed rest. He led the horse to the stable. There was fresh hay and he forked some into the manger. He stripped off the gear and left the horse free to eat or to roll in the dust of the corral. If anyone did come he wanted to appear unworried and unhurried.

He took a handful of hay and rubbed the horse down, talking to it as he did so. A man had to talk to somebody and most cowhorses received a lot of confidential chatter which they were in no position to repeat. That was one thing about a horse. You could say almost anything to it as long as you treated it decent.

Walking outside he sat down on the bench that circled a huge cottonwood. The soft wind stirred the hair over his damp brow. It was good, good to stop if even for a little while.

Stan Brodie was twenty-two and had been an orphan since he was nine. He had never had anything like a home since his folks passed on, but he knew what a home could be like.

Once when he was eleven a man needed a boy to do some chores around the place, but when Stan arrived the man was not yet home so the maid showed him into the parlor and warned him, "Now just you set, and don't you touch anything."

He had seated himself on the very edge of the sofa, holding his cap in his hands. The carpets were deep and soft, and there were pictures on the wall and some glass-doored bookcases holding books in red and gold or black and gold leather. There was a lamp with a fringed lamp-shade and the room was all red plush, so quiet that his breathing worried him.

Finally he tiptoed over to the bookcases and read the names on the books. Scottish Chiefs, by Porter; Lord Halifax, Gentleman, whose author he couldn't make out; Pilgrim's Progress, by John Bunyan; and The History of the Five Indian Nations, by Cadwallader Colden. He was staring longingly at the books when a man entered.

"What is it, boy? What are you looking for?"

Guiltily, Stan had stepped back quickly. "I . . . I was just looking at the books, sir."

The man was pleased. "Well . . . I haven't many. About thirty, I'd guess, but I've read them. Most of them several times. Can you read, boy?"

"Yes, sir. I can do sums, and I can write. I went to school in the orphan asylum."

"Orphan? You've no parents?"

"No, sir. Not that I know of, sir. My mother died when I was nine and my father was off somewhere and nobody knew where to find him. I ran away from the asylum, sir."

"Why?"

"I wanted a job, sir. I wasn't getting anywhere in that school."

He had worked for Alec Winters for two months, cleaning up the yard, cutting grass, sawing wood, and exercising his horses. Then Mr. Winters got him a job herding cattle.

Not that he was a real cowboy. He had to be sure that no cattle strayed and to bring them into the big corral at nighttime. He stayed with the job all summer and when he left Mr. Winters he had seventy dollars. He put ten dollars in his pocket and hid the rest in his belt at a place where the stitching was broken.

Two men grabbed him as he left town. Peterson was an itinerant laborer of doubtful background, the other man he did not know. One held him with his face in the dirt while the other went through his pockets. They found a little more than seven dollars because he had bought a pair of shoes.

"Where's the rest of it?" Peterson demanded angrily. "Winters paid you seventy dollars."

"No, sir," Stan lied. "There was the deducts. He deducted some for this, some for that. There was no more than ten dollars left when he got through."

They did not want to believe him, but they did. Deducts were a common experience and more than one workman had found himself broke at the end of a job. There were deductions for time lost, for tools broken, for any excuse an employer could find. Why should Winters have treated this youngster any different?

They argued, slapped him around a little, but he held to his story. Then they let him go, telling him to keep going and that they'd beat the life out of him if he came back and told anyone.

He kept going.

That was in Illinois. In St. Louis he cleaned boots and shined them, in Louisville he was a printer's devil. In eastern Kansas he helped with the harvest, and in Fort Smith he worked for a printer again, delivered newspapers, and swept out a saloon every morning before opening time. He earned two dollars a month from the printer and fifty cents a month from the saloon-keeper, but he actually found the equivalent of four or five dollars a month in the sawdust on the saloon floor. Or he did until the saloon-keeper found how well he was doing and began sweeping his own floor.

When he was fourteen he joined a cattle drive that had been turned west short of Baxter Springs and drove to Abilene with it. He drifted south when the cattle were sold and joined another drive starting near San Antonio.

He drove an ox team from Westport to Cherry Creek, Colorado, tried placer mining, worked on other men's mines, swung a sledge driving spikes on a railroad, and then one night he helped a drunken man home.

The man's wife was a plain-faced, pleasant

woman who took her husband and put him to
bed. She glanced critically at Stan. "Should
I know you?" she asked.

"No, ma'am. I'm Stan Brodie. I've been
laying track for the Denver and Rio Grande.
Your husband got a bit too much and asked if
I'd help him home. I never saw him before."

"You're a good lad. Will you have a cup of
coffee? That's the least I can do."

"Yes, ma'am. Your husband was talking to
me for some time, ma'am. Said some mighty
fine things about you."

"He's a good man. He just can't handle
whiskey. He never could. Mostly he stays
away from it but when he starts . . . What
worries me is the paper."

"Paper?"

"We publish the _Bugle_. He does it all, but
without him we'll have nothing and now we're
apt to lose it all."

"But he'll be sober in the morning."

"Not him. He will be drunk for weeks, if I
know Tom. We can't afford it."

Stan put down his cup. "Ma'am, I could run
your newspaper. I have done it before."

When morning came he appeared at the
newspaper office, which was below the rooms
where he had taken Tom Hayward the night
before. Mary Hayward opened the door for
him. "It isn't much," she said, letting him
in. "Can you handle a Washington handpress?"

"Yes, ma'am. I used one in Fort Smith."

"There's the type. Most of it is there.
There isn't enough of the letter 'k' so

Tom's been using 'q' in its place. Most of
our readers are used to it by now."

"All right, ma'am. In Fort Smith we didn't
have any 'f' and we made do with 'ph.'"

"The paper is due out tomorrow and I am
afraid he doesn't have anything done.
There's a few items he's set up over there,
mostly local news. The patent-medicine ads
are set." She looked worried. "There will be
a lot of space to fill, I'm afraid."

"Yes, ma'am, there nearly always is. Don't
you worry about it." He held out his hand.
"You might give me that key. I've got to run
down the street for a few minutes."

Gebhardt was sitting over his breakfast in
the Stockman's Restaurant where Stan had
known he would be. He dropped into a seat
opposite him.

"Gep, do you still have that St. Louis
paper I saw you with?"

"It's over in the wagon. Mighty handy out
on the road to have a paper around. Why?
D'you want it?"

"I need it. That paper isn't more than a
week old, is it?"

"Week? Why, that paper is just two days
old! Got it from a Pony Express rider."

"Can I have it?"

"Sure enough. You'll find it down on the
left side of the seat."

Stan picked up the newspaper and glanced
over it on the way back to the office.

Inside, he sat down and read through the
last few copies of the Bugle, capturing the
essence of the style used by Tom Hayward.

Then he set up the type for a story on the candidacy of Ulysses S. Grant for president lifted from the St. Louis paper.

He found another story on a speech by Schuyler Colfax, who was to be Grant's running mate, on payment of the national debt in gold.

He also included a brief item to the effect that an organization calling themselves the Jolly Corks had formed a new organization to be called the Benevolent and Protective Order of Elks. He also reported the robbery of a train at Marshfield, Indiana, by a gang reported to be the Reno brothers.

Stan remembered that day and those that followed. Most editing was done with scissors and a paste-pot, newspapers borrowing liberally from each other but careful to give credit. Where additional space had to be filled, he added bits and pieces from memory, a poem by Lord Byron, and an historical question about the name of the great-grandson of Cleopatra who became emperor of Rome.

He chuckled, remembering that. Nearly every subscriber had written in wanting to know who the emperor had been and how it happened. "Caligula" had been the answer and historical or sporting questions had become a regular feature of the paper from that day on.

He was startled from his reverie by the sound of horses' hooves . . . a lot of

horses. He started up, then suddenly
realizing he could not run, he removed
his coat quickly, folded it, rolled up his
sleeves, grabbed a bucket, and started
toward the house.

They rode in and drew up sharply, dust
swirling about them. "Howdy!" The man wore a
star, as did one of the others. "Mind if we
have a drink? We're huntin' a killer."

"You don't say?"

"Held up the stage an' murdered his
partner, but we'll get him. He ain't gone
far."

"I've seen nobody." He gestured toward the
well. "There's water, and I've just pumped
the trough full. Help yourselves."

"He didn't come this way," one of the
posse volunteered.

"This was the closest water so we circled
around." He looked at Stan again. "Do I know
you?"

"I haven't been around long," Stan said.
"Just came in to help out a little."

"Well, they can use it. Carrie's all right
but she's not up to all she has to do. I
hope you can help her, son. I hope you can."

He heard the buckboard coming as they led
their horses to the trough. He felt his
mouth go dry.

Several of the men had remained in the
saddle. His own horse was unsaddled and in
the stable. He was trapped, his stomach gone
hollow, his heart beating with slow, heavy
throbs.

The buckboard came up in a clatter and a

rattle and swung into the yard. A pair of matched grays driven by a girl. A girl with red hair and freckles.

The girl from the hotel.

CHAPTER 2

The red-haired girl's eyes were upon him. Her surprise obvious.

"I'm sorry, ma'am," he heard himself saying, "I haven't done much yet. But I'll get to it."

"I guess we interrupted, Carrie," the man with the badge said, "comin' up the way we did. But I'm glad you've got some help until things get straightened out. If there's anything we can do . . ."

"No, Mr. Blake," she replied, "Stan will take care of things. I have an idea he will prove to be the best hand we ever had. If he doesn't," she added, smiling, "you will be the first to know."

"'Day, ma'am. We'll be ridin' on."

"I think you must be, Sheriff. There's been a hanging."

Stan felt a chill finger run along his spine. He stood very still. "They caught a man in town, and he'd been spending that new gold . . . like that stolen from the stage. When they searched him they found a lot of it and, well . . . I believe they were kind of hasty."

Blake's face showed angry impatience.

"Damn it, I--!" Then he looked to her.
"Sorry, ma'am, but they should have held him
for trial. This here lynching has got to
stop."

He swung his horse and rode out, followed
by his posse.

For a moment Carrie and Stan simply stared
at each other, then she said, "Put up the
horses. Then come into the house. I think we
should have a talk."

She got down from the buckboard before he
could move to help. She looked straight into
his eyes, a cool, searching glance.

She was pretty, he realized suddenly, very
pretty. The few freckles only made her more
attractive. He had always liked girls with
freckles, anyway.

He took the team into the shadowed
recesses of the stable and stripped off the
harness, hanging it on hooks left for the
purpose. He took his time, trying to think
it out.

Where did she stand in all this? Why
hadn't she given him away? How had she
gotten his name? Was this her ranch? What
had she meant when she added that comment to
the sheriff that if he did not pan out he
would be the first to know?

He could saddle up and run, but his
direction was the way the posse had been
searching, and if he left here now there
would be questions, too many questions.

He dried his hands on his pants, wiped
the sweatband of his hat, and started for
the house.

Coffee was on and it smelled good. When he removed his hat and stepped into the house there were two cups and saucers on the table along with bread and butter and some cold slices of meat.

"Sit right down," she said, "I'll be only a minute."

He sat down carefully, holding his hat in his hand. It was a cool, pleasant room with window curtains, rag rugs on the floor, and a couple of oval, tinted pictures on the wall. One was of a man with a round head and a collar that was a size too large, the other a dignified-looking woman with her hair done up on top of her head except for three curls on each side of her face. They looked like all the other pictures of people he had ever seen.

There was a Bible on the table, a big, square old-fashioned Bible with heavy leather covers. There was a coal-oil lamp and in the corner some shelves with books, about twenty of them, and some stacks of Godey's Lady's Book. The room was neat, clean, and quiet.

In a moment she came in, poured coffee, and sat down. She looked across the table at him. A pretty girl, he thought again, but a stubborn one.

She smoothed her skirt over her lap, then she lifted her cup. "The first thing you must understand," she said, "is that you are my prisoner."

"What?" He was not sure he had heard right. "What did you say?"

"One word from me and you would be
arrested, perhaps hung. I shall not give
that word unless I must. If you do your work
properly and conduct yourself correctly I
shall not give it."

"I have done nothing," he said, which was
a small lie. He had participated in a
holdup, even if it had been done without
criminal intent.

"That is no concern of mine," she said
primly. "That would be for the courts to
decide . . . if it ever got so far. My
concern is this ranch. My father has been
injured. It will be weeks before he is able
to work, and it may be months. In the
meantime, I have you."

He did not believe it. He stared at her,
shocked. "Now see here," he began, "I--"

"You see here! As you noticed, the sheriff
is a friend. So is every man on that posse.
So are many of the people around here. If
you leave before I permit you to leave, or
if anything happens to me, you will be
caught and hung . . . hanged."

He studied her for a minute. "You know,"
he said, "you're not a very nice girl."

She flushed to the roots of her hair, but
her chin lifted. "My character is not under
discussion. Each day until you understand
the situation here I shall lay out your work.
Each day I shall expect a report that the
work has been completed.

"The weather is good. You will sleep under
that farthest cottonwood. When you are on
the home ranch you will have your meals here

with me. You will attend strictly to
business. From time to time there will be
visitors. Talk to them as little as possible
and perhaps I can keep you alive."

"What about wages?"

"You--? You speak to me of _wages_?"

"Yes, ma'am. I will want wages. Slavery
has been outlawed in this country. I shall
want thirty dollars a month and found,
payable at the end of the month. If you
don't want it that way, turn me in."

She stared at him, uncertain whether he
was bluffing or not. His features were
bland, unreadable. Suddenly uncertain
herself, she wavered. Then she said, "I see
no harm in that. If you were not here I
should have to pay someone else.

"Also," she continued, "I shall want your
gun. You will not need one here."

"I have no gun. I have no firearm. Neither
rifle nor pistol. They were taken by the man
who murdered Bud Aylmer."

Obviously, she did not believe him, but
before she could speak he said, "Please
think back. You saw me in the hotel. If I
had been carrying a weapon you would have
seen it."

He finished his coffee and stood up. "If
you have no further need of me, I'll be
going. In the meantime you might list the
things that need to be done."

He went outside and stopped in the morning
sunshine. He should get out of here, get as
far away as he could, yet he was certain she

would do just as she threatened and Stan had
no doubts about that sheriff--he was a tough
man.

Her name was Carrie . . . Carrie what?

What kind of a spot had he gotten into,
anyway? How long did she expect to hold him
here? Until her father returned? And what if
he never got well?

<u>Stan Brodie</u>, he told himself, <u>play it
cool, play it smart, and when the chance
comes . . . run!</u>

He had never been given to idleness, and
the presence of work was the occasion for
work. He started by repairing the corral
gate, which needed fixing. Then he forked
hay to the horses. The hay started him
wondering. It was good meadow hay, and the
meadows spoke of low ground, possibly water.
He had seen little water coming here and
most of the range closer to town was
indifferent, at best.

He led out his horse and saddled up. As he
tightened the cinch he looked across the
saddle at the house, and she was standing in
the door with a rifle in her hands.

"You wouldn't be thinking of leaving?" she
suggested.

"Just thought I might ride out and see
where that hay came from. If I am to be of
any help I'd better get acquainted with your
range."

He rested his hands on the saddle. "You
know, if you're going to keep an eye on me
you'd better ride along. I might just decide
to take out of here."

"There's the sheriff," she replied, "and that posse. Then there's that rough crowd in town who might want another hanging. I am not worried about your leaving."

She lowered the rifle. "Ride north two miles. That point of rock with the white streak of quartz in it marks our corner. Then ride east for six miles or just about that. You will see a hole in the rock, high up. That's the Keyhole. Everybody around here knows it. Ride south four miles to Two Cabin Creek and about a quarter of a mile further on you will come to our line fence. Then come back here."

"Sounds like quite a layout."

"It could be. If you see any riders over toward Two Cabin, stay clear of them. They won't be friendly."

"May I ask why?"

"They want the water in Two Cabin. They settled over beyond there knowing they couldn't make it without our water and knowing it belonged to us."

Stan Brodie considered that. "What happened to your father?"

"His horse fell with him."

"Where's the horse?"

"We had to destroy him. He broke his leg."

This was a wide and empty land where the short-grass plains ran up to the mountains and lost themselves in the open mouths of the canyons. Yet it was a deceptive land, for viewed from afar it seemed only one vast plain of gently rolling hills with here and there a butte or mesa standing stark against

the sky. Riding over it one found that the
plains and rolling hills were cut by shallow
canyons and the dry streambeds that ran only
in the hours following heavy rain.

Stan Brodie had punched cows in just such
terrain, and rode warily. Without a gun he
felt naked and exposed. He had climbed
somewhat and the grass seemed greener, due
no doubt to some pattern of prevailing winds
and rainfall. Miles away he could see what
he was sure was the Keyhole, the rock Carrie
had mentioned.

There were a few longhorns mingled with
some of the whiteface cattle they were
beginning to bring into the country. Dipping
into a grassy hollow near an arroyo he came
upon the ruins of an adobe house, gutted by
fire. A lean-to barn some distance away was
also burned . . . Indians probably.

Suddenly a buzzard flew up, then another.
He rounded a turn in the arroyo and before
him lay the remains of a dead horse. Two
more buzzards flew up and he drew near. This
must be Carrie's father's horse.

Buzzards had been at work on the carcass,
but the forepart was little damaged. He
glanced at the broken leg. It had been a bad
break, offering no chance to save the horse.
He was about to ride on when something else
caught his attention. Swinging from the
saddle, he walked back.

Across the front of the horse's leg right
above the break the skin was broken, a
straight-across gash that had cut to the
bone. The animal must have run full tilt

into something, maybe the bottom wire of a fence, tripping the horse and throwing the rider.

He returned to his horse and mounted, but he did not ride away. That horse had ridden into something, a taut wire it looked like, yet such a wire in a canyon like this was unlikely. He looked around, studying the rocks and the ground.

Whatever tripped that horse had to be close by. No horse was going far with a leg like that.

He wished he had a gun.

He walked his mustang down the canyon, then pulled up. A lot of hoof tracks . . . This must be where the horse had fallen, then it stumbled up and hobbled around.

The horse would have been killed when they found Carrie's father.

What _had_ that horse tripped over? Had Carrie guessed that the horse tripped?

No wire.

The canyon widened a little and there was a cove on each side. He walked his horse over and checked one cove. Nothing. In the other he found the tracks of two horses and the stubs of cigarettes smoked by men who waited here. One of them smoked his cigarettes tight and small.

But were those tracks and cigarette stubs left before or after the accident?

He glanced back toward the dead horse, out of sight now. Walking his horse, he studied the rocks on both sides of the small canyon.

Turning, he strolled back down the canyon,

keeping his horse beside him. One wall of
the rocks was honeycombed and pitted, and
suddenly he saw what he had been expecting:
a place on the edge of one of the holes
where something had chafed the rock.

Squatting on his heels, he glanced into
the shallow hole. It joined another hole not
over a foot away. A wire had been run into
one hole and out the other, then tied to
itself outside the holes.

He stood up and glanced directly across. A
juniper, squat and gnarled, stood just
opposite. Walking over he could see where
something had scratched the bark.

He walked back, brushing out any tracks he
might have made, then mounted. Someone had
stretched a wire across the canyon at that
point, then somehow, by a shot or some other
means, had startled Carrie's father or the
horse into a run. Hitting the wire he had
spilled over, breaking the horse's leg and
injuring himself.

Stan glanced around quickly. He had better
get away from here, and fast. Quickly he
turned his horse into some deep sand in the
bottom of the arroyo where no defined
hoofprints would be left, then he climbed
out of the arroyo and lost himself along a
hillside covered with juniper. It was
scattered, but in places it was quite heavy.
He was barely under cover when he glimpsed
three riders. Reining in, he waited in a
clump of five thick juniper trees, watching
the riders.

He had never been one to decorate bridle

or saddle with flashy ornaments and he was glad for that now, for they picked up the sunlight and could be seen for miles. The three riders came along up the hill on a line that would take them within fifty yards of where he sat.

There was no escape. The best thing he could do would be to sit still and hope they did not see him.

Stan Brodie was without illusions. Nothing in his twenty-two years had given them fertile ground for breeding. Still, he had his own dreams and aspirations, and none of them included being killed. He had no enmity for any man but trusted few of them.

If these riders did not ride for Carrie they had no business being where they were, and if they had no business there it was likely they would not wish to be seen.

He had no loyalty to Carrie. She had taken advantage of his seeming guilt to use him for her own purposes, and he had no choice but to go along until he could choose a time for escape.

What he wished to avoid was getting in deeper while he waited.

He was positive an attempt had been made to kill her father, and if it had not succeeded it was not for lack of trying. The attempt was sufficient to convince him they would stop at nothing . . . and here he was, unarmed, and within easy rifle-shot of them.

He spoke softly to his horse, whose ears were pricked toward the oncoming riders.

That these men were among those who were

trying to get Carrie's water he had no
doubt, and they would assume he was a spy.

He had made a fool of himself once and he
did not intend to do so again. Every time
he had gotten into trouble it was from
keeping bad company . . . but how was he to
know about Tex? Yet, he admitted, he had
known. He had not trusted him from the
first. It was the whiskey that mellowed his
doubt of the man.

The man they hung in town? Could that have
been Tex? Possible, but unlikely. It was
more likely that stranger he met on the
trail had gone back, looked, and found the
stolen gold Stan had hidden under the pack
rat's nest.

Yet Tex could still be around. Certainly,
he had known that bartender.

The riders turned sharply away from him
and began to spread out. Then for the first
time he saw that several head of whiteface
cattle had come into the open below him. The
three riders rode toward them and hazed them
off toward the west. That they were Carrie's
cattle he could not doubt, but he was
unarmed and men who had killed once would
not hesitate to do so again.

With the cattle drifting west the three
turned back and rode up the hill toward him.
Suddenly one of them pulled up sharply and
called out.

Stan swore bitterly. They had found his
tracks. One glanced up the hill toward the
clump of trees, then scanned the side of the
hill to right and left.

Abruptly they turned and rode down the hill. Stan mopped his brow. Of course, they did not know if he was still up here, nor would they guess he was unarmed.

And that gave him an idea.

CHAPTER 3

When he rode into the ranch-yard Carrie came to the door. "Supper's ready."

A thought came to him that was disturbing. "When you drove up in the buckboard you called me by name. How did you know it?"

"I heard somebody call you that in town."

Now a gentleman did not call a lady a liar, but that simply was not true. Nobody in town knew his name. Tex and Bud had only known him as Montana, a name he had given himself on the spur of the moment. So how could she have known?

"I saw three riders," he commented at supper.

"On our ranch?"

"Yep."

"Did you order them off?"

He gave her a wry smile. "Three armed and unpleasant men? And me without a gun?"

She was irritated. "Well, perhaps I was foolish. You'd better wear a gun. Get yours out and carry it."

"I don't have one."

She started to reply angrily, then stopped. "But if you don't have a gun, then how--?"

She was wondering how he could have held up the stage, and he saw no harm in letting her wonder. "I don't have a weapon of any kind," he said, "but this knife." He put his hand on the haft.

"That man . . . the one they found in the hotel . . . he had been killed with a knife. They found it."

He drew his own. It had an eight-inch blade and had a nice feel but it was obviously more of a working knife than one that would be chosen to kill a man. "I still have mine," he said quietly.

That she was disturbed and puzzled was obvious. Evidently this information did not conform with what she had believed.

"We have rifles," she said.

"All right, I shall carry one."

For a few minutes they ate in silence. There was an occasional crackle from the fire, and the subdued rattle of knives, forks, and dishes. It was pleasant, that he admitted, and she was a pretty, in fact a very pretty girl. A very pretty girl who now held him captive.

He finished his coffee and pushed back from the table. "You'd better let me pick out a rifle. Those men were running off your cattle today."

"I'll tell the sheriff."

"All right, but I doubt if it will do any good. They won't have the cattle where they can be seen, or if seen, be tied to them. Let me take care of it."

"You?"

"I'm slave labor, don't you remember? I'm the man you blackmailed into working for you."

She flushed angrily. "Don't be like that! I needed somebody, I--!"

"And I was handy, is that it? And I didn't have any way out?" He turned and looked at her. "What about you, ma'am? A woman can use a knife as well as a man. You were in that hotel, too!"

For a moment he thought she would strike him. He waited, but she simply stared at him, her eyes hot with anger. After a minute he said, "Better let me have that rifle, ma'am. And some ammunition . . . a lot of it."

"They'd never believe you."

"What?"

"I mean they'd never believe you saw me in that hotel, and they'd never believe I killed that man."

"Did you?"

"Of course not! I did not even know there'd been a killing until somebody found the body. I heard them talking of it downtown."

"And thought of me."

"Who else?"

He shrugged. "All right. I am a possible suspect and I know I did not do it. You are a possible suspect and you say you did not do it. So what became of the man who did it?"

"Who would that be?"

"A tall, high-shouldered man with black eyes and a lean look about him."

Carrie got to her feet and picked up the dishes.

"There must be many such men. Anyway, he is probably gone."

She took the dishes to the sink, then turned on him.

"Do you wish to leave? I won't report you to the sheriff."

"No." He went to the rifle rack. They were good guns. There was one Winchester there of which he liked the feel. He took it in his hands and held it for a moment. Then he replaced it in the rack.

"Take your pick," she offered. "There are two or three pistols in the drawer at the foot of the rack."

He opened the drawer. There was a gun-belt and holster there, then two six-shooters, an Army Colt, and a newer Remington.

He took out the holster and belted it on. It felt good around his waist, too good.

"I'll take the Colt," he said, his voice cold. He took the Winchester down. "And this rifle. I am sure your father won't care."

"Do you really mean to stay? There'll be trouble, I know."

"I'll stay for a little while," he said. Now, more than ever, he wanted to know what was going on . . . a part of him had to know. "When will your father be up and around?"

"Three weeks, I think. Three weeks at least."

"All right. You can count on me until then."

* * *

Outside in the darkness he shifted his bed to a hollow among some rocks. No use to advertise the place where he slept. He touched the gun, then drew it. For a moment he stood holding the pistol, then holstered it. "Stan Brodie, you'd be better off a-runnin'. Curiosity is what killed that cat, isn't it?" he muttered.

The guns he had taken were his own, taken from his room the night Bud Aylmer was killed.

CHAPTER 4

The place he had chosen to sleep was on a small, rock-covered knoll some fifty yards from the ranch house but overlooking the area. There were fifty or sixty boulders scattered across the top of the knoll, ranging in size from the size of a barrel to twice as large. Between them were grassy hollows free of stones. In one of these, where he had merely to turn his head to see the house, he bedded down.

Once he was settled, he kept an eye on the house, but his mind was busy, and there were a lot of questions to which he had no answer. What he should do was cut and run, yet if she called the sheriff there was small chance of him getting out of the country before they caught him. They knew the area far better than he.

How had his rifle and pistol, apparently taken from the room the night Bud was murdered, showed up here?

What had become of Tex?

Carrie had obviously not been aware that the weapons he chose to take were his own. Who had access to that house other than Carrie and her father?

Off across the hills the coyotes began to yap. It was a familiar sound and one he had never found unpleasant. He lay, hands clasped behind his neck, thinking.

The stars overhead were very bright, and the night was cool. He listened, vaguely aware of movement . . . cattle? He wanted no part of this mess. He wanted to get away, but he suspected the sheriff or some of his posse were already a little suspicious-- after all, where had he come from so suddenly? And there were a few people who could place him in town.

He awakened suddenly, having no memory of falling asleep or of even being sleepy. It was morning.

Getting out of bed he gathered his bedding and rolled it carefully, stowing it in the corner of the stable he had taken for his own. Carrying his rifle he went to the house, where smoke was coming from the chimney. As with many such ranch houses there was a basin at the back door and a towel hung on a nail near a small hand mirror fastened on a board.

He shaved in cold water, turning occasionally to look over the hills around the ranch. If he was going to be in the saddle so much he would need more horses, which brought another thought. If this was a working ranch, where was the saddle-stock?

He wiped his feet at the door and went inside. His breakfast was on the table, obviously just put there for it was hot, although there was no sign of Carrie.

Drawing back a chair, he seated himself, then feeling something under his foot, he glanced down.

Mud . . . soft mud . . . several crumbs of it and one good-sized piece that might have fallen from the edge of a boot.

Somebody either was here or had been here, somebody who had recently stepped in mud that had not had time to dry. He ate his bacon and beans, a couple of slices of home-baked bread, and then finished his coffee. The only place he remembered seeing any mud was near the horse trough. There might be a track.

He got up from the table, pushing his chair back and purposely making some noise, but Carrie did not appear. Was the visitor still here? Or had Carrie been outside herself?

He went out, closed the door behind him, and dumped a little water in the basin to rinse off his fingers. In the mirror he studied what he could see behind him, shifting position for a better view.

Nothing . . .

He went to the stable and saddled his horse, leading it outside. As he walked up

to the trough he glanced in the mud.
Somebody had deliberately scuffed a foot
across the mud, smearing any track that
might have been left.

Stan Brodie swore softly. What was going
on here, anyway? Her father was in the
hospital . . . so who had been here? A
lover? Despite himself he was suddenly
jealous. Then he laughed for being so
foolish.

What was she to him? A girl he knew and
worked for. What was he to her? A drifting,
probably no-good cowhand.

He shoved his rifle into the boot and
stepped into the saddle. He was not going to
let them see him scouting for sign, but he
intended to do just that. He meant to find
out what was going on.

In the meantime there was work to do. He
found a few steers and drifted them back
away from the Two Cabin area. All morning
long he rode, stock was scarce and he
wondered how many had already been stolen.

Several times he saw tracks of small
bunches of cattle, usually driven by two or
three riders. Those he found he turned back.
The range was in tolerable shape and that in
the area around the Keyhole was the best.
Beyond it was wild country.

The sun was straight up by the time he
reached the Keyhole so he rode into as much
shadow as there was near the rocks, picketed
his horse on a patch of good grass, and
climbed up the rocks. He had neglected to
fix himself any kind of a lunch and Carrie

hadn't fixed one for him, so he was hungry, but he had often been in that fix. Settled down with his back to the rocks, he studied the country.

Stan Brodie was not a big man, being a shade under six feet and rarely weighing over one-sixty, carrying most of it in his chest and shoulders, which was partly a result of driving spikes on the railroad and work with a pick and shovel.

In the orphan asylum one of the men who supervised them had liked to see them fight so he would tie gloves on the youngsters and let them go to it. Stan was often whipped, until he realized that the boy who just kept coming usually won. So he began to simply pile in swinging, throwing punches until the other boy began to back up. After that Stan usually won. Here and there in the years that followed he had picked up a little more know-how as to fighting and survival.

The other day they had found his tracks and lost them, but they had been curious, maybe a little worried. A guilty man can find a lot to worry him in something he does not understand. Well, that was something he could do. He could worry them.

From his position he could see over quite a lot of country, and it could save him miles of riding. He spotted several groups of cattle feeding on slopes or draws over toward Two Cabin. These he would drift back away from the borders of the ranch as he had done the others.

Coming down off the rocks he mounted and

rode back to the south and west, pushing
cattle ahead of him. Once, in the distance,
he glimpsed a rider, but he could not make
him out, and disappearing into a draw the
man vanished from view.

When he came within sight of the ranch he
swung around it in a wide circle. He could
see no horses at the hitching-rail nor at
the corral. He picked up the old tracks
of the posse coming and leaving, and almost
a mile further along, the tracks of another
horse that had gone to and returned from the
ranch. He glanced at the sun. Almost an hour
before sundown. Turning his mount he walked
him along the trail of the lone rider. He
followed the trail into the low hills until
he came to a small spring with a trickle of
water that sub-irrigated a meadow below it.
Here he found where another rider had
waited, smoking many cigarettes, until the
visitor to the ranch returned. They rode off
together.

He studied the hoof tracks so he would
know them if he saw them again.

Carrie was setting the table when he came
up to the door to wash his hands. "Who are
those fellows over at Two Cabin?" he asked.

"I don't know them all. There's the Tutler
brothers, Brockey and Red Fitz Tutler.
There's Shang Hight, and a man named
Trainor. They are a bad lot, and I doubt if
any of them is using the name he was born
with." She paused. "Stan, be careful. If
they killed Pa, they would kill you. Of

course, they did not kill Pa, but they tried, and they would have."

He offered no reply, but seated himself at the table. She filled his cup. "Where did you come from, Stan?"

"I'm a drifter," he replied, "just a loose-footed saddle tramp."

"I don't believe that. You sound like an educated man, sometimes."

"You'd be mistaken. Most of my education I got in an orphan asylum or a newspaper office."

She brought food to the table, and sat down opposite him.

"If I were you," he said suddenly, "I'd be very careful, and be sure your father is well guarded."

"Guarded? He's in the hospital, such as it is."

"His fall was no accident, you know."

"Of course it was. His horse fell with him, that was all."

"Your father's horse," he said, "was tripped by a wire stretched across the canyon."

"What? I don't believe it."

"Anybody who took the trouble to look could see where the wire cut the skin on the horse's leg. I found where the wire was tied. Somebody came down out of the rocks and took up the wire while your father lay there on the ground. He just let him lie, thinking he was dead or dying."

"You mean somebody tried to kill him?"

"It's obvious, isn't it?"

"I'm not going to leave."

"Then you'd better get ready for a fight. I doubt if they will wait until your father is up and around . . . if it is the place they want."

"Do you doubt it?"

He shrugged. "I'm just a passing stranger, ma'am. I don't know anything about you or your father. But somebody tried to kill him and I think they will try again."

"Can you stop them?"

"Seven or eight men, maybe? That's asking a lot from a man you only got to stop by using blackmail."

She flushed. "I was all alone, and I needed help. Maybe it wasn't nice of me but--"

"You've got other friends," he replied quietly. "Get them to help you."

"Other friends? Why, I don't--" She paused. "What do you mean by that? What friends?"

Stan did not reply. For a moment there was silence and then she said in a somewhat lower voice, "I don't know what you mean."

He stood up. "If you will excuse me? I am quite tired."

She looked up at him, wide-eyed and embarrassed. Then she stood. "Oh, by the way. You spoke of reading. We have a few books if you'd like to read them."

"I would, indeed. However, I doubt if a campfire that would provide enough light to read by would be good for my health. Not if

you have as many enemies about as I
believe."

"You could come in here. I wouldn't mind."

"All right, but not tonight. I believe I
should be outside. I had the distinct
impression," he added, "that someone was
around last night."

He stepped outside and closed the door
behind him, then moved along the wall to the
corner before stepping into the shade of
the big tree. He remained there for a
moment, listening.

Every instinct he possessed warned him
that something here was radically wrong.
Unless the ranch had had a lot more cattle
until recently but they'd been stolen, it
had too few to be a worthwhile operation. To
make ranching pay they'd need to run at
least six hundred head, and if they had half
that they were lucky. The herd was a mixture
of Hereford and longhorns but the latter
predominated . . . and where were their
horses?

Was the operation simply a cover for
something else? But if so, why have him
around?

The answer to that seemed obvious and
unpleasant, for the only reason he could
imagine was simply to have him here as a
suspect in case anything went wrong.

The place he chose for his bed that night
proved a bad one. He slept restlessly and
awoke irritated with himself and his
situation. He was getting nowhere here, and
it was time for him to get away, to move on.

He had lost enough time in drifting and it was the moment to make a decision as to where he was going and just what he intended to make of himself.

He shook out his boots, knocking a centipede four inches long from one of them. He swore and tugged the boots on, then got up and looked around. The prairie was a uniform mixed green and brown, the hills rolling, the sky somewhat overcast.

Taking his rifle he walked down to the house and washed his hands and face. Carrie put her head out of the door as he threw the water from the washbasin into the yard. "Come on in. It's ready."

First good thing he'd heard all morning. At least, he told himself, the cooking was good. He started to turn away toward the door when he looked again at the small mirror. It was held to the log wall by bent-over nails. He turned two of them aside and, taking down the mirror, dropped it into his pocket.

This morning it was pancakes and eggs. Where she had gotten the eggs he could not guess but obviously there was somebody around the town who had chickens. He ate them with pleasure.

Sitting back, he looked across at her. "You set a good table," he admitted.

"My father likes to eat, so I had to become a good cook."

"How's he doing?"

"He's still unconscious." He glimpsed the

worry in her eyes. "He must have fallen very hard."

"Or was slugged on the head before he could get up."

She stared at him. "You don't believe that?"

"I believe it's likely." He hesitated, then said, "Where's the riding stock around here? I need a fresh horse now and again."

"Oh! I didn't think! I've been so worried, I . . . Stan, there's a place about a mile west of the Keyhole. It's a small valley there and there's some water in it and we've fenced the ends. The walls are steep enough so that's all we have to do to make a corral that has about sixty acres. We have a dozen head of horses in there.

"Catch up the gray or the Appaloosa. There's a dun there who's the best horse of the lot but nobody can ride him since my brother--" She broke off, then added, "Ride him if you can, but he's mean."

Finding the valley was easy enough, and they had a nice place for holding stock. A small, isolated valley kind of tucked into a corner of low hills, and the grass was good. I roped the gray and saddled it, meanwhile keeping an eye out for trouble.

An idea had been working itself around in my mind for some time but whether it would work or not would depend on how many of the cattle gathered by the Tutler brothers and their friends were longhorns.

Now a longhorn is no ordinary cow-beast. A

longhorn is a wild animal, as much so as any elk, buffalo, or deer. Even though occasionally rounded up and herded by men, they remained wild, very skittish, and likely to stampede on the slightest provocation. A sudden whiff of a wolf-hide, the drop of a tin pan, a shot . . . many things might cause a stampede.

A Hereford, or whiteface, was less likely to stampede, but if one started the rest would go along with the crowd. There was no way I could tackle that bunch of land-grabbers head-on, but there were several ways I might give them trouble. The first thing I had to do was to worry those longhorns. They were probably nervous enough but I'd leave nothing to chance.

So far as I'd been able to see they had altered no brands. They had simply drifted cattle over to range they claimed, and as cattle often strayed far afield nobody could then move in and brand whatever cattle there were.

Until now they had been doing all the scaring and the threatening. If all went well we would see how they liked it when somebody put a saddle on their own horse.

Mounted on the gray I scouted their camp. There were

COMMENTS: Yes, that is exactly how this story ends! Its beginning has something in common with the "suddenly out of place" situation found in Louis's novel *The Man Called Noon* and it also harkens back to a few of his noir or crime thrillers from the days when he was writing for the pulp magazines.

Like "Borden Chantry" and several of Louis's other stories, this looks like it is headed toward being a melding of the mystery and Western genres. I can never quite figure out how they did it, but Louis wasn't the only writer who tried to create and solve mysteries in just one draft. I had a couple of conversations with novelist Tony Hillerman about how to pull this off, and it's not easy. However, as in quite a few of the works in this book, I think Louis finally got to a point where he needed to do some more figuring before he continued. Here are a few lines out of his notes on this story:

```
    Somebody seems to have visited the
ranch during the night.
    What was CARRIE doing in that cheap
hotel where Bud Aylmer was killed?
    Where are CARRIE'S cattle? Where are
the horses? Why are the horses kept some
distance from the ranch house?
```

Some of these questions may simply have been things that Dad figured he'd better clarify, but others may have been intended to be part of the mystery. Your guess as to which is which is as good as mine.

JACK CROSS

The Beginning of an Adventure Story

CHAPTER I

The name is Jack Cross, John Cross, if you want to be particular, and I'm a guy in need of a fast buck. So I'm standing on the Avenida de Almeida Ribeiro in Macao with ten dollars in my pocket and a .45 Colt in a shoulder holster.

Sure . . . I'm broke . . . but this is my backyard. Or it used to be, 'way back before the war. They knew me here in those old days, and they knew me on Malay Street in Singapore, in Shanghai's Blood Alley, and on Grant Road in Bombay . . . and in a dirty little bar in a backstreet of Bangkok there's a guy who holds mail for me.

Profession? Well . . . what can I say? I'm a guy who has been around, a guy who knows most of the answers but is quite sure he doesn't know them all. I'm a guy who can use his mitts, a guy who can handle a rod, and I've run a machine gun a couple of times in wars that didn't belong to me.

Beginning? Maybe there was never a beginning, and maybe there was a map of the world hanging on the wall when I was born. Maybe it was reading Jack London and Stevenson and Conrad. More likely it was a melody of foreign names, the sound of names that rang little bells in my brain, or great gongs. Names like Bangalore, Gorontalo, and Taku Bar.

Way down in my guts there was something that liked the sound of those strange and far-off places. Samarkand . . . Makassar . . . Kuala Lumpur . . . Chittagong . . . the Malabar Coast . . . the Banda Sea.

Education? Mostly the kind you get from learning what to do when somebody stabs a fast left for your mouth or when a guy comes at you with a shiv or sticks a rod into your belly.

The kind of education that enables you to take a Browning apart in the dark and under fire, or tells you how to tell the feel of gold from silver, or how to con a ship through a reef-strewn sea somewhere south of the Line.

Sure, I've read a book. In fact, I've read a lot of books, read them in the aimless, casual way of a man who loves to read and loves books for themselves. I've read them in fo'c'sles and bunkhouses from Magallanes to the Yukon, read them all, Plutarch, Thucydides, Homer, and Shakespeare, from the classics to the fast action magazines, and found plenty of interest in all of them.

What did I want from life? The sound of

bow wash about the hull . . . the slat and
slap of empty sails on a dead calm sea . . .
the smell of copra and tar and musk and the
acrid smell of burning camel dung.

Sure. And temple bells and elephant gongs,
the hot, excited bodies of tan-skinned
girls . . . the feel of a Colt butt bucking
in my hand . . . the solid thrill of a hard
punch landed . . . the knowledge of far-off
places and seas untracked and unmarked . . .
the smell of opium in the Shanghai
"Trenches" and all the fierce, hard, lonely,
beautiful intoxication of living all of life
that I could get hold of.

Put it down in your book that I'm an
unreconstructed savage, that I'm born out of
time, that the Spanish main is gone and the
free companies are gone and that Drake and
Hawkins and even O'Reilly and Christmas have
passed the way of all flesh. But put it
down, too, that there's always a war
somewhere, always a fast buck to be made,
and always a man or a woman who will take a
chance when the going is rough. And put it
down that the old spirit isn't dead yet, and
that if tomorrow, in spite of all those boys
who are still babies at eighteen, if
tomorrow somebody said they would need a
crew to build a bridge on the moon, they'd
have the office jammed within an hour.

Put it down that I'm a fool, that I'll
find my finish someday cursing my luck on
some lonely reef in the wash of a weedy sea,
or in some barroom with a knife in my back
or some lead in my guts . . . but put it

down that when that day comes I'll have
lived. I'll have seen it all, known it all,
and tasted it all.

So it's been . . . and so it was last
night when I heard that sampan paddle
chunking astern of the freighter, the
freighter that had been my home for the past
three months.

It was past two a.m. and the ship was dark
except for the anchor light forward and a
bulb by the gangway where the night watch
was loafing. We were due to put out to sea
shortly after daybreak and I was restless.
Standing beside the rail looking at the
lights of Macao, I heard the paddle moving
in its locks.

Then I saw the sampan not far off the
stern, and just like that my mind was made
up. He came at my low call and waited
alongside. So I got my gear and lowered
it with a heaving line then went down
beside it.

It was an ugly part of town where he
landed me and an ugly hour of night, but
I'd landed in a lot of towns and this was no
worse than many. Finally, I found a sleepy
rickshaw coolie and shook him awake.

So I was on the beach again . . . like
that first time, so long ago in Shanghai.
Oh, those had been the good, hot, wonderful
days! I'd landed there with forty cents, had
a fight in the ring for a few bucks, a fight
won quickly. . . . Then there was the matter
of some guns up the river in piano boxes,
and of a man who ended his career with his

head on a piece of pipe. . . . There was a
poker game up the Yangtze near Yichang with
twenty thousand dollars on the table at one
time. . . . There had been jai alai games
and horse races and dog races. . . . And
then there had been some tribute silk
smuggled from the Forbidden City in Peiping
in the darkness of a rainy night and sold to
a Greek with a sweat-soiled collar. . . .
There had been dinners at the Del Monte, and
dancing with Rose Marie of the Lido . . .
the Peach Blossom Palace and there had been
trips to that Venice of China, Hanchow.

There had been songs and laughter and
stories told, and there were fights in
the streets and there were dark-eyed
Eurasian girls and sad Russians and turban-
wearing Sikhs and a fortune teller who
failed to tell his own and there was a dark
night and a dark street and a time when two
good British seamen jumped into a fight to
help me and were killed for their
pains . . . but several of the Chinese
rivermen died, too, and I came away with a
bloody coat and a half-dozen minor cuts and
a gun in my pocket that I forgot to
use . . . which comes of fighting with your
hands until it is second nature to think of
no other weapon.

And those wonderful hours of talk over
wine or whiskey, talk of the names of which
history never speaks, the men like General
Lee Christmas, Tracy Richardson, Tex
O'Reilly, One-Arm Sutton, Rafael de Nogales,
Larson of Mongolia, and Rajah Brooke, and

other names that echo down the brassy halls
of warlike memory.

These were the men of whom we talked for
these were the men of our kind . . . and
some of them were there among us.

So I was back again . . . back on the
beach in the Far East and north of me there
was war . . . and all over the East there was
a stirring and moving of new forces
rising . . . the Malays, the Chinese, the
Tamils, the Bengalese . . . all of whom were
feeling their own urge to freedom, to throw
off the old shackles of colonial government,
to remove the burden from the white man (who
relinquished that burden bitterly), and to
look around with a new awareness. But it was
my East, the place I knew best.

The fingers of dawn felt their way down
the quiet avenues of Macao, life began to
stir again and the working citizens began to
go about their business. I found my way to a
seaman's hotel and checked in, and after
breakfast I started making the rounds.

Haig . . . he might be in Macao. The last
I'd seen of him was before the war and
probably he had been recalled to service.
Giacomo . . . where was he?

It was past noon before I saw a familiar
face. I was behind a table in a little
bistro on a side street off the Avenida when
he came in . . . Jimmy Pak Lung.

He turned quickly when I started up and
then his face smoothed out and he came to
me, his grin spread wide, his hand out.
"John!" he said. "You're back!"

We gripped hands and stared at each other and I never felt better. Jimmy was born in California, but nobody would have guessed he was anything but Chinese. He could play the cynical denizen of a treaty port or a wide-eyed rube from the interior, but he had all the mannerisms of an American, too.

So we talked, and the hours went by, and then he said, "You want to make a spot of cash?"

"Who doesn't?"

"You've been up-country in China. I know a man who wants to go there."

"Now?"

"Right now. And he's got money, plenty of money."

"What's he after? He's not a Russian, is he?"

"He's a Yank, like you. I don't know what he's after, but it smells of money."

So there was talk of this and that again, and finally back to this American, Jonathan Spurr, who wanted to fly into Red China at a time when Americans were hated by many and especially by the government. It was just such a trip as appealed to me . . . full of risk, yes, but a quick reward too.

So we went to see him, this Jonathan Spurr. . . .

He rolled a fat cigar in his lips and he looked at me, and he didn't like what he saw. I've read that look in the eyes of too many men before this and didn't like it any better from him. I'm a big guy, six-one and an even two hundred pounds, but I carry no

scars and your average punk who has never
been across the street from home thinks a
tough man should swagger and talk out the
side of his mouth and act hard. It always
irritates me because I've licked fifty guys
who were just like that.

"You've been to Kansu?"

"Yeah."

"Ever hear of Choni?"

"I've been there."

That surprised him. He looked at me with
more respect and some doubt. That I could
understand, for Choni is one of the most
out-of-the-way places in the world. Wars and
revolutions had passed and repassed over
China without ever touching it.

"Are there any white men there?"

A test question. "There was. A missionary,
some kind of a Scandinavian. He'd been there
a long time."

"What were you doing there?"

When he asked me that I just looked at
him. "We're talking business, not history,"
I said.

He didn't like it and I didn't give a
damn. This guy was used to throwing his
weight around, used to being obeyed. He
would be hell to get along with until I'd
broken him in . . . and I was ready to start
just anytime.

"Could you take us there? In a plane?"

"Who," I asked, "is 'us'?"

"There will be four of us. The plane will
carry eight and some freight. It's an
amphibian."

"For enough money I'll take you any place you damn well please."

He rolled his cigar in his fat lips. "I've heard you were tough. You don't look it."

It was a stupid remark. The remark of a fool or some romantic girl who has never been out of her home circle. "And what," I asked him, "does a tough man look like?"

"I know one when I see one."

"You're fortunate. It will save you a lot of trouble while you're looking for one." I got to my feet. "Look, friend, you'd better not tackle this sort of deal. You're not going to be up to it."

My hat was in my hand and I started around the table toward the door.

"What's the matter?" he demanded. "You walking out?"

I turned back. "You may know a tough man when you see one but to me you assay like a forty-eight-carat sap."

His face got red and he started to say something he would have been sorry for-- after I'd hit him.

Then from behind me was another voice. "Take it easy, Jonathan. I think this is our man."

He came into the room, a lean-bodied, older man with cold gray eyes and white hair. His face was weathered with the fine lines at the corners of his eyes that come from looking at too many hot suns.

"No man can talk to me like that!" Jonathan Spurr was a big wide-beamed man and he came blustering around the corner of his

desk. He came around the corner of his desk
and I stood there waiting for him, knowing
how much I was going to enjoy it. Maybe he
saw something of it in my eyes, maybe some
little sixth sense of caution warned him
he was running into trouble. Anyway, he
slowed down.

"What's the matter?" I asked him. "Don't
you want to lose some teeth?"

"Forget it!" It was the older man. "Take
it easy, Cross. Spurr's just on edge, that's
all. This is a big deal and we've got to
keep our heads."

Spurr mopped his face. "All right," he
said, more quietly, "let's forget it. No
need to go off half-cocked. If you've been
in Choni you're just the man we want."

Right then the door opened again and a
girl walked into the room. She was a blonde
with a golden tan, and lovely blue eyes with
a hint of Hell in them.

She came right up to me, and Spurr said,
"Mr. Cross, my niece, Joan Iveson. And Doc
Pardee, a friend of Joan's father."

"How do you do, Mr. Cross?"

"Better," I said, letting my feelings show
in my eyes with an overcoating of insolence.
She stiffened a little. "Much better."

Then I turned away from her and said to
Spurr, "All right, lay it out for me. What's
the score? What's in Choni that you want bad
enough to risk your life to get?"

"Research," he said. "I'm doing some
research into the--"

"Nuts," I replied shortly, "save that for

somebody who will believe it. Talk turkey
with me or get yourself another boy. You
never went after anything in your life
unless there was money in it."

That he didn't like, either, but he chewed
on his cigar and then Pardee said, "Go ahead
and tell him. He'll have to know anyway."

"Joan's father had an uncle who was a
missionary in western China. He saw
something very valuable in a remote place.
We're going after it. We're going to bring
it back."

He rolled his cigar in his lips and looked
at me. "I want a man who knows that
country," he said, "and one who can handle a
gun."

CHAPTER II

"It will cost you," I said, "it will cost
plenty. Is there enough up there to pay for
the trip?"

"There is," he said, "and more."

"Know anything about that country?"

"A little. We looked it up, studied it in
books and magazines." Then he indicated
Joan. "And she has her great-uncle's notes.
He was very accurate as to details."

"That will help. As for the books and
magazines, few of them can give you anything
that will help in that country. In the first
place, nobody out here knows what has
happened back there. Not even me. Choni has

lived under the rule of a hereditary prince for many years, and maybe it still does. It is an out-of-the-way valley green and lovely, and not too easy of access. But the Reds have been getting in everywhere so they are probably there, too."

"We expected that. However, we heard that a little money . . ." Spurr rubbed his fingers together suggestively.

"Maybe. Money used to buy almost anything in China, and with some of them it will yet. But a true Communist? Forget it. Money won't work and whatever you bring with you they can take by force. Any plane that can make it in there will be especially valuable."

"We've thought of that. That's one reason why we want a man who can handle a gun."

"Is what you want right at Choni?"

"No . . . it is beyond Choni."

Beyond . . . mountains and gorges, high, cloud-piercing peaks, black canyons, trackless and lonely, boiling rivers of black water laced with white. The strange, bleak, lonely land lost in the interior of a vast continent. The very thought of it made me stir restlessly, for it was that sort of thing that had drawn me back.

That vast and lonely land where Tibet meets Sinkiang, the land of the Kun Luns, the Altin Tagh, the Chang Tang. A land of lonely ice lakes and forbidding mountains, the land of the white bear and the snow man, the land of the Lolos and the Ngoloks. A bitter, savage mountain fastness where the outside world was a rumor and nothing more,

where the wars and dynasties of China were
only travelers' tales and the doings of the
outside world were misty legends, faintly
known and altogether, to those people,
unbelievable.

A land without roads . . . a land of camel
trails or yak paths . . . a land of passes
and mighty mountains, a land where the
highest peak on earth might be and yet
nobody could say for sure whether it was or
was not . . . fantastic, mysterious, remote.

"Beyond Choni," I said musingly, "that's
the loneliest place on earth, excepting,
perhaps, the Antarctic . . . and even less
known." I looked up at Spurr, for I had
seated myself and he was still standing.
"What is it you're after?"

He hesitated, brushing the ash from his
cigar, studying the ash as if to read the
answer there. Doc Pardee stirred a little
and then said quietly, "An idol of gold
encrusted with gems. It is in a long-
forgotten temple, unknown and lost. Charles
Iveson actually saw it."

"You're sure of that? It wasn't just a
legend he repeated?"

"He saw it," Joan said, "and he described
it in detail. He even brought home two large
diamonds from it. The money from their sale
paid for my education."

"It's worth a fortune," Spurr said.

"It belongs in a museum." Joan spoke
almost on top of his words.

Right there was the problem in a nutshell,
not to mention that it really belonged to

the locals. The communists wouldn't value a religious artifact but they certainly weren't going to hand it over to foreign thieves either. None of that was my problem, I intended to have money in the bank before we took off.

"Alright, you said four would go? Who are the others besides you?"

Jonathan Spurr nodded at Pardee. "Doc will go, Joan, and Bob Landes."

"Joan?" I was surprised. "You want to go into that country?"

She smiled, her eyes bright with excitement. "I wouldn't miss it for the world!"

"That's no place for a woman," I said, "and the less of a load we have, the better. I don't see any sense in carrying excess baggage."

"I'm not excess baggage!" she flared angrily. "I can cook, I can shoot, I know first aid, and I've flown a plane! I'll do my part!"

Doc Pardee smiled. "Also," he said quietly, "she has the location of the temple. The rest of us only know it approximately."

That settled that. I know better than to argue with a woman when her mind is made up. Besides, she'd be nice to take along. Right then she must have read my mind because she looked at me, her eyes cool and carrying a challenge. "Bob Landes," she said, "is my fiancé!"

Jonathan Spurr and Pardee were eager to

talk about it. Spurr began telling me about
the plane, and I listened, then nodded
toward Jimmy Pak Lung, who sat quietly by the
door. "Jimmy goes along," I said.

Spurr stopped abruptly. "Nothing doing,"
he said, "we can't afford the weight."

"You weigh twice what he does," I said,
"so suppose you stay behind? You or this
Landes guy?"

His face got red. Jonathan Spurr did not
like me. He was not going to like me under
any circumstances. "Landes," he said, "is
a fine rifle shot, a skilled woodsman, and a
very useful man aside from being Joan's
fiancé. I," he added grimly, "am running
this show . . . and financing it."

That I would have bet on. Leave it to the
Jonathan Spurrs of this world to have
money . . . no matter what they have to do
to get it.

For that matter, I was in no position to
speak myself. I suspected myself of some
ethics, somewhere along the line. If my
methods were not always strictly legal,
there was at least a sense of fair
play . . . as long as they played fair with
me. But I was not a disciple of the "turn
the other cheek" school. In my book it was
every man for himself when the playing got
rough. I had my own feelings about Jonathan
Spurr, and a good hunch that he did not
intend to share any more of that gold than
he could help. And then he brought up the
key consideration.

"How much," he asked, "will you want for this?"

It made me smile because I knew I was going to hit him where it hurt. "Five thousand," I said, "in cash and on the line . . . and twenty percent of the take."

Jonathan Spurr's face and neck grew red. For an instant he could not bring himself to speak, or lacked for words. And he was not the only one. Both Joan and Doc Pardee were staring at me as if I were insane.

"Preposterous!" Spurr flared. "Why--!" He stopped, then turned abruptly. "All right! Forget it! We'll get another man!"

That made me smile. "Spurr," I said, "you're a chuckle-headed idiot. You ask a man to risk his life flying almost four thousand miles over enemy country, in danger every minute he's out of Macao.

"You ask him to go into a country where any man is a fool to go unless at great profit, even in peacetime, even when the people are friendly. You won't find anybody else who is crazy enough to go; furthermore, if you go around talking about it the government here won't let you take off with gas enough to get you there. They want no trouble with Red China.

"And I might mention this: You won't find anybody in Macao who knows Choni. If there's one man in the city who knows of the place, I'll pay off any bet you'd like to make. And you seem to imagine you can fly in there, pick up this idol, and fly out. You'd better think it over, and think it over a lot."

So I started for the door, and then
hesitated, Jimmy at my elbow. "You've
exactly five hours to change your mind. I'll
be having dinner at the Hotel Central and
you can find me there at that time.
Furthermore, I won't bargain: Five thousand
in my hand when the deal is closed . . . and
twenty percent of the take. I'll pay Jimmy."

We walked out and closed the door after
us. Jimmy chuckled, then shrugged. "Well, it
would have been a mean trip, anyway," he
said cheerfully. "We'll find something
else."

"We won't need to," I said. "They'll meet
our terms. You wait and see. Who else could
they get?"

He was silent a few minutes, and then he
said slowly, "One way they could get it--
just one other way. They could go to
Shuksan."

That stopped me. "Petro Shuksan? He's
here?"

Jimmy looked at me seriously. "Yeah, I
should have told you. He's not only here,
he's the biggest operator in town. He's got
a hand in everything."

Petro Shuksan was a half-caste, half-
Portuguese and half-Chinese, and a renegade
in any language. He had been, when I first
knew him, a petty thief and a runner for a
waterfront girl-house. He had graduated from
that to smuggling, thieving on a larger
scale, and running a house of his own. On
one occasion over at the Nine Islands I had
slapped him until his nose streamed blood

and his lips were smashed. That was for trying to kidnap a girl I knew.

Since that day his hatred for me had been a living and ugly thing, and if he was a big wheel in Macao then I'd better get out of town or kill him, but fast.

"It was the kidnapping," Jimmy said, "of Dr. Lu. He arranged that, and it was he who notched his ear and received the money. He dealt with the Japanese during the war. He trades with Red China now, and he has great influence with them. If he learns of what is planned he will not hesitate to warn them or to come in himself."

So there it was. A man like Shuksan could have another man killed by a simple word or gesture. And in Macao it would mean nothing. That he would find whose palms to grease was certain, he would grease them generously. And in my own pocket was a lone ten bucks.

There was no avoiding the issue. Shuksan was the worst enemy I had in the world and the years that had passed would not have dulled that feeling in the least. He would never be satisfied until I had suffered for the beating I'd given him. Every minute I was in Macao was a danger.

"He'll know, Jack," Jimmy said. "You'd better stay away from the Central. The place is full of his spies. Get your gear from the hotel and move out to my place. He doesn't like me but he doesn't watch me, either."

"Tonight we go to dinner at the Central," I told him, "and after that, we'll see."

The hours between were not wasted. Jimmy

Pak Lung briefed me thoroughly on the events since our old Shanghai days, and we went to look at the plane, then stirred around among the dives, talking to this person and that person.

No, Haig hadn't been seen since the war. Last anyone heard he had been a colonel in the British Army in Burma. Giacomo had remained in Shanghai for the first year of the Japanese occupation and then he had vanished.

"Killed?"

"No," my informant said, "I don't think so. He went back inland somewhere."

Everywhere we heard rumor of what went on inside of China. There were purges . . . rewards were given for denunciation. The call for political purity was being used to repay old grudges . . . to prevent being denounced by others . . . to gain favor.

Yet beneath the surface old China went on as it always went on, and I was satisfied that when the present furor was over China would have absorbed communism as it has absorbed all religions and all philosophies. In the end communism would be turned out as they were, as something distinctly Chinese. A hundred years or so of nearly continual war had driven the Chinese to welcome almost any stable government. Chiang had failed in twenty years to bring reform or any real change to the great mass of the people; now they seemed ready to let the Communists try.

"Shuksan," I commented later to Jimmy,

"would take them, but good. He'd keep it all for himself."

"But do they know that?"

No, they did not, that was the rub. And Shuksan was a glib talker, just the sort who would know how to handle Jonathan Spurr.

Nevertheless, I went ahead with my planning and thinking the thing out. Of course, it was no trick to realize the main problem was the matter of gasoline. The plane could not fly there and back without refueling, and there was no gas that I knew of in Choni.

"Jim," I said, "remember that field outside of Takwan? I wonder if it could still be used?"

Pak Lung shrugged. "Could be. I was in there once--it was in '46. It had been deserted for months, then." He started to get up. "I could find out. I know a guy . . . he was a Nationalist flyer. He deserted to the Reds, didn't like them and got out. He's in town."

"See him, then meet me at the Central for dinner . . . at eight." He sauntered to the door, a slim, shabby young man in a soiled drill suit. "And ask him what he knows about Meitsang."

Jimmy was curious. He looked at me, quick and interested. "In the Min Shans? What's there?"

"You ask him; don't volunteer anything. If he knows anything, he'll talk. Just get him to tell you about it."

Jimmy Pak Lung went out and I sat there

alone in his room. And when a man is alone
there is no reason to kid himself. I was a
sap, of course. I was a worse sap than
Jonathan Spurr, because I knew better. The
Red Chinese were eager to lay hands on any
American illegally in the country. A spy
trial would fit into their propaganda
program very nicely right now.

In another sense, it hinted of disloyalty
to even make the effort, for it could deal
the USA a political blow. Wryly, I reflected
on what would be said. The fact that I had a
reputation could give the State Department
their out. I'd fought for cash in China
before . . . and I'd been a smuggler. And
they could drop the whole thing--Spurr,
Joan, and Doc--under my cover.

On the other hand, and this I considered
seriously, I might learn a good deal. I'd
been an Army man, and renegade or not, I was
a Yank. Maybe I was out to make a fast buck,
but not at the expense of my own country. I
might find out a great deal if I got out
safely. If . . .

It depended on so many things. Leaving
here would be the first one, for the town
was full of spies. All planes departing in
that direction would be reported. If we were
sighted flying inland they would send
fighters after us. If there was any hitch in
our refueling we would be dead ducks, and as
for getting out again . . . The whole
operation was insanity.

Who was I to talk? Sitting here with ten
dollars in my pocket and a dinner ahead of

me that would cost at least that. If they failed to show and talk business I was a goner. This had to go through.

The room had grown dark as I sat there thinking. Starting to rise, I stopped suddenly. There was a man loitering outside, staring at the building.

Relaxing in the chair, looking out the window, I watched him. He hesitated, lighted a cigarette, then leaned against a lamppost.

This was it then: Shuksan was suspicious. Or was it somebody else? For some other reason?

My eyes strayed to the dial of my watch--it was past seven and time to be moving. When he turned his eyes from the window I came out of the depths of the chair and slid into my shoulder holster, then my coat. There was a back door to the alley. . . . I turned that way, searched the alley with care, then stepped out into the night.

Flattened against the building, I waited. Nothing moved. I went to the end of the alley, looked around and saw nothing. And then I stepped out into the open street and walked quietly away. And I was smiling.

This was my backyard. . . . I was home again. . . . The street smelled of ancient fish, of dust, and the remembrance of heat, but I was back. . . . This was Macao. . . . This was living.

LT

COMMENTS: This fragment is related to "China King," the story fragment that you will read next. That is not to say this one was written first, but they probably were created within a few years of each other. Mentioned here is the "tribute silk" caper that makes up the backstory of "China King." Both stories have a foundation in the era of chaos that reigned in the Far East before and after World War II.

Louis often had his protagonists express a litany of odd jobs and experiences. This was always a general reflection of his own life and varied employment history but in a few cases, this being one of them, the list held even greater resonance. Occasionally, Dad mysteriously suggested that he returned to the Far East after his first trip in the mid-1920s. Supposedly, a few of the details mentioned in this story— jumping ship with forty cents in his pocket, a fight in the ring for some quick money, inside knowledge of the fake arms sale that ended with the con man's head being impaled on a pipe driven into the gravel of a Shanghai parking lot— were events from his life. The latter incident is more specifically described in the short story "A Friend of the General." In my opinion, the jury is still out regarding the veracity of these tales. What is more likely true is the story about the fight between the British seamen and the Chinese river pirates. I know that Dad was in Shanghai for four days and that story sounds like something that might well have happened along the Huangpu waterfront.

A few of the people and places mentioned here might be familiar to the soldiers and sailors of the time. "The Trenches" was a tough neighborhood of dope dens, gambling houses, and brothels outside the control of the Europeans who ran the International Settlement, or Treaty Port, of Shanghai. Del Monte's was a popular nightclub in Shanghai, as was the Lido Gardens ballroom. Notoriously—or perhaps mythically—beautiful White Russian women (the "Whites" fled Russia to avoid the "Reds," or Communists, after the revolution of 1917) were paid to dance with the male clientele at many of the clubs. Sikh bodyguards from India were hired to chaperone these girls, and "taxi dancers" were, supposedly, only there to dance. Of course, the White Russian women of Shanghai were also some of its most legendary prostitutes, so the rules may not have been as cut and dried as all that.

Lee Christmas, Tracy Richardson, Edward "Tex" O'Reilly, Francis "One-Arm" Sutton, and Rafael de Nogales were all famous mercenary soldiers, though not all in the same part of the world or at the same time. Frans August Larson was a missionary and explorer who managed to travel through some very remote parts of China, Mongolia, and Siberia. Most notably, James Brooke became the first "White Rajah" of Sarawak (an area of North Borneo) when he was given the territory by the Sultan of Brunei for his help in putting down piracy and a rebellion. The Brooke family ruled Sarawak from 1841 until conditions during and following World War II forced them to cede the country completely to Great Britain. All were Europeans who sold their abilities, often violent ones, in the hinterlands of Asia and Latin America.

"Haig" is not just a character in this fragment, but a man Louis claimed to have known, a British intelligence officer in China who had become a Buddhist and was an opium addict. There is a good deal of crossover between potentially real and totally fictional versions of this man, some of which occur elsewhere in this volume. While I have done my best to separate what is true from what is not, there is no way to tell how much truth, or fiction, there is to many of these stories.

From references in the text this seems to have been written in the early 1950s, when the Chinese Communists were still solidifying their hold on the western sections of the country. Louis did spend some time in China prior to World

War II and his brother was there right afterward as part of Ambassador Patrick Hurley's mission just before the Communists took over in 1949.

It is interesting, in light of all the Red Scare paranoia of the time, the horrific drama of China's Great Leap Forward, and then the Cultural Revolution, to see that Louis's predictions about Red China have turned out to be, at least so far, correct:

```
    . . . I was satisfied that when the
present furor was over China would have
absorbed communism as it has absorbed
all religions and all philosophies. In
the end communism would be turned out as
they were, as something distinctly
Chinese.
```

Dad had great confidence that China would emerge from its Communist period in a manner that was both prosperous and fundamentally Chinese. He didn't think the totalitarian idealism of communism stood a chance in the long run when compared with the Chinese interest in doing business with the rest of the world.

———————————

CHINA KING

———————————

The Beginning of a Crime Story

When I opened the door he was sitting
there with a gun in his hand. He was a lean
and evil man with a scar on his cheek that
had not been there when I saw him last and
the stench of unwashed clothes about him.
There was another scar on his upper lip
which I had reason to remember. My fist put
it there in a brawl on a ship's deck one hot
night off the mangrove coast.

"It's been a long time, Jack," he said,
grinning at me, "a very long time."

If there was any change it was not for the
better. He was older, of course, and his
tongue-tip kept touching the thickness in
his lip where the scar was. That wasn't a
good sign.

"How'd you get in?"

"A few years ago you wouldn't have asked
that. You'd have known." The smile left his
lips and his eyes veiled a little. "Ask me

what I'm here for and I'm not going to
like it."

He was an inch taller than my six-one,
though a good thirty pounds lighter. But I
made no mistake about China King. Even
without the gun he was no bargain in any
kind of fight.

"Want a drink?" Ignoring the gun, I
crossed to the sideboard.

"Sure," he said, "just so I watch you
mix it."

When he had a bourbon in his hand he took
a sip, then grinned. "Taste, kid. You got
it. But you always had it. Clothes, liquor,
and women."

He chuckled then. "Whatever became of the
Malay babe you picked up in that place on
High Street? When you moved in there I
figured you were due for a throat-cutting.
Her old man was a big muck-a-muck up in the
Federated States."

"We got along," I said. "We got along all
right."

This was trouble, real trouble. Nor was it
anything I had coming to me. China King and
all like him were a thing of my past, my
drifting days. That was over now, and I
wanted no part of him. When a man drifts
from port to port and lives as he can, he
meets many people, good and bad. China King
was poison.

"Nice place you got, kid. The first time I
met you was in Shanghai. You were broke and
on the beach."

"All right." I was a little irritated. "What do you want, China?"

His face changed as if he'd been slapped. His thin shoulders hunched and there were ugly lights in his eyes. "You know what I want! I want fifty thousand dollars! I want it right here in my hand, an' don't try stallin' me!"

"I haven't got fifty grand and never had it."

Something in my voice made him look twice at me. "It had to be you!" he said angrily. "Only two of us got out alive."

"Maybe."

"What does that mean?"

"What about Forbes?"

"That limey? He's dead. I killed him."

Opening a drawer in my desk I put my hand in. "If it's a gun," he said, "I'll kill you."

"It's a magazine," I told him, and took it out. The magazine was more than three years old. The picture I showed him was a group of three men . . . three top-flight business executives representing three separate airlines celebrating a merger into Trans-Orient. The man on the right was the new president of the company, Paul Greenway.

China swore. "How could I have missed? I had him dead to rights."

"You didn't get me, China. And you had me right where you wanted."

"You." There was no bitterness in his tone. "You were always a fool for luck."

Fifteen years can be a long, long time.

And the Far East was a wide world away and in those days it was a place to make a fast buck. Gunrunning, pearl poaching, smuggling, buying and selling the stuff big ships couldn't afford to handle, looting, gambling . . . fifty ways to make it and a hundred to lose it again.

Seven of us were in on the deal, seven men from all over the world and every man out for himself. We were lifting tribute silk from the Forbidden Palace in Peiping and peddling it to a Greek who sold it again in India. It was not stealing . . . not in the usual sense. We were under orders from a Chinese official; ostensibly the money went to buy guns but that was none of our business. Only we made our share in the process.

Up to a point, we did. The Chinese decided on a double cross . . . cutting out the Greek and the rest of us once the pipeline was set and the connections made. When we brought out the second load they were waiting for us with guns.

It was a hijack. A good old Yankee-style hijack. Only it didn't work. It didn't work because we were a suspicious lot of lads, and all of us had been around a little. We knew what the score was, and when that dark boat moved in alongside and they ordered us to stop, we took our time.

We knew the voice: It was our Chinese official. We would have stopped for nobody else. Then we saw three men rise out of the waist of that boat with tommy guns. We were

ready for trouble, and even as they opened
fire we dropped flat and heaved three
homemade grenades into their laps.

That was it. One of our boys copped it. He
was gone before he hit the deck, and a
Chinese boatman with him.

Six of us left, and a load of silk.

We never stopped, just kept going down the
coast. We didn't go near Shanghai and we
avoided Hong Kong. We went to Macao, made a
quick deal, and we were sitting on top of
three hundred thousand dollars.

Three hundred thousand dollars . . . six
men from nowhere. Forbes was an Englishman,
he had been chief mate on a Chinese steamer
line but did too much smuggling on his own
hook. There was the Portugee, a beachcomber
named Finley, a little rat named Joe
Hollinger, China King, and me. Fifty
thousand apiece, if we all lived. If some of
us died, there would be more to split.

That idea came to all of us, I think. For
myself, fifty grand was plenty, more than
I'd dreamed of having at this stage of the
game, but I knew the rest of them.

"We'd better get away from here," Forbes
advised. "There's too many in Macao who have
wind of this."

So it was Hong Kong we started for, and
Hollinger opened the game. He picked a fight
with the Portugee and before anybody knew
what had happened, the Portugee was on his
knees with his gut ripped open. Hollinger
was short, mean, and ready for trouble. "He

asked for it," he said, and I slipped the
safety off my Colt.

Five men and nobody felt sleepy. We were
off Tingkao village in the approaches to
Hong Kong when the lid blew off. Who started
it I never knew. Suddenly, everybody was
shooting at once. Forbes shot Hollinger and
China King shot at me, and I did some
shooting, too.

Somebody splashed in the water, and then I
went over the side myself. The water was
shallow in that wide sandy bay, and I got
to shore. There was another shot, then
silence . . . but I did not go to Hong Kong.
Instead I went to Canton and from there flew
to Shanghai . . . and safely in a room in
Shanghai I counted my money.

When everybody started to shoot, King shot
at me and I went into the bottom of that
boat, stuffed my shirt with money, and went
over the side. They thought I was gone when
King shot, and they were busy killing each
other. My take was seventy thousand. . . . I
neither knew nor cared what happened in the
junk, but it was pleasant in Europe that
spring, and from Paris I went to Rome, then
to Nice and through North Africa. I was
broke when I got back to the States, but it
had been worth it.

Hollinger, Finley, the Portugee . . . they
copped it.

"Somebody got away with the boat," King
said. "It had to be you or him."

There was no need to mention the seventy

thousand. "It was a long time ago. It's best forgotten."

He sneered at me. "I ain't forgettin' it. I'd figured it was you," he scowled, "but you never drank nor gambled them days, an' I know you hit the beach in the States flat busted. You never drank enough to wet a man's whistle. You couldn't have gotten rid of three hundred grand so fast."

He was right about that. Even seventy thousand had given me trouble.

He got up and poured himself a straight shot of bourbon. "I think I'll see Forbes."

"I wouldn't," I said. "I'd lay off."

He left me then, and after a while I went to bed. But I couldn't sleep. Forbes had always impressed me as a cold-blooded proposition, and certainly he had done his share of the shooting, but whatever else had happened, that was past. He had gone on and made a place for himself in the world and I couldn't let him look into the eyes of murder without a warning. So I rolled over and picked up the telephone.

It took me more than an hour to get to him. When I did his voice was brusque and impatient. "Yes? What is it?"

"Greenway, if your name used to be Forbes, I just want to say that China King is in town. He wants to see you."

His hesitation was brief, then he said in a quiet, perfectly cool voice, "This is Paul Greenway. My name was never Forbes. I do not know any China King. Good evening."

So I went to sleep. If he was not Forbes

he had something to wonder about. If he was, he knew what was in store for him. No matter what happened, the burden was off my shoulders.

Two nights later I came up to my door and dug for my key. My hand stopped there and I listened.

My radio was playing, and louder than I usually play it. Somebody was in my apartment, and that could only mean it was China King.

At first I thought about calling the cops. Then I shrugged and opened the door and stepped inside. It was King, all right, only he wasn't sitting on the divan waiting for me. He was lying on the floor and he had been shot twice in the stomach. What he failed to get that night off Tingkao he had now, a bellyful of it.

And so had I.

There was no gun, but I had a very good hunch. Opening the drawer of my desk I looked for my pistol. It lay just where it had always been. I sniffed the barrel. . . . It had been fired.

There could have been a lot of men who wanted to kill China King, but I did not believe more than one of them was in Los Angeles . . . and trust Greenway to have known about me, and to have guessed who the call was from.

Sitting very still in my apartment with a dead man at my feet, I tried to remember all I had known of the man we had called Forbes.

It summed up to very little. We called him a limey, but whether he was actually English or not, I did not know. We had met in Shanghai the way drifters do meet. None of us had known the others well. I'd known the Chinese who got us all into it, had seen King, Finley, and Forbes around. Forbes was a cold-blooded fish, a good poker player, and a cool head under fire. He would be a dangerous opponent, and now, of the seven, only two remained.

Knowing something of the man, I knew he would have an alibi; I knew also that he would have arranged to point this killing definitely at me. It was not enough that it be clear, but there must be no mystery to invite inquiry, and I was the only one who could point a finger at Greenway.

The only one . . . In that case I'd be better off dead, from his viewpoint. Dead, I could not talk. Dead it would appear that either I had shot King and killed myself, or had been wounded and died later, or was killed by a friend of King's or the police.

Hence, his best bet was to kill me. The man I had known as Forbes would reason just that way.

How much did he know about me? That would be important now. What would he decide that I would do upon finding the body of King?

Call the police? Or remove the body to some other place? He would suspect me of the latter move. If that was so, and if he wanted to kill me, then he or his killer would be someplace near my car, which was

parked in the space behind the apartment
house.

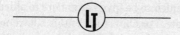

COMMENTS: This is a much more interesting story fragment than it may seem on the surface. The underlying idea,
that a group of desperate characters, near strangers to one
another, perform a dangerous or illicit act in order to gain a
"treasure" and once they do can no longer trust one another,
can be found in more than a half dozen of Louis's stories and
novels. These include "What Gold Does to a Man," "Desperate Men," *Kid Rodelo* ("Desperate Men" was the short story
that became the novel *Kid Rodelo*), a couple of story fragments here in *Louis L'Amour's Lost Treasures*, and the best of
all of them, the short story "Off the Mangrove Coast," to
which this piece has certain connections. It will also show up
as a subplot in Louis's soon-to-be-published first novel, *No
Traveler Returns*.

The basic idea contains elements of B. Traven's classic
The Treasure of the Sierra Madre, but in "Off the Mangrove
Coast," Louis added a brilliant refinement: It's not much of a
treasure. The fact that there really isn't enough money to go
around increases the likelihood that one of the men will try
to kill the others for the chance to get it all.

Was there some element of this story that was true to
Louis's life? Is that why he returned to this plot over and
over? He did tell some stories to this effect, but so far, I have
no way of knowing if they actually happened. One thing that
appears in this story that is true is that he did run into a man
named Joe Hollinger, both at sea and with the Hagenbeck-
Wallace Circus. And, it seems, a knife was Joe's preferred
weapon.

This is also a sequel of sorts to the story fragment titled

"Jack Cross." The "silk caper" mentioned is referenced in both stories, and the time period seems right. At a guess, "tribute silk" was silk either given the Chinese emperors in tribute or intended to be given as tribute to allied governors or heads of state. Possibly stock of this silk remained in the Forbidden City for some time. The other oddball crime mentioned here is "pearl poaching," which probably refers to sneaking into Australian territorial waters without the appropriate permits and diving for pearl shell. Before cultured pearls, the real market was for mother-of-pearl from the inside of the oyster (it was used for many of the things we now make out of plastic, like buttons, combs, and the keys on musical instruments). The pearls themselves were so rare that it was a waste of time diving in the hopes of finding one. However, if you were in the mother-of-pearl business and earned a living from the thousands of oysters you brought up, the pearls themselves served as a windfall profit.

Contrary to what one might think from reading some of the overtly macho material Louis wrote, he was a fairly mild-mannered guy. He had great presence, but certainly by the time I came along, he had little to prove in any way other than just trying to be a good writer. Though he could certainly tell adventurous tales about his life, he was a gentle man who could inspire that same gentleness in others.

TAP TALHARAN

The Beginning of a Western Story

He made camp where the rising sun found
frost on the hill, bedding down under a
clump of aspen that lined a small hollow on
the slope. He was dead tired with the miles
behind him, and when the picket pin was
driven in he fell into his blankets and
slept.

The next thing he knew was a boot in the
ribs and a harsh voice, "Get up out of that!
Get up, I say!"

His gun was hanging on an aspen near his
hand but one of the three men had been
thinking of that and held a shotgun on him,
grinning as if to say that he should go
ahead and try it.

Tap Talharan sat up. "What's the matter?"
he asked mildly.

He was in trouble. He was no pilgrim and
he knew it when he saw it. These were hard
men, riding a hard way, and no give to them
at all.

"We want no saddle tramps on this range."
The man was slab-sided and hatchet-faced.
"Get on your horse and get out of here."

"Look," Talharan said mildly, "I rode all
night. I'm dead beat. I've been asleep maybe
thirty minutes. When I've had some rest I'll
be moving."

"You'll move now."

"What's the trouble? I don't even know
you, or the country. Why push me out?"

The stocky man with red hair was a
fighter. He had a broad, tough face and
scarred knuckles. He packed a gun but a man
could see he liked to fight with his fists.

"You can leave now," he said, "or be
buried here."

Talharan walked to his saddle and grabbed
it. When he was cinched up and had his
blanket roll he belted on his holster, but
they had taken the gun.

"Give me my gun," he said.

The big man just looked at him and the
wiry, sallow-faced one snickered.

"I've had that gun a long time," Talharan
said.

"You've got thirty seconds," the big man
said, "thirty seconds to start moving. You
get no gun."

Talharan looked at him a slow five seconds
and then stepped into the leather and rode
away. He rode steadily for fifty yards and
then slapped spurs to the buckskin and took
off. Talharan realized then that he was mad.

He was not a man who often became angry.
It had been several years since he had last

lost his temper, but he needed sleep and he
did want that gun.

When he reached the crest of the ridge he
looked back and could see the three riders
sloping off across the country, following a
trail diagonally opposite his own. In the
distance a thin trail of smoke pointed a
questioning finger into the sky.

Talharan was three days unshaven, and four
days tired, and had but six silver dollars
in his pocket, but he turned toward the
smoke that suggested a town.

Two hours later he had walked his horse
down the dusty street to the livery stable.
The buckskin was dead beat and had to rest.
And Tap Talharan was no man to kill a good
horse. He walked up to the livery stable and
found he had arrived late.

The redheaded man was sitting on a bench
at the wide stable door. There was an older
man beside him but the redhead did the
talking. "When you don't know a country," he
said, "it takes a longer time to get places.
Now you keep moving."

Talharan looked at him. "You're pushing
me," he said. "Why?"

The redhead grinned at him. "Maybe we
don't like your looks. Maybe we just don't
like strangers. Maybe we don't want your
horse eating our grass. Maybe we think you'd
live longer if you kept going."

Talharan nodded. "Maybe you're right about
that last item. Trouble is, I'm a most
stubborn man."

He walked his horse down the street and saw the sallow-faced man loitering in front of the general store, and the big man in front of the saloon.

"Well, Buck," he said, "this looks like a closed town. And it isn't much of a town, either."

He rode steadily west until he saw the churned-up ground where a number of cattle had been driven across the trail. He turned there and lost his hoof tracks amid those of the cattle and the riders who drove them. He followed the trail across the prairie into a grassy bottom where a small stream found a winding way among the trees. Entering the stream he doubled back, riding toward the trail he had left until he found a clump of willows. Entering the willows he pushed on until he found a bare space that was open. There was a little grass there, and he picketed the horse again and stretched out in the sun.

Voices awakened him in the late afternoon. The buckskin was standing with its ears pricked and he whispered to the horse to prevent it from nickering. The buckskin flicked an attentive ear and relaxed. Tap Talharan sat up and listened.

His camp in the willows was not fifty yards from the trail, but these men were off the trail and closer.

"The gun has seen a lot of use." It was the voice of the redhead. "Who do you think he was?"

"A drifter . . . saddle tramp. Just as well to get rid of him."

"I don't think you have," Red was saying. "Look, Talbot. You took his Winchester and his Colt. I don't think he would leave without an argument."

"He's gone."

"I thought at first he might be one of the Macken Boys."

"Don't be a fool. Johnny Macken was the last of them and he was killed in Texas. The old man's alone now."

"He's a tough old man."

"He was tough." Talbot was speaking. "Now he's just old."

When they had passed along, Talharan got up and looked at the sky. It was about two hours by the sun until nightfall, so he saddled up. The buckskin had done well by the grass within the small clearing, and now he drank from the stream.

Talharan had a deep hunger within him, but knew there would be no food for him in the town. If you could call a store, one saloon, a post office, and a stable a town.

Macken had been the name. An old man named Macken. The name sounded some memory deep within him but he could not place it; however, the name Johnny Macken did mean something. Macken had been a Texas Ranger, killed fighting rustlers the year before, and a good man, by all accounts.

Talharan took a long drink of the cold water and then got into the saddle. Macken had an outfit, and the chances are it was

back behind him . . . back where he was
camping when they came on him first.

Their pushing him out of the country made
no sense unless they were afraid he was
going to work for Macken, against whom they
must have some sort of plan. If Talharan
could find Macken then he might get a real
meal and a gun. Looking for him was not
smart, but Talharan had never thought of
himself as very smart. However, he was
stubborn to the point of mild insanity. And
he did not like to be pushed. When pushed he
was inclined to dig in his heels.

He circled widely, getting a feel for the
lay of the land as he did so.

Under the late afternoon sky the hills lay
tawny with autumn, and through the cresting
pines gold fingers of light found their way,
but already the valleys were gathering
shadow. Tap Talharan rode warily, enjoying
the cool of the evening, but realizing he
would ride warmer with a filled holster.

On a far, high slope some cattle grazed
and the land lay empty between, and then
when he topped out on a new ridge Tap
Talharan saw a cluster of shabby buildings
lying at the end of a long sweep of a
magnificent valley.

Twice he saw M Bar brands on cows and
decided this must be the Macken brand, so he
rode on, walking his horse to approach
slowly. The sky was painting its clouds for
sunset before he rode into the ranch-yard.

Several horses were in the corral, good

stock. The place looked down-at-heel and
needing a handyman around, and he went into
the yard and hallooed the house.

"All right," the old man's voice came from
the open doorway of the barn, "speak your
piece, and while you're talkin' keep it in
mind that this here's a .56-caliber
Spencer."

"Mr. Macken"--Talharan drew a foot from
the stirrup and hung his knee around the
saddle horn--"I'm a wandering man. The last
few weeks I've come a far piece on mighty
low rations, hunting the sun and of no mind
to stop where there'll be snow.

"Last night I rode all night because I
bedded down for a couple of hours' sleep in
the sunshine.

"Three men came along, a man named Talbot
and two others. They kicked me awake, took
my rifle and six-shooter, and told me to get
out of the country.

"Mr. Macken, those men have trouble with
you. Of its sort and kind I'm not familiar,
but I've a mind to do something about what
they've done to me."

"You'd be safer to keep riding."

"You are right. But I've a fat streak of
meanness running through me that makes me
want to see those men again when I am
standing upright with a gun belted on."

"You're a fool."

"I'm a hungry fool. How's for some grub?"

The old man came from the stable with the
Spencer in the hollow of his arm. "Nobody
ever left this ranch hungry. Come inside."

When Macken opened the door, light streamed out, and the kitchen was warm and cheery with the smell of baking, and there were curtains at the windows and a cloth on the table, and then Tap was removing his hat hurriedly, for there was a girl there, too, a girl with sandy hair and green eyes.

"I am Ruth Macken." She held out her hand and Talharan took it and looked very foolish. "Sit down," she continued. "I was just putting supper on the table."

Tap looked at her and turned quickly away to the washbasin, where he washed his hands and face, then slicked down his hair.

"You're riding the grub line?" she asked.

Talharan was riding it, all right, when he had a chance, but admitting it to a girl like this was something he could not do. "No, ma'am." He remembered the six silver dollars. "I can pay.

"It was the frost that did it, ma'am. When the first frost came to Montana this year it came early, and when the frost comes, I ride. So I threw a hull on my horse and started south."

She went about putting supper on the table and when she had seated herself, Macken looked across the table at Talharan. "They've been driving cattle at night, driving them across my land, and I would not have it. There were other trips at night, too, times when they rode fast and hard, cutting across to the breaks along the river."

"You work the place alone?"

"There were two hands, but they ran them off."

"The sun is brighter down Arizona way, but if you'll have me until the trouble is over, I'll abide."

He went outside when the meal was over and forked hay to the stock in the corral. There was work to do around the place and he stayed with it until sundown.

When the red arrows of the sun shot into the high clouds, he saddled up and rode away, and glancing back, saw Ruth Macken watching him, and he thought how pleasant it was to see a woman standing in the doorway, seeing him go. Yet it left an uneasiness on him, and for a moment there was a feeling that Arizona was far away and he had better waste no time.

Lights were in the windows of the saloon when he rode into town. There was a lantern over the door of the livery stable, and two more inside, hanging from the roof beams. Tap drew up outside the stable and saw the hostler sitting there on the bench. "Where's Red?" he asked mildly.

The old man drew on his pipe, it glowed briefly, and after a moment he said, "I've seen your kind before, and you belong nowhere. Ride on. . . . There's country you haven't seen."

Tap Talharan considered that in the slow way he had, and knew the old man was right. This was not his fight. He should look upon his guns as the chance of the trail; they might as easily have been lost fording a

stream. He should ride on. It was safer, and
there was nothing at issue here.

He shifted in the saddle, and the words
he spoke came unbidden. "You are one hundred
percent right, but there's something else.
They began trouble with me, took my guns
when I was asleep."

"It isn't reason enough."

Talharan remembered the girl in the
doorway, and he remembered the quiet way she
had, serving the food, and the direct way
she looked at him across the table.

"A man has to stop somewhere," he said,
and walked his horse toward the saloon.

Behind him he heard the old man say, "He's
alone, but not for long."

Tap tied his horse at the hitch rail and
felt the emptiness in his stomach that he
remembered. It was still possible to get
into the saddle and ride on. Yet he mounted
the steps, knowing he was not a brave man,
and a little curious about what bravery
really was, and then he opened the door and
went in.

It wasn't much of a place. A sheet-iron
stove, two tables and some chairs, and a short
bar not over eight feet long. Red was
sitting at a table and there was a bartender
behind the bar. Two men sat quietly at a
table nearby and he knew them for small
ranchers like Macken.

Red looked up at him and grinned and Tap
walked over to the table where he sat, and
Red's expression changed, a flicker ran
through the muscles of his face, and he

started to get up. Tap remembered the way
they had come on him asleep and he swung a
long right that caught Red rising and
knocked him back over his chair.

Red sprawled in the wreckage of the chair
and stared up at Tap, and then started to
gather himself, and when he was almost ready
to get up, Tap kicked him in the solar
plexus. Red grabbed at Tap's leg, too late,
retched violently, and then Tap reached down
with a big hand and jerked him to his feet.
He pushed him away and swung at his face
with both hands, and the big fists smashed
dully in Red's features, and the blood
started from a broken nose and smashed lips.

Red pawed at him with weakened hands but
Tap slapped them down and, reaching over,
took Red's gun and dropped it into his own
holster.

Coolly, he pushed Red against the bar and
hooked a hard right into the man's stomach,
and let him fall.

"You didn't give him much chance," the
bartender said mildly.

"He made his own rules," Talharan replied,
"about daylight this morning."

Boots sounded on the steps outside and the
door opened. The big man was the first
inside and the sallow-faced one followed
after.

Talbot saw Red lying on the floor,
struggling to rise, his face bloody. He
stopped and he turned partway around and saw
Tap Talharan. Red's pistol was in his hand.

"I've got a gun, Talbot. You can drop your

gun-belts, or you can die right here, it
don't make no matter to me."

Nobody moved or spoke. A moth fluttered
about the coal-oil lamp, and Talbot stood
darkly against the light.

"You've got the drop," Talbot growled.
"Give me a break."

"Just what you gave me this morning? You
drop your belts, both of you. I'm not going
to count, I'm just going to start
shooting."

The other man's hand went to his belt, and
very delicately he unfastened it and let it
fall. Talbot hesitated, not liking it, the
hot fury showing all through him.
Reluctantly then, he unfastened the buckle
and let his belt fall.

Talharan moved them back and gathered the
gun-belts. He took the guns and thrust them
behind his belt, and coolly, taking his
time, he removed the shells from their gun-
belts and shoved them into his own pockets.

"Now put your money on the bar."

Talbot started to speak, then stopped.
None of the ranchers moved to protest.

They piled it on the bar, some thirty or
forty dollars. Talharan gestured at it.
"Pour them each a drink," he said. "And one
for Red. Talbot's buying."

When the glasses were filled, Talharan
said, "Now drink it. This one is for luck.
Just toss it off."

Talbot looked at the whiskey and started
to speak, but Tap said quietly, "You booted
me in the ribs this morning, Talbot. I

could kill you for that, like you threatened to kill me. Now drink up."

He sat down then, and when the bartender had filled their glasses again, he had them drink again.

An hour later they were drunk, and unable to walk straight. The sallow-faced man was the first to pass out, and Red was the second. Talbot lasted another hour, and it was close to midnight when he slumped to a sitting position on the floor.

Talharan gathered up the change and put it back in Talbot's pocket. Then he stopped and picked the big man up and carried him outside, the ranchers and the bartender watching. He tied Talbot in his saddle and did the same with each of the others. Then he released the horses and tied the bridle reins to the horn of the saddle on each one. With a hat he slapped each of the horses over the rump . . . only taking time to slip a Winchester from the scabbard on Red's horse.

The three horses clattered off down the trail, their drunken riders bobbing in their saddles.

Tap Talharan walked back inside. "Sorry to have kept you open," he said.

"Worth it," the bartender said.

COMMENTS: A careful reader will recognize Ruth Macken's name. This is not intended to be the same character who is the resourceful widow in the novel *Bendigo Shafter.* That woman would have been married to a man named Macken, whereas this one seems to be the daughter or daughter-in-law of the man who owns the ranch. This is simply a case of Louis reusing a character name he liked.

THE DARK HOLE

The Beginning of a Crime Story

CHAPTER I

There were deer tracks in the dust, and nothing more. Dia was gone.

He hesitated, looking around into the gathering dusk. She could not have gone far. He called . . . and his voice echoed, then lost itself lonesomely against the far walls of the canyon.

It was unlike her to walk away, and she had been tired. She had remained behind to rest while he took an exploratory walk up a branch canyon. He could have been gone no more than ten minutes . . . or fifteen.

He called again, and the echoing voice made him cringe inwardly, for this was a place of silence.

The meadow was shadowed and still with the late evening. There was sunlight upon the mountains, but in this deep hollow it was gone. The parched grass was matted and yellow, offering concealment for nothing larger than a fist.

He called again and yet again, but there was no answer, no sound, no faint reply.

He paused before the boulder where he had last seen her. Her tracks were there, where she had walked up and seated herself. He could see where she had shifted her feet several times, but no sign of her leaving.

Dia, his gentle, fragile Dia . . . gone!

But where could she go? He called again, mounting worry giving rein to irritation.

Then he saw something else. A small, circular spot in the dust, such a spot as is made by the toe when one rises and suddenly turns.

He lifted his eyes and looked to where hers must have looked. He was staring at a dark finger of woods. A finger of dark trees pointing at the rock on which she had been seated.

Dia had risen suddenly--something had moved there, something that startled her. But Dia was not easily frightened. Slender, fragile, yes . . . but with courage.

What then?

He walked swiftly, half-fearfully because of what he might find. He was careful to walk wide so as to obliterate no tracks. He paused within the shadow of the trees, straining his eyes to see.

It was darker here but he could make out fallen trunks, a few boulders. . . . He searched among them but there was nothing, simply nothing at all.

Dia was gone.

He called, and his voice lost itself down the empty canyon.

It was twelve miles to the nearest town. Seven miles to the ranch through whose gate they had come to reach this place. He called again, and yet again, walking beneath the trees. It was dark, yes, but light enough to see her body if it had fallen here.

Her body.

His throat tightened.

Then relief flooded over him. Why, what a fool he was! Knowing it would be too late to go on farther into The Dark Hole, she had simply started back toward the car, knowing he would soon catch up!

Wheeling about, he started back, disgusted with himself for his foolishness. He set out the way they had come, then began cutting a zigzag trail to find her returning tracks. He was good at reading sign and at times had followed deer for miles. . . . But there were no tracks.

Only the tracks they had made as they neared the place, that was all.

He stopped again . . . and called. His voice echoed down the canyon toward the outer world, and there was no other sound. Somewhere, far off, a nightbird called.

Could she have gone on, up the canyon, deeper into The Dark Hole?

Perhaps she felt that she moved too slowly for him, and had gone on. She knew his curiosity about this place, and that he would not want to go back when they were so close to seeing the end of it. It was unlike her. . . . He hurried on across the meadow and started up the narrowing canyon again.

It was darker here, and there were many water-worn boulders, some of them gigantic. He stumbled up, calling again.

His wife was gone. Dia was gone.

Suddenly, he knew. He could not find her. She was certainly gone. He must go out to the ranch at once, call for help, get the sheriff out here with a searching party. It was too late and he could cover too little ground alone. She must have gone away, started away. Possibly she was lying in some crevice now, hearing his cries, her own voice lost to weakness.

No tracks . . . Now there was a star in the sky. The cliffs had turned to edges of solid black against the pale cloudless gray of the oncoming night. Under the trees where he had searched for Dia there was ominous darkness now. Fear clutched at him.

"Dia!"

His voice rang out against the cliffs, echoed down the canyon and up the canyon in twin voices, weakening with increasing distance. "Dia, Dia, Dia . . ."

But only his own voice called into the silence, and only his own voice answered, and there was no other sound; there was nothing, not even the wind.

Magill forced himself to think. He forced his mind to be cold. He ruled out fear and doubt. He fought to abandon emotion. To think.

She had suggested waiting. After all, he

would be gone only a few minutes, and she
was tired. When he was exploring he was
always overeager and sometimes he forgot
that others lacked his enthusiasm and his
physical condition. Yet today he had
remembered not to hurry, to think of Dia, to
take his time.

He considered the situation. After all, he
was a thinking man. It was through thought
that Man had risen above the beast, yet at
the first sign of fear, of panic, of danger,
he was apt to stop thinking and to act
blindly, instinctively. And man could in
most cases no longer trust his instincts. If
he was to find Dia, he must think.

The canyon's line was roughly east and
west. To north and south were cliffs that
would be difficult to climb, even for him.
Nor could she have climbed them in the time
he had been gone. Therefore, she must have
gone down the canyon toward the car, or up
the canyon and deeper into The Dark Hole.

He looked down-canyon for tracks and found
none. He had looked up the canyon and found no
tracks either. Nor had he seen any tracks
leaving the rock where she had been seated.

The canyon leading into The Dark Hole was
narrow and almost floored with boulders.
Only at the side, sometimes along one wall,
sometimes along the other, was there room
for a path.

A path that was a game trail, nothing
more. The walls of the canyon were not rock,
although there was much rock in them. They
were of cretaceous formation, but almost

sheer, reaching up for all of seven hundred feet to the rim.

There was some brush on the cliff, sparse stuff, mingled with poison oak. In the canyon bottom there was a mixture of trees, dark pines or oak, with an occasional cottonwood. Once, halting to gasp for breath, he paused beneath a cottonwood.

He called again, "Dia!" It was incredible that she could disappear, but disappear she had.

He stood alone in the bottom of this narrow crack in the earth. He was in the middle of California, but he was utterly alone. There were cities not far away, crowded with people; there were intervening villages, farms, homes. . . . Yet he was alone, all, all alone. And Dia was gone.

There was danger where there were people, but here there were no . . . But how did he know? Could he be sure they had not been followed? That some unseen madman had not lurked under the trees? Possibly some creature of feeble mind but great strength? He had heard of such things.

Yet he had seen no tracks. Not even so slender a girl as Dia could leave without tracks. And he had followed the trails of rabbit, deer, and wolf.

He was gasping and bathed in sweat. He had a horrible feeling that she might be in desperate trouble, that he might be running away from her rather than toward her. Perhaps she was held silent by some criminal who even now was watching him. But that was imagination. He had no reason to think such a thing.

He started on, then stumbled and fell. He got slowly to his feet, his hands torn by the gravel. He was scarcely conscious of the pain. It was then he thought of a fire.

He would go back to the meadow and build a fire. She would see it and come to him . . . if she was alive.

He gathered wood. There was plenty of it-- no fire had been built in this place for a long time. He put sticks together, and soon had a blaze going. Under other circumstances it would have made a peaceful camp. He was a quiet man, interested in wildlife, in trees, shrubs . . . open country, mountains, and forest. He had always lived quietly. Violence had no place in his life.

The flames leaped up as he added dry sticks to make a bright blaze. A big fire, that was what he wanted. Yet he was careful, even now, to keep it from spreading. He let a little circle of grass burn off around the spot, letting it spread only a few inches at a time. Soon he had a border of blackness where no chance spark could ignite the dry grass if he had to leave the blaze.

He gathered wood in a pile. He moved away from the fire, listening. There was no sound but the crackle of the flames. He paced anxiously; he waited. He thought of a thousand things. Nothing made sense. Dia would not wander off by herself. She never had; she wasn't the type. She would have waited for him. That was just it--none of it made sense.

His Dia gone . . . It was impossible.

Footsteps.

He came quickly to his feet and sprang away from the fire. "<u>Dia</u>!" His voice rang. "You've . . . !"

It was not Dia. Three men had walked to the edge of the firelight. One was the rancher, Rorick. The other two were strangers, but one was obviously a forest ranger.

"Don't you know you can't build fires in here?" The ranger's voice was patiently angry.

"It's for my wife. She's gone."

"Gone?"

"Lost, I guess. I left her sitting here. . . ." He started to explain, trying to talk coolly, to remember everything.

"But that's ridiculous!" The ranger was irritable. "Where could she go? In this canyon you can go up and you can go back. Unless she could go up the wall."

"She wouldn't do that."

"There was a girl in the car with him," Rorick said, "a pretty little thing."

"Look," the ranger insisted, "if your wife came up here with you she's got to be here now."

"You passed my car?"

"It was empty."

"You passed no one?"

"Wouldn't we have mentioned it?"

"Then she must be up in the canyon, if she isn't dead."

Their eyes all turned to him, startled. The ranger's eyes seemed to grow more intent. Or had he imagined that? "Why would she be dead?"

"I've been yelling. She would have answered, wouldn't she?"

The search lasted two hours. There were four of them now and they walked abreast up the canyon to the head. They found nothing . . . or almost nothing.

The head of the canyon was a cliff down which water fell during heavy rains. The rocks there were polished and smooth. There was, nowhere, any sign of Dia.

Returning, they stopped at one place. It was a fresh slide. The ranger, whose name was Bronson, threw the beam of his five-celled flashlight up the slide. It was still somewhat damp.

"After sundown," Rorick said, "or maybe an hour before. The sun would have dried it out."

"Maybe." The ranger walked around the pile and studied it with his light. "The sun only reaches the bottom at midday. That's why they call it The Dark Hole."

They lingered, and Magill shifted from foot to foot. Dia . . . where was Dia? Somewhere out in the dark, Dia who never wanted to be alone, who hated to be alone. She was out there, somewhere alone in the dark.

"Do we have to stand here?" His irritation

was in his voice. "My wife may have fallen somewhere. She may be suffering."

Bronson straightened, brushing off his breeches, taking his time. "Mister," he spoke slowly, carefully. "Your wife did not come down the canyon. She isn't, so far as we can see, up the canyon. If she was alive, we would have found her."

"I don't think so anymore. If she was dead we would have found her. We've been over every inch of this canyon."

Bronson nodded. "That's right, mister. We have been over every inch of it . . . almost."

He stared from one to the other. "What do you mean? Almost?"

"We've been over every inch of this canyon," Bronson repeated, "except what's under that rock pile!"

CHAPTER II

Bronson turned away from Magill and began gathering material for a fire. The third man helped, and after a minute or so, Magill did also. He felt numb . . . shocked. He could not look toward the debris but kept his eyes averted.

Rorick conferred quietly with Bronson, then started off into the darkness. They could see his light bobbing down the canyon for several minutes, then it disappeared.

The third man was short, stocky, and

quiet. "My name is Don Matthews." He moved over beside Magill.

"Mine is Magill. Morgan Magill."

The forest ranger was squatting beside the new blaze, feeding it with fuel. He looked over his shoulder at Magill. "Not the Morgan Magill? Who wrote the book on tropical birds?"

At Magill's nod, Bronson turned back toward the fire, vaguely disturbed. If that was true, then what he had been thinking would be absurd . . . or would it?

He had read the book, and loved every page of it. Here was a man who not only loved birds, knew them well, and understood them, but who could write.

Yet how could one tell? Murder came to the most unlikely places. Considering this big, quiet, easy-moving man behind him, he decided that Magill must be around thirty-five, possibly a year or two younger. And he had been around a lot. Exploring for birds in Borneo, New Guinea, Halmahera, Indo-China and Brazil. Looking for rare birds and studying their habits.

"Been married long?" Matthews asked.

"Four . . . almost five months. We met in Honolulu on my way home. Dia was there on vacation."

They waited, keeping the fire going. At last, Magill could stand it no longer, and moving to the rock pile he began lifting away the larger rocks. Steadily, quietly, he worked. Finally, the others joined him.

By the time Rorick returned with shovels,
all the larger rocks had been moved.

Carefully, taking their time, they began
work with the shovels. There was no chance,
nor had there ever been any chance of
finding anything alive under that pile. Many
of the rocks were large and they had come
down with great force.

When the pile had become quite small,
about to the limits of a small human body,
they rested. Bronson rubbed his jaw and
looked around uneasily, avoiding Magill.

For the first time Magill noticed the butt
of a pistol sticking up out of Rorick's
pocket. It had not been there when he left
to go for the shovels. Magill lifted his
eyes to Rorick and found the man watching
him. He must have seen Magill's eyes on the
gun. After a moment, without seeming to do
so, Rorick moved back, farther from Magill.

Morgan Magill suddenly felt very tired.
There was no coolness left in him. He was
simply exhausted now, emotionally and
physically. He backed up and sat down.

She was not under that pile. She could not
be. Not his lovely, fragile, beautiful Dia.
Not crushed and broken and . . .

More footsteps . . . He came to his feet
instantly, tight with awareness.

No . . . they were not light-stepping
feet, but the heavier scuff of men walking.
Then a bobbing light and after a long minute
two men came into the circle of firelight.
One wore a badge on his coat.

"Hello, Bronson . . . Rory." He glanced

once at Magill, then at the pile. "All
right, uncover it."

The men went to work, with their hands
this time. Magill sat very quiet, suddenly
aware of a new tension, a new feeling in the
air.

The sheriff . . . they thought he had
murdered Dia.

He got swiftly to his feet and the sheriff
turned on him, his eyes alert, his hand near
the edge of his coat.

Magill flushed. How silly could you get?
But he said nothing at all. Now they were
down . . . Rorick got up.

"Nothing here, Sam." With the shovels they
moved the last of the debris. There was
nothing there. No Dia . . . nothing.

"She's alive then," he said. "She's got to
be alive."

Bronson looked over at Rorick, frowning.
"You're sure there was a girl in that car?"

The rancher was impatient. "Of course! I
brought her a cup of water from the well.
Gave it to her with my own hands."

"Then," the sheriff asked quietly, "where
is she? Don't tell me she climbed over those
seven-hundred-foot cliffs in the dark?"

Magill shifted his feet. "Sheriff," he
said quietly, "it was not dark when I first
missed her. It didn't become dark for almost
thirty minutes. I looked under the
trees . . . everywhere."

"You think she climbed out?"

"I think the idea is absurd. Dia did not
like heights. At least, I could never get

her to climb. Besides"--he looked around at their faces--"where could she go? And what would be the object of it?"

Nobody had any answer to that. The sheriff moved off to one side and held a low-voiced conversation with Bronson. Don Matthews remained beside Magill. He seemed sympathetic. "You were very much in love?" he asked.

"She was the only woman I ever loved. In fact, she was the only woman I ever knew very well."

"You must be well-off," Matthews suggested. "Those trips must have cost money. I've read a couple of your books."

"The trips didn't cost so much as you'd imagine. I came back from overseas with a little money saved. That paid for the first one. I sold a few articles, then I got a grant from a foundation and took the second. It was not difficult after that."

"Did your wife have money?"

"Dia? No . . . nothing. She had been a librarian somewhere in the Midwest before we met. We . . . we married rather suddenly because she was almost broke and if she returned to her job we would be separated. I didn't want that and neither did she."

Matthews dropped to his haunches and poked absently at the fire. Magill was a handsome man in a rugged sort of way, but seemed more the scholar than the explorer. Leaving Bronson and Matthews beside the fire in case Dia might be alive and lost and the fire might lead her to safety, the sheriff and

Rorick started back toward the ranch. The
other man had disappeared somewhere in the
darkness.

"Just relax"--the sheriff's name was Sam
Gates--"we've done all we can do tonight. By
daylight we'll have searching parties moving
in from both sides. That's wild country but
we can cover it. If she got out of the
canyon, we'll find her."

They returned silently to their vehicles
and Magill found himself back at the
farmhouse. He paced the floor restlessly,
and finally, just as the sun was rising, he
fell asleep in a chair.

He awakened with a start. Instantly wide
awake and on his feet. He looked at his
watch, but it had stopped. He wound it, then
checked with the clock in the kitchen.

The backyard was full of men. Not far from
the window, which was raised a little at the
bottom, was Sheriff Gates. Rorick and
several other men were standing with him.
"If you hadn't seen her," Gates was saying,
"I'd say she never existed."

"Killed her an' hid her body, if you ask
me." The speaker was a burly, unshaven
man. "Plenty of places a body could be
hid. I figure that there slide was started
a-purpose. It was just a blind."

They all looked at the man. "How do we
know," he continued, "she ever got as far as
the Hole? We saw where he left his car.
There's plenty of canyons open off the trail
before you get to the Hole. Has anybody

looked in that old quicksilver mine? I say
she never got to the Hole."

Magill backed up and sat down heavily. The
sleep had cleared his mind, and he was a man
who was accustomed to dealing with problems.
He was possessed of two facts of which they
could not be sure. He _knew_ his wife had
reached the canyon, and he _knew_ he had not
killed her. Therefore, where was she?

If her body had not been found, it was
not there. The only place where the earth
was disturbed had been examined. Hence, if
she was not there she had gone away or been
taken away.

Yet he had found no tracks and Dia would
have been unable to cover a trail sufficiently
to deceive him. And why should she wish to?

Suppose someone had come upon her
suddenly . . . But there had been no
evidence of a struggle. Unless she had been
knocked unconscious. Little by little he
began to examine all the possibilities, all
the situations that might have arisen.

Again and again his thoughts returned to
the slide. Something had to start a slide.
It could have been a coincidence, but it was
almost too much of one. And it was the only
thing in the area that seemed in any way
different than usual.

A woman had vanished . . . and there had
been a rock slide. Had anyone scouted the
rim above the slide? She might have been
knocked out and carried up the cliff. That
might be accomplished by a man of unusual
strength . . . but it was improbable.

Turning his head he glanced at his
reflection in the mirror. He was a big man
with rumpled light brown hair and quiet gray
eyes, but now those eyes had dark circles
beneath them, and his mouth looked drawn.

Dia . . . gone.

He remembered how they had met. It seemed
like yesterday, and yet . . . in some ways
it seemed a faraway, impossible time.

He had devoted four months of his life to
Halmahera in the East Indies . . .
Indonesia, it was now. He'd spent most of
those four months in the jungle, away from
the coasts, and without any preconceived
plan. He had just started out with four
native boys and rambled from place to place.

Returning, he had decided to spend two
weeks in Honolulu assembling his material.
It would be more pleasant, and he might take
a few short trips to the more remote islands
and add to his knowledge and his
collections.

For the first three days he had held
to his plan. He had worked hard, cataloguing
his finds, spending his evenings planning
for three trips among the islands . . . and
then on that never-to-be-forgotten morning
he had taken a walk down the beach.

It was not much of a beach. It was away
from the populated centers and actually, it
was more of a picturesque shoreline with,
here and there, patches of sand.

She had come along the edge of the sea
that morning, her skirt whipping in the

wind, her blond hair blowing. She was
walking toward him, oblivious of his
presence, and she was singing a tune in a
pleasant, if untrained voice.

She drew abreast of the rock on which he
sat, and he applauded. He grinned,
remembering her embarrassment. But they had
talked, and although she had refused his
invitation to lunch, she did agree to have
dinner with him.

That had begun it. The two weeks fled by
and he forgot the island trips he had
planned. They lunched together, walked,
danced, worked together. Once she discovered
what he was doing, she began to help him.
She knew a little of birds . . . not of
tropical birds, beyond a few scattered and
largely mistaken ideas about parrots and
parakeets, but the birds of her home state,
and she had read several articles about
penguins. However, it was her librarian's
patience and organization that made the
greatest contribution. She could understand
the smallest difference in the most
insignificant bird, and if she wondered that
he was content to pass his life in such a
way, she never mentioned it.

When the subject of marriage first came
up, he did not exactly remember. It seemed to
have been about the time she first mentioned
leaving; by that time he was used to her and
the thought of her going away dismayed him.
Nor could he recall who had first mentioned
the subject, but it had remained on their
minds, and had come up again.

She had told him, frankly, that her money was almost exhausted and she must return to her job.

His response had been automatic. "Why not stay here with me?" He started to add that he would gladly pay her whatever she was earning at wherever she had been working, but somehow she had misunderstood him and the first thing he knew she was accepting his proposal.

Flustered, he started to explain, but there had been no chance, and as she talked happily on, he began to think of the advantages . . . a home, Dia . . . It was more, really, than he had ever expected.

Now, looking back, he was forced to smile at the way it had all happened. Dia . . . but Dia was gone . . . gone.

And he was accomplishing nothing. He must get out and join in the search. He glanced at his watch. It was not yet eight o'clock in the morning. He could not have slept more than two, possibly three hours. He had been awake thirty minutes at most.

He walked back through the house to the bathroom and washed hurriedly, then combed his hair. He was thinking again of the problem at hand, and where to search. He would work, as he always did, by himself. He knew where they had been, knew exactly where he had last seen Dia . . . and he would investigate that slide.

Perhaps she had rested a few minutes, then wandered up the canyon. Frightened, she might have started up the wall. Frightened

by what? A snake . . . a skunk . . . a
steer . . . almost anything might have
frightened her. The slide might have started
and she might have believed it was easier to
continue on to the top than to return.

Back in the kitchen he selected a cup and
poured coffee. It was only lukewarm but he
gulped several swallows, then put it down
and started for the door.

Passing the window he stopped abruptly.
They had something. He looked again. It
was a scarf of Dia's. . . .

A scarf . . . but Dia had worn no scarf!
He was a man who gave attention to detail,
and he could describe in detail what Dia had
been wearing, and there had been no scarf.

Yet the scarf was here; he remembered
buying it for her. The scarf was hers--and
it was dark with the stain of blood!

COMMENTS: The Dark Hole is in Kings County, California. Louis's journal shows that he first visited the area in
November of 1951. Indonesia, the country of Magill's orni-
thological studies, only came into being in 1949, so it seems
very likely that this was written by the mid-1950s.

I like the character of Morgan Magill. He's a more normal guy than a lot of Dad's heroes. It's amusing to see Louis
commenting:

When he was exploring he was always
overeager and sometimes he forgot that
others lacked his enthusiasm and his

    physical condition. Yet today he had
    remembered not to hurry, to think of
    Dia, to take his time.

That was Dad. I think most of the memories I have of him when we were hiking were from behind. Dad was always moving on, barely waiting for whoever was with him. He might pause, but as soon as my mother, sister, and I caught up, he would head off again.... If we wanted to keep up we didn't take time to rest, we just kept plodding!

_____

SAMSARA

Three Beginnings for an Adventure Novel,
and a Treatment

SAMSARA:
    We find nothing new, only change, always and inevitably, change. Is it not more logical to believe in re-birth than to believe in an endless creation of new souls?
    Scientists find energy and matter indestructible, only their form is changed, so what of these new souls?
    The memories of other lives remain with us just as do the feelings and ideas received from books read long ago. We cannot call to mind with any exactness either those memories or the words, but the impression remains.

A toe prodded me in the ribs. "Get up," a voice said, "here they come again."

And then I was conscious of the sun's heat, and the smell of blood, sweat, and dust. From afar I heard a thunder through the earth, and grasping my broken spear, I stood.

We could scarcely see them for the dust, and our ranks were thin. I, who had stood in the third rank of the phalanx, now stood in the first row. My spear, which had been twelve feet long, now measured less than half of that. My skull throbbed and

the pounding grew louder and they came out
of the dust, a solid wall of horsemen. To
my left they crashed upon our points. There
was a screaming of animals and men. A sword
swept down and my shield shattered under
the impact.

I saw the fierce glare of eyes, a face
only half revealed because of the helmet,
and as the sword lifted to strike again, I
thrust upward with all my strength.

The point of my spear took him below the
breastbone and went into him like a driven
spike. We crashed to the ground. He swept a
hand up, brushing back the helmet, and for
the first time I saw his face.

His eyes were wide, his lips already pale
with death, twisted with words. "Apollodorus!
It is I--Rameses, your friend!"

My name was not Apollodorus and I had
never a friend named Rameses, yet something
stayed my hand. "My horse!" he gasped. "Get
my horse . . . quick! There is a book--!"

That ended it. He died like that, leaving
me staring at him, this man who seemed to
know me as someone I was not. Still, the
horse was there, and it was my prize, along
with what armor and possessions the man had.
But as I grasped the bridle, a hand reached
over mine to take it, an officer of
Alexander.

"The horse is mine," I said, gripping the
bridle. "I won fairly."

"You shall have him," the officer replied
shortly, "but first there will be
questions."

"Forget it then. I want no questions."

The battle was over. I picked up a shield and a whole spear before leaving the field, for our leader looked with no favor upon a weaponless man.

As to the man Rameses, I despoiled him of a ring, and two bracelets from his arm. His sword was a handsome weapon with a fine, beautiful feel to it, so I chose it for my own. Then I walked away, but twice I looked back upon him. He had been so sure he knew me, and even knowing he was dying he had sought to do me well. He had mentioned a book. I had nothing to do with books, but to mention a book at such a time . . .

I wished for the horse. Not that I could do ought but trade him, for I was a foot soldier.

Back at camp I cleansed myself with fresh sand, for water there was none. I rubbed the sweat and dust away, then hunted for wine. I had none, nor had Crates, the one who had kicked me out there after I had been felled. My head still ached from that one, or from something else, for there was an uncertainty in me that I had not known before.

The officer who had taken the horse came to me. "He wishes to see you."

I was shocked, and frightened, too, for I knew what might come of his displeasure. We who served him thought well of him, for he was brave and wise in battle, a wiser man than his father, whom I had served as a boy.

"Be quick--he does not like to be kept waiting."

* * *

He was sprawled in a chair just inside the door of his tent where he could drink wine and watch the camp. I had seen him like that before, and he missed nothing. It was said that he had eyes and ears everywhere, and we believed it.

Alexander was a handsome man, arrogant and proud, but as fine-looking a man as ever I had seen, and he wore more gold than I had ever seen upon any man or woman. Some said he wore it as a challenge to enemy soldiers. To kill him and take what he had in battle would make a man wealthy. My mouth watered at the thought, but I'd no wish to kill him, only to serve him. As much as he appeared the dressed-up one, he was a fighter. Few of us could have stood up to him in even battle.

"What is your name?"

There was something in this that puzzled me, and I agonized trying to think what I had done that was wrong. But there was a curious look in his eyes. He was not looking at just a soldier, he was looking at me. Besides, he knew my name well enough. He knew the name of every man in his army, and always had.

"Carlax," I said.

There was movement behind me and I glanced around, though I knew I shouldn't, for when you talked to him you faced him.

It was the horse. They had led him right up behind me.

"Carlax," he said, "you fought well today.

You fought very well, as you have always done."

He straightened in his chair and studied me; still dusty from the field he was. "A good soldier," he said, "and a fighting man. I have watched you. You do your job well--no recklessness, no heroics, just a good steady job. I like that in a man. We would win nothing if it were not for your sort."

He seemed to ponder, and then casually, he asked me, "Who was that man you killed? I hear he called himself Rameses, but I also know that was not his name."

"I never saw him before."

"He knew you. I saw it with my own eyes. I was there to see if the charge would break upon you spearmen, as it did. He seemed to know you well, and wished you to have his horse."

He studied me in a disturbing way. I did not like it and wanted to be away. He seemed to feel I was concealing something, and I had heard it said he had a way of sensing things unspoken. The man knew so much. Aristotle was his teacher, after all. Whenever there was no fighting he had a way of gathering the wise men around him . . . those from the land around . . . and he asked them many questions, far into the night, prodding them to debate with one another.

"He was sure he knew you. He called you Apollodorus."

"It is not my name."

"And he called himself Rameses, and that was not <u>his</u> name. I have prisoners. They

have looked at the body and told me his
rightful name. Do you wish to know what
it is?"

"What for? He is dead."

"Ah . . . ? Yes, of course. He is dead.
And death does come to us all, does it not?
Too soon, sometimes."

He glanced around at Ptolemy. "A chair for
our friend. We have much talking to do."

Uneasily, I sat down. He sat there for a
long time, watching the camp bring itself
into order. Crates would be opening a bottle
now, and slicing a haunch of mutton. I was
hungry, and ill at ease, wishing to be free
of all this. I did not know the man I had
killed. . . . Did they think I was a spy?

"You have served me long. How old are you,
Carlax?"

"Twenty-nine, I think. I have been
fourteen years a soldier."

He was in a strange mood, silent, musing,
yet there was friendliness in him. "You
fought well at the Cilician Gates," he said
to me, "and you prevented a fight at Soli."

This was a surprise. My way was the
soldier's way, and I did what had to be
done, not looking to be seen or praised for
it, unaware that it had been noticed.

"You did not think I had seen," he said,
"but believe me, Carlax, there are twenty
thousand of you whose worth I know as well
as this ring." He tapped the heavy gold ring
with the red stone. "It is the commander's
task to know." He looked around at me.

"Battles are won by men, not by tactics alone."

The minutes dragged by. Wine was poured, and I drank, feeling better. Some of the tiredness left me. "You fought in the army of Philip," he said. "Did you know Aristotle at all?"

"When I came for the first time to the army," I said. "He had questions, that one."

He looked at me. "He asked you questions?"

"He asked me an odd thing: Had I ever been to Samothrace, or to Delphos."

He did not look at me now, but at the plain where the tents were pitched. "And had you?"

"No."

He shifted his seat somewhat, impatiently, I thought. "He was not one to ask the foolish question, Carlax. Why did he have questions for you at all?"

I shifted uneasily. "There was foolish talk. Some comrades of mine began it. We had come up to a mean village, a petty sort of place on a low hill beside a stream. I found a corner of wall . . . it was some ancient ruin . . . and I dug down and found a vase filled with coins."

The shadows had vanished; the fires were showing bright against the darkness. Still Alexander sat there, staring out over the plain. "Had you been there before?"

I hesitated. "No . . . no, never. Only . . . it reminded me of something I couldn't put a name to. As for the gold, well, I just tried to think where I might

bury some gold. . . . It was a fortunate
chance."

He was still silent, and after a long time
said, "You can ride?"

"Yes."

"Keep the horse. You will not be with the
phalanx any longer. I shall want you close
to me."

He had said nothing about the book, but I
knew that I was dismissed, and got to my
feet, leading the horse away.

Out in the darkness, I stopped to think
about what had been said, but it made no
sort of sense. Yet I could not get the face
of the man I had killed from my thoughts. It
stayed with me, open, smiling, as no dying
man's face was expected to be when he looked
into the eyes of the man who had killed him.

What had Samothrace, Aristotle, Delphos,
and the discovery of a small vase of gold to
do with this?

COMMENTS: Thus begins just one version of what is
probably the strangest story in this book—and in Louis's
career. It was an idea that he experimented with in different
forms for nearly thirty years. The story of a man, or a group
of people who, at some point in their lives, realize that they
have been reincarnated and that the knowledge from their
past lives can be recovered. From generation to generation,
these reborn souls or identities have moments where they
can recall those lives and, if the conditions are right, find
repositories of information cached in order to help them re-

member more and move forward in whatever plan fate has in place for them.

I do not possess every version of these manuscripts, nor a complete set of Louis's notes. Whether the other pieces were lost in one of Dad's moves, thrown in the waste can in frustration, or suffered some other fate I do not know. What I do know is that a few other fragments remain. Here's an alternate version where, instead of telling Alexander the Great about finding the hidden coins, Carlax tells a more mysterious story:

He sat there staring at nothing for several minutes, then he called to the man holding the captured horse and told him to bring the saddlebags. But he let them lie unopened.

"Tell me, has this ever happened before? Have you been recognized by anyone else?"

"No," I said, and then hesitated. He waited expectantly, and I replied that there had been one other occasion.

"It was in Crotona, when I was a lad. I had come there for the first time that morning and a passenger aboard our ship wished to see the school where Cythogorus taught. So I took him there--I do not remember how it was that I knew, but I did.

"He was curious, and asked me many questions. He, too, said I looked like someone he knew."

"And . . . ?"

"That night he tried to kill me."

We sat long over our meal and the wine

that followed, and he asked me many
questions about myself. Yet what was
there to tell?

I was a soldier. I had been a man of
the sea from boyhood, but joined
Alexander when he marched into Asia.

COMMENTS: When Dad wrote the majority of these drafts
he was in his sixties, and I have often wondered if his work
on *Samsara* may have been an attempt to confront his own
mortality. He collected dozens of books on the subject of reincarnation and on the various religions and mythologies
that dealt with the transmutation of souls. Although a spiritual man, he was not an adherent of any particular religion.
I have often wondered if his interest in writing this story
(especially, as you will see, since his efforts took so many
forms) didn't come from some desire to feel that there was
something beyond death, some continuation of the soul's
narrative.

Below is a piece of either a series of notes or part of one
of the various forms of this story that explains a certain
amount of what Louis had in mind:

It is not surprising that some know
and others do not. Some men are content
with a little knowledge, others would
not be content with all knowledge. Some
wish to know enough to get along from
day to day, some wish to know enough to
progress in their particular field, but
there are always a few who wish to reach
out, farther, and still farther.

Long ago there came a realization to such a man: perhaps an ancient memory from some past life, perhaps a recognition of some other such as himself. He approached the other, discussed the question, felt his way carefully along until he knew that this man also remembered. So a pact was made. An agreement to find a way to meet again in some future life, to share experiences, and to plan for the future. This must have happened so long ago that when these men planned to cache a few treasures against a future life, all they could leave would have been a stone ax or perhaps an amulet.

Over the years, over the centuries, a few such men and women banded together, and from this derived the Eleusinian Mysteries, and many secret orders had their beginning in this desire to preserve this esoteric knowledge for themselves in future lives, and for others like themselves.

These people chose themselves and as a result of their mystical experiences and thinking, planning, and mental preparation they became able to control the processes of rebirth, and they shared this knowledge among themselves. Few could pass on the new knowledge, and fewer still had the discipline necessary to cope with it, or to use it. Some of the elect died before they could effect

plans for their future, and after
several such deaths or failures to
locate the repositories of knowledge,
some of the elect forgot the old
knowledge. In other places it became
mingled with ineffective superstition
and only the superficial forms of the
practices were followed, and thus the
effect was lost.

Each of the elect made it a practice
to exchange knowledge with the others,
but also to leave behind in some form the
knowledge he had, and the knowledge that
he would need in the future. Among the
ancient Egyptians and some others it
came in the form of murals on the walls
of tombs, or tools and equipment, much of
it fallen to dust, that had been left
for the future. Many of the tomb
robberies were done by the former
occupants of the tombs, returned to find
that which was needed for a future life.

Most of the elect deliberately court
obscurity, and they learn very early to
be wary of sharing any part of what they
know, for skepticism, resentment, and
persecution often follow.

COMMENTS: Now, here are two chapters of a very different version of the story, or perhaps simply the story of another incarnation in the wheel of many lives that the soul of
our narrator has lived.

CHAPTER 1

When it began I do not know, nor in what land, for it was in a time before the names began.

The legend is that I myself was the first to understand. I, and the wise Adapa, although what name was his at that time I do not know. He was the second.

It began, we believe, with the memory of a spring.

Upon a certain day, in a time when all men wandered in search of game and gathered nuts, roots, and berries as they traveled, and when men had not yet learned to plant seeds, my people had come to an ending.

There had been a great dying of plants and animals; the sun shone hot each day and the clouds did not gather, nor did the rain fall. Our band had taken up our few things and wandered in search of food, in search of water, and we had found nothing but more sun, more dust, more pools of cracked mud.

The last of our food was gone, and only a little water remained and many had come to sit and wait for death.

They said, "Why must we struggle when it is only to die? There is no more grass, and there is no more water. The time has come for dying."

Then I stood and pointed. "Yonder where lie the blue hills there is water, and there will be food."

My people stared at me, their eyes wide
with hunger and suffering, their bodies thin
and worn. Their will had fled from them and
all they wished was to lie still.

"Hills? Where are these hills of which you
speak? We see no hills."

"Yonder," I said, "another day only."

They did not, they could not, believe, but
one man looked at me, with understanding
upon him, and said, "This man has become the
voice of a god--follow him."

They stared at him, and then at me, and
they laughed, a terrible laughing from raw,
parched throats. "He? We have known him from
birth. What manner of foolishness is this?

"He is young and we have watched him grow.
He is not the voice of any god. He is no
more than any of us."

"One more day of walking," I said, "just
one more day. A green valley lies there with
a stream that is cold and swift. Wild sheep
are there, sheep that have seen no man, and
wild cattle as well."

"How is it that you say this? Have you
looked into the smoke?"

"It is there. Are you children that you
lie down to die when water is near? Lie
then, if you wish. I shall go on, and
tomorrow I shall drink deep of the cold,
cold water."

Taking up my spear and sling, I started
forward, although my feet were sore
from wandering, and my muscles from
struggling on.

And they followed. . . .

The sun rose higher but we plodded on. The heat grew great and there was no green . . . only the vast sky, only the long grass bending before the wind.

They stumbled often, and sometimes fell, but they arose again and continued, no longer thinking, no longer planning, only putting one foot before the other in a kind of stupor, moving through the trembling air, their throats parched, their tongues drying within their mouths.

And suddenly there was a low purple line across the horizon, which only a few noticed, and of which they did not speak, thinking it born only of their desires, but after a while it grew larger, and they began to see these were mountains indeed, with peaks and shoulders and great ridges.

Now their steps quickened, and I, who had known, walked before them, pointing my way with my toes toward the distant loom of one opening jaw of hills.

No one stumbled now. There was a breeze from off the hills, a hint of coolness. Day began to wane and the glare of the sun departed. Still we marched, and then we could see trees, though only a scattered few.

"There is water?"

"There will be water. There will be much water," I said, "and there for a long time we will stay."

Into the darkening canyon we walked, and into a broad open valley within the mountains, and they asked me, "Where is the water?"

"It is there," I said, pointing, "beyond those trees." And they ran ahead, and there were cries, and the others ran, and there was a stream, running cold and clear, and they drank the water, and then drank again.

A wild ox came down from the hills and stared at us, head up, nostrils distended.

Choosing a rock I put it in my sling, and I swung a mighty blow and the rock flew, striking the ox between the eyes.

He dropped, and running forward I finished him with a spear thrust. And after their thirst was quenched they came to cut up the meat, and to eat it. Some was eaten raw from hunger, and some was roasted above the fire.

The old man came to me, he who had said I had become the voice of a god, and he said, "You knew."

"Yes," I replied.

"How did you know?"

I thought of that and said, "I remembered."

"Do not tell them so. Tell them you saw it in the smoke."

"You wish me to lie?"

"Only to let them believe. How, they will say, could he remember? Have we ever seen this place? Have we ever come so far? And has he not grown up among us? What could he remember that we could not?"

"I saw nothing. I simply knew."

"Perhaps that is the way of it," he said. "I think we must be careful, you and I.

People do not always like those who are wiser than they; they do not like to believe that some know and others do not."

Something within told me this was wise, so when Pied Bull said, "How did you know?" I shrugged and said, "I did not know. It was a lucky guess."

Pleased, Pied Bull said, "I thought so," and he went to tell the others.

Pied Bull aspired to be our chieftain, and was an arrogant man, a strong warrior but a man of small judgment and much impressed with himself. He was among them now, making little of my leadership in this case.

"It is well," the old man said. "Let them not know too much."

His eyes turned to mine. "This has happened before? I have seen it."

My reply was guarded. "Who knows?"

"Even as a child, you hunted with a warrior's skill, and when you looked for berries, you knew where to look."

"It was my good fortune," I said.

"You remembered," he replied, "just as you remembered this place. You have been here before."

"That cannot be." I hesitated, then said, "You know my life. None of us have ever been so far."

He waited for a while and then said, "Sleep well tonight, but unless I am mistaken in the night you will remember other things. You are one of Them."

"Them?"

"Those who remember," he said. "Once when

I was very young the shaman told me there
are some who remember, and to be alert for
them."

"And you think I am one?"

"I know it. I have known it these ten
years."

"Long ago I might have heard this place
spoken of, in a time when I do not remember.
Perhaps some hunter . . . some visitor to
our camps . . ."

"Perhaps." He got to his feet. "Eat," he
said, "and rest. We will talk of this
again."

Eat, I did, but no rest came to me.
Warily, I let my eyes look about. Did I know
this place? Was there more that I could
remember? I wiped the grease from my hands
upon the grass and went to the stream to
drink again.

I drank, then took from my feet the
sandals I wore, and I bathed my feet in the
cold water.

Hot water, I thought, might be better. Yet
who had ever heard of heating water for the
feet? I had better not think of that or they
would know me for a fool.

When I had rested a little, my back
against a tree, I became restless to walk
about. Taking up my spear and sling I walked
away among the trees, and then stopped where
I could look up at the walls of the canyon.

It was a wide canyon with meadows and
trees, the stream offering water. We would
stay in this place, for there seemed to be

game. Everywhere I saw the tracks of
animals, but none of men.

And then my feet found a path.

It was a hidden way, a winding way among
rocks and old, old trees. How I came upon it
I do not know, but suddenly it was there and
my feet were walking it as if . . . as if
they _knew_.

The path led along one wall of the canyon
but close to the foot of the cliff, and it
was a good way, a very good way where one
could come and go and be unseen from the
valley below. Then, I stopped.

Someone watched me.

Turning from the path . . . a path that
left nothing for the eyes to see except at
great intervals when there seemed to be
places a little worn . . . I went into the
trees. Suddenly I saw Pied Bull.

"Where do you go?" He peered at me, his
small eyes prying and cunning. I shrugged my
shoulders. "I look for the droppings of
game. I do not know if there are deer, or
more of the big oxen."

"You are a fool," he said contemptuously.
"There are droppings everywhere. I have seen
them. And there are tracks. This is a good
place."

"Well," I said, "you are a great hunter.
You would know best."

He looked about, and his curiosity
satisfied, he went away. He had not seen the
path.

Yet . . . had I really _seen_ it? Or did I
see it because I knew it was there?

The way grew steeper; it wound around
among great fallen slabs of rock, then up a
narrower canyon where the sun did not shine.
Now I was far from our place beside the
stream, and I was alone.

What if there were men here? I could be
attacked and killed, and then they would
come quietly upon my people and kill all of
them, for we were few, only sixteen men,
twenty women, and the children. It was a
small tribe, for we had lost many through
war and hunger.

I paused. There in the sand was a spear-
head.

I knelt to examine it. It was very small,
very neatly done. The flakes of stone struck
from it were done with great skill, nothing
like our own clumsy spear-heads. But such a
spear must have been used by very tiny
men. . . . It was like nothing I had seen.

Straightening up, I looked all about me. I
was in a shadowed place, a spirit-place. The
canyon walls towered above me, and somewhere
I could faintly hear the trickle of water.

I knew this place.

I knew this place well. And this chipped
point of stone I held in my hand was not a
spear-head. It was another sort of
thing . . . something for which I had no
name.

Yet now, suddenly, I knew where to go, and I
ran on, swiftly, along the trail . . . and
stopped.

Cut into the sandstone were steps leading
steeply upward. Steps leading to what?

They were much worn, old; many rains and winds had beaten upon them. I started up.

Fear kept me from looking down. I climbed, across a shoulder of the rock and into a crevice, a split in the rock where the steps were natural and easy and it was wide enough for only one man at a time. I went swiftly up to a wide ledge.

I stopped.

Before me was something I had never seen before. Something . . . Yet, had I not seen this?

Stones fitted together to make a wall, an opening in the wall for air. I walked slowly forward. Past the corner there was a door.

I stepped inside, my spear poised.

It was shadowed and still, but upon the floor lay the skeleton of a man. The bony hand held a knife, a strong thin blade of chipped stone.

I sat down and looked upon the man long dead. I took the knife from the skeleton fingers. It was finely done, much better than my own.

The room was bare. The floor was of neatly fitted stones, upon one side a wooden seat. I looked at it, studied it, then stood up.

The dead man had been killed, and he looked to have fallen while running. Bending over him I saw something else. On the floor beneath him, under his ribs, was another of those small spear-heads.

Looking at it, I scowled. There was something about it that I should know, but

did not know. Something I should have . . .
<u>remembered</u>?

There was another door. The spear in my
hand, the newfound knife held low in my
other hand, I went through that door. A long
room . . . a shadowed room.

Empty.

Crossing it with running steps I went into
the room beyond. Smaller, almost square
except for a sort of closet in one corner, a
closet or space but with no door. The door
might have been of wood, and burned. Peering
closer I could see the frame of the door was
charred as from fire. At the opening I stood
peering into the alcove.

There was nothing there, yet there should
have been.

From room to room I went. Some were in
ruins, roofs or walls fallen in, a few more
scattered bones, signs of fire. There had
been a fierce fight here. At one place the
center of the floor had ashes and the marks
of burning as if something had been piled
there and set afire.

For a moment I felt a chill of fear at the
sight of that fire, but I did not know why
it should so affect me.

I went out again into the air and looked
around. The place where I stood should have
been perfect for defense, and it needed only
one or two men to protect it from invasion.
Yet it had been attacked and its people
destroyed. How, I could not guess.

It was late, and I knew I should go back.
But I was hesitant to leave. I looked all

about me, disturbed by thoughts whose origin I could not guess. Somehow I believed I should have found something here, that I had been guided to this place by some strange influence, perhaps something from within myself.

In the dim light I went down the steps in the stone, then turned back toward our camp.

Emerging from the narrow canyon into the wider, I paused. The valley fell away before me with only the slightest of grades, and leaving out the trees the land was flat. I looked at it, and something nudged hard at my consciousness. . . . Why should it impress me so?

At the camp the fires were burning small, our place was hidden as well as might be, and our people were eating again, restoring their strength against the days to come.

The old man looked up at me, and in his eyes there was a question. But also upon me were the eyes of Pied Bull, the one who did not like me.

Did I like him? I thought of that and decided he did not matter to me. I had no feelings of liking or disliking, only of wariness. The man was too curious, too envious, and was dangerous because of his jealousy of me.

"You bring no game," Pied Bull said.

"I did not look for game," I said. "I looked for others, and there are no others. I think this is a good place in which to stay."

He shrugged. "There is game. The women
have found roots. We can stay for a while."

Something stirred within me, and there lay
before my eyes the wide valley, the almost
level fields with grade enough for water to
flow.

"We would do well," I said, "to move no
more. This is a good place to stay."

Pied Bull looked his disgust. "And when
the game is gone? And we have eaten the
roots and fruit?"

"Where these roots grow, and these seeds,
more will grow. We will plant seeds and they
will grow for us."

"Plant? What is plant?" The woman who
spoke was Wolf Boy's woman. She was quick
and sure in her movements, one of the best
tanners of skins, one of the quickest to
find the food we gathered. Her name was Moon
Daughter.

There was a knowledge within me I dared
not tell, yet there was a logic she would
grasp.

"We have seen where seeds fell upon the
ground, and where seeds have spilled when we
were eating, and later when we came again
the seeds had grown to plants.

"Why only gather what we find? Why not
open the ground and spill the seeds into it,
then close the ground over the seeds and
when they grow, take what we need? We can
eat some, the rest we can store in dry
caves. Then we need move no more."

"It is foolish," Pied Bull said. "How do

you know the seeds will grow? And can you grow meat?"

"We can," I said quietly. "Do you remember the baby deer Moon Daughter's child kept? Why can we not keep a dozen such, or many more? Let the children guard them, and when they grow we can eat them as we need, and need no longer trust only to the hunt."

The old man who was my friend spoke quietly. "You speak wisely, my son. It is good, what you say. And it can be done."

"It is foolish," Pied Bull said irritably.

"No. It is good," Moon Daughter said.

Our chief, who was very old, sat quietly and listened. I had noticed this of him, that he let much talk go by before he spoke, and he listened well and then said what it seemed most of the people wished, or perhaps what he suspected they wished even when they had not spoken.

"We can stay here for a time. There is game. There is food. We have seen no signs of enemies. Our dry time has been bad, and we have suffered. Now we will rest, and we will grow strong again."

"And we will plant," I said. "All who wish to plant with me shall meet when the day comes at the meadow's edge, each with a sharp stick."

When they had scattered to their beds the old chief remained. He looked at me, his eyes old and wise and hard with thought. "Is it that you would take from me that which is mine? I am the chief."

"You are the chief. I speak only to help.

To come here was hard. The way was long, and
the land was dead and without water. Now we
are here. Perhaps there is no one here.
Perhaps no one has been here for a long
time. Why should we move from a land of
plenty?"

The old one, my friend, had come up to us.
"Heed him," he advised. "Your troubles will
be less."

The chief scowled, staring off down the
canyon. "I am tired," he admitted. "We came
far, and we are a small clan. Perhaps no one
has ever crossed that waste before."

"Perhaps not," I suggested, but I was
remembering the houses of stone. "Or if so,
not for a long time."

"We will stay," the chief said, "while
there is food. You may do what you will with
your seeds."

CHAPTER 2

When morning came twenty-one people came
to the meadow, men, women and children. Each
brought a sharp stick.

The day before walking through the canyon
I had come upon a wide place where grew a
sort of grass that had many small seeds. As
I walked through the grass the seeds fell
from the grass, striking the ground with a
sound like rain.

With Wolf Boy, Moon Daughter, and two of
their young ones we had returned and in the

evening had filled baskets with the seeds.
Now we gave some to each and they walked in
a wide-spaced rank down the meadow, making a
hole with a sharp stick at each step. Four
times each of us walked the field's length
dropping the seeds, and then we returned to
camp.

It was in my thinking to go back to the
place I had found, to the houses of stone,
but I did not wish anyone to know where I
was going, nor to find them, not even my old
friend. It was something within me that
warned me, so I was wary, and when in the
late afternoon I went out of camp, I watched
behind me with care.

So it was that I saw Pied Bull following
me. I had seated myself on the bank of the
stream before he arrived and when he came
upon me I was staring into the water. He
came up to me and peered over my shoulder
into the water. "What do you look at?" he
demanded.

"The water," I said.

"The water?" He was puzzled. "But it is
only water. What is there in it to see? Are
there fish?"

"I do not know," I said solemnly. "I think
the water wishes to speak to me."

"What foolishness is this? You have lost
your wits."

"Listen! Can you not hear it? It tells me
things. Secret Things."

"You are foolish." He turned from me. "I
do not know how they can listen to you."

He strode away, leaving me alone, and when

he had been gone some time I got up and went
on my way. When I started into the canyon I
could look back and see him heading for our
camp.

This time the climb was quicker. My toes
were ready for the narrow holds cut into the
rock, and I went up swiftly. Once on the
ledge I paused, took my spear from the strap
over my shoulder with which I'd carried it,
and went into the building.

The bones lay where they had been, and I
stepped past them and went forward into the
third room. Puzzled, I stood before the
alcove. There was something I must do here,
something I should remember.

Each time it had come to this, this moment
when one must not turn aside.

Each time?

Into the alcove I looked, and saw nothing.
Only bare walls, only the fitted stone, the
silence of years. But there was within my
mind the haunting sense of recognition. But
how? Why?

The old man said, "You knew," and I had
answered, "I remembered."

There was no time now--something warned me
of this. I might go away and never find the
opportunity to return here alone, and to sit
down and think was not the thing, not now.

There are memories within the muscles,
memories of actions performed long ago: the
hurling of a spear, the dodging of a blow;
these things become instinctive. Stepping
into the alcove, I raised my hands and
touched the wall before me. I found a crack

opposite my chin, my fingers dug, a brick
came loose. Behind the brick an opening, and
in the opening a gripping place.

The grip was also of stone, a dark stone,
smooth and polished. I put my hand in and I
pulled.

For an instant, nothing happened. I braced
my toe and pulled the harder.

The wall swung toward me. . . .

I looked into a black, rectangular cavern.
It was deep and wide, and in the center, on
a stone table, lay a long box . . . a box as
long as a tall man.

Inside the room were other things. On the
wall, a shield, beside it, crossed, a spear
and a sword.

No man in my tribe had seen such a weapon,
but it was a sword. I knew it at once, knew
its uses.

What was happening to me?

I stepped into the room. There were two
smaller boxes against the wall. There were
other weapons . . . and the long box?

I took hold and lifted the lid.

It raised easily under my hand, no squeak,
no groan, no grating of stone on stone.

From within came a faint scent as of
something musky, something faintly fragrant,
and I looked upon the skeleton-face of a man
long dead.

He wore a breastplate of thin and shining
stone, on it a deer with one head and three
bodies, a strange symbol.

The skull wore a heavy hat of the same
thin stone and there were fragments of a

robe. A hide? No, some different material.
It had fallen to bits. . . . It had been
purple.

There was a circle about the bony finger
of the right hand, a ring of strange design.
And in the hand there was a sort of
blackened box as long as my forearm, the end
square, each side of the square as long as
my thumb.

With careful fingers, I took the box from
the skeleton-hand, took it reverently,
gently.

I had forgotten where I was, forgotten who
or what I was. What I was doing . . . it was
something I had been destined to do.

Now I knew that our tribe's trek north had
not been only to save them, to escape from
enemies into a land where there was water
and a chance to live. I had needed to come
to this place. My feet had followed a trail
traced out by my mind, by some strange
design woven into the fabric of my genes.

What was it the Old One had said? <u>You are
one of Them</u>. <u>You are one of those who
remember</u>.

The man who had been buried here in that
long box had once been <u>me</u>. It had been my
hand that held that now tarnished silver
box, awaiting the time when I should come
again and take the gift I held for my
sometime self.

Gently, I removed the gold ring from the
finger and fitted it to my own, then
carefully I closed the coffin and, taking
the silver box, I stepped back.

Tucking the silver box into my waist I took from the wall first the sword, then the spear. I glanced at the chests. . . . What awaited me there?

Well, they could wait.

Perhaps for another day, perhaps for another time, or another life.

Out into the dusky twilight of the square room I walked, and turning, I took the handle, closed the door, then replaced the brick. Taking dust from the floor I blew some from my palm into the thin cracks around the brick.

Then I walked outside to the ledge and looked down the canyon. I could see the narrow opening into the valley, the sky overhead with its few stars, and I stood there breathing the cool air, knowing now that when I went down those toehold steps again I should no longer be the man who climbed them, but something else.

Seating myself on a block of stone I placed the spear and the sword at hand.

It was a short sword, no longer than the length of my arm without the hand, as wide at the hilt as the length of my thumb, tapering only slightly to a short but sharp point. Each edge was a cutting edge, unbelievably sharp.

Taking the box in my hand I placed it across my knees and felt it carefully. It was so dark I could see only the glint of metal, but it was embossed with some strange design. Suddenly my thumb halted.

A small knob or button. Was it a catch? A means of opening the box? The box seemed to have no opening, yet from its weight it could not be solid. I pressed the

WHEN IT BEGAN, I DO NOT KNOW, NOR IN WHAT LAND, FOR IT WAS IN A TIME BEFORE THE NAMES BEGAN.

THE LEGEND IS THAT I MY-SELF WAS THE FIRST. I, AND THE WISE ADARA, ALTHOUGH WHAT NAME WAS HIS AT THAT TIME I DO NOT KNOW, WAS THE SECOND.

IT BEGAN, WE BELIEVE, WITH A MEMORY OF A SPRING.

UPON A CERTAIN DAY, IN A TIME WHEN ALL MEN WERE NOMADIC AND NO MAN HAD YET LEARNED TO PLANT SEEDS, MY PEOPLE ROAMED INTO A FAR LAND BECAUSE OF THE GREAT DYING OF ANIMALS AND PLANTS.

A handwritten version of the beginning of this draft.

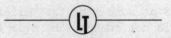

COMMENTS: I have as many questions about this story as you do. Who are these people? On what continent do they live? Who is the man in the coffin and what civilization is he from? What matters really, however, is that Louis has given us one indication of how this concept of reincarnation and the discovery of knowledge handed down over generations might function in other variations of this story.

The versions you have read so far have been some of the

later ones, possibly written in the mid-1970s. It all fits in
very well with the alternative spirituality of the time, a time
when Louis was experimenting with stories about mysti-
cism and other universes in novels like *The Californios* and
Haunted Mesa. However, the first time Louis sketched out
the beginnings of his reincarnation concept was in the mid-
1950s, in a proposal for a television series—an idea that was
likely twenty or thirty years ahead of its time.

SAMSARA OR THE WHEEL OF LIFE

A Television Series
by Louis L'Amour

Who can say what mysteries lie within the
soul and mind of a man? Who can say that he
alone has the answers to all questions?
Since the beginning of time Man has longed
for immortality in the Western world, and
feared it in the Eastern. To every man and
woman comes at some time the belief that
this life is not enough; there is the desire
to live on, to live in another world or in
another life than this.
    Beyond the grave lies hope, and many
religions offer the promise of immortality;
but only in the belief in reincarnation, or
metempsychosis--the transmigration of
souls--is there something tangible,
something real, something all men can accept
and understand.

More people of the world believe in
reincarnation than disbelieve, and many
millions look longingly and hopefully in
that direction.

This series will have romantic appeal for
men and women, who can escape the treadmill
of everyday life by imagining the people
they once might have been; it has enormous
appeal and identification in that the hero,
by moving through his past lives, has access
to and command of all the knowledge and
wealth of the universe.

He may know where lie the still unfound
Maya libraries; or where the Pharaoh was
buried and where he lies in his golden
sarcophagus, awaiting the lucky
archaeologist. He could know where
Alexander's ships went, where Cleopatra
buried her treasure. There is no secret
he cannot plumb, no life into which he
cannot go.

Yet do we say we believe in reincarnation?
Not necessarily. In the person of the
scientist, the psychologist DR. RICHARD
MARKHAM, we introduce in each episode a
different and varying word of caution in his
conversations with VAUBAN, our hero.

Perhaps the experiences come from
stored-up knowledge of history; perhaps from
books of fiction; perhaps from the very
articles Vauban sells. We introduce much
speculation through the psychologist, and
all of it will be cogent, entertaining,
and stirring to the imagination.

This is not fantasy; it is an adventurous
step into realms of spirit, of the unknown.
Man may return to dust after death, and
that may be all, but millions believe
otherwise.

MICHAEL VAUBAN is an importer of art and
antiques; he is young, handsome, athletic,
and he lives among the vases, the carved
stones, the jewels, the weapons of bygone
years.

To his shop one day comes a woman to buy a
rare vase; she is waited upon by a clerk
while Vauban writes busily nearby. She likes
the vase, and is assured that it is a rare
Etruscan piece. She, however, wants a pair.
The clerk assures her this is the only one,
that there is no other.

Vauban, still writing, comments aloud,
"But of course there's another! When
Karchamal made that one, he made another,
identical to it."

The woman is surprised, the clerk
astonished. Vauban looks up, realizes he has
spoken, and is confused.

After the customer has gone, the clerk
comments, "I had no idea there was another.
How did you know?"

Vauban shrugs it off, but he is disturbed.
He leaves that night, and walking down the
street, goes to the home of Dr. Richard
Markham. He explains, and he adds that this
has happened not once, but several
times . . . and more than once his hunch has

proved to be correct. Can he be clairvoyant?
Markham discusses the idea, suggests he try
an experiment: Go home, relax, breathe
properly. . . .

Vauban does so and emerges panting and
gasping from the sea. He is a galley slave
who has escaped from a wrecked galley. He
has various adventures.

In successive trips into the past he is a
Roman Legionnaire; a priest of Isis in
Ancient Egypt; a king of the Hittites; a
wandering mendicant in Mughal India; a
traveling minstrel in eleventh-century
Europe; a prince of India.

But there is danger. When in the trance
states he is in a state of suspended
animation and if so found he may very well
be taken for dead.

This actually happens, and he comes to in
a coffin just before the funeral. This
frightens him, and he knows if he is to
venture into the past again he must have a
room no one can enter but himself. It must
be fireproof, thief-proof, etc.

He goes into the past and watches the
burial of a Pharaoh; he is himself the
priest; then he comes back in his twentieth-
century life and excavates the tomb. With
the wealth he gains from this sort of
activity he builds a secluded home.

There is a young woman with whom he has a
strange relationship. He sees her on the
street, they exchange glances, but she
evades him. She is dark, lovely, myste-

rious. He finds her in his dream-travel.
He realizes that certain people have an
affinity for one another in the reincarnation
process.

Another time he wishes to see a girl whom
he loved and lost in another life. He finds
where she is in this life, but she is an
ugly old crone who runs him off, flinging
things at him.

There is much humor, for he learns to
distinguish who people are in this life,
recognizing them from the past. A man comes
to his shop to sell antiques whom he recalls
as a trickster in ancient Tyre. He refuses
to buy. He passes a pig in a marketplace
that he knows is an acquaintance in another
life, and he says, "Just as I thought. I'd
have known him anywhere!"

For this series there is no end. It is
adult entertainment, but it has romance, it
has many talking points, in that each
chapter will begin or end with a speculative
comment by Dr. Markham.

The hero can venture into any world, into
any life, can be anything, always returning
to his own life. There are many dangers. He
always knows he will live again, but he does
not know when he will die in each life he
returns to. And in some of them he will
die. . . . Here, for the first time, we have
a hero who can be killed and still appear in
the next chapter.

He can be anything, do anything, go
anywhere.

* * *

REINCARNATION: the successive habitation
of many different bodies by the same soul.
The belief that the spirits or souls of men
pass after death into other bodies is a
feature of many religions, especially in the
East, and is still held by the Buddhists and
by many Hindus, and, of course, by the
modern Theosophists. It was taught in
Ancient Egypt, by the Orphic priests of
early Greece and by Pythagoras, was
discussed by Plato, and was believed in by
some Christians.

My background to be the writer of this
series, and I would write all the episodes
myself, is excellent. With due apologies I
might say that I have read several hundred
books on psychology, metempsychosis,
hypnotism, the occult sciences, yoga,
psychometry, multiple personalities,
clairvoyance, the subconscious, and the
earliest and latest ideas on the human mind.

I have an extensive knowledge of the arts,
music, and literature of ancient times; I have
read widely in the history and archaeology of
all nations, am an amateur archaeologist
myself, and have at hand both the knowledge
and the library for essential research.

My travels in many lands have fitted me
with the background to handle this series,
and it is a theme that intrigues me with its
romance and unlimited scope. Before us lies
the entire field of world history; there is
no avenue we cannot explore. A Viking in
early America? A Phoenician sailing beyond

the gates of Hercules? A castaway in the
time of Rome?

Many of the early stories can be done with
an eye on the budget, but there are no
limits to the possibilities.

Throughout the series there can be this
one mysterious woman, one to whose life
cycle Vauban is bound, who continues to show
up in the lives he leads. Sometimes he is
old, sometimes young; he is a cripple, a
blind beggar, a gladiator; he is Alexander
the Great, he is anybody.

This is a series without a chance of being
stereotyped. It cannot become monotonous. It
appeals to the spirit of romance, adventure,
and speculation. It will stir controversy.
It will demand comment. And no man,
anywhere, can say it is impossible. We will,
in the person of Dr. Markham, offer, as I
have said, alternative solutions. We make no
claims; we offer stories and we offer
explanations. The viewer can choose the
truth he likes the most.

COMMENTS: *The Wheel of Life* is obviously a simpler approach than the first two versions of this concept. It's a more
straightforward, "time travel through past lives" situation,
where there is not so much mystery, though perhaps a
greater variety of adventure. It was also an easier concept
for a writer to pursue because the television series of the
1950s were essentially episodic and open-ended, and thus it

wasn't so important to work out what the conclusion or meaning of the overarching story was going to be.

I have always wondered if Vauban's shop was based on one belonging to a very dear friend of ours, Harry Franklin. Harry had a narrow storefront in Beverly Hills and inside it was a cabinet of wonders. He specialized in primitive and oceanic art and there were giant carvings from New Guinea, masks and drums from Africa, and Roman and ancient Chinese jewelry. As a little kid I found it to be both a fascinating and a kind of scary place—a shop very much like the Harry Franklin Gallery also appeared in "The Hand of Kuan-yin," a story of Dad's that was used as the pilot for *Hart of Honolulu*, a TV show which, if the pilot had been picked up, might have become the first detective series shot in Hawaii.

Over the years Louis made other attempts to get the novel version of *Samsara* started and to figure out how to write it. The most powerful and personal version is the one that follows.

CHAPTER I

A man with gold rings in his ears . . . a vase of ancient glass . . . a fragment of carved stone . . . and a girl.

Yes . . . a girl.

These things caused a door to open, a door I cannot close, a door I am not sure I wish to close, yet a door that has opened the way to a haunted past.

Alone I am, and alone I have ever been except for those days, those moments even,

when from out of the beyond I have found
again those whom I love, and who love me.

For the one thing I have discovered is
that love need not die, need not end . . .
for even after millenniums I have known it
to endure.

Yet never have I been so alone as now when
I possess a knowledge I cannot share. Not,
at least, in its entirety.

The man with the gold rings in his ears,
the fragment of stone . . . the girl . . .
these were not a beginning but rather a
culmination of something that began . . .
how can I say where? Or when? Or how?

When I was not more than five years old a
Gypsy said things to me that I have not
forgotten. That Gypsy set me upon my path.
My father was a veterinarian who also dealt
in farm machinery, and not far from the town
in which I lived were some farms owned by
Gypsies. In the spring they came to plant
their crops, vast fields of wheat in those
days, and when the wheat was well above
ground they would depart, returning only for
the harvest.

They built no house upon the land,
preferring their own caravans, but often
they came to visit my father and to trade
horses with him, a business at which my
father and the Gypsies both were adept.

One year at harvest time they came to my
father to buy a complete threshing outfit; a
steam tractor, separator, water-tank wagon,
cook car, hayracks, and even pitchforks.

Several days of discussion and bargaining

preceded the actual purchase, but the deal
was finally consummated in my father's
office.

This was a small room in the corner of the
great red barn used by him as a veterinary
hospital. It contained a rolltop desk, a
swivel chair, and an old leather settee and
had linoleum on the floor.

It was a day I shall never forget.

The Gypsies began to arrive at daybreak.
The men wore black suits and had bandanas
tied over their heads under their black
hats, and some had gold rings in their ears.
The women wore brightly colored dresses and
shawls, with many necklaces of gold coins,
and bracelets upon their arms. By the time
the last had arrived there were at least
thirty in our yard.

They knew my father and liked him, so there
was much talk and laugher as they relived
old horse-trades in which first one and then
the other had been bested, before they
settled down to business.

When the time came for payment they paid
in cash on the floor of my father's office.
And they paid in gold.

The women lifted their outer skirts,
revealing a series of petticoats containing
hidden pockets around the waist. From these
they each took several gold coins until my
father was paid in full, a shining heap upon
the linoleum floor. It amounted, I believe,
to six or seven thousand dollars. I always
intended to ask my father the amount merely

to satisfy my curiosity, but now it is too late.

Too late?

Perhaps not . . . perhaps in some other time, further along down the years.

Among the Gypsies who came that day was one who took no part in the proceedings, for he was a stranger among them, a man from another tribe, another land.

He was a tall old man, though very straight and strong, with piercing black eyes, white hair, and a fine, high-arched nose and high cheekbones. He sat alone on a bench beneath the cottonwood tree at the end of our porch, and the others treated him with great respect, perhaps even fear.

He was sitting on the bench when I emerged from the office, following some others. I felt his eyes upon me. Others walked between us yet his eyes did not waver, so I stopped at last and stared at him and he at me.

"So?" he said. "Here you are."

"Yes," I said.

"Do you know me, then?"

"I believe I do."

The sun was hot and I stood in the sun. The others had drawn away, not seeming to be aware, not talking at all, nor seeming to listen.

My father was in his office sacking up the gold, and I could hear the chink of coins and a fly buzzing. A horse stamped in the dust near the corner of the barn.

"It has been a long time. A very long time."

I said nothing, for I had few words, yet

within me there stirred a kind of awareness,
a kind of knowledge, and a listening.

"You will have much to learn, but it will
come to you quickly, to you above all."

The afternoon was still. Within the house
dishes rattled and soon my mother would
call me.

"You were born to him?" His eyes indicated
the office where my father was.

"Yes."

"He is a good man, a strong man. This I
have heard."

"Yes."

"You will be like him, I think. Like him,
but different, for you will know. You, of us
all, will surely know."

What he was saying to me was unlike
anything that had been said to me before,
yet the words seemed right and I found
nothing strange in them.

"You will <u>coor the drom</u>," he said, "and if
you need to know more, come to me in the
springtime at the Sea Mary Church on the
Gulf of Lyon, or at Burgos in the fall . . .
and if you should meet a man with a golden
dorje, tell him who you are."

My father came from his office then, and the
Gypsies were drifting to their wagons. The tall
man got to his feet and rested his hand on my
shoulder. He looked at my father and said,
"You have a fine son. Let him go his way."

When they were gone my adopted brother,
who had stood listening, asked, "What does
it mean? To <u>coor the drom</u>?"

574   LOUIS L'AMOUR'S LOST TREASURES

"To go tramping," I said. "He meant that I should travel across the world."

Yet I could not have explained how I came to know Romany words.

Only a short time before I had become fascinated by maps, having them always before me. Already I could read the simplest books, and knew the continents and countries by their names and shapes.

"Pa," I asked later, "where is the Gulf of Lyon?"

"On the coast of France," he replied, and accustomed to my questions he did not ask why I wished to know.

That was the first indication, but nothing happened again for a long, long time.

And yet . . . ?

On a summer's day I had gone with my father into the country, and while he discussed business I walked up a low hill to where the sun lay warm upon the grass, and lay down near a big, old tree. After a while I dozed, yet what I then experienced was no dream, or if a dream it was unlike anything I would normally think of as such.

For I was not asleep. Distantly I heard the sound of a mowing machine, the murmur of my father's voice as he talked, and the lazy drone of a bumblebee. Occasionally wind stirred the grass, but when it ceased there was only the warmth of the sun on my back.

Beneath all of this I had been for some time aware of another sound, a faint but definite beat that grew in volume until suddenly I knew, I who at the time had seen nothing larger than a rowboat, that what I heard was the rhythmic beat of many oars moving in unison.

At the same time I gradually became aware of movement, of water rustling about a hull, and the realization that I myself was aboard that boat, moving with it, looking along the boat's length from some high point near the stern.

The sun was warm upon my back, for the sunshade above me possessed neither back nor sides. My finger stirred, and the hand I looked upon was my hand, yet much older, and upon the second finger was a ring bearing a strange device, a triangle with a peculiar design upon it. The ring, I knew, was important for what I was about to do.

"I will cross the bridge," I seemed to be saying mentally, "and enter the Red Pavilion."

The remark was puzzling, out of context, and did not belong to what I was then doing or thinking. Yet it was the first of such random thoughts, all part of a reconstruction that had begun to take place within the boy that I was.

The boat glided to a stop, grated against a stone-faced quay, and two slaves offered me their hands. I stepped from the boat into the hot, bright sun, and looked upon a city.

Turning, I glanced at the boat, seeming to really see it for the first time. There were forty rowers, twenty to a side, a high, curved prow, and a still higher decked stern over which was stretched a fringed awning of green. Under that awning was the single, fixed chair in which I had been seated.

"We have been waiting, Master. We have waited a long time."

Turning my back to the boat I found waiting for me a covered chair with four stalwart bearers and two armed guards. The man addressing me was a tall man with a fine, high-arched nose and black piercing eyes.

"Mine was a far journey," I heard myself saying, in a voice that was mine, yet not mine. "I had duties. I could not come until now."

"A useless journey, I fear. They will not listen, Master. They have been too long at peace, and they cannot envision what will happen. The will to fight, if they ever possessed it, is gone from them. They wish to treat with the enemy, and believe he will come in peace."

"We cannot permit it. If this is lost, two thousand years of knowledge goes with it."

Once more I looked at the river. The waters were brown, moving with infinite power. Far off, where this river began, its waters were clear and cold, flowing down from mountains where glaciers were, down through dense forests among green ferns and over moss-covered rocks. I had come from there, and even beyond there. How long must I remain in this hot and humid land?

Turning to the chair that awaited me I heard my father's voice calling, and the chair seemed to fade, and the hot, white glare of the sun, and I smelled the warm green grass below me, and the dark, rich earth. So I got to my feet and walked back down the slope to where my father waited beside the car, and I walked as in a dream, a strange question alive within me.

Who was I? What river was that? What was I? Above all, what had I been?

By that time I had been several years in school, my education no different from those about me. Ours was a pleasant, attractive, and busy town where two small rivers met in a valley. I played a little basketball, hiked along the rivers, boxed in the gymnasium, and spent long hours in the library. Of the dream, or whatever it had been, I said nothing at all, to anybody.

It remained within me, and with it a sense of waiting, of preparing for something that was to come. Preparing to begin something . . . or was it simply to begin again?

My mind was impatient with its progress, demanding more and ever more. When each day's school was complete, I hurried to the library, searching for I knew not what. Yet sometimes in my reading I would chance upon a name . . . or unbidden a name would come into my thoughts and I would search feverishly through books and maps to find it.

Thaneswar.

Why did such a name come to me suddenly, from out of nowhere?

There were other names, names found in no book, upon no map.

Sanathirtha . . . Jalandhar . . . Hari-Yupuya.

Suddenly I knew that last name. It was the city where I had left my boat to stand in the hot, white sun. Yet nowhere upon any map could I find such a city.

Of these things I said nothing, and after a time the memory of the boat and the landing grew dim, and I rarely gave thought to it.

Often, however, when reading old books I would find myself upon familiar ground as if some bygone knowledge had awakened within me. This struck me as absurd, yet it became increasingly necessary to guard my tongue to avoid seeming anything but normal.

Not that I came suddenly upon wisdom, for the foolishness every youngster must go through to grow up was still upon me. Often I succeeded in making an ass of myself, in saying or doing things that in a future time would make my ears grow red with embarrassment. Yet in those areas where I concentrated I found my thoughts leaping ahead, knowing what was to come, understanding arguments before they were offered.

Each year the Gypsies returned and several times they visited us and once I visited them with some youngsters of my own age.

The old man with the rings in his ears was not with them, nor could I learn anything about him. He had traveled with them a short time only. Vaguely they implied he had come from Hungary or Romania and was known to them through some obscure family connection.

There had been something familiar about him, something remembered or half-remembered.

More and more I spent time in the library, reading avidly from first one book, then another. Once, looking through an old book, rarely read by the look of the checkout slip stuck to the flyleaf, I came upon an etching of an ancient temple door. Under it was the caption: Unknown Ruined Temple.

Yet that temple was not unknown to me, for surely as I looked upon the picture I knew what lay within that door, knew I had been there, and upon occasion I had climbed those steps, stood within that door.

"Too much imagination," I told myself, and turned the page.

These things filled me with restlessness, and occasionally I wondered what would happen if I tried those same conditions again . . . lying on a hillside, the warm sun on my back . . . or possibly if I just relaxed and waited?

Yet even after the idea came to me I did nothing; it was not from lack of faith in the experiment, but simply the demands of day-to-day living. For the time had now come for me to go wide upon the world, to find my own destiny, in my own way.

CHAPTER II

There were bleak years before me, and
hardships to endure. There were books to
read, there was music to hear, and paths to
explore. Often my feet were blistered with
walking and my hands with work. Hunger made
spare my flesh, and thirst parched my
throat, yet I grew in strength, for strength
does not grow out of softness but out of the
use of strength.

My hands took easily to the ax and shovel.
Never did I despise labor, nor the sweat of
it. I hauled on the heavy lines on tramp
freighters, swung a double-jack in the
mines, or worked in lumber camps or on
construction jobs.

Always I studied, finding my way slowly to
knowledge, learning to strike quick and hard
when the occasion demanded, and to move on
before I became too deeply involved in
situations not good for me, or ways foreign
to those I preferred.

In San Pedro, while waiting for a ship to
anywhere at all, I lived the best I could,
for hard times were upon the land, and many
were the men I met there. One of them was
Sleeth.

He came from where I knew not, and when he
passed he went to somewhere beyond my
knowledge, yet for a few weeks we spoke
often.

When first I saw him he was coming into

the library of the Seaman's Church
Institute, a dark, slender man with good
shoulders. He was of a medium height or
somewhat less, wearing neat but shabby
clothes, and he did not look like a seaman,
although the place was a club for seamen.

What he read in that library I do not
know, but after a while we talked, of books
and ships and far-off lands. He was a
romantic, as men who follow the ships are
apt to be, but what else he was or why he
was there he did not say.

Often I saw him about the hall, playing
checkers or chess, and at both he was a
wizard. Nor was there any limit to what he
could do with figures. He was fantastic.

Several times I saw him watching me, and
one day he said, "When you get a ship, where
would you like to go?"

"To the Far East."

"Why?"

I shrugged, I guess. "I don't know. It has
always interested me."

"Yes, I suppose it would."

"Have you been there?"

"Many times. I am going back, someday."

"What's a dorje?"

He was tying little knots in a cast-off
string, quaint, intricate weavings that he
created deftly with amazingly quick
movements of his fingers. It was a way he
had, playing with string. At my question his
fingers stopped.

"It's a Buddhist symbol," he said, "a
thunderbolt symbol. In fact, that's what

'Darjeeling' means . . . <u>dorje-ling</u>. The place of the thunderbolt."

He stood up, putting his string in his pocket, then drawing his palms along his thighs as though drying them. "Where did you hear about a dorje?"

I laughed, to make nothing of it. "Oh, a man I met when I was a kid . . . he was a Gypsy. He told me if I ever met a man with a golden dorje I should tell him who I was."

He did not look at me, merely said, "Stick around here at night. When the shipping office is closed and a ship comes in to refuel sometimes they'll take the first seaman they can find."

"I don't have an AB ticket. Just a couple of discharges as an ordinary seaman."

"I know a man who has one you can use. He took it as security for a loan and never saw the man again." He paused for a moment, looking out the window at the gently falling rain. "I think I can get it for you."

"Thanks," I said.

He looked down at his hands. They were skilled, capable hands, hands of strength. The sort of hands one might imagine a sculptor to have. "I wish we'd met further along," he said suddenly. "There's so much you could tell me, so much I want to know."

He looked at me suddenly. "I am caught in the middle, you know, and I can't remember some of the things I must remember. You could tell me how, you more than anyone.

"Look"--there was desperation in his tone--"do you remember anything at all?"

His words made no sense, and yet, in a strange sort of way I understood what he was getting at. "A little, I think. I . . . I'm not sure."

"I have an awful feeling I'm needed," he muttered, "but I don't know where, or how to find out. When I first saw you . . . there in the library . . . I knew you, all right. I just couldn't believe it. You of all people. And then to discover that you haven't arrived . . . that you can't help me."

I had no idea what to say, so I said nothing, yet I was perfectly aware that something was happening to me, that I was approaching a point of no return.

"The Gypsy . . . do you know where I could find him?"

"At Burgos, in the fall. Or at the Sea Mary Church on the Gulf of Lyon. That's what he said." And then a thought came to me. "His name was Adapa."

"I thought so. My God, Adapa! I've got to find him." He put the accent on the first syllable, as I had, and the sound of it gave me a curious sensation. "I hope nothing's happened to him."

He looked at me sharply. "You're going out east, then. Get word to me, will you? You'll know all about it soon, and when you do, get word to me. Maybe by that time I'll not need it, but do what you can."

He paused again. "Somebody has to get into

Central Asia. Somebody who knows where to
go. We need a new location, something
farther west. Or somebody has to write
something . . . you know . . . with the key
words and a guide for us. It's hell to have
to blunder along.

"For so many years there were a half-dozen
places a man could go. You, for example,
if you had access to the records you could
put yourself in tune within hours. You
could arrive."

The following morning I was drinking
coffee at a restaurant counter, with only
thirty-five cents left in my pocket. Sleeth
came in and sat down beside me, moving
quickly as he always did.

"There it is," he said, "the ticket.
There's a lifeboat certificate, too. It
might help.

"I know about a ship," he added. "It left
Newport News to go through Panama and was
shorthanded. I am sure they'll need some
men, and they won't be too particular. It's
a hungry ship, but it's a living and it
will take you where you want to go. Most
of the ships of that line call at Japan
first.

"I can't help you there; maybe your own
sense will guide you. But there's an old man
in Shanghai, he's all crippled up. Tortured,
to make him talk. He never did, and they
left him for dead. He's in Shanghai most of
the time now, deals in arms for the warlords
or anybody who's buying. He will know you,

and he will be able to help. If you can get
into western China . . . Well, leave it to
him. You could save us, put everything
right."

"How will I find him?"

"He'll find you. His runners meet all the
ships, anyway. He won't be able to come to
you himself, as he should. The man has
difficulty moving, but he'll know. . . .
I'll send a cable.

"If you reach Rangoon, go to the Shwedagon
Pagoda at dawn or sunset. There are usually
some people there to hear the temple
bells. . . . Don't miss it."

The restaurant was almost deserted, for
the hour was late. When the waitress
refilled our cups, he said, "I've never been
able to settle down. Some of the others
have, but I've left too much behind. There
are too many memories.

"When I was in Los Angeles I saw a
girl. . . . I knew her, but I did not.
When she started to go into an apartment
house she stopped suddenly and turned to
face me.

" 'You must go away,' she said. 'I waited,
but you've come too late. I am married now,
and happily. There's nothing to be done.'
She went into the building and I stood
there, looking after her. She had known me,
all right, but all I remembered was that I'd
known her before, and I didn't know where or
when."

He turned suddenly and looked at me. "How
old are you?"

"Seventeen," I admitted. "I've been passing as twenty-two."

He swallowed some coffee. "Seventeen . . . You're about due. You say you saw Adapa?"

"I was very young."

"But he knew you? Well, he would. He would know, or Nabu. The first time I arrived I was in Jenbeskala, and Nabu was there. In those days they spoke one language or a dialect of it from the Aral Sea to the Indian Ocean, we were all Munda-Dravids of one kind or another, and I'd come to the town just before the attack.

"We had no chance. They came riding in off the desert and into the town before we could close the gates. I was a warrior, but long since I'd learned there was no sense in dying for a lost cause, so I ran.

"I knew nothing about the town, you understand, and when I ran into this long stone-walled passage I thought I'd had it, yet something made me run on, even though there was nothing but a thirty-foot stone wall at the end. . . . Only there was.

"A section of the wall drew my attention, a large boulder, worked into the mortared stone, solid, and yet . . . I pressed myself into a man-sized divot in the rock. It was hardly big enough to conceal me but something, desperation or some form of knowledge, moved me. The rock moved behind me, rotated on a heavily greased column. I whirled as it moved to close. I was in a long room. There was a table at one end and a man was working there.

"'Sit down,' he said, 'I will be free
shortly.' And there I stood with a bloody
sword in my hand, gasping for breath with
blood and sweat running off me, and he never
turned a hair. That was my first meeting
with Nabu."

Sleeth rambled on, talking of things of
which I knew nothing, yet I did not wish him
to stop and I found my mind waiting
anxiously for each word, even while another
part of me was filled with questions.

I had told him the old Gypsy's name was
Adapa, but nobody had told me that, so how
could I have known?

"What happened then? When you met Nabu?"

"He continued to write, then sat back in
his chair. 'You came right to this place and
it is a hidden place,' he said. 'How did you
manage it?'

"'They will find me,' I said. 'I am one of
the last of the defenders. They were close
behind.'

"'They will not find you. In fact, they
have already gone on.' He smiled at me.
'They think they just imagined that you
dodged into that dead-end passage. They will
be looking for loot now, not you.'

"'Suppose they come here?'

"'They cannot.' He gestured around. 'We
are inside a rock. Unless they knew, as you
did, they could never find the place.'

"'I? I knew nothing.'

"'In this life, no. But there have been
other lives for you before this, and there
will be others after. It is well you came

when you did.' He looked at me. 'I am Nabu.'

"The Wise One." Sleeth looked at me as he said it. "I knew who he was but did not know how I knew. In the next few days he told me a lot, let me see what was happening and what I was a part of. Not over two hundred people know what we are . . . are what we are."

Outside in the street a taxi went by. The door opened and a man came in, shaking the water from his slicker before hanging it up. He was an old man, unshaven, and he looked tired. He sat at the counter a few stools away and ordered pie and coffee.

The cup holding my coffee was thick and heavy. It had to be, in such a place as this. So it was with us. We had to be durable.

"Would it be better if we never knew?" I asked the question of Sleeth, and he shrugged. "For me it is simple. I must know. I am like Ivan Karamazov, who did not want millions, but an answer to his questions."

"These men? Do they know each other?"

"Men and women. Yes, of course. One may be taller or shorter, but the type remains the same, and the sex, of course. Besides, there's something . . . a subtle thing, but something we all recognize. You'll see it, eventually.

"There have always been places we could meet if there was need, and our own libraries where we could bring ourselves up

to date if the hiatus was too long. All
that's hard to reach now. Inaccessible
because of politics or war or natural
barriers.

"I wasn't one of the first. In fact, I
arrived late. I wasn't like Adapa, Nabu,
you, or some of the others." He looked at
me. "You were the first, I think. You and
Adapa."

"I don't know. All this, it's very
strange. I am talking without even . . . I
mean, I really don't know anything about
this."

"No dreams? No day-dreams? No sudden
recollections?"

"Well . . . maybe." I told him about my
dream or day-dream, of the boat coming to
the landing, and the old man waiting for me.
"It was Adapa."

"Think of that!" He looked at me. "You
did not make it, you know. We'd all been
waiting, hoping for your arrival before the
invaders came. We hoped you could make the
rulers realize what was happening to them,
and if that failed, perhaps keep
everything from being destroyed. We
realize so little so late; we spend most
of our lives catching up . . . we can't
move fast enough to stay ahead of all the
events around us."

"You said I did not make it?"

"You never got away from the riverfront.
The street ran along one side of the state
granary . . . a high brick wall. There was
another on the other side, and they were

waiting for you. If you'd been a young
man--"

"What happened to Adapa?"

"Him, too. You see, the idea of a fifth
column is not new. They had agents within
the walls of Hari-Yupuya months before, and
somehow they knew you were coming to stop
the fighting, so you were killed."

"The city was destroyed?"

"Not only the city . . . everything. The
people fled to the countryside or the
jungle, and civilization dropped from them
like a worn mantle. Fifty years later it was
as though it had never been. Worse yet, one
of our first libraries was lost. If there
was ever a way to see how all this started
we'll have to remember it, if we can.
History, you know, it's chaos. So much is
destroyed."

It was strange. I sat with a man I had
seen first only a day or two before, and we
talked of places of which I knew nothing and
events I could not understand. And yet . . .
and yet I did.

It was as if we talked of an old story we
both knew, only somehow the feeling was
sharper, more intense. There was a sense of
loss, of loneliness, something that I could
not account for.

We sat there together and drank another
cup of coffee. "You're ready," Sleeth said
quietly. "It isn't good to arrive when
you're too young. A kid just can't cope, and
he talks too much."

I stared into my empty cup. It was time

to be moving on, yet I was reluctant to go,
for there was so much to learn, and I had
only the faintest grasp of what was
happening.

The old Gypsy, and now this man.

"Adapa spread the word, that once you
arrived again we could reorganize. We must
have new centers, some farther west, in some
safe place . . . if there is any place that
is safe."

He got up suddenly and shook my hand. "I
never expected this. Not to meet you, not
like this, anyway. You get that ship now,
and go to the old man in Shanghai. He'll put
you on the right track, help you to
reconstruct. . . . But it will come fast
for you, and you'll remember more than any
of us."

We started toward the door. In the street
he turned suddenly. "Something I have always
wondered . . . how it all began. I mean
there at the very first. It must have taken
some doing."

"I don't know."

"Well . . . well, anyway, the best of luck
to you." He put his hands in his pockets and
went away down the street. I looked after
him, then turned toward the waterfront. A
big Dollar Liner was coming up the channel
from the sea. It had come from Asia, where I
would soon be going.

COMMENTS: Though very much a mixture of fact and fiction, these two chapters contain a lot of legitimate details about Dad's life. There were Gypsies that came to Jamestown, North Dakota, in the years that he lived there. My grandfather, Dr. L. C. Lamoore, did, reportedly, sell them some farm equipment and my dad often told the story of the Gypsy women taking the gold coins out of their petticoats. Louis had an adopted brother, Jack, who was just about his age, although I don't believe that Jack was around when Louis was five. The description of the Jamestown property is pretty accurate also.

The same situation holds true for the chapter set in San Pedro. Louis was "on the beach" (meaning out of work and waiting for a ship) there for many months. True or not, he has told other stories of Sleeth; you can read one of them, called "It's Your Move," in either *Yondering, The Revised Edition* or *The Collected Short Stories of Louis L'Amour, Volume 4*. And Dad did hang out at the Seamen's Church Institute and did ship out under similar and somewhat mysterious circumstances for the Far East.

This last draft also contains a wonderful metaphor for Louis's life: a child and a young man discovering the fertile imagination that will eventually allow him to blossom into a prolific fiction writer. Those "past lives" could be seen as the lives he would live in stories. When the writing is going well, a writer often feels like a channel or a medium for a flow of information that is coming, so it seems, from somewhere else. Another life? The spirit world? The collective unconscious? You are creating other lives and other times, and sometimes it feels like you are drawing on other realities to do so. I have had that experience occasionally, and my father had trained himself to live in it for hours a day.

Louis rarely mentions writers like Talbot Mundy or James Hilton as significant influences on his work, but in this book we see material that is a good deal more mysterious and spiritual than he is typically known for. In this particular case, it may be that Jack London's *Before Adam* had some influence. Though he probably first encountered it earlier in his life, I also remember Dad reading it to my sister and me at the breakfast table in the late 1960s or early 1970s.

It's also pretty obvious that Louis's experiences in, and study of, Asia had a profound effect on his creative life. Of course, his earliest successes both creatively and financially were in writing about merchant seamen and adventurers in Asia. Later, he occasionally even attempted stories like "May There Be a Road" and "Beyond the Great Snow Mountains" and *The Golden Tapestry* (included in this book) with Asian or Eurasian protagonists. In these versions of *Samsara*, we not only have a character marching eastward with Alexander the Great, but we have reincarnation, secret societies, and occult information hidden in "Central Asia." I'm thinking that Mundy and Hilton and maybe a few others I haven't yet discovered were more influential than I thought!

Now, just like our young/old protagonist, we are off to the Orient and a mysterious city that lies beyond the Jade Gate.

———————————

JOURNEY TO AKSU

The Beginning of an Adventure Novel

COMMENTS: *Journey to Aksu* is mostly set in western China in an area called Xinjiang or, in the westernized spelling of the time, Sinkiang. Sinkiang is to the north of Tibet at the base of the mountains that support the Tibetan plateau, wedged between modern China, Siberia, and Mongolia.

Though Louis worked on these drafts intermittently between the late 1940s and the mid-1960s, the story is set in the mid-1930s. It was a time when much of China was ruled by local warlords, only some of whom cooperated with Chiang Kai-shek's Kuomintang government. At the time, Sinkiang was, along with certain areas of central Africa and Antarctica, one of the most isolated areas on earth. Its isolation, however, did not keep it free from the sort of chaos found in the rest of China; political intrigue and warfare were common throughout the decade. The population of Sinkiang, especially in that time period, were mostly Turkic, rather than the Han people Westerners more typically think of as "Chinese."

There is a canyon in the Altyn Tagh, far west of Sukhain-nor, from which, in a thousand years, no man has ever returned alive.

This story is told in the marketplace of Suchow, east of the Jade Gate, and it is whispered among the camel drivers of Kashgar, far to the west, beyond the great desert of the Taklamakan.

Yet it is but one of many such tales, for this is a land that breeds legend and the story you hear tomorrow in Tashkent or Hami may be the story that was told in the same cities, and with the same inflections, at any time since the first camels slogged westward, their goods bound from far Cathay to Egypt, Rome, or Byzantium.

The massive, ice-sheeted range of the Altyn Tagh and the mysterious Kuen Lun forms a vast rampart dividing the province of Sinkiang from the fortress land of Bodh, known to Westerners as Tibet. Yet that gigantic wall, seemingly impassable, is penetrated here and there by canyons and passes that allow access to the farthest reaches of the mountains and the lands beyond. Some of these passes lead from Sinkiang to Tibet . . . but who can say, who dares to even guess, where others may lead?

To the north, along the Tien Shan mountains and the far edge of the great basin, the camel and truck caravans bound west from the Jade Gate now travel the route that leads from Hami to Turfan and Aksu.

It was not always so. Two thousand years

ago the silk route lay to the south along the foothills of the Altyn Tagh and the Kuen Lun. But with the passing of time the bed of the Tarim River found a new course. The great lake of Lop Nor vanished, creeks and springs dried up, and the southern route was all but abandoned.

Still, in the wastes of the Taklamakan, one of the earth's most formidable deserts, there remain ancient walls and towers, the ghosts of forgotten cities. Sometimes seen, sometimes buried by drifting sands, their ancient walls are blackened by time, polished and hollowed by abrasive winds. Others sink in salt-rimmed marshes, lost in forests of dying reeds.

In the heat-waved distance mirages shimmer and mirror fabulous towers and lush gardens where shadowy figures move along cloistered halls and among sparkling fountains . . . phantoms in the sky, images of another world. And sometimes the men who look too long wander into the sand and are seen no more, nor are heard from again.

Whispered in the bazaars and on the street corners of towns bordering the great basin are stories of djinns and hidden gold, of dragons and ghost caravans that move by night, almost soundless and almost unseen.

Any man who has traveled these lonely wastes, who has camped at night under the black loom of the Altyn Tagh, with the vastness of the Taklamakan stretching away to the north, will but agree that he has heard or seen the shadows of these caravans.

At night when the camels are resting and the dung-fires lend their thin smoke to the desert's emptiness, there will sometimes come sounds from the distance. And then suddenly, the talk will still, the camel drivers will avert their eyes, the dogs will whine and bury their heads in the blankets of their masters . . . and out beyond the firelight, out where it is dark and yet not quite dark, there will be a ghostly movement, a soft shuffling of feet, a jingle of accouterments, the muttering of camels and the far-off cough of a man: A caravan is passing.

Nothing is said of the caravan, nor is anything said when morning comes. . . . Only, there are no tracks. The thick trail dust is unmarred, undisturbed. What manner of men and camels are these, who leave no tracks behind? Who pass, almost soundlessly, in the night?

The foothills and boulder-strewn slopes of the Kuen Lun are said to be haunted by a species of devils who, as the water left the springs and the riverbeds grew dry, withdrew into the deeper fastness of the mountains, emerging only at times to prowl the desert. Sometimes if one looks quickly around, one may see the flicker of their shadows as they dodge back among the boulders. Sometimes, on the brightest day, one may see a shadow where nothing stands.

Far west of the Sukhain-nor there is a narrow canyon that opens upon a boulder-

strewn slope, and this canyon is crossed by
a stone wall that is very high and of a pale
blue color. In the center of this wall there
is a massive and very ancient wooden gate,
but the trail that leads to this gate has
been grass-grown these many years, for now
that caravans no longer come and the rivers
have died, the trail is no longer used, the
gate no longer opened, not even for a
walking man.

There is about this town, looked upon
from the basin side, an appearance of death,
yet the town is not dead, and not dying. For
this town has lived and continues to live.
Nurtured by what well of vitality no
outsider can guess, it knows the hard-won
secrets of survival. It lives, and yet now
it fears. For armed men move along the
southern road once more and the grapevine of
the desert whispers a warning to the
sentries in the mountains above the
town . . . a warning of trouble, of men who
come to capture or destroy or, simply . . .
to change.

The man in the sheepskin short coat was
cleaning a pistol, but beside him on a flat
rock, and close to hand, lay another pistol,
fully loaded. The man in the sheepskin short
coat was not given to taking chances.

Along the banks of the tiny stream were
scattered sixty-four men who were bathing,
washing clothes, or cleaning their weapons.
In the narrow-mouthed cove in the mountain

wall four mounted men watched over a herd of horses.

At either end of the camp, well away from the stream and the small noises made by the working and resting men, were mounted sentries.

All the men were dressed alike in round sheepskin hats and <u>poshteens</u>, the knee-long sheepskin coat common to the area. All wore hand-stitched boots without heels. From time to time the man cleaning the pistol turned his head to look toward the sentries or at the blue wall that blocked the canyon.

There was no outward indication that the gate had been approached in many years, but the man cleaning the pistol was not given to accepting the appearance of things.

The waters of the stream were cold, clear, and fresh, flowing down from melting snows in the glaciers far above. All the way from Suchow there had been a scarcity of water and now the soldiers basked in the warm sun and drank deep and often of the stream.

There was about these men a tough competence, the appearance of battle-wise comrades who know their own strength and have confidence in their weapons.

The man in the short coat had a face darkened by desert sun, honed by wind to a bleak hardness. The shirt under the sheepskin was faded navy blue wool, the wide belt of hand-tooled leather clasped with a silver buckle kicked from the sand at the crossing of the Su-lo-ho.

A hired fighting man, a mercenary in the

ever-changing armies of China, he had almost
a year ago been given a mission that had
more to do with lining the pockets of a
general than with any military value. With
thirty-two men he had started west from
Kansu, but long ago that mission had been
abandoned and now his little army, its
numbers increased, functioned as an
independent unit, existing by and for
itself.

It has been said of China in the twenties
and thirties that anyone who could feed an
army could have one, and this was a force
that lived well.

The beat-up, worn-out weapons which had
been theirs at the start had been discarded
for modern, more efficient weapons from a
cache along the way or captured during the
fighting. Their firepower had been increased
by the addition of five light machine guns
and two mortars. They had learned that care
of their weapons came first, their horses
second, and themselves third.

Only three of the number were Chinese. Six
were Ladakhis from a country once part of
Tibet. The Ladakhis were wanderers,
mountaineers, and fighting men. Twenty-two
were Torgut Mongols, scarcely changed from
the time of Genghis Khan, twelve were
Kazaks, nine were Tocharis, four were Lolos,
fierce tribesmen from eastern Tibet, never
conquered by the Chinese, and four were
Buddhist monks. These monks were much more
given to brawling and fighting than to

prayer and meditation. The remainder were
Tungans.

They were men from the bazaars of a dozen
cities, men who had been camel drivers, yak
herdsmen, thieves, and bandits. Of the
original command only a few remained, and
those the toughest and best. During the
months that had passed they had won
consistently in battle, had acquired better
equipment, horses, clothing, and food than
they had ever known, and they were a solid,
closely knit group.

They fought for money and the goods they
needed, taking what they could from the
warring factions of China's far west. On
occasion they had brokered peace, or at
least the temporary truce, based on their
alliance with one side or another. And they
avoided direct conflict with the powers
that could destroy them, the Kuomintang,
the Chinese Communists, and the Soviets.

The man in the sheepskin coat closed the
cylinder of the first pistol and tried the
mechanism. It worked smoothly, so he
reloaded the gun and placed it on the flat
rock. He began to strip the second pistol.
This one was an automatic, smaller, more
compact. . . . This one was insurance.

The sentry nearest the wall spoke
suddenly, sharply. The man with the pistol
glanced up, waved a reply to the sentry's
signal, and resumed his work.

He was seated upon a rock in a shaded
place near the stream. It was cool, and the
breeze from off the mountain was pleasant.

His back was toward the empty space of the
Taklamakan Desert, which lay, a low and
shimmering brightness, beyond the trees.

When he lifted his eyes again there were
three men entering the trees, and they rode
horses that could only be from the Kara
Shahr or Bar Kol oases, noted throughout
western China for their fine animals.

What was the old saying about tribute to
the emperors of China? Horses from the Kara
Shahr, melons from Hami, grapes from Turfan,
and girls from Kucha.

For the emperors, nothing less than the
best of everything.

The riders stopped, uncomfortably aware of
being surrounded by armed men and waiting
for him to respond to them. Deliberately, he
continued to work upon the pistol. Two of
the men were Europeans, that in itself a
surprise.

"All right, gentlemen. What the hell do
you want?" As he spoke he looked up,
sweeping them with a glance.

One of the men was tall, stooped, wearing
glasses. "This is . . . well, it is
unexpected. We had no idea . . . I mean, we
did not expect a white man."

Or perhaps they had sent out the two
Europeans precisely because he was a white
man. He peered down the gun barrel, checking
its cleanliness. "All right, what's on your
mind?"

"As a matter of fact, we are preparing for
an attack."

"So?"

"We . . . well, we hoped we might prevail upon you to ally yourself with us."

"How would that benefit me?"

The little man interrupted. "It is a matter of survival, my friend. Together we might cope with the situation. Alone you would be defeated."

"You assume too much. First, that I should remain here to receive an attack, and second that we should be defeated. The assumption is unwarranted and altogether stupid."

The little man stiffened. "Stupid? When you would be outnumbered ten to one?"

The man in the sheepskin short coat glanced over his shoulder and gestured, speaking sharply as he did so. A Torgut Mongol walked over and placed a Czech light machine gun on the rock.

"We have several of these and mortars. I know the force you expect to attack. They are a hungry rabble. My men are better trained, better equipped, more efficient in every respect.

"However, when we are rested we shall ride on. Marshal Chu will not arrive in time to disturb us, and I am sure he would like to avoid such a meeting."

The three exchanged glances. Obviously the meeting was not proceeding as they had intended, and the obvious unconcern of the commander of the small force worried them.

"Perhaps if you could come into the town," the tall man suggested, "we could talk to greater advantage." Then realizing his

oversight, he added, "I am Phillip Laurent,
and this is Signor Villani . . . and Mr. K'o."

"I am Medrac," the man with the pistol
replied.

"It is a French name, is it not?"

"I'm an American, not that it means
anything out here."

"Marshal Chu is going to attack us if we
do not agree to his demands. He wishes our
young men for his army, and our women. He
has also made demands on our flocks, and his
force is noted for their looting."

"The precedent is timeless. It is the way
of armies."

Villani nodded. "I agree. The Huns--"

"Signor Villani"--Laurent was impatient--
"this is not the time for a dissertation."

"You have come to request a favor." Medrac
slipped the clip into the automatic and
stowed it away under his coat. "So far you
have said nothing to the point."

"Mr. Laurent or Mr. K'o," Villani said,
"are more competent to discuss that aspect
than I." His manner became pompous. "I am
accustomed to dealing with matters after the
fact. After all, I am an historian."

"Which probably means that you are an
artist in ignoring all that does not conform
to the truth as you wish to see it. I have
small use for historians."

"We are not here to discuss history,"
Laurent said stiffly. "No doubt this
officer--" He hesitated delicately. "What is
your rank, sir?"

"Rank is only important to martinets or

officers' wives." Paul Medrac got to his
feet. "I take it you have remained
undisturbed for some time?"

"Since 1892," Villani replied proudly.
"That was the last time we were attacked. We
have, I believe, developed survival to a fine
art here. In fact, we are dedicated to it. As
you can see, our town is remote, far from the
beaten track, and out of the mainstream of
events. Consequently we feel no need to share
in wars, famines, epidemics . . . nor to pay
duties or taxes. We particularly," he added,
"dislike taxes."

"Who doesn't?"

"We have received a demand from Marshal
Chu," Laurent persisted. "Three days ago an
advance party appeared, and they informed us
that Chu was advancing with a vast army--"

"Six hundred men."

"--and that we must provide them with
quarters, food, recruits, and women.
Otherwise they would capture, loot, and burn
our city."

"We have never paid tribute," Villani
said, "not even to the Mongol khans."

"We have strong walls," Laurent added,
"and an ample food supply."

The walls did not interest Medrac, but the
food supply did. Walls are of little use
against a determined enemy and there is no
more determined attacker than a lean and
hungry soldier outside a fat and prosperous
city.

He was far more interested in the people
themselves than in the walls, for the

strength of a city or a nation does not lie in its guns or walls, but in the hearts and backbones of its people.

"You will join us, then?"

"Nothing I have said implies any such decision. You ask me to risk my life and the lives of my men. . . . What do you have to offer?"

"But you're a white man!" Laurent protested. "There are white women here! I . . . we thought surely . . ."

"You were mistaken." Medrac picked up the other pistol from the flat rock and returned it to its holster. "I'm not of the opinion that a white woman suffers any more from rape than a Chinese or a Mongol. So if you have any idea of trading upon any inclination of European chivalry, forget it. Such a sense in me is comfortably dormant.

"Furthermore, let me tell you this: I have here one of the toughest, best-trained outfits of fighting men in Asia. We are few in numbers, but competent. I shall not risk their lives without reason.

"However, I am willing to entertain an offer for our services, but before you decide upon the size of the offer, let me point out a simple fact. If we want your town, we will take it."

Mr. K'o cleared his throat. "If price is a consideration, I believe we can talk to some purpose."

"Price is the consideration. And may I suggest you begin with your best offer? We can grade it up from there." Medrac glanced at K'o. "I am sure we will continue to understand each other."

Laurent started to interrupt, but Mr. K'o spoke quickly. "You will accept an invitation to my house? I am but a guest in the city, but my poor house is at your disposal. Shall we say, for dinner?"

"You are a guest? How long have you been here?"

Mr. K'o smiled. "Twenty-seven years." His eyes twinkled. "At eight, then?"

"At eight."

Medrac watched them ride away, then turned to the stocky Chinese with the scarred face. "Chen, I want five men in that town within the hour. They will go quietly to shop for fruit, and to inquire about horses.

"While doing this they will check the defenses of the town and the morale of the people. Also, how many Europeans? Have they modern weapons? How long since a caravan was here? They will be back no later than seven o'clock with the information."

Chen departed and a tall young Mongol came swiftly up. "Shan Bao, take four men and swing around behind the town. Check the canyons leading into the mountains and get a rough estimate of the flocks. I have an idea you'll find a number of connecting valleys and canyons, rich in grass and water. Don't take more than two hours. I want this information before I enter the town."

Seating himself again, Medrac drew from a musette bag a handful of maps. Each was a beautifully drawn map of some section of

Sinkiang, and two of them were very good
maps of the region where they now camped. A
Chinese in Lanchow had provided these maps.

To the north and some distance away was
the vast, salt-encrusted bed of old Lop Nor,
the vanished lake. Rumor had it that the
lake was filling with water again after many
centuries. The Cherchen-darya River was to
their west, and behind the nearby town
loomed the massive rampart of the Altyn
Tagh. Beyond that range lay Tibet, or to be
more specific, that region of Tibet called
the Chang Tang, and relatively unknown.

The town behind the pale blue wall was
marked on no map at all, and from here the
town might easily have been passed by as
merely another of the ancient ruins
everywhere along this route. Yet it
presented a new factor, and a disturbing
one, intriguing to the mind of any curious
man. This town was a relic, something left
over from the past, yet obviously not
without some contact with the outside world,
as illustrated by the presence here of
Laurent and Villani.

Still, the town must have been known in
the days of the caravans before the springs
dried up and Lop Nor vanished. So how had it
been forgotten? And there were white women
here, too. But why not? There were white
women in Tashkent, Samarkand, and probably
in Aksu. So why not here?

Thoughtfully, Medrac considered the
situation. The trek from lower Kansu to this
point had been long and hard, and during the

first part there had been almost continual
fighting. Due to some luck they had been
able to resupply ammunition for their
rifles, but their food supply was running
short. If they stopped here it would give
them a much-needed rest and a chance to
renew their supplies and repair equipment.

As for Marshal Chu, Medrac had learned of
him long ago. The old bandit leader was no
bargain. They had so far not crossed trails,
but Chu was shrewd, cunning, and capable as
a military man. He had no political
convictions, no leaning toward the
Communists and less toward Chiang Kai-shek.
But Marshal Chu's weapons were worn and old,
his equipment was in bad shape, and his men
were the rag ends of a half-dozen bandit
forces.

The Mohammedan outbreak had come on the
heels of earlier fighting, putting too many
strong forces in the field with which he
could not cope. Also, the Russians were
showing indications of moving into Sinkiang,
which they had been trying to do off and on
for a couple of hundred years--whenever, in
fact, their country grew strong. Russia had
always, whether czarist or Soviet, wanted
this area, three times larger than greater
Germany.

If Chu could take the town behind the blue
wall he might settle down in that relative
obscurity and outlast the current chaos.
Chiang Kai-shek had failed to live up to his
promises with twenty years in which to do
it, his regime was coming apart at the

seams, and now disturbing reports of a full-scale Japanese invasion were filtering in from Peking and Shanghai. The people of China were looking for relief, and Marshal Chu wanted a storm cellar to last out the trouble.

Shan Bao rode in at a spanking trot and dropped to the ground, executing a smart salute. He was a lithe, quick man with intelligent eyes, and he cared little for anything but riding or fighting.

"You were right," he said, "there are many deep, well-watered canyons. It is impossible to reach them by circling, but we could see into some of them. They have herds of sheep, goats, yaks, and camels, and there are a number of great orchards and vineyards. This is a very rich village, sir!"

"Anything more?"

"There are well-traveled trails leading into the mountains, but the way to all the trails is through the city."

"Any fortifications on the hills?"

"I believe so. There were rows of rocks that might be natural, but I believe are in part constructed, and there are clumps of trees and brush that might offer a hiding place for men or guns."

"Thanks. You'll be in command while I'm in the town. I'll take Jepsun and six men with me."

He walked out to the edge of the trees, and looked toward the town. Already the gate was only a darker shadow against the wall. Medrac felt a growing excitement. A forgotten city on an abandoned caravan trail!

Down the long basin behind him the rays of the dying sun touched the distant yardangs of the Taklamakan with a fringe of crimson. Shadows crept out from the ancient hills, and far off, the towering mass of a great, snow-covered peak gleamed like a great white tower above the basin. Far out over the wastes, a jackal called.

To the north and east there was a dark blotch on the gray face of the desert. This was one of the great forests of reeds that covered what had been an ancient lake--reeds that were sixteen to twenty feet high; once lost in that forest no man could find his way out. It was said that many of them grew from a deep slush, crusted over enough to bear a man's weight in places, but if a man fell through it was like quicksand, and there was no escape.

The jackal called again. Medrac walked back and sat down. Jepsun would come soon with his horse, and they would ride to the strange gates . . . and beyond them.

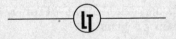

COMMENTS: Although there is no hint that mercenary Paul Medrac is the youthful narrator of the last draft of the *Samsara* fragment, at one time, at least some of the pages you have just read were intended to be part of that story of reincarnation. The City of the Blue Wall was likely intended to be a repository of information that allowed the "arrived" reincarnated people to learn more about the process of reincarnation and their greater purpose.

In one out of the dozen drafts of *Journey to Aksu*, Louis's initial description of Sinkiang, the mysteries of the Taklamakan Desert, and the City of the Blue Wall were followed by these words:

```
    For I, at last, had come to this
place, a place I remembered, yet did not
remember, brought here by a series of
seemingly casual meetings, objects,
ideas . . . even dreams.
    And by several people . . . a Gypsy
man in my own backyard, by Sleeth in San
Pedro, a Buddhist monk on the Irrawaddy,
and by Haig, that causal wanderer.
    The night winds rustle the
leaves. . . . The desert waits, softly,
like a cat, crouching.
```

Then the manuscript goes into a flashback that is, for all intents and purposes, the version of the *Samsara* fragment that begins in young Louis Lamoore's home in Jamestown, North Dakota:

```
    A man with gold rings in his
ears . . . a vase of ancient glass . . .
a fragment of carved stone . . . and a
girl.
```

There is no indication of how we get from the boy who meets a mysterious Gypsy in his backyard, or from the uncertain young man trying to go to sea, to the cynical and worldly professional soldier, Medrac. Perhaps there were many other adventures between the time he shipped out and when he arrived in China, adventures that brought maturity and toughness. Certainly, the story mentions nearly a year spent in the west of China. . . . However, it is best to remember that these were *drafts*, written at different times and with different intents. It is fun to look at *Samsara* and *Journey to Aksu* as one consistent story, but that is not the only possibility.

It is much more likely that, over the years, Louis split this story into two separate tales, or was combining two tales to make just one. . . . I cannot tell.

What I do have is some other pieces of the narrative, so we can put together a bit more of what he intended. All in all, Dad left behind twenty-two separate fragments of *Journey to Aksu*. He attempted to begin it over and over. Sometimes these attempts were nearly identical and other times quite different. On many occasions, we have only a page or two from the midst of a more complete manuscript. The rest of the clues to what Louis was attempting are lost forever.

The following is from a flashback that deals with Medrac's first arrival in China:

To be frank, I was puzzled over my situation, but had accepted it with caution. From my arrival in Shanghai with forty cents in my pocket to my present predicament, events had moved without seeming purpose.

From that first evening when I came ashore from a sampan at Wayside Pier, my situation was clear. I needed money. Forty cents was not going to get me far.

My assets, except the obvious physical ones, were few. I was tall, dark, and broke. A satisfactory able-bodied seaman with the rudiments of navigation, a good hard-rock miner, a fair to middling lumberjack, and better than average at prizefighting, judo, and karate. None of these talents seemed calculated to help me find a place to sleep or anything to eat in a town where none of them were particularly in demand.

The theoretical skills that I possessed were hard to evaluate and had never been tested. From my grandfather, an officer in the Civil and Indian Wars, I had learned the basic fundamentals of military tactics, developed by much discussion of the methods used by Grant, Lee, Stonewall Jackson, Sherman, and Thomas, to name a few. Along with some mildly profane comments on Nathan Bedford Forrest and John Singleton Mosby, there had been out-and-out respect for the Sioux.

That initial curiosity had led me to a study of the tactical writing of Sun Tzu, Vegetius, Marshal Saxe, Napoleon, and a few dozen others. And along the way I had picked up the working fundamentals of various guns and weapons. In the China in which I had landed these were marketable talents.

My first move after landing was to find a seaman's hangout on the chance that I would come across someone I knew who would stake me to a few dollars until I could find a job or a ship. What I found was a girl.

Or she found me.

Contrary to the movies, merchant seamen do not go ashore in their working clothes; several of the men in the place were fairly well dressed, and most of them were neat, although occasionally one was rumpled and unshaved. These were usually the ones who had been ashore several days and were obviously influenced by the cup. My own suit was dark blue, tailored on London's Bond Street, my hair trimmed, my shoes polished. Looking like someone to the manor born, I had in my pockets just the price of a bottle of beer.

COMMENTS: Could the girl mentioned above be the one referred to in the opening lines of *Samsara*? Was she the emissary of the crippled arms dealer known to Sleeth? I have no idea. What I do know is that Medrac's background of learning military tactics from his grandfather is identical to my father's, and the story of jumping ship in Shanghai, which is also described in the *Jack Cross* fragment, is one he told too.

From Shanghai, the information we have picks up Medrac in Suchow (Suzhou) a city in the western Chinese province of Kansu (Gansu). This would have been weeks or months after his arrival in China, and certainly weeks or months before his arrival at the City of the Blue Wall. At some point during his stay in Shanghai, Medrac has been hired to perform a minor military mission by a corrupt Chinese general. He has traveled to the western edge of China proper, and with his small detachment of troops, is just about to head into Sinkiang. He must decide whether to follow the north-

ern route or the more obscure southern Silk Route around
the Taklamakan Desert to Aksu near the Soviet border:

"You go to Aksu?"

"Those are my orders."

"On the northern road there are Tungan
soldiers, soldiers turned bandit since
General Ma was defeated."

"Nonetheless . . ."

"Of course. It is your duty."

The words were gently spoken, but they
posed a delicate question also, a question I
had been asking myself. How much duty did
I owe?

The Ladakhi with the pockmarked face was,
it appeared, a chance traveler, also going
west. "A man must follow his destiny,"
he said. "If your journey is to Aksu, so
be it."

He must have guessed my uneasiness, must
have seen how alone I was. For that matter
he was also alone, or appeared to be.

Throughout the day he had loitered about
the camp, talking to me whenever the others
could not listen, reaching out with
tentative fingers toward my plans. Had we
not been soldiers and well armed I should
have suspected him of being a spy for
thieves, but at the time I had thirty-two
men equipped with modern rifles, five
machine guns, and two mortars.

"Even to Aksu the southern way is best.
You will find no Tungans there, and at a
point due south of Aksu you may strike north

across the Taklamakan and come easily to its
gates. That is, if you still wish . . ."

The note was crumpled in my pocket and he
had been close by when the ragged boy
brought it to me. Had he seen it? The boy
had been clever, so it was unlikely that the
loiterer had seen anything. Yet the note was
itself mysterious.

Using one hand only I had thumbed open the
folded paper and glanced at it by firelight.

Come to the House of the Five Dragons.
The one who loaned you the Tao-Te-Ching
sent me. I have only three hours.

There was no signature, and I knew it
could be a trap. Suspicion is a friend to
the stranger, yet who could know about the
loaning of the Tao-Te-Ching?

Only Haig had been present that afternoon
in the apartment on Avenue Edward VII in
Shanghai.

The wind was rising. Ragged clouds raced
the moonlit sky. A wall of wind struck the
building in whose courtyard we were camped.
Ancient timbers creaked, dust swirled.

Kicking dirt over the fire, I smothered
the coals. The man with the pockmarked,
knife-scarred face had wandered off. When I
stepped over the collapsed timbers of the
gate the wind tore at my throat, blowing the
breath back into my lungs.

The House of the Five Dragons had been
pointed out to me as one of the oldest in

Suchow, dating back to the time of the Old
City.

The midnight streets were empty of all
save the wind that roared in from the
western desert, bringing with it a driving
storm of fine gravel and sand.

Several times I hesitated at corners or in
the shadow of a wall to look behind me, but
I seemed not to have been followed. I had no
idea why I should be followed, but I was in
a strange land, among strangers, and the
circumstances were unusual. Lately, I found
myself growing suspicious. That was why we
were still here when two days ago we should
have gone on, toward Aksu.

The vast old structure of the House of
Five Dragons was dark and silent but for the
ocean of wind that beat against its walls.

Undoubtedly I was a fool to have come
here. Who, in this place, would know Haig?
Or know that I knew him? Yet Haig was a
peculiar man, with friends in all manner of
odd places, and he had, so I'd heard, a way
of disappearing for months on end, going off
somewhere inland. But why should Haig send a
message to me across more than a thousand
miles of China?

There was a huge wooden gate, and beside
it, a door. Lifting the latch--there was no
question of knocking on such a night--I
stepped inside. Behind my belt my pistol was
a comforting thing, and I unbuttoned my coat
with my left hand.

The outer court was bare under the moon.

An ancient cart leaned drunkenly against the far wall, poplars lashed about with slender limbs so the wind might know their agony, and down a long arcade there was a faint gleam of light. Like the house where we had camped, this was an abandoned place . . . or so it seemed. The wind thundered among the roofs. Opening the door, I stepped inside.

The room was large, drafty, and high of ceiling. At the far side was a k'ang . . . a raised portion of the floor heated by a stone fireplace and used as a bed. At a small table alongside the k'ang a solitary man sat smoking a cigarette. A lean, raw-boned man with a narrow, tough face and a lantern jaw, he wore a leather jacket unbuttoned down to the last two buttons, a gray wool shirt, and a scarf tied around his throat, cowboy style. His hair was rust-colored and there was a hint of freckling under the skin. "I'm Milligan," he said.

A battered coffeepot stood at the edge of a fire, and from the edge of the k'ang he took a spare cup and saucer and filled the cup with coffee, black and steaming.

"You got a friend, Medrac. A mighty good friend."

"How do you happen to be away up here?" I asked.

"I get around. Flew up to Kanchow for a fella. I got my own ship. Fly charters for whoever." He rubbed out his cigarette and started to shape another. "Haig asked me to tip this hand for you." He looked at me over the cigarette he was building, his eyes

slate-gray. "You're in trouble, _amigo_,
plenty of trouble."

"I've had a hunch."

"Why do you think you were picked for this
job? Because you're a foreigner, you're the
fall guy. If anything goes haywire, you get
the ax . . . and I mean _ax_."

He lighted the fresh cigarette. "Haig
steered me into half the money I've made in
this godforsaken country."

The coffee was good. The last time I'd
tasted coffee like that was in a cow-camp
down in the Big Sandy, in Arizona.

"Did you ever think why the general picked
you for this job? You ain't been in the
country long and he's got you figured for a
greenhorn. If anything goes wrong, if his
buddies find those guns are going to the
Communists, then this is _your_ deal, not his.
You get knocked off and you can't talk and
nobody can prove anybody was in it but you.
If you bring it off, then the general has
sold a big load of contraband at four or
five hundred percent profit."

"I was told to drive back six hundred
horses."

"From Aksu? They've got horses there, all
right, and those horses will be loaded with
goods brought over from Alma-Ata, in Soviet
Russia.

"As for horses, there's no need to go as
far as Aksu if they want horses for the
army, like they claim."

"Nothing was said about those horses
carrying packs."

"Of course not. But you'll find they are. And the packs they carry will be machine guns, rifles, mortars, and ammo."

"The general is a Kuomintang man."

"Don't kid yourself, friend. He's like all the rest, feathering his own nest, playing both ends against the middle. I don't know about Chiang, but that crowd around him are a bunch of highbinders. They rob the country and they rob each other."

He gulped the hot coffee, then took up his cigarette.

"Look," he said after a pause, "you picked yourself a hot package. The way I see it you got two choices. First, you drop it right here and fly out with me, then grab yourself a ship out of Shanghai, work-away or anything you can get."

"And the other choice?"

"Go ahead with the deal. Accept the goods all innocent as you please, then meet me somewhere and we'll take your cargo and fly it elsewhere. We sell the goods to the highest bidder, split the take, and scram.

"Now you take Feng . . . the Christian General . . . I know him and like him and he'd give his eyeteeth to lay hands on that cargo. Say ten percent off the top for squeeze and we split the rest any way you want it."

He squinted his eyes through the smoke. "You got any idea what that cargo will be worth, delivered in the middle of China today? A quarter, maybe even a half-million dollars. I know at least three places I

could turn that cargo over for gold
money . . . cash on the barrelhead."

He paused again, finishing his coffee.
"There's one thing. Like I said, if anything
goes wrong you get the ax, and the man
who'll use it on you is right along with
you."

Well, I just looked at him.

"Fact," he said. "Haig told me that, too."

Mentally, I considered the men with me.
There was no reason to doubt it; certainly
none of them owed any loyalty to me.

"Did he have any idea who it was?"

"No . . . and there might be more than
one. I'd guess there would be at least two."
He grinned at me. "The general would be
worried for fear one might sell out."

Of course, Milligan was right. The
quickest, simplest, and smartest thing was
to cut and run. Drop the whole thing now,
fly out to Shanghai, and grab the first ship
off the waterfront.

The trouble was I was tired of being
broke. At fifteen I'd left home and since
then had worked in construction camps,
mines, and lumber mills, drifting from job
to job, going to sea occasionally and
prizefighting when the chance offered. It
all added up to nothing except that in the
process I had gotten the edges of an
education in libraries and from books
carried along as I traveled.

Milligan picked up the cups and rinsed
them out with what remained of the coffee.

"I got to take out." He dumped the pot and the cups into a canvas sack.

"Thanks. I'll stay on."

"Your funeral." He glanced at me. "You got a rod?"

Pulling back my coat, I showed it to him.

"May be the only friend you got. Keep it handy." He started buttoning his coat. "You bring that stuff here, to this house. I'll find a buyer. We split and I'll fly you the hell out of the country."

He picked up an old baseball cap and put it on. "You get caught with this stuff and they'll shoot you. The Chinese will believe anything of a white man; you're just a renegade. That's why they picked you."

There were thirty-two men waiting for me on the edge of town and any one of them might be the hatchet man. And they spoke a language I did not know, except for the two noncoms, who spoke English.

"You get back with those guns and stash them here. There'll be a man around, a man you can trust."

Suddenly, he seemed to think of something. "Look, you'll go from here to Anshi. Now in Anshi there's an old house"--he drew a design on the wall with his finger--"it stands about <u>there</u>. In that house there's a small cache of guns and ammunition. Might be helpful, for your men or bribes or some such.

"Joe Davenport was a buddy of mine. We did a piece in the Marines together when I first came out. When he got his discharge he went

into the munitions business, smuggling and
selling. This lot in Anshi he was supposed
to deliver to General Ma, but after he'd
cached them some trigger-happy son-of-a-
bitch went and shot him. So far as I know,
those guns are still there."

"You've been here a long time."

He hunched his shoulders against the wind
and grinned at me with one side of his
mouth. "I'm an old hand, son. I came out in
'21 with the Marines, and there was eight
years of that; when I paid out of the
service I stayed on, wanting to make a fast
buck.

"Well, I learned to fly, bought myself an
old crate, and went into business. This is
my third ship."

"How about the fast dollars?"

"Oh, I had 'em! I had 'em three or four
times, but have you ever been in Shanghai
with twenty thousand dollars in your kick?
It doesn't stay there long!"

He dropped his cigarette and thrust out
his hand. "All right, boy . . . Luck. You'll
need it."

He turned away from me and started off,
walking into the wind, and for a moment or
two I had to fight down an impulse to run
after him. But I stood there until he
disappeared in the night and then I turned
and went back to camp.

My orders had been definite. Follow the
route north of the Taklamakan to Aksu . . .
but suppose I didn't? Suppose, without even

suggesting it to any of the others, I cut
off to the south?

It was a rare Han Chinese who liked the
desert or the wild country, and from ancient
times until now, these western deserts had
been considered the end of the world. The
route to Anshi and beyond would wind among
the dunes somewhat, and there would be
several changes of direction. Suppose I
followed the advice of my pockmarked friend
and went off to the south; how would that
affect the plans of those with me, whose
mission it was to eliminate me if anything
went wrong?

Suppose I got them into wild country where
nobody but me actually knew where we were?

By the time I had slid into my sleeping
bag I had decided. At first light I would
move them out to Anshi, telling no one my
plans. Barring the unforeseen, we could then
leave Anshi before daybreak, lose ourselves
in the desert, then strike south toward the
oasis of Tun-huang and the Caves of the
Thousand Buddhas.

Lying on my back looking up at the stars
and listening to the wind, I had another
idea altogether.

What I needed was control, but not the
sort of control I possessed now. The men I
had were supposed to drive and guard the
returning horses. From the first it had
seemed like a lot of men but now it made
sense. . . . There was going to be a
treasure trove of arms and ammunition too.

I had read Machiavelli and Kautilya. The

answer was plain enough. I needed more
men . . . my men.

What did that suggest? First, that they
not be Han . . . or if Han, then local men
holding no loyalty to that far-off general.

Back in Shanghai I had heard an Englishman
in the Astor Bar say, "Anybody in China
today who can feed an army can have one."

Well, conditions were bad and that
Englishman had been right: The Chinese
alternative to famine was soldering or
banditry, often nearly the same thing.
Suchow itself was filled with drifters. The
Mohammedan rebellion had stopped the
caravans, and the town was filled with
jobless, homeless men, many of them thieves
or worse. I had seen them standing or
sitting around, men of a dozen
nationalities, for in the mountainous
corridor through Kansu to Sinkiang a Han
Chinese was apt to be the exception. Here
one found men of all sorts and no particular
loyalty.

The pockmarked Ladakhi . . .

Obviously, he had a reason for wishing me
to take the southern route, but that could
be dealt with when the time came. For now,
he might prove useful.

Suddenly, I sat up in my sleeping bag and
looked out through the gate to where several
men huddled in a corner of a wall about
fifty yards away. They were big, raw-boned
men carrying old-fashioned rifles. Each had
a saber slung across his back, the hilt

showing above his left shoulder. The right shoulder was bare.

They talked to no one, and apparently had almost nothing to eat. I had watched them because of the way they had been looking at our horses, which I was sure they intended to steal.

Pulling on my boots and sheepskin coat, I picked up my rifle and walked over to where they lay. Two were asleep but as I approached, the three others sat up, as ready for trouble as ever men could be.

"Do you speak English?"

They merely stared at me.

"Do you want horses? Food to eat?"

They grasped the word "horses" quickly enough. One of them got up and tried me in what was probably a bastard Chinese, but I knew none of it.

Squatting on my heels I drew a rough map in the sand showing where we were. Touching the man nearest me with the drawing stick, then myself, and gesturing to show the country around, I made an X with the stick. "Suchow."

"Suchow!" he agreed, his voice harsh and strange.

"Anshi." I made another mark. "I give you new rifle!" I slapped the Mauser that lay across my knees. The men's eyes widened. "I shall go here." Drawing a line as I spoke, I indicated the Tun-huang oasis, the Kuen Lun Mountains, the crossing to Aksu.

"You"--I indicated them--"come with me. You ride"--I drew a horse--"and you eat."

Gesturing to my mouth was enough for that.
"Maybe we fight." I mimed shooting, slashing
with a sword, and indicated a place for them
on either side of me. When I stood up, I
looked from one to the other. "You are not
Chinese. What are you, then?"

One of the men, who wore a thin mustache,
said, "Ngolok." Then taking up my stick he
drew a region south of Tun-huang and
considerably beyond it, drew the big bend of
a river, then pointed to the space inside
the bend and indicated that it was their
country.

Turning, I walked back to camp, and they
followed. I served up what was left of our
supper and when I got back into my sleeping
bag they grouped themselves around me.

Looking from one to the other I realized
that for better or worse I had acquired the
services of five fighting men. I knew
nothing then of the Ngolok, the wildest,
fiercest tribe in Asia, a nomadic people who
have defied for centuries all efforts to
penetrate their land. Nor had I any idea how
rare it was to find any of them outside
their own country.

Lying in my sleeping bag, I knew what it
was I would do. I'd recruit, not an army,
but a force at least comparable to the one I
now had, a strong force of men whose loyalty
lay only with me. Moreover, my recruiting
must be done at once and before anyone could
circumvent my efforts. By the time those
whose mission it was to watch me realized

what was happening, I wanted my force
doubled.

At daylight I was on my feet and the Ngoloks
with me.

We mounted horses and rode into the
outskirts of Suchow, and with me was
the pockmarked Ladakhi, who had appeared
from out of nowhere once more.

If there was nothing else I knew, I knew
fighting men, and it was fighting men I
sought. The first was a Mongol with a gold
ring in one ear, a stocky, powerful man with
broad, high cheekbones.

"You!" I pointed a finger at him. "I want
to talk to you."

He merely looked at me, then stared off
down the street with an air of contempt that
was beautiful to see.

"There is fighting to do, and traveling to
a far land. If you are a coward, stay here."

My pockmarked friend, called Serat,
translated for me, and the Mongol got to his
feet and spoke.

"He wants to know where you go."

"Tell him that if he comes with me he will
eat each day, ride a good horse, and fight,
and that if he asks any more questions I do
not want him."

Serat translated and the Mongol looked at
me, a hint of a smile on his lips, then
spoke and, turning, went behind the
building. "He will get his horse," Serat
said, looking at me curiously. Then he
asked, "Where do we go?"

"Where there is fighting," I said grimly.

"If you come with me, you shall go where
I go."

"Where else?" He looked about him. "How
many men do you wish?"

"Thirty . . . if I can find others like
these."

We found them. And we could have found a
hundred . . . perhaps two hundred more. In
Suchow that day there must have been a
thousand aimless, footloose wanderers.

Brigands, some of them, and leaderless
soldiers, too. No doubt many were camel
drivers and truck drivers rendered jobless
by the unsettled conditions, but the men I
chose, I chose because they looked like
fighters and because of their readiness to
go. Any who quibbled or asked questions I
ignored, for I wanted only those willing to
commit themselves.

They were a hodgepodge of languages and
nationalities, most of them in rags, all of
them hungry, all of them potentially
dangerous, and scarcely one who did not bear
the scars of battle. Yet diverse in origin
as they might be, most of them spoke enough
of the argot of the caravans to make himself
understood. I alone was deficient in that
respect. I, and those Chinese soldiers who
were in my command.

Of the original thirty-two, only five had
actually been Chinese from the coastal
provinces, and of these two spoke English
enough to translate and to make themselves
understood. Yet I now had Serat, if he
proved loyal.

Serat was a doubtful quantity. Where he had come from and what he wanted were a mystery. Possibly only a job, a horse to ride, and food to eat, yet he was too glib, too ready with explanations, and a bit too concentrated on that southern route.

Certainly, it was not unexpected to find such a man in this part of China. The caravan route had made it a land of wanderers and the harsh conditions made it the home of nomads; in most places little had changed from the time of Genghis Khan or Marco Polo.

No stranger or more mysterious place lay on the face of the globe. Even Tibet was an open book by comparison. Up to a point the history of Sinkiang was a history of the Silk Road and life around the string of oases, but there had been a time, long before that, even long before the time of Christ, when vast, civilized cities had thrived there.

Who were the people who lived in those cities? What books did they write? What pictures did they paint? Who were their heroes? Their enemies? What was their history, their origin?

There was no use lying to myself. I was going south. It was good advice to avoid Ma's now leaderless soldiers along the northern route. But it was far less the whispered suggestions of Serat than my own desire to go south, into that never-never land west of Tun-huang.

* * *

Liu Hung, who was second in command, was pacing about and talking excitedly when I rode back into the court with Serat. The five Ngoloks were close behind.

"We leave in one hour," I said, and immediately moved to start organizing the camp for departure.

"We cannot, sir. No. It is too late in the day."

"It's not too late. I don't care if we only make thirty li. We're moving!"

He stopped, about to speak again, then he looked at the Ngoloks who stood around me.

"These men, what do they do?"

"They ride with us," I replied, "and there will be more."

"More?"

"The news is," I explained, "that the route is dangerous because of Ma Chung-yin's soldiers. The obvious solution is more men, a stronger party." It wouldn't do to suggest I was thinking of anything but the northern road. . . .

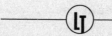

COMMENTS: So now we have one adventure leading to another. We learn the young mercenary, Medrac, hired to retrieve a herd of horses from the farthest frontier of China, has actually been tricked into running guns to the Communists by a corrupt Nationalist general. Medrac's friend in Shanghai, Haig, has sent the pilot Milligan to warn him, and Serat, the mysterious Ladakhi, is steering him toward the southern Silk Road and the City of the Blue Wall—a city that has staked its survival on secrecy, on no one ever leaving, or surviving an escape attempt. A city that certain drafts of Louis's *Samsara* fragment hint might be the repository of information archived by those who have "arrived"—those who can remember their previous lives, or incarnations.

Again, because of the way the bulk of the drafts of *Journey to Aksu* are written, I do not believe Louis seriously considered melding *Samsara* and *Journey to Aksu* into the same story for very long . . . but he did toy with the idea.

The most interesting part is that, just like the autobiographical aspects included in the last version of *Samsara*, this story is also strangely connected to Louis's life. Haig, Milligan, and the apartment on Avenue Edward VII are all part of the greater universe of "semi"-autobiographical L'Amour stories. Mercenary pilot "Tex" Milligan shows up in "A Friend of the General," with "the General" using Milligan as a method of escape:

> There was a charter plane at the
> field. You knew him, I think? Milligan?
> He would fly you anywhere for a price
> and land his plane on a pocket
> handkerchief if need be. Moreover, he
> could be trusted, and there were some in
> those days who could not. . . .

Haig, and his apartment in Shanghai, make an appearance elsewhere in this book, and in the short story "Shanghai, Not Without Gestures":

> It was not just a room but a small
> apartment, pleasant in a way. Drifting
> men have a way of fixing up almost
> any place they stop to make it
> comfortable. . . . Yet the apartment was

```
not mine. I'd been given the use of it
by a Britisher who was up-country now.
His name was Haig, and he came and went
a good deal with no visible means of
support, and I was told that he often
stayed up-country months at a time. He
had been an officer in one of the
Scottish regiments, I believe. I had a
suspicion he was still involved in some
kind of duty, although he had many weird
Asiatic connections.
```

Again, the apartment, though not the man, is mentioned in "The Man Who Stole Shakespeare":

```
When I had been in Shanghai but a few
days, I rented an apartment in a narrow
street off Avenue Edward VII where the
rent was surprisingly low. The door at
the foot of the stairs opened on the
street beside a moneychanger's stall, an
inconspicuous place that one might pass
a dozen times a day and never notice.
```

And, most interestingly, Haig is also mentioned in *Education of a Wandering Man* . . . a book that is, supposedly, nonfiction! Louis describes "the old crowd," a type whose "ranks are thinning" but could be found "in every large seaport city." They were men who were smugglers, dealers in information, and those who wanted to "avoid the eyes of officials." He claimed a man named Oriental Slim, whom he met while "on the beach" in San Pedro, first put him in touch with this group:

```
My first contact in Shanghai came in a
sailors' joint called, if I remember
```

correctly, The Olympic, having nothing
to do with the games--although games of
other kinds were played there.

It was a perhaps-accidental meeting
with a Scotsman, a former British-India
Army officer named Haig. He had left the
service and become a Buddhist, but I
always suspected he was with British
Intelligence.

I am not going to get into all the questions about Louis's
actual experiences in Shanghai. Those questions are many
and I wonder about them constantly (and uselessly). I will
say that I have proof he was there, but at a time prior to
when this story seems to be occurring ... and at that time,
he was there for only a few days. Did he return? It is still an
open question.

Last, there is one final piece of the *Journey to Aksu* manuscript that has survived through the years, a denouement
of sorts ... not enough to satisfy but enough to suggest
some sort of closure:

. . . the city behind the blue wall
remains in my mind . . . no bit of it
forgotten, and I find myself wondering
how they are faring there and if through
all that has happened since they have
survived, they who understood the art
of survival better than anyone.

There is little about Sinkiang that is
Chinese, but even less than that of the
city.

Perhaps the sharp reality of all my
impressions derives from the state of
heightened sensibility in which I

undoubtedly was. Not so much from the
task for which I had been retained,
but what I knew would come after. Even
at that moment I knew that once the
danger to the city itself was removed,
then they would find some means to
remove me also, for fear that I in turn
should become a menace.

There were people there whom I called
my friends, and I flatter myself that
they thought of me in the same way, yet
where the city and its survival were
concerned there was no friendship. The
city itself came first, and it always
had, and that was the price of its
survival.

In the end it was a whim of mine that
made the difference, a whim and a sharp
sense of the reality of things even in
that most unreal of all places.

It was odd that I, a newcomer to
China, and in many respects an
innocent, should come upon the city
behind the blue wall. Haig, who knew
more of China, I think, than any other
foreigner, knew of the city only by
rumor, and he did not quite believe in
it. The story, if one could dignify the
vaguest of rumors by such a name, was
flimsy indeed. It had none of the
qualities of legend or mystery, nothing
but a whisper here and there among the
marketplaces that such and such a place
had once existed.

Shanghai, the Shanghai of that era, is gone, erased by a world war, a revolution, and what was supposed to be a Great Leap Forward. Haig, Milligan, "the General," Oriental Slim, the apartment on the alley off Avenue Edward VII, the Olympic Cafe. I can't say it's all fiction, not by a long shot, for Dad left this tucked between the pages of a disintegrating scrapbook:

The Cafe Olympic

First Class Restaurant

and Cabaret.

1343-8 WAYSIDE

SHANGHAI.

Flimsy evidence indeed, but more than a whisper that such a place existed.

ACKNOWLEDGMENTS

I would very much like to thank my mother who has been our cheerleader through every iteration of this project, Paul O'Dell (who worked on the earliest incarnation of this book and came up with the title for this entire program), Jeanne Brown, Angelique Pitney, Charles Van Eman, Sonndra May, Daphne Ashbrook, Jamie Wain, Jayne Rosen, Jessica Wolfson, Mara Purl, Cathy Sandrich Gelfond, Trish Mahoney, Jordan Ladd, and Paula Beyers for all their help and the sorting and transcribing of the original manuscripts.

On the publishing end of things kudos go to the great Stu Applebaum, Gina Wachtel, Ratna Kamath, Nina Shield, Elana Seplow-Jolley, David Moench, Kate Miciak, Joe Scalora, Cynthia Lasky and her crack team, Scott Shannon, Matt Schwartz, Paolo Pepe, Scott Biel, Heidi Lilly, Ted Allen, Larry Marks, Bill Takes, Libby McGuire, and Gina Centrello.

It took every name on this list and many more to make this book a reality.

ABOUT THE AUTHORS

Our foremost storyteller of the American West, Louis L'Amour has also thrilled readers with his work in the adventure, crime, and science fiction genres. He wrote ninety-one novels, a book of poetry, and over two hundred short stories. There are more than three hundred million copies of his books in print around the world.

Beau L'Amour is an author, art director, and editor. He has also worked in the film, television, magazine, and recording industries. Since 1988 he has been the manager of the estate of his father, Louis L'Amour.

louislamour.com
louislamourslosttreasures.com